CRISPED + SERE

TJ KLUNE

BOATK Books

Crisped + Sere

Twenty-one days.

In a world ravaged by fire and descending into madness, Cavalo has been given an ultimatum by the dark man known as Patrick: return Lucas to him and the cannibalistic Dead Rabbits, or the town of Cottonwood and its inhabitants will be destroyed.

But Lucas has a secret embedded into his skin that promises to forever alter the shape of things to come—a secret that Cavalo must decide if it's worth dying over, even as he wrestles with his own growing attraction to the muted psychopath.

Twenty-one days.

Cavalo has twenty-one days to prepare for war. Twenty-one days to hold what is left of his shredded sanity together. Twenty-one days to convince the people of Cottonwood to rise up and fight back. Twenty-one days to unravel the meaning behind the marks that cover Lucas.

A meaning that leads to a single word and a place of unimaginable power: Dworshak.

For Mrs. Benz and Mrs. Phifer,
You told me one day you'd see my name on the cover of a book.
This was, of course, after reading my story about an evil Jet Ski.
Thanks for believing in me.

And for the season it was winter, and they that know the winters of that country know them to be sharp and violent, and subject to cruel and fierce storms.

—William Bradford, *Of Plymouth Plantation*

the map

THERE WERE nineteen days left when Cavalo stood on the outskirts of Cottonwood, snow blowing harshly against his face. The sky buried the morning in gray clouds, and Cavalo wondered if he would survive the winter to feel sun on his face again. He didn't think he would. Not now.

Bad guys? Bad Dog asked him, eyeing the southern gate into Cottonwood warily. *BigHank? AlmaLady?*

"No," Cavalo said. "Not bad guys."

WarMan bad guy?

Cavalo closed his eyes. He wasn't surprised the dog had picked up on his thoughts. If he could do that at all, that is. "Maybe. I don't know what Warren was."

He was not your man, the bees whispered, sounding like Patrick. *Did you know that?*

If WarMan was a bad guy, then maybe BigHank and AlmaLady bad guys, Bad Dog said. *Maybe all of them bad guys.*

"That would make things easier."

How?

"We could leave."

Where? Back home?

"No. We would find a new home. Far away from here."

How far away?

"Very."

Tin Man? Smells Different?

Cavalo sighed. "I don't know."

Bad Dog huffed. *Can't leave them.*

"We can't?"

No, he panted. *Can't. They fit.*

"With what?"

Us. Me. You and I. Tin Man is a rust bucket, but he's ours. Smells Different makes blood come out of people, but as long as he doesn't do it to me or MasterBossLord, he's ours too.

"That's... comforting."

Can't leave 'em. Can't leave here.

"That simple?"

Yes. If BigHank and AlmaLady good guys, then they need Bad Dog to protect them from monsters. Bad Dog barked to show his ferocity.

"We don't know who the monsters are anymore," Cavalo said. He looked back at the southern gate. He could see faint figures moving along the walkway near the top of the wall. The Patrol hadn't yet seen him. They'd know soon enough.

Are we monsters? Bad Dog asked.

"You're not," Cavalo said. "You're a good guy."

Bad Dog was not fooled. *And you?* He bumped his head into Cavalo's knee.

"I don't know."

I do.

"Oh?"

Good guy.

"You only say that because I feed you."

7

Probably. Bad Dog turned toward Cottonwood and sniffed the wind. *This isn't going to go well, is it?*

"Doubt it. We killed people the last time we were here."

Bad guys, the dog reminded him. *They were hurting Smells Different.*

"At least we know what for now." He pulled the hood of his jacket over his head.

Does it make a difference?

"It will. One day. Come on. We don't have much time."

Bad Dog fell into step at his side. He didn't bound through the snow or become distracted by the call of a bird from the trees. He knew his place well.

Cavalo was the same. He kept his eye on the gate. On the Patrol that had yet to see him. He didn't allow his thoughts to drift to the robot and the Dead Rabbit left back at the prison. He didn't think about the lines on the Dead Rabbit's skin and what they would mean or the way the robot had said they were incomplete. That half of the schematics were missing. He didn't think about where the other half would be, though he had an idea. The bees tried to speak, but he waved them away.

He knew the second they spotted him. One moment they were lax and loose, and the next it was as if they'd been struck by lightning. Shouts could be heard above the wind and snow. They pointed at him, raised their weapons at him. He could have gotten in without them noticing, but it wasn't part of the plan. He needed to walk through the front gate. Needed all of them to see him so they could understand he was not hiding. That he was not running.

At least not today.

"Stop!" one of the men on patrol cried. "Don't come any closer!"

Cavalo did as he was told. Bad Dog stopped beside him.

"Who are you!"

He must be new, Bad Dog grumbled. He barked once.

"Is that... Bad Dog?"

Yes, you maybe bad guy! Let me in before I decide to bite you!

"Oh shit," the man groaned. "I was almost off shift. Couldn't you have waited until later, Cavalo?"

Cavalo looked up at him. He was a squat fat man with wide eyes. His name... his name. Frank, maybe? Fred. Something close to that. The barrel of the rifle he had pointed at Cavalo's head shook.

Cavalo shrugged.

"Get Hank," Frank or Fred snapped over his shoulder. "Tell him we've got a problem."

"But he's—"

"Now!" Frank or Fred shouted. He turned back to Cavalo. "You're in deep shit, you know that?" He tried to make his voice sound tough, but Cavalo could hear the tremor in his words.

"Figured," Cavalo grunted.

"You killed them."

Cavalo said nothing.

"Deke shot you."

Cavalo scowled. "Don't remind me." He still couldn't believe that happened. He should probably consider punching Deke in the face while he was here. Or at least scaring him quite badly. It was only fair.

Frank or Fred's eyes grew wider. "How in God's name are you alive? You took a bullet to the chest!"

"Robots," Cavalo said, sure that would explain nothing. "And I'd like to avoid that this time around, so point that gun elsewhere before there's an accident, Fred."

"You don't get to tell me what to do!" He jabbed the gun toward Cavalo. "And the name's Frank!"

"That was my other choice," Cavalo told Bad Dog.

He a bad guy?

"No. Though if he doesn't stop pointing that gun at me, we're going to have a problem."

Put down the boomstick! Bad Dog snarled up at Frank. *Put it down before I eat your eyes and haunt your dreams!*

"What did he say?" Frank asked.

"You don't want to know," Cavalo said.

The gate began to open.

"Easy," Cavalo said quietly as Bad Dog began to growl. "Easy."

BigHank, he said. *Others. They have boomsticks. What do I do?*

"Calm," Cavalo said. "They're not going to do anything." At least, he hoped. He remembered the power of mobs.

Calm, Bad Dog said. *Calm, calm calm. I'll bite them all.*

Hank stood on the other side of the gate, a stern look on his face. He was flanked by four men on either side of him, each of them armed, pointing their guns at Cavalo. Only Hank was unarmed. Cavalo was unsure if that was something to be thankful for.

"Cavalo," Hank said.

"Hank."

"Didn't think we'd see you again."

"I'm full of surprises."

Hank chuckled ruefully. "That's one way of putting it. Just you two?" His gaze flickered to the snow-covered road behind Cavalo.

"Yes."

"How's the chest?"

"Still pulls a bit."

Hank nodded. "You're lucky that's all it does. There was a lot of blood. Didn't know how much of it was yours."

Cavalo shrugged. "Some, I guess."

Hank sighed. "We've got a bit of an... issue here, Cavalo."

"Figured."

"Questions need to be asked."

"Yeah."

"Are we going to have any problems?"

"Putting me in jail, Hank?"

Hank rubbed a hand over his face. "I suppose. We can see how it goes from there."

"You know how it's going to go."

"Then why'd you come back?"

"Would you have come for me?"

Hank nodded. "In the spring. There were... plans."

This didn't surprise Cavalo. "I could have been long gone by then."

"No."

"No?"

"You would have stayed."

"How do you figure?"

"I know you, Cavalo. Whether you like it or not, I do. You would have stayed."

"I suppose."

"You carrying?"

"Yes."

"I'll need it all."

Cavalo reached for the knife at his side. All the guns pointed at him tracked the movement. He had to fight every instinct he had to kill them all where they stood. One or two of them might get lucky and wing him, but they'd all be dead before they realized what was happening. It wouldn't take much. He'd prefer not to get shot again, but it was an acceptable risk. The bees agreed with him, wanting to see blood splashed against the snow. Even Hank would not be safe if he raised a hand against Cavalo. It would be unfortunate, but necessary.

Cavalo curled his hand around the knife and zeroed in on Frank as the first to go, the knife to his right eye. Adjust for the wind. Adjust for the broken fingers. It truly was regrettable that everyone here would die. But then, they should never have pointed guns at his face.

Somehow, he stopped himself. Cavalo tossed the knife toward Hank. It landed in the snow in front of him and sank down out of view. His pistol followed. Then his pack. The rifle and bow were back at the prison. He'd wanted to travel light, without an arsenal. Like he was coming in peace. Like he meant no harm.

They didn't seem to believe him. Every movement he made was

scrutinized. He wondered which one of them would accidentally fire first. He bet on an older man whose name he did not know standing to the right of Hank. There was sweat on his brow even though the cold was biting. The barrel of his rifle was still shaking.

"Watch it there, old-timer," he said.

The man's eyes went wide. He licked his lips. Blinked away the sweat.

"That's it?" Hank asked.

"Traveled light."

I still have my teeth, Bad Dog reminded them all. *You can't make me give them up.* He showed them all his teeth.

"We're good," Cavalo told him. "No teeth."

Bad Dog huffed but subsided.

Hank shook his head. "Some days I think I've got you figured out."

"And other days?" Cavalo asked, curious.

"Other days, you do something that makes me think I don't know you at all." Hank bent down and retrieved Cavalo's belongings.

"I'll want those back," Cavalo said.

"I'm sure you will." He nodded toward Bad Dog. "Gonna be a problem?"

Yes! Bad Dog barked.

"No," Cavalo said.

Hank handed Cavalo's pack and weapons to the old-timer with the shaky hands. Cavalo could see the pressure on the trigger momentarily grow tighter before it was released to fumble with his possessions.

Hank turned back toward Cavalo. He reached into his back pocket and pulled out a pair of handcuffs. He tossed them at Cavalo's feet.

Lose something, Charlie? the bees asked.

But they weren't Charlie's. He'd seen these before.

"Put them on," Hank said.

"Warren's?" he asked.

"Used to be," Hank said. "The town's now."

Everything screamed at him to lash out as he bent down and picked the cuffs out of the snow. To kill them all. To head back to the prison and finish what he'd started. Then, he could sleep. Then, he could dream.

He closed each cuff tight against his skin, his hands secured out in front of him. He never took his eyes off the men that stood before him. He knew they heard each click of cuffs. They thought it a trap. Cavalo almost wished it had been. They were bound to be disappointed. For now.

Hank walked toward him. Bad Dog tried to put himself between them, but he made the dog stand down. "We're okay," he said quietly. "We talked about this."

Doesn't mean I like it.

Hank stopped a few feet away. Close enough to be heard, but far enough away in case Cavalo or Bad Dog lashed out. It was smart.

He said, "He's pissed, huh?"

Cavalo shrugged. "A bit."

"Why?"

"Why what?"

"Everything."

"That's a lot."

"This isn't a game. People are terrified of you."

"They should be."

"Deke still can't sleep."

"He shot me."

Hank's eyes softened. "Feels real bad about that."

Cavalo snorted. "I'm sure he does."

"Why did you come back?" Hank asked, lowering his voice so as to not be heard by the gunmen.

"I need to talk to you," Cavalo said. "Something's happened."

"What?"

13

Cavalo shook his head. "Not here. Just you and me."

"I'm not going to like this, am I?"

"Depends."

"On?"

"If you're willing to fight."

"For?"

"The future."

Hank chuckled. "Son, just what do you think we're doing out here?"

"You're surviving," Cavalo said. "Barely. It might not be enough anymore."

"That's almost funny coming from you."

"There are things...."

Hank waited.

"The Dead Rabbit."

"What about him?" Hank asked. Cavalo could not ignore the way his voice hardened.

"He's.... It's not what you think."

"And what do I think? That he's a monster? A murderer? That he killed those men in cold blood?"

Cavalo shook his head. "What does that make me, then?"

"And you care about that now?"

"I don't know," Cavalo said honestly. "Things have changed."

"I can't make promises," Hank said. "Let's get you inside and we'll see what we see." He turned back toward Cottonwood.

"Hank."

Hank stopped.

"They came for me. At the prison."

"Who?"

"Dead Rabbits. Said they heard of me from the town."

Hank stiffened but did not turn.

"Did you know?"

"About?"

"Warren. He was theirs."

"Was he?"

"Yes."

"It makes sense."

"Does it?"

Hank shook his head. "You miss a lot when you hide away, Cavalo."

Cavalo said, "I've never asked for much."

"You've never asked for anything," Hank said. "Withering and sere, remember?"

"This, my most immemorial year."

"Which is why I can't quite figure this out."

"You have to trust me." Hollow, those words. Cavalo knew this.

"Do I?"

"I am asking for this. This one thing."

"For you? Or for him?"

"For all of us."

Hank nodded. "They'll want your head. The town. They thought those men were hope. They thought we were saved. Promises were made. Even though it was shit, the words were pretty. You took that from them. You and the Dead Rabbit."

"Let them try," Cavalo said coldly before he could stop himself. "I'm already damned. More blood on my hands won't matter."

Hank laughed bitterly. "There's the Cavalo I know." He said nothing more as he walked toward Cottonwood.

And the man and dog followed.

THEY WANTED HIS HEAD, YES. HE COULD SEE IT IN THEIR EYES.

Though it was just past dawn, and although the snow fell heavily, they stood outside their doors. They peered out through their windows. They whispered his name with malice and rage in their eyes.

Flanked on all sides by men with guns, he followed Hank through Cottonwood. Bad Dog crowded him closely, ears flat back

15

against his head, a low rumble emanating from his chest. They'd tried to put a rope around his muzzle as they entered the gates, but Hank must have seen the black murder in Cavalo's eyes and held them off. They could chain him up all they wanted; they would not touch Bad Dog in that way.

As he was led through the town, he braced himself for the first raised voice. For the first thrown stone. For the first signs of the mob forming and writhing toward him, ready to take his life and the life of his friend for what they'd done. He would fight back, he knew. He couldn't *not*. But they'd be overwhelmed, and the last thing he'd see would be the faces stretched in fury above him as they cursed his name and tore at his flesh. It would just take one stone cast. One insult hurled in anger.

But it did not happen.

He could feel their hatred, yes. It all but rolled over him. However, their fear of him was stronger.

They were scared of him and every step he took. They wondered at him with wide eyes. They knew what he was capable of, having seen the aftermath of his destruction. Maybe they thought it a trap. Maybe they thought he'd turned against them and Dead Rabbits were hidden amongst the trees, waiting for his signal.

None of them spoke against him, but his name was whispered again and again and again until it became how the Deadlands sounded when wind blew through the lifeless trees.

Bad guys, Bad Dog growled. *All bad guys.*

"No," Cavalo said quietly. "Confused. Scared."

Smells like bad guys.

"Calm," he said.

Yes. Yes.

As they neared their final destination, there were three more:

Deke, who caught Cavalo's eyes before looking away, hiding his face, hands tightening around the rifle he held.

Aubrey, who held Cavalo's gaze. She had no fear on her face, only worry. Bad Dog wagged his tail briefly when he saw her, and for a moment, she looked as if she'd reach out to pet him. Her father shook his head and she took a step back.

And finally Alma. Always Alma. Alma, who stood on the porch of the small office that had belonged to her brother before he'd been murdered and eaten with only his head left behind as warning. She looked fierce as the snow fell around her, her mouth a thin line, her eyes narrowed. He remembered the song he'd heard her sing about good-bye, good-bye, saying good-bye.

"You're alive," she said when they stood before her.

"Yes," he said.

"I thought you might not be."

He said nothing.

"Cavalo," she said. "Do you know what you've done?"

"I've done many things."

"I know. But now... the others."

"What others?"

"The UFSA," Hank said. "They came from Grangeville. Looking for Wilkinson."

"And you sent them to me," Cavalo said. "Because you knew what I'd do. If I was still alive."

Alma looked away.

"It wasn't her," Hank said quietly. "Or me. Someone else in town. Don't rightly know who. Can't say I blame them, though. I told you, Cavalo. You took away their future."

"Where are they?" Alma asked. "The ones who went up the mountain."

"In the ground," Cavalo said coldly.

She nodded tightly, as if she expected nothing less. "They'll come for us now."

"Not for the reasons you think," Cavalo said. "Crisped and sere."

Alma raised an eyebrow. "And what does that mean?"

"I don't know. But we don't have much time."

"Hank," Alma said, dropping her arms to her sides. Only then did Cavalo see the tin star attached high on her coat. He was sure it was the same one her brother had worn. "Bring him in. Bad Dog too." She turned and walked into the office.

I HATE BEING IN JAIL, BAD DOG GRUMBLED, STARING FORLORNLY at the metal bars as he lay his head on his paws.

"We live in a jail," Cavalo reminded him. He tested the bindings on his arms, cuffs attached to chains that stretched to the wall. There was some give to it, the metal grating against the hooks they slid through. They were strong. He wondered where they'd been found. He didn't remember them from when Warren was here.

No. We live in our home.

"It won't be for much longer." He didn't know if he believed that.

AlmaLady didn't even give me a bone.

"She's angry."

With me?

"No. With me."

Uh-oh.

"Yeah."

The door opened. Alma walked in, followed by Hank. He closed the door against the cold. Alma glanced back at him and then turned toward Cavalo. She stared at him through the iron bars for what felt like an age. Then, "I half thought you'd be gone already," she said. "Some magic trick into thin air with chains laying on the floor."

Cavalo shrugged.

Hank surprised him when he opened the jail cell door, grunting as he slid it to the left. Cavalo took a step back until he was pressed against the wall. Bad Dog growled low, but stayed at Cavalo's side when Hank and Alma entered the cell, keeping the distance between them. Cavalo didn't know what they were doing, but he wasn't going to take any chances. These people were his friends, or as close to friends as he'd ever had. But he would kill them if the situation called for it. He would mourn for them, but his hands were already stained with blood. He wouldn't mourn for long.

"Why'd you come back?" Alma asked.

"Lucas. They're coming for him."

"Who's Lucas?"

"The Dead Rabbit."

Her eyes widened. "He can talk?"

"No. He wrote it in blood on the walls."

"Do I even want to know?"

Cavalo shook his head. "It doesn't matter. Things are different now. He's...."

"He's what?" Alma asked.

"Marked. It's why they came for him."

Cavalo did not miss the shared look between Hank and Alma. "Marked how?"

"Tattoos. All over his body."

"Of what?"

"How much longer can you keep the lights on here?" Cavalo asked.

Hank didn't seem fazed at the change in topic. "Through the winter," he said. "Maybe a little longer if we ration."

"And the water?"

Hank hesitated. "The snow helps. For now. We're storing as much as we can. Our purifier is running. For now."

"Because everything else is radioactive," Cavalo said. "And it will eventually kill you to drink it. After the purifier goes."

"And the droughts don't help," Hank agreed. "Summer rains are getting farther and farther apart. Not that we can really trust what comes down."

"And when was the last time you saw a batch of potassium iodide?" Cavalo asked. "Or any other antiradiation pills? The caravans ran out of their supply a long time ago."

"There was a rumor that someone found a DTPA cache up north a while back," Hank said. "But I don't think anything came from it."

"And how many dead?"

"Cancer?"

"Yes."

Hank shrugged. "Depends upon how far back you go. Dozens."

"Cancer isn't the only thing that kills you here," Alma said, her words harsh and biting. "What's your point, Cavalo?"

"Then why do you stay here so close to the Deadlands?"

Alma stared hard at him. He thought she wasn't going to answer. Then, "Because there's nowhere else to go."

"That's not true. There's an entire continent."

"Full of only God knows what," Alma said. "You've heard the stories just like we have, Cavalo. Of monsters and men. Of stretches of irradiated land that go on for miles. Yes, they may be just that. Stories. But we have survived here. We have made a home here. Why take the risk?"

Bad guys, Bad Dog agreed. *Scary bad guys with big teeth that live in the trees.*

"Sometimes," Cavalo said, "a risk is all there is."

She laughed bitterly. "Those words mean nothing coming from you. Tell me, Cavalo. What risks have *you* taken? Why do *you* stay?"

"Because this is all I have," he said honestly. "But sometimes, that's almost not enough." He thought of the tree that danced in the haunted woods. The tree that whispered poison in his ears.

"Then what changed your mind? You've never given a damn about anything other than wasting away in your prison."

The words stung. "There's more now."

"What?"

"Lucas."

"The Dead Rabbit." She was good. Her voice gave away nothing. "Yes."

"You know what he is."

"Yes."

"What he's done."

"Yes."

Now the anger came. "Did he do it?" Her eyes flashed.

He knew what she meant. "No. He had nothing to do with Warren."

"Is that what he told you?"

"Did you know Warren was working with the Dead Rabbits?" It was out before he could stop it.

She slapped him. He tasted blood. Bad Dog growled viciously at his side. "No," he said, pointing toward the ground. Bad Dog lay back down, but his ears and tail were rigid, and he watched Alma with a curl to his lip.

There were tears in her eyes. Alma, who said that tears were a useless thing. A sign of weakness. He understood then.

"You knew," he said.

She looked away.

"There's much you don't know, Cavalo," Hank said quietly. "Choices had to be made."

"You both knew," Cavalo said. "About Warren." The bees screamed in his head. "What have you done?"

"We ensured our survival," Alma said.

"I'm sure Warren doesn't see it that way."

"I could kill you," she said. Cavalo believed her.

"He came out of the woods one day," Hank said, looking down at his hands. "We thought he was a drifter. We get them, every now and then. He was charismatic. He laughed. He smiled. He ate with us in my house. With my children. And then one night, he told me just how easy it would be to take Aubrey into the woods. How pink her skin was and how it would taste under his tongue. How it would crack and boil over a fire. She would scream, he said, as he peeled it away. Fear did something to the flesh. Gave it more of a tang." He took a shuddering breath. "And we would watch. He would make us watch as he devastated my daughter. Then the rest of us would follow."

"Patrick," Cavalo breathed.

Hank nodded. "It's been a little over two years now. Only the three of us knew."

"You son of a bitch," Cavalo said. "What did he want? In return?"
Neither answered, nor would they look at him.

What did he want?

"Supplies," Hank said. "Information. Caravan routes. How often they came through. Grangeville. How many. How often we traded. The surrounding area. The mountains. Rivers. Dams. Never told them about the prison. They never asked."

"That's it?"

"And people."

Cavalo closed his eyes. "To recruit?"

"No."

Cavalo felt sick. "How many so far?"

"Five," Hank said. "The first was from Grangeville. The second was from a caravan. The third was found wandering the woods. I never even knew her name. The fourth was a man from the south who had raped a woman and left her for dead."

"And the fifth?"

"He couldn't do it anymore," Alma said. Her voice was flat, like SIRS when caught in the grip of his insanity. "He said this isn't who we are. He told us we had to stop. That it was time to rise up and fight back."

"Warren," Cavalo said.

Alma nodded. "He went out one day. Said he'd be right back. That he was just going to talk some sense into them. The Dead Rabbits. I begged him not to. I begged him to stay. You know what he said?"

"What?" Cavalo croaked out.

"It's not what Cavalo would do. Cavalo wouldn't stand for this. Cavalo wouldn't let this happen." She wiped her eyes. "Always Cavalo with him. Cavalo, Cavalo, Cavalo. You would have thought you walked on water rather than crawled in the dirt."

Without thinking, Cavalo rushed them both, forgetting the chains that bound him to the wall. All he could think about was his hands around their necks. To squeeze until blood vessels burst in

Patrick. The Forefathers, whoever they are. They didn't know Patrick had divided it up. They thought he was nothing more than a pet. A psycho fucking bulldog. A means to an end. But he's more than that. They didn't know what they had. They never stopped to look. Lucas is the key, and I guarantee you Patrick is the lock. Whoever opens that door... will have the power to control everything. You have made a deal with the devil, and in nineteen days, he is coming to your doorstep to collect."

of bees and men

THEY LEFT him chained to the wall, Bad Dog fretting at his feet.

He pulled on the chains. They clanged against the hooks on the wall. There was no give in them. He wondered how many of those the town had fed to the Dead Rabbits had been kept in here, arms bound to the walls.

His throat hurt. He couldn't remember the last time he'd spoken so much. They promised him water but never came back. He expected as much. It was okay. He'd survived worse. He knew there was a guard out in the front office but did not call out to him. It would not have done any good. Besides, he was sick of people. He'd seen too much of them lately. Of this town with all its secrets. He wanted to be alone while he had time left to do so. Once the sun rose, he'd either be killed by the town or fed to the Dead Rabbits. Of that he was certain.

As the sky grew darker, the snow stopped and the clouds parted here and there, leaving patches of stars and sky he could see through the small window behind him. He even saw the moon, the sliver that it was, when he craned his neck uncomfortably. He couldn't remember the last time he'd seen the moon. Men had gone there once, he knew. In their ships that spat fire. Much like the space in which the moon drifted, it was something Cavalo couldn't quite fathom. He wondered what the moon looked like up close. And how quiet the space around it would be. All dust and stars.

Bad Dog curled around his feet protectively, huffing quietly in his sleep as his legs jerked. Cavalo wondered what he chased in his dreams. He wished he could follow his friend there. It would be better than staying trapped here in the real world where people he would have trusted, people he thought far better than himself, had shown they were exactly the same as he. It should have provided him comfort to know that others made hard decisions like he did. Those decisions that no one else would choose to make. But it was Alma. And Hank. And Warren. They weren't supposed to be like him. They were supposed to be different.

And why are you letting it affect you so? the bees whispered from their hive. *They are nothing to you. They are no one. You are alone as you've always been. As you will always be. That's what you've wanted. And that's what you'll get. They are already dead. Why did you even come here? What did you hope to achieve?*

He closed his eyes against the bees. He could feel them pricking about in his head. He couldn't tell them (or even himself) about that strange, soaring hope that burst through him when SIRS had started to explain the marks on Lucas's skin. He couldn't tell them of words foreign to him like *hope* and *future* that danced across his mind. Even as the blood had dripped down the Dead Rabbit's neck where he'd almost cut his throat, Cavalo had been filled with a terrible wonder. And even with the scrape of the knife, he'd bent his head and scraped a kiss against the Dead Rabbit's lips. He didn't know why he did it. Maybe he meant it as a good-bye. Maybe he meant it to say he was sorry for what he was about to do.

Or maybe he was fucking tired and fucking lonely and maybe he couldn't get the fucking psycho out of his head. He was always there, mixed in with the bees. Cavalo hated him. He hated everything about him. And even as *hope* and *future* had risen in his mind, so did *change* and *destruction*, and wasn't there a moment where he'd almost grabbed the knife and finished what he'd started? Wasn't there a moment when he thought that it'd be easier if Lucas was dead, his head separated from his body, Cavalo's hands drenched in his blood?

There *was* such a moment, and it was a battle that Cavalo had almost lost.

Why he stopped himself was a curious thing. Cavalo thought it had to do with the Dead Rabbit always being in his head. Cavalo wished, not for the first time, that he'd killed Lucas the day they'd met. All of this could have been avoided. He might have gone the rest of his life never knowing what Hank was capable of. Alma. Warren. The town. This place.

He wondered what the morning would bring.

"If you can get away, you run," he told Bad Dog.

Bad Dog opened his eyes and looked up at him. *They bad guys now?*

"I don't know."

We bad guys?

"I don't know."

Can't leave you, Bad Dog said.

"You have to."

Can't.

"Why?"

Home. You're my home.

"Stupid dog." There was no heat to the words.

Stupid MasterBossLord. Stupid man who thinks Bad Dog will leave him. I will never leave you. Where you go, I go. And if they come, they will see my teeth and run because I am Bad Dog.

"The most ferocious," Cavalo said quietly.

Bad Dog closed his eyes and slipped back into his dreams, curling closely to Cavalo to stay warm.

Cavalo watched him sleep.

Hours passed. The cold air through the window prevented Cavalo from sleeping. It seeped through his deerskin coat and chilled his flesh. He thought of many things, none of them good. The ruination of flesh. Blood splashing against snow. The gnashing of teeth. A little boy, hands outstretched, with a live grenade in his lap. A lady with turquoise hair. A lady who danced amongst the trees. Of Charlie, who lost something. Of a woman with an infected cut on her foot opening a door to snarling animals. Of robotics. Of machines that purified. Of machines that destroyed.

And of Lucas. *I am Lucas*, always there in his head. Lucas, who had the audacity to kiss him in the lookout and ruin everything he knew about himself to be true. Lucas, who had the gall to watch him as he did, like a predator hunting prey. Lucas, who had the temerity to exist at all, to bring Cavalo's ordered little world crashing down as if it were constructed of nothing but ash and smoke.

Lucas, Lucas, Lucas.

Cavalo's skin hummed at the thought of him. He wished Hank had not taken his knife so he could have attempted to cut Lucas out of himself. It was the only thing that made sense. Lucas was a sliver underneath the skin that had become infected. Cavalo needed to cut him out.

And on and on it went. Those circles in his mind. Round and round. The bees screamed. Cavalo gritted his teeth. It would never stop. It would never—

Bad Dog raised his head. Sniffed the air. Cocked his head.

"What?" Cavalo asked.

The dog's tail thumped once. Twice. *They're here.* He sounded surprised. He stood. Shook himself. Glanced over at Cavalo.

"Who?" Cavalo asked.

Smells Different.

"For fuck's sake," Cavalo muttered. "Has he killed anyone?"

No. No blood. He won't let Smells Different kill. We don't know if they're bad guys yet.

"Who?" Cavalo asked again.

Tin Man. Tin Man's here too.

"SIRS? SIRS is here?"

31

Yes. Yes. Bag of bolts came down off the mountain. Has he ever left before?

Not in all the years Cavalo had known him. Not once. "This can't possibly be good," Cavalo said.

All together again! Bad Dog said with a low bark, spinning in a circle. *Like at home!* He stopped, and his tail drooped. *Except we're still in jail.*

Cavalo stood. "I doubt it will be for much longer."

Really? Bad Dog asked, looking up at him.

Cavalo shrugged. "Either that or we're going to die a whole lot quicker."

I pick the first one. I don't like being dead.

"You've never been dead before."

Yes, but I know I wouldn't like it.

Cavalo turned toward the window. The chains pulled at his arms. He prayed Bad Dog was wrong, though Cavalo knew in his heart he wasn't. If they were here, it meant they'd come to rescue them. It meant they worried, SIRS more than Lucas. Especially for the robot to have left the prison. How Lucas had convinced the robot to leave, Cavalo didn't know.

He waited. Nothing moved outside the cell. The moon peeked through the clouds again, and shadows shifted and changed.

Then:

Fingers curled around the bars. A face appeared, dark eyes cloaked in a black painted mask, a hood over his head. Lucas's eyes narrowed as they peered between the bars, but then his gaze found Cavalo. The scowl turned into the shark's grin. *Found you,* that smile said. *I was hunting you and now I found you.*

"Why are you here?" Cavalo asked.

Lucas glanced over his shoulder, then looked back at Cavalo. He tugged on the bars once. Twice. *Because you're in jail,* he said.

"We knew this might happen."

Lucas rolled his eyes. *Because you're a shit messenger.*

"It's a lot to take in," Cavalo said. "They need time to think."

We don't have *time,* Lucas reminded him. *He's coming.* He pulled on the bars again, jerking his arms. One of the bars spun slightly in its groove but nothing more.

"That's not going to work."

Lucas glared at him. *You don't say.*

"Lucas!" a voice hissed from out in the snow. "You vile creature! I told you to *wait* for me! I could have gotten lost! I had to hide from a man with a *very* large gun. If he'd spotted me, our cover would have been blown! I am positive that—what on earth are you doing hanging from a window?" Glowing orange eyes appeared next to Lucas's head. "Ah! Now it makes sense. You know, Cavalo, these humans made it very easy to sneak in to a supposedly fortified town, and I've never snuck into anything before in my life. And you think they'll be able to fend off Patrick and a group of Dead Rabbits? I think our chances are infinitesimal. Let me break down these walls and we can go back home. There is a lesser chance of being eaten hiding behind the walls of the prison. And we have defenses that they do not have here."

"Could you be any louder?" Cavalo asked. He glanced back at the door. Nothing moved.

The robot's eyes flashed. "I am sure I could. Shall I?"

"You left the prison," Cavalo said.

"At great risk to the remaining shreds of my sanity," SIRS said. "Why, even now I can feel my processors shutting down. I undoubtedly am facing an imminent death. The things I do for you. Can we go home now? I find I don't like the outside world very much. It's too real."

"I told you not to come."

"Our psychotic little friend here seemed to think something would happen to you. Funny, that."

"Did he?" Cavalo asked. "Maybe because he already knew what they did here." He hadn't thought of this. Not until now. He didn't know if that made it better or worse that Lucas had thought he needed help.

They do many things, Lucas told him solemnly. Lucas pulled on the bars again. *Can't go this way, too loud.* His eyes flickered over Cavalo to the door. His feral grin returned. *We can go through the front.*

"You can't kill anyone," Cavalo said. "Do you understand?"

The smile turned into a frown. *Why not?*

"These people don't deserve it." He wondered if he believed that. Surely they deserved *something*. Much like Cavalo himself did.

I thought they were maybe bad guys? Bad Dog asked. *We kill bad guys with our teeth. Maybe bad guys too because it's safer than sorrier.*

"Not here," Cavalo said. "No one dies."

What's the point? Lucas asked with a scowl.

I never get to kill anything anymore, Bad Dog said.

"What happened here?" SIRS asked.

"Not now. I need to get to Hank."

"And then?"

"I'll figure it out."

"This isn't going to end well."

"Does it ever?" Cavalo asked. "One guard that I can tell. SIRS, do not let Lucas kill him."

"What about maiming?" The robot sounded amused.

"No maiming."

"I tried," SIRS told Lucas.

I will maim if I feel like it, Lucas said. He reached in between the bars and gripped Cavalo's face tightly. *I could maim you right now. Spill your blood.*

Cavalo waited.

Lucas released him and shook his head. He pursed his lips and buzzed. *All those bees*, he said. *They want many things from me.* He looked back up at Cavalo. *I will get you out.* He dropped down out of sight.

Cavalo sighed. "SIRS, make sure he—"

"I know, I know. No violent bloody murder. You know, maybe you should have just a little more faith in him."

Cavalo ignored him, looking back up toward the house. It was dark. Dawn was still hours away. They'd be asleep. Deke. Aubrey. Hank. He'd be quiet. Get his answers. Then he could think about the next step. It was that easy.

Don't get shot again, Bad Dog said. *Tell Boy Deke to put down the boomstick.*

"I won't," Cavalo told him. "And I will."

"Are you sure this is a good idea?" SIRS asked.

"No. But it's all I've got."

He started toward the house.

And was stopped when a hand reached out and grabbed his own, pulling him back. He glanced down and saw Lucas's hand holding his own. He didn't understand. The grip tightened, grinding his bones together. He looked up at the Dead Rabbit. His eyes glittered in the oily mask.

Cavalo waited.

Lucas appeared to war with himself. He looked away, toward the dark house. His mouth stretched into a thin line.

"I'm coming back," Cavalo said. He didn't know why he felt the need to reassure Lucas. He didn't know why Lucas was here at all.

Lucas nodded tightly. He let go of Cavalo's hand and took his knife out once more. Flipped it and caught it by the blade. Held the handle out to Cavalo. *Take it,* he said.

Cavalo hesitated. "I don't think I'll—"

Insistent. *Take it. Take it.*

Cavalo took the knife. "What about you?"

Lucas gnashed his teeth. *I don't need it.*

"No eating anyone," Cavalo said sternly, pointing the knife back at him.

Lucas just smiled.

Cavalo took a breath and left his strange group hiding in the shadows.

The house was quiet as Cavalo stepped onto the porch.

He tried the front door. Locked, of course. Cavalo would have been disappointed if it'd been that easy.

The front window was locked too. That was easier. He stuck the knife between the frame and bent it back until the wood cracked, and the window popped up with a low groan. He stuck the knife in his teeth as he propped the window up with a small slat of wood set against the frame. He climbed in, feeling strangely guilty about the act.

This is Hank, he told himself.

Who is not who he seemed, he told himself.

The house settled around him as he stood in an old mudroom. He took the knife from his mouth.

Low lights flickered through a doorway off to his left. Little flashes of orange and red. Dancing shadows. Cavalo thought it beautiful.

He walked through the doorway.

The fire in the fireplace burned brightly. The room was warm.

From his chair in front of the fire, Hank said, "I wondered how long it would take you." He didn't look at Cavalo.

"Waiting long?" Cavalo asked quietly. He listened for the sounds of an ambush: the quick intake of breath, the light steps of feet. There was only the pop of fire and wood, the shifting of the old farmhouse.

Hank shrugged. "There are many answers to that question, Cavalo."

"Cryptic doesn't sit well on you, Hank."

"I don't mean to be," he said with a sigh. He lifted a glass filled halfway with a dark liquid to his lips and drank. His throat worked, and Cavalo gripped the knife tightly in his hands. The blade flashed against the firelight. "Scotch," Hank said as he lowered the glass. "One of the caravans had it. Never opened. Cost me an arm and a leg, but I had to have it. From 2004." He shook his head. "Hard to believe there was ever such a time as Before."

"I don't know what year it is now," Cavalo admitted.

Hank laughed, but there was no humor in it. "It is the year of our Lord 2123. Give or take a year. I don't think anyone knows for sure."

"SIRS does. Probably."

"He here?"

Cavalo said nothing.

"Of course he is," Hank said. "And Bad Dog. And your Dead Rabbit. What happened to Jacob?"

"Jacob?"

"The guard."

"Will wake up with a headache," Cavalo said. "Nothing more. Though you should tell him to clean his gun. And actually put bullets in it."

Hank winced. "Saw that, did you?"

"Yes."

Hank looked over at him for the first time since he'd walked into the room. He looked older than Cavalo had ever seen him, and his eyes were bloodshot. Cavalo wondered how much of the scotch he'd had tonight. "Thought you might."

"You knew I'd get out."

"Maybe. Probably. You never were one for cages, except for the ones you made for yourself."

"Deep, Hank."

Hank glanced down at the knife. "Are you here to kill me, Cavalo? I thought us friends once."

"No."

"To which? Killing or friends?"

"Does it matter?"

"It might."

"The first."

Hank nodded. "We were friends, weren't we?"

"I think so."

"But not anymore."

"I don't know."

"Why him?"

"Who?"

"The Dead Rabbit. Lucas."

Cavalo knew what he meant, even though he didn't want to. "I don't know. He... smells different, I guess."

Hank arched an eyebrow. "Oh?"

Cavalo shook his head. "No. That's what Bad Dog calls him. Smells Different."

"Ah," Hank said, as if it all made sense.

"But he is. Different."

"Than what?"

"The rest."

"You didn't seem to think so when you brought him here with a rope tied around his neck."

"Things change."

"They do. Who would have thought you'd be standing in my house in the middle of the night after breaking out of our jail, deciding whether or not you really want to use that knife on me?"

"I don't."

"Your eyes say differently."

"It's the bees," Cavalo said.

"That buzzing in your head."

"Yes."

"It wants you to use that knife."

"Yes." The bees wanted him to end this once and for all and leave this foolish man to the fate he'd created for himself.

"Can you control them? The bees."

"For now."

"And Bad Dog? Lucas? SIRS? Can they control theirs?"

"Yes." That felt like a lie. He remembered the sound of his bones breaking as SIRS bent his fingers. The blood on the Dead Rabbit's teeth.

"You know what's at stake."

"Yes."

Kill him, the bees said. *Stab him and let his blood out to see what colors it would make in the firelight.*

"If Patrick finds out about Dworshak. If he gets Lucas back. If he gets power. Water. It'll be over, Cavalo. For all of us. It won't be long before there are missiles and bombs. Satellites with lasers. This has all happened before, and it will all happen again. If he wins. If we give him what he wants."

"All you've done is given him what he wanted," Cavalo retorted.

Hank closed his eyes. "Because there was nothing else we could do. Before."

"And now?"

"There's a chance."

"For?"

"A life. For my children. For their children. For others."

"Do you think of them?" He took a step toward Hank, gripping the knife again.

"Who?" Hank did not look afraid as he opened his eyes.

"The people you've killed. The people you've sent to die."

"Every day." Hank's voice shook. "I don't sleep much anymore. I see them all when I close my eyes. That look. That look of understanding. Of what we were doing. Of what would happen to them. Have you ever seen that look, Cavalo? All fear and anger and hatred rolled into one."

"Like a cornered animal." A bear in a cave.

"Yes."

"I have," Cavalo said. He bent over until he was level with Hank, the knife pressed against the side of Hank's head. "I see it in you right now."

The bees screamed.

Hank took a deep breath.

Cavalo stepped away.

"Grangeville," he said.

"What?" Hank asked. A tear trickled down his cheek.

"We have to tell them. About what's coming. They'll need to help. They'll need to hide. Cottonwood would be easier to defend."

Hank shook his head. "We can't fit all of them here. We'd be bursting at the seams." He sounded dazed.

"I know. That's why those who can't fight—the children, the elderly, the infirm—they'll go to the prison with SIRS. The defense grid will hold them. It'll be tight, but they should fit."

"You have enough power?"

Only just. "Yes. And Dworshak. You'll need to send a team to Dworshak. To make sure it still stands. That the Dead Rabbits haven't found it. People you trust. People who can move quietly. Send two or three who know what to look for."

"And you?"

"I'll take Lucas to Grangeville. They'll want proof. We'll be gone only a day. We can't take any more than that."

"What will I do?"

Cavalo looked into the fire. "Prepare," he said. "We have eighteen days."

"They'll need convincing. The people. Cottonwood."

"Then I suggest you think of something. You'll tell them later today."

"And Patrick? How... we need him. His... skin. If he's got the other half."

"I know." Cavalo hadn't gotten that far yet. He was surprised at how much he'd already said. He should have killed Hank and left. Talking always messed things up. "I need to sleep. Is the house down the way still vacant?"

"That's it, then? You think I will just let you go?"

Cavalo chuckled bitterly. "You don't have a choice. Not anymore. Is the damn house vacant?"

"Yeah. Go. I need to think. And sober up."

Cavalo turned and was almost out of the room when Hank called his name. When Cavalo glanced back at him, the big man had stood from his chair and stepped toward the fire. "Does it ever stop?"

44

"What?"

"Seeing them. When you close your eyes."

"No," Cavalo said. "And sometimes, you see them even when your eyes are open. That's how you know you're well and truly fucked."

He left Hank sitting in the dark.

THE DOOR TO THE EMPTY HOUSE WAS UNLOCKED. IT WAS COLD inside. SIRS found some blankets in a closet. They were musty, and Bad Dog sneezed as he curled up against Cavalo for warmth.

"I'll keep watch," SIRS said. "But we have to hurry, Cavalo. I have to get back to the prison." He sounded desperate. "I can't be out in the world like this for long. I am slipping. I can feel it already."

"Won't be long. I promise. I have plans for you."

"Okay." A bit of relief crept into the robot's voice. "I miss our home. Funny, that."

Cavalo propped his head up and looked beyond the robot. Lucas stood near the door, flipping his knife again and again. The scowl was back. "You should sleep," Cavalo told him. "You'll need it. You and I are going on a trip."

I'm not going anywhere with you.

"You will."

Go to sleep, Lucas said. *Go to sleep so I can cut your heart out.*

"There's a blanket there if you need it. It's going to be cold." He looked away before he could see the reply. He turned toward Bad Dog, who huffed at him.

"What?" Cavalo whispered.

He wants to come down here too. Smells Different wants to be in our Bad Dog pile.

"No."

Yes. His bees are too loud, though.

"You can hear them?"

Yes. They scream. Like yours do sometimes. Except his are all the time.

"Go to sleep."

Bad Dog did. And somehow, Cavalo followed him.

Until he was awoken a short time later.

He opened his eyes. Bad Dog snored against his chest, his tail twitching against Cavalo's leg. And from behind him, a warm body pressed against his back. Cavalo turned his head and found eyes glittering in the dark, a knife pressed against his ribs. Cavalo thought it possibly a dream. Surely it felt like one. The man and Dead Rabbit watched each other for a time. No words were spoken. For once, the bees did not make a sound. It was in this incredible silence that Cavalo realized he did not want to look away.

Eventually Cavalo laid his head back down. He brought his hand up to the Dead Rabbit's and pressed down. The knife dug into his side. Not enough to break the skin, but enough to sting. The scrape of the knife told Cavalo he wasn't dreaming. The scrape of a kiss behind his ear told Cavalo he wasn't sane. And with the breath of a clever monster upon his neck, Cavalo slept again.

When morning came, the town of Cottonwood gathered around them, distrust and fear in their eyes. They whispered to each other. They pointed fingers. They bowed their heads. They swayed like trees. Cavalo wondered if all they saw when they looked at him was blood. On his hands. On his face. In his teeth. Every part of him told him to run. To run and never look back. And when he looked up at the town around him again, he saw the blood on their hands. On their faces. In their teeth.

They were no different. They thought themselves better, but they were no different.

Cavalo glanced down at Bad Dog at his side. His posture was rigid as he eyed the townsfolk. A low rumble came from his chest. Every now and then his teeth flashed.

Cavalo looked to SIRS next to Bad Dog. His posture was rigid as he eyed the townsfolk. He clicked and beeped. Every now and then his eyes flashed.

Cavalo looked to Lucas on his other side. His posture was rigid as he eyed the townsfolk. His black mask was smeared around his narrowed eyes. Every now and then, his teeth flashed.

They were the same. He thought they were better, but they were no different.

Hank spoke. He said many things about power and water and Dworshak. About light and darkness. He spoke of their fallacies. About the blood on all their hands. Of the decisions made in the past. Of choices that had to be made in the days ahead. He spoke of who the Dead Rabbits wanted. Of what they would do if the town complied. About what the town would do if they did not. Of cycles ongoing. Of cycles broken.

Alma stood with the crowd. She caught Cavalo's eye once. Held. Looked away.

The questions came as Cavalo knew they would. People could not live this close to the Deadlands and have seen what they'd seen without questions. Especially when it involved a Dead Rabbit. There was disbelief in the words as they were shouted. Skepticism. Even anger. Cavalo thought of mobs forming. Like a hive filled with bees. He started to dig his feet into the earth, cataloging those that would be the most immediate threat. They would be the first to fall, their life's blood spilling onto the dirt before they even knew what had happened. It would be regrettable, but necessary. The sight of blood would either cow the rest or send them all into a frenzy. Either/or would do Cavalo just fine.

He tasted the dusty tang of copper in the back of his throat. "Be ready," he muttered to those at his side. "Be ready."

And it might have ended there, this story, with the spilling of blood and the deaths of dozens in this little town on the border of a radioactive wasteland. Humanity, after all, cannot always contain the rage within. The hive could have split, and a swarm of bees could have descended and crawled on the eyes of all those present, clouding their visions from nothing but death.

It was close. The hive cracked. Voices raised. Fury spilled over.

But it did not happen.

Instead, Lucas stepped forward.

The town of Cottonwood sighed as they took a step back. Cavalo thought of the tree-wife who danced in the haunted woods. Cottonwood sounded like the wind through the tree-wife's leaves.

Lucas lifted his shirt up and over his head. Gooseflesh raced along his arms and back. His breath streamed from his mouth. The fat scar around his neck paled sharply in the cold. He dropped the shirt onto the snow. The black tattoos on his skin were bright against white flakes dropping from the heavy clouds above.

He raised his arms and turned slowly, just as he'd done in the cell block before. And when his back was to the town, his gaze met Cavalo's. A snowflake landed on the thick mask around his eyes. It melted upon contact, and a black tear tracked its way down his cheek.

As the town of Cottonwood looked on in horrified wonder, Lucas watched only Cavalo.

And Cavalo, knowing how truly pleasurable it was to burn, did not look away.

push

THERE WERE SEVENTEEN DAYS LEFT. Cavalo stood near the southern gates of Cottonwood, the sun not yet risen. Lucas stood behind him, twirling his knife, pack slung over his shoulder. Bad Dog sniffed the metal gate, anxious to get on the road.

"We'll be back by tomorrow," Cavalo told SIRS and Hank, tightening the strap of his own pack. "Afternoon at the latest, barring any storms. Are your people set?" He slid his bow over his shoulder. SIRS and Lucas had brought it down from the jail, along with his rifle.

Hank nodded. "Bill knows more about electricity and such than anyone else around. He's kept the lights on this long. He's the best we got. He's taking his son Richie with him."

"They know what to look for?" Cavalo asked, though he knew Bill knew his stuff. He'd come to the prison once to help Cavalo and SIRS with a short circuit that SIRS could not track down.

Hank shrugged. "As much as possible. It'd be easier if SIRS went with them."

SIRS stiffened. "That might be so," he said, "but the world is *far* too big and the chances of getting lost are extraordinarily high, and even *if* I wanted to—"

"Not an option," Cavalo interrupted. "I need him at the prison. It will make things easier. They'll have the walkies. You said they're long-range. Are you sure they'll work?"

"Never tested them that far," Hank said. "I guess we'll find out. They'll be heading east, then north on the old US 12 toward what used to be Orofino. There's a caravan route to follow. It'll take them through higher elevations, but SIRS said we're clear of any major storms for at least a week or so."

"And who's the third person going with them?"

Hank hesitated.

"Hank."

"He's a good boy, Cavalo. What happened was an accident. He asked to do this, and even though it goes against my better judgment, I agreed. I think he sees it as his penance."

"Deke?" Cavalo asked. "Shit. Are you sure that's a good idea?"

"Not sure of much anymore."

Cavalo felt the scrape of a knife against his arm. He had to stop himself from lashing out instinctively. He looked over at the Dead Rabbit. There was a question in his eyes. He made an L shape with his thumb and forefinger and pointed it at Cavalo.

"Yeah. That was him."

Lucas glared at Hank. Jabbed the knife at him. Motioned between Hank and Cavalo. Jabbed the knife again. Pointed at Bad Dog.

Hank didn't appear to be put off in the slightest. "What'd he say?" he asked Cavalo.

"Said you better make sure Deke knows if he's going to point a gun at someone, he'd better be ready to use it."

"That's all he said?"

"Yes."

Lucas scowled at Cavalo. Waved the knife again.

"That wasn't all," Hank said sagely.

"I'm not going to say that," Cavalo told Lucas.

Lucas pressed the knife against Cavalo's stomach. The tip poked through the outer layers and dimpled his skin underneath.

Cavalo sighed. "And if Deke ever points a gun at me again, Lucas will cut off his arms and feed them to Bad Dog."

And I will eat them with great satisfaction, Bad Dog said with a growl.

"And Bad Dog will eat them."

With great satisfaction, Bad Dog instructed.

"With great satisfaction," Cavalo muttered.

"Duly noted," Hank said. Cavalo could hear the hidden smile in his words. "Let's keep that to ourselves. For now."

"Tell Bill to keep his head down. They move quick and quiet. If there is any sign of trouble, they run."

"Bill knows. Should take them five days or so. Couple of days there, a day at the dam, couple of days back."

"And any caravans come through, you get all the ammo you can. And if they won't stay and fight, you tell them to run."

Hank was amused. "I'll make sure."

Cavalo nodded. "We should go."

Lucas sheathed his knife and grinned at Cavalo. He turned toward the gate as it began to rise.

"Do be safe, Cavalo," SIRS said. "This is the most excitement we've had in years, and I would surely hate it if it ended with all of your heads on a pike as a warning to others. I think that would be a most painful way to die."

"Thanks," Cavalo said. "I think. You know what to do?"

The robot's eyes flashed. "Oh, I don't know. I'm *only* capable of understanding complex quantum mechanics. I don't know how I'll ever shepherd a bunch of meat suits to my prison."

"You understand quantum mechanics but can't figure out the rest of the schematics?" Hank asked.

"You aren't allowed at the prison," SIRS said. He beeped loudly, and his eyes went dim. His head rocked back with a loud creak and he blared, "G.H. LEWES WROTE THAT THE EMERGENT IS UNLIKE ITS COMPONENTS INSOFAR AS THESE ARE INCOMMENSURABLE, AND IT CANNOT BE REDUCED TO THEIR SUM OR THEIR DIFFERENCE." His head came forward as the lights of his eyes grew brighter. "Why are we all standing around talking?" he asked, sounding affronted. "We have work to do!"

"We'll be ready," Hank said.

Cavalo wasn't sure if he believed him. "Alma?" he asked quietly.

Hank shook his head. "Give her time, Cavalo. She's—*we've* made mistakes. Terrible choices. It's hard for her. For all of us."

"Could you tell her...." Cavalo stopped himself. He didn't know what he wanted Hank to tell her. Words were frivolous things, and he'd used more of them in the past few days than he had in the past few years. He was tired of speaking.

"You can tell her when you get back," Hank said quietly, as if he only wanted Cavalo to hear. "She's just not sure about"—his eyes flickered over to Lucas—"everything."

"It's not—"

"He fits," Hank interrupted. "Like the missing piece of a puzzle. He fits, Cavalo. With all of you. I can see that. And so does she."

"It's not...," Cavalo tried again.

"It's not what?" Hank asked kindly.

Cavalo didn't know.

"You know what you have to do. You have to push."

"Push what?"

"The Dead Rabbit. For everything he knows. It's better if...."

"If?"

Hank looked away. "If it's done away from other people."

Cavalo understood. "In case he... reacts." For a moment, he hated Hank more than he ever had before. It was a flash of white-hot rage where Cavalo almost shot Hank in the face. It faded as quickly as it'd come.

Hank gave a grim smile, unaware of how close he'd come to death. "Reacts. Yes. He knows, Cavalo. More than we ever could. If we're to do this, we need to know what he knows. Every little detail. It's our only chance."

And that's what worried Cavalo. How much the Dead Rabbit knew. How much he'd give up.

And if he's really on your side at all, the bees whispered. *Or if he's playing you. Pushing his way in like a worm into a rotting corpse until one day, when you least expect it, you look down and see his knife buried in your chest, his teeth biting into your skin as he begins to feed.*

"I'll do what I can."

"Travel safe." Hank squeezed his shoulder.

Cavalo nodded tightly and turned toward the southern road, suddenly dizzy from the burst of bees in his head. He did not miss the way Lucas frowned at him, the knife again in his hand.

THEY FOLLOWED THE SOUTHERN ROAD, OR RATHER, WHAT remained of the southern road. There were curious legends, faded green signs that let them know they were traveling on what used to be known as the US 95, back in Before. Mountains were in the distance to the west. Ahead of them and east stretched snowy white fields as far as they could see. They were out in the open, but they could see if anyone approached them. But it also meant they could be seen by anyone *as* they approached.

Cavalo could not remember the last time he'd traveled to Grangeville through the old farmlands as they did now. It'd been months. Possibly even a year. Surely before the snows fell last. Maybe a bit longer. Hank had said that the bigger town was still run by Cordelia, an older woman who looked like someone's grandmother until you crossed her the wrong way and she brought out her gun. She may have been old, but she was a tough old broad who didn't take shit from anyone. And for some reason, she liked Cavalo. He wasn't sure why. He thought she'd help. Or she'd shoot at him until he left. For all he knew, she'd had a similar deal going on with the

Dead Rabbits. Cottonwood and Grangeville were the only towns within a hundred miles this side of the Deadlands.

He didn't know what she'd make of Lucas. Perhaps she'd shoot him and Cavalo would be rid of him once and for all. It would certainly be easier.

Bad Dog wandered ahead, his nose low to the snow, ears twitching.

Lucas walked beside Cavalo. The knife was still in his hand, his grip on it tight. Cavalo wondered who he wanted to stab. He decided it wasn't an answer he wanted that badly.

They continued on in silence. Cavalo continually scanned the horizon. He thought he saw a smudge of black against the white clouds off to the east, but his eyes weren't as sharp as they'd once been. It might've been nothing. Still, when US 95 turned east and the smudge was ahead of them, he couldn't take his eyes off of it.

It was slow going, the snow thick under their feet. They kept to the road as much as possible, but the old highway was split and cracked, large chunks rising up out of the earth at sharp angles. The frames of farmhouses and barns stood off in the distance, some crumbling, some charred. Cavalo wondered, as he sometimes did, who had lived there Before. How had they lived? How had they died? These were questions he could not answer. He wasn't sure he wanted the answers.

They passed a pile of wood sticking out of the snow. Lucas stopped, cocking his head at the rotted wood. Faded reds and greens mixed with the white. *What is it?* he asked, pointing the knife.

"Billboards," Cavalo grunted. "From Before."

What's a billboard?

"A sign. For food and places. People."

Food? Bad Dog asked hopefully, sniffing around the wood.

"You've never seen one before?" Cavalo asked Lucas.

Lucas shook his head.

Cavalo had. A few times. Most were destroyed. Those that had still stood were illegible. One had been high in the air, somehow still standing after all else around it had collapsed. The words and pictures were almost gone, but he could still make out the smiling man with the large teeth next to the words *BEEN INJURED IN AN ACCIDENT? CALL DICK LEWIS FOR HELP! 1-800-GET-DICK! WITHOUT HIM, YOU WON'T GET DICK!* The billboard had been falling apart. Dick's face sagged. Some of his teeth had torn away, and metal struts showed through. He looked like a monster. Cavalo had hurried past him and never looked back. That had been in his wandering days. Before Elko.

"They sold things," Cavalo said now, though he wasn't sure if that was quite right. "Told people what to buy."

There's no food here, Bad Dog grumbled. He lifted his leg and watered the wood and snow. *This is also mine now. I own many things.*

Lucas pointed at the sign and shrugged. *Why would people buy what they were told?*

"I don't know. It was how the world worked, I guess. Dick Lewis told them how."

Lucas scowled. *Fuck Before. Fuck Dick Lewis.* He kicked at a piece of wood. It broke off and fell into the snow.

"Fuck Dick Lewis," Cavalo said softly.

Fuck Dick Lewis! Bad Dog barked excitedly. He pissed on the billboard again and put his nose back to the ground.

We fit, he thought.

Cavalo looked down the broken road after the dog. The black smudge wavered in the distance. They were still alone. He wondered how much longer that would last.

They passed the burnt-out shell of a truck, the rubber tires long since rotted away. The door to the truck was open, the seats inside cracked and covered in mold. Dead blue bunchgrass poked through the seats, black and frozen stiff. Bad Dog sniffed around it, as he sometimes did, but they didn't stop. There was no point; what had been in the truck, if anything, had been ransacked long ago. Cavalo knew from personal experience that had he looked inside the cab, he'd have seen a small curved seat lying upside down under the dashboard. All that was left of the child that had been in that seat was a small skeletal arm fused to the floor, the third and fourth fingers missing. The bone of the arm was splintered and pockmarked with little divots. Cavalo hoped it was an animal that had chewed on that arm. And that the child had not been alive.

He wondered if Lucas had ever caused teeth marks in bone. He thought it possible. He was a Dead Rabbit, after all.

He can't fit, Cavalo thought. *Whatever I am. Whatever I've done, I'm not like him.*

At least Jamie hadn't ended up like the child in the truck, not that it was possible. Jamie had been nothing but a crater left in the ground. Pink mist and shards of bone. That was all that had been left of the boy who sometimes stuck his tongue out between his teeth when he thought hard on something.

Lucas buzzed at him, pursing his lips and blowing. *I can hear your bees,* he said. The knife had been put away when Cavalo hadn't been watching.

Cavalo said nothing, keeping his eyes on the black smudge on the horizon. He thought he knew what it was. He hoped he was wrong.

I can hear them over mine, Lucas said, wincing as he grabbed the sides of his head. *They have to be loud for me to hear that.*

"Sometimes," Cavalo allowed.

What happened?

"When?"

Now. To make your bees come. He pulled the fur-lined hood of his jacket up and over his head.

"The truck."

Truck?

"That... vehicle. In the road."

Lucas shrugged. *What about it? They're all over.*

"Yeah."

So?

"That one's different."

How?

"There's an arm in it."

Lucas glanced back the way they'd come. The truck was out of sight. *So?* Lucas said again. *You've seen worse.*

"Have I?" They hadn't talked much about before. Not Before, but before Lucas had first held a knife to his throat in the clearing of the haunted woods.

Yes. It's on your face. In your eyes.

"Is that why you hide yours? Behind the mask?"

I don't hide. He covered his face with his hands.

"Sometimes you don't wear the mask." *You have to push,* he thought.

I don't need it.

"But most of the time you do."

Stop it.

Cavalo chuckled bitterly.

Lucas glared at him.

They walked on. Bad Dog was ahead of them. Cavalo was waiting for him to pick up on the smell of the black smudge that lay ahead. If it was real, it'd be soon. Cavalo hoped it was nothing but the bees playing a trick on his mind. They'd done it before. They'd do it again.

"Did it hurt?" he asked eventually. *Push, push, push.*

What?

When Patrick cut your throat. "The tattoos," he said instead.

Lucas didn't answer. He pulled the knife back out instead. Bared his teeth.

"You don't scare me," Cavalo said.

I scare everyone.

"Most everyone."

I scare you. I can hear it in your bees.

"Not for the reasons you think," Cavalo said before he could stop himself.

What reasons?

"Did the tattoos hurt?" The wind was cold against Cavalo's face. The bees laughed.

Lucas scowled. Pointed the knife at him. Cavalo thought about breaking his arm and taking the knife away but decided against it. They didn't have time to stop. Still, it'd almost be worth it to hear the bone snap and wipe that look off the boy's face. If they survived the next few weeks, he'd do it then.

He thought he'd receive no answer from Lucas. Then, a shrug. *Maybe.*

"There's a lot of them."

Maybe.

DEFCON 1. WE'RE AT DEFCON 1. "And it'd have to have been done in the last few years. Since you're still a kid. They would have stretched otherwise."

A jab of the knife. A gnash of teeth. *Maybe. Maybe. Goddamn you, maybe.*

Dangerous ground, this. Cavalo had never been one to ignore warning signs. Like the black smudge ahead that looked more and more like a black cloud trailing up from the ground toward the sky. "It's like a joke, isn't it?" he asked. "What came first, the scar or the tattoos?"

Maybe. Maybe. Lucas's shoulders tensed. His back arched as if electrocuted.

Lose something, Charlie? "The scar," Cavalo said. "That came first. Patrick wouldn't have taken the chance of marking you only to try and kill you."

A stuttering step. *Stop,* Lucas said. *This is done. Billboards. Tell me more about billboards. Bones. The bones of children in the husks of cars. Why your bees make noise whenever you think of children. Tell me of that. Tell me of all of that. Just stop. Stop with your mouth. Stop with the noise. Stop making your bees touch my own. Stop it, stop it stopitstopitstop—*

"How long did it take? Months. It had to be. There's too much there to be done all at once."

The knife flashed. *Stop. Stop.*

But he wouldn't. Cavalo was tired of secrets. He'd learned too many over the past few weeks. Enough to last him a lifetime. Hank was right. He had to push. At least out here, Cavalo would be the only one to die. "His pet, huh? Sucking on your dead mama's tit when he found you. Raised you. Cut you. Marked you." *Fucked you,* Cavalo thought, and the anger that roared through him was hot and slick. It curdled his stomach. All of it did.

Kill you, Lucas said with a snarl. *Kill you.*

For every step Lucas took toward him, Cavalo took an answering step away. Bad Dog hadn't yet noticed the shimmer in the air. Cavalo had. He knew what it was. What they'd find. *Push now,* the bees whispered. *Push now before they realize what the black smudge truly is.*

"Does he have the rest? Patrick."

Hurt you. Stab you. Split your skin.

"You put on a good show. For the town. Bought yourself some time."

Break you. Smash you. Make you bleed.

"But what happens when they find out you're only part of the solution? That you're not even whole?"

Hate you. Fuck you. Kill you. Lucas stopped walking. His hand tightened on the knife.

"You'll be just another Dead Rabbit then."

Bastard. I want to hurt you.

Cavalo turned away from the billowing smoke in the distance. Lucas was coiled, ready to spring. "They'll see nothing but a monster. And I can do nothing to stop them."

You should have killed me.

"So many times," Cavalo said.

Lucas's eyes narrowed. *And yet you didn't.*

"I still can."

You won't. You need me.

"I don't need anyone."

The bees screamed. A strong wind blew along the fields, blowing up snow. It swirled around him like a snow globe.

Lucas took a step toward him. Cavalo did not take a step back.

They all need me. What's on my skin.

"We can scan it," Cavalo said. "Once you're dead."

But you. You want to touch my skin.

"Fuck you," Cavalo said hoarsely.

Your bees give you away.

Cavalo pulled his gun. "Stop."

MasterBossLord? Bad Dog sounded worried.

"Stay back."

But I smell—

"Stay back!"

I hear you, Lucas said with a nasty smile, *at night. You call for him. Jamie. Jamie. Jamie.* He was only a short distance away from the barrel of the gun.

"One shot," Cavalo swore. "That's all it'll take."

And her. You beg her. In the night. Don't go. Don't take him! Please come back. Please!

"Kill you," Cavalo whispered.

Bad Dog barked.

And Alma. I see the way you look at her. You fucked her.

"Leave her alone."

You fucked her, but you want to fuck me too. Alma's clean, though. Isn't she? Not as much blood on her hands as yours and mine. We're the same, you see.

"Stop. Now."

Bad Dog barked again, sounding far away.

Lucas stood before Cavalo. He pressed his forehead against the barrel of the gun. Grinned. Pressed the knife on the side of Cavalo's chest, aiming for his heart. *Do it,* he said, his eyes wide in the mask. *Do it. Do me. Do it, and I'll do you. We can both go. Just a little push.*

Pressure on the trigger. Almost enough. Lucas wouldn't have time to shove the knife into his heart. And so what if he did? Cavalo knew what awaited them in Grangeville. He knew what would happen from here. He knew they didn't have a chance. Not against Patrick. Not against the Dead Rabbits. The UFSA. The Forefathers. None of them. He was just one man who wanted to exist until he didn't anymore. That was all.

The bees swarmed in his head.

He didn't think he had any rubber bands left to break.

The tables had turned on him. He didn't know how it happened. The snow globe was shaking so hard Cavalo thought the glass would shatter.

Lucas, saying the things he did, even though he couldn't say anything at all. It wasn't real. It was all in Cavalo's head.

It was just a matter of bees and men.

The scrape of knife and kiss.

The last half pound of pressure on the trigger. Cavalo thought Lucas's brains would spatter prettily over the snowy southern road.

He'd wanted it before. And it was something Cavalo could give.

But that was too easy.

MasterBossLord!

"Patrick," he said, surprised at how even his voice was, this close to death. "You were his pet. His toy. His psycho fucking bulldog. And unless you tell me what I need, I will make sure his hands fall on you again. I will give you to him myself."

Lucas's eyes were black. Cavalo doubted there was any part of the Lucas he knew left.

Lucas pressed his forehead against the gun barrel harder until the skin split. Blood trickled into the mask around his eyes. Cavalo pulled the gun back slightly to avoid pulling the trigger. Lucas stepped closer. Cavalo could feel his breath on his face. It was hot in the cold air. It steamed up around him, and Cavalo wanted to lick the blood from his eyes. It hit him, this dirty thing, this nasty thing. It hit him in the base of his spine, oily and hot. Lucas was right. Cavalo did want to kill him. He wanted to fuck him too. The bees told him he could do both. Fuck him. Shoot him in the head. It was simple enough.

Sex and murder reflected back at him in those dark eyes.

He didn't know how it had come to this.

"Tell me," he said. "Everything."

I want to eat you up, those eyes said.

And then, a curious sound:

A long mournful howl came from behind them.

Cavalo's eyes cleared.

Lucas sucked in a deep breath.

The howl echoed over the both of them. The hairs on Cavalo's neck stood on end.

He turned. Bad Dog sat on his haunches, his head tilted back. He cried mournfully again. It rolled over the empty fields.

Cavalo dropped the gun to his side.

The knife fell away from his chest.

Drops of blood from Lucas's forehead fell into the snow, little red dots melting into little red tunnels.

"Bad Dog," Cavalo said. "It's...."

Bad Dog howled again.

Lucas touched his arm. Pointed to his ear. *What'd he say?*

"Smoke," Cavalo said. "Fire." He closed his eyes. "Death."

grangeville

THEY KEPT low to the ground as they covered the last few miles approaching Grangeville. They left the southern road and cut across the snowy fields. Dead wheat and shrubs poked up through the snow, brown and frozen. Cavalo didn't think it was enough to hide their approach. If anyone was watching them from the walls around Grangeville with binoculars, then they didn't stand a chance. There wasn't enough around them in the dead of winter to blend in. It was made worse when the gray clouds above broke apart briefly and weak sunlight shone through. Almost a month straight of snowstorms and the one time Cavalo needed one, the sun came out.

The plume of smoke loomed over the horizon, and as the outer walls of Grangeville took shape, the air became acrid and heavy. There was a cloying sweetness that came with the smoke that caused Bad Dog to sneeze and Cavalo to take shallow breaths. He knew that smell. He'd smelled it before. In Elko.

They came to a small hill outside of Grangeville. The two men and the dog crawled on their stomachs to crest the hill. Cavalo pushed the snow out of the way, laying his pack and bow against a small tree with black and peeling bark. He pulled his own old pair of binoculars out of the pack. "Stay down," he muttered to Lucas and Bad Dog.

Bad smell, Bad Dog whispered to him. *Hurts my nose. All smoky and bad.* He flattened his ears against his skull and whined.

"I know." Cavalo scanned the wall. He saw no movement. The column of smoke seemed to be rising from what Cavalo thought to be the town square. Whatever was burning seemed to be contained. The main gate into Grangeville was closed and secured, but there was a ragged hole farther down, the wall torn and blackened, as if something had exploded.

"Shit," Cavalo muttered. He handed the binoculars to Lucas and pointed toward the hole in the wall. "Is it them? Your people?"

Lucas frowned as he looked down at the wall. He shook his head.

"It's not them? The Dead Rabbits?"

He glared at Cavalo. Then nodded. *Yes, but they are not my people.*

"They were. And I think most people would disagree with you."

I still want to stab you.

"Feeling is mutual," Cavalo said, taking the binoculars back and pointing them toward Grangeville. "What'd they use? Grenade? Dynamite?"

Lucas hesitated. Shook his head. Made his hands into half circles, one in front of the other, inches apart. Put them near his right shoulder. Jerked them back. *Boom,* he said.

"Boom," Cavalo said. "Rocket launchers."

Lucas nodded.

"We're fucked."

Lucas shrugged.

We're fucked? Bad Dog asked. *Big boomstick?*

"Yeah. Big boomstick."

I hate boomsticks, Bad Dog growled. *I hate big ones even more.*

"They still here?" he asked Lucas.

Lucas hesitated again. Shook his head. Shrugged. *No. Maybe.* He sighed. *Probably.*

"We have to go down there."

Lucas shook his head again. *No.* He pointed back down the hill. *We have to go back.*

"We have to see if there's anyone left."

There won't be, Lucas snarled. *You know this. You know what's happened.*

Still no movement aside from the smoke. He could see tracks in the snow through the hole in the wall, but he couldn't tell if they were coming or going. "I know. But this is on me. And you." And it was. Every death in the town below was on Cavalo's head. Patrick had been one step ahead of him. He'd known that Cavalo would reach out to Grangeville. He'd known how to strike them down. Cavalo tried not to think about the last time he'd been in Grangeville, walking through the town. All those children who had been in the streets. Laughing. Playing.

I'm not going down there, Lucas said. Cavalo wondered what he was scared of.

"Then stay here." He glanced over at Bad Dog. "You know what I'm going to say."

Bad Dog rolled his eyes. *Stay here, Bad Dog. It's safer. I am a big bad human, and I make decisions that are dumb when I should be listening to my Bad Dog.* He huffed. *Stupid MasterBossLord. I go where you go.*

Cavalo reached over and grabbed Bad Dog's snout and pulled his head toward his own until their eyes met.

"You follow my lead," he said.

I follow you, for you are my MasterBossLord, Bad Dog said.

"You listen for my commands."

I listen to you, for you are my MasterBossLord.

"I will have your back."

And I will have yours.

"Together."

Together.

He let go of Bad Dog's snout. Lucas was watching him again, a strange look on his face. "What?" he asked, putting the binoculars in his pack before shouldering it again.

Lucas pointed at Bad Dog, then back at Cavalo. *He trusts you. You trust him.*

"He's my friend."

Lucas pointed at himself and shook his head. *You don't trust me.*

"No," Cavalo said. "I don't. Stay here. If you're not here when we get back, you're getting left behind." He pulled himself up and over the top of the hill. He slid down the other side on his stomach, the heavy coat protecting his skin from the ground underneath. He heard Bad Dog following down behind him. They reached the bottom and crouched low. Cavalo scanned the wall as they moved toward Grangeville. He did not hear voices. He did not hear screams. He thought maybe the time for screaming had already passed. He could hear the creak of the wooden walls. Somewhere, a winter bird called out. His own breath sounded like shotgun blasts in his ears.

He debated the rifle. He debated the pistol. He thought of the knife. He decided on the bow. Nocked an arrow.

The hole in the wall was bigger than it seemed on the hill. The black scorch marks radiated down the wall. They reminded Cavalo of a black mask. Chunks of blackened wood littered the ground.

He pressed up against the wall. Bad Dog crowded his legs, sniffing the air.

"Anything?" he asked quietly.

Smoke, he said. *Fire. Death.* His ears twitched. *Maybe. Inside. Blood. MasterBossLord, there's blood.*

Cavalo looked down at the ground. The snow here was dirty and flattened. Footsteps going in and out. Looked like more going out. He hoped. "Hold," he said to Bad Dog.

Bad Dog froze.

Cavalo waited. The wall groaned. Water dripped. Wind cooled his heated skin.

The bees told him to run. Run until he could run no more.

He took a deep breath. Pulled on the bowstring. Let out his

breath. Peered around the wall.

Houses. Shops. A weathervane squeaked as it spun. He pulled back. Took another breath. Let it out again. Swung his body around, keeping low. He pulled the arrow back. It scraped his cheek. Swept left. Clear. Right. Clear. Up. Clear.

It was almost normal except for the lack of activity and the quiet. It was almost normal except for the footsteps fanning out in the snow from the wall. It was almost normal except for the splashes of maroon over the snow. The walls of the houses. The boarded walkways.

Blood, Bad Dog whispered from behind him. *Blood.*

And it was. Trails of it in the snow, as if someone had been dragged away. Scrapes in the wooden posts that Cavalo thought had been made from fingernails. The blood on the walls looked to be almost dry. The blood on the snow looked frozen. It'd been there for some time.

They came at night, Cavalo thought.

Run, the bees said. *Run. Run.*

He leaned back against the wall. Released the tension in the bowstring. "Stay low," he said. "Follow me. Move until I say. Stop when I say. Don't leave my side."

I will follow you, Bad Dog said. He bumped his head against Cavalo's knee. *Forever.*

Cavalo knew he would. He wished he could tell his friend that it would lead only to death, that it was inevitable for Cavalo, but he knew it would fall on deaf ears. The dog was blind to any other way except following his MasterBossLord. Cavalo wondered how much longer they would last. Perhaps today would finally be the day. If it was, he hoped the bees did not follow them to whatever happened next.

Until then, though.

Pivoting on his heel, he brought the bow and arrow up. Pulled on the string. His line of sight followed down the arrow's shaft. Four steps and he was in Grangeville. Four more and he was pressed against the side of a house. Took a breath. Stepped out.

He followed the footprints. The trails of frozen blood. He could see the story in them. Of doors barricaded to keep the monsters out. Of doors smashed in as the monsters swarmed. Pieces of clothing caught in the wood as people were dragged from their homes. Bullet holes. Windows shattered. An axe in the middle of a dried blood splatter, the handle splintered in half.

No bodies. No people. No voices. No screams.

That sickly sweet smell in the air.

The black smoke rising over the rooftops.

No one walked the planks atop the walls.

No one moved inside the houses.

No one called out to him as he moved quietly through the town.

No one tried to kill him as the sun disappeared behind the clouds.

He stopped, blocks away from the center of Grangeville where the smoke rose to the sky. The snow at his feet was all red now, a mixture of slush and gristle. Cavalo was sure he saw a tongue mixed in with the dirt. A finger. A clump of hair.

Blood, Bad Dog muttered. *Blood, blood, blood, blood*. His whiskers dripped with it, his legs a rusty red.

Cavalo knew what burned ahead. Knew what he'd find.

Run, run, run, the bees chanted.

The air was so thick. So sticky sweet. Like meat cooking on a fire.

He picked a house at random. One close to the center of Grangeville. The door had been torn off its hinges. The furniture on the lower level had been overturned. Bad Dog's toenails clicked on the wooden floors. They passed the kitchen. Dishes broken on the floor. Blood on the cabinets. He found the stairs and went up. Passed a child's room with drawings on the walls, the bedsheets strewn about the room.

The hallway toward the back of the house was covered in debris. On the wall to the left, red words dripping in obscene streaks: *I LIKE IT WHEN THEY RUN* and *THESE ARE SOME GOOD EATS*.

There was a photograph hanging on the wall at the end of the bloody graffito. A man and woman. A child. Cavalo couldn't remember the last time he'd seen a recent photo. Cameras were rare. A nail had been hammered into the man's head. The glass had cracked. A human eye hung from the edge of the nail. It was small. The iris was blue, fading to gray. Cavalo wondered which of the people it'd come from.

Blood, Bad Dog whispered. *There's only blood here. MasterBoss-Lord, there is so much blood.*

"I know," Cavalo croaked out.

They reached the far room. It was mostly undisturbed. The covers on the bed had been thrown to the side, as if someone or someones had been awoken in the middle of the night to the sounds of the crashes from below or screams from the child's room down the hall. How many of them had there been? How many other houses looked this same way? He wondered if he'd known the people who lived here. He wondered what it meant when someone such as him couldn't stop shaking.

He approached a broken window that overlooked the town center, shards of glass on the floor below. He told himself he knew what was out that window. What he'd see. What to expect. What it would mean.

But when he saw the hundreds of bodies piled up in the snow, the hundreds of bodies of men and woman and children thrown atop each other as if they were garbage, he found he wasn't prepared for it. Their faces. Their open mouths. Their silent screams. Their arms and fingers. Feet that stuck out into the air. Little faces that had seen things no little face should ever have seen.

And they were all on fire.

The dead had been piled high into the air and lit on fire. The sweet smell of burning flesh clung to the air. The smoke from the blackened skin rose toward the gray sky.

Dead. The town was dead.

Grangeville had never stood a chance. Not in the middle of the night. Not if they didn't know what was coming. Not if they—

Movement, near the burning mountain of the dead.

He raised the bow and aimed the arrow.

Held.

Cordelia, the de facto leader of Grangeville, on her knees in the snow, disheveled hair around her face. Her head bowed. Little drops of blood dripped from her nose. Her hands were bound behind her back. She was only ten yards away. Cavalo could see the lines on her face. The tense set of her jaw.

Next to her was a man Cavalo recognized as her grandson. Mac? Was that his name? Once he'd been drunk in the bar where Cavalo had gone for a drink. Young, foolish thing that he was had tried to get Cavalo into his bed. Cavalo looked at his youthful, innocent face with faint disdain and had turned him down. Repeatedly. That face was now swollen with bruises. Split lips. Blood oozed down his chin as he stared up at the sky with bruised eyes.

Another man on Cordelia's other side.... Cavalo didn't recognize him. He looked no older than Mac. His arm was obviously broken, resting at an odd angle, what looked like bone poking through the skin of his forearm.

There were others, yes. A small group standing in front of the three people on their knees. Four men. One woman. All but one of them laughed at their prisoners. They spat on them. Kicked them. Rubbed the flat side of knives against their cheeks. The woman slapped Cordelia viciously, her head rocking back, blood spraying into the snow.

"Leave her alone!" Mac cried.

The woman laughed. "Leave her alone! Leave her alone!" She struck Cordelia again with a closed fist.

Her first, Cavalo thought. *Arrow through her eye. Another arrow. The farthest man. In his heart. Another arrow. The smallest man through his throat. Another arrow. The laughing man. In his mouth. Another arrow. Last man. Last man. Last—*

The last man turned his head. Cavalo saw him in profile.

Patrick.

Bad guys, Bad Dog whispered. *Bad guys and blood. Scary man and blood.*

Sweat trickled down Cavalo's neck.

Kill him. Do it now. Do it—

And he would have. He would have let the arrow fly then, straight into that smiling monstrous face. It would have been the end of this, at least this part.

But he didn't. He didn't fire the arrow because more Dead Rabbits began to come out of the shadows. From behind the houses on the other side of Grangeville. From storefronts. From behind the burning mountain. Dozens of them. Men and women. Black armbands on around their biceps. Some carried shovels. Bats with nails jutting out. Guns. Knives. Machetes. Swords. Grenades. RPGs. Blood on their clothes. Hands. Blood in their teeth. Sores on their faces and arms. Some had growths on their bodies. They moved quietly, like shadows.

And they gathered behind Patrick. The light from the burning mountain flickered on their faces.

"You had your chance," Patrick said. His voice was almost kind. "I warned you what would happen if you chose to side against me."

Cordelia raised her head. Even beaten down, Cavalo could see the steel in her eyes. *Tough old broad.*

Patrick smiled at her. "Fire," he said. "Just like him."

"You'll never get what you want," Cordelia said. "People like you never do."

"I guess we'll have to agree to disagree," Patrick said. "I'm okay with that."

Cordelia said nothing. The unknown man on his knees groaned. Mac's shoulders shuddered.

"Such savage business," Patrick sighed. "Things didn't used to be this way."

"This is your doing," Cordelia snapped at him. "This is you. This is all because of you. There were children. They were just *children.*"

"No," Patrick said. "This is on him. For taking what belonged to me. For standing there in front of me with disdain and anger and fire burning in his eyes. Like I was *nothing*. Like I was *no one*."

"You *are* nothing," Cordelia said. "You *are* no one." She spat blood and mucus at his feet.

Patrick shook his head sadly. "No. I am the man who has brought you to your knees. I am the man who has taken everything from you. But it didn't have to be this way. You forced my hand. This, my dear, rests on you. I gave you a chance. I gave you an opportunity. I told you how it could be for you and your people."

"He will beat you," Cordelia said. "If I know anything about him, it's that he will be the one to kill you."

"Cavalo?" Patrick laughed. "He is a broken man hiding in a broken prison. He will be nothing but memory soon enough."

Cavalo almost fired right then. Somehow, he held.

The unknown man next to her groaned.

"What was that?" Patrick asked, cupping his ear.

The Dead Rabbits laughed. It sounded like broken bones rubbing together.

"Just... tell him...," the man said through gritted teeth. "Please... Cordelia... just give him... what he wants."

"There is nothing left to give," Cordelia snarled at him. "Thomas, he has taken everything from us. We are not him. We are not the Dead Rabbits. We will never join them. We will never fight with them. That is not who we are."

The female Dead Rabbit slapped her face again.

Thomas cradled his broken arm. "If I... tell you," he said to Patrick, "will you let me go?"

"I think that can be arranged," Patrick said with a smile. Cavalo thought him a liar.

"In.... Cottonwood. There's a person. Who. Works for... them. I overheard the others. When they were here. Before they left to find Wilkinson."

"Who is it?" Patrick asked. "Give me a name."

"It's—"

But that was as far as he got. Cordelia lunged at him, her teeth going to his throat. She bit down, and blood poured over her face. Thomas screamed. It echoed over the burning mountain. Cordelia pulled back, tearing out his throat. Thomas fell forward, blood spilling out onto the snow. He landed facedown. He twitched once. Twice. A shudder rolled through his body. Then he was still.

Silence. The Dead Rabbits watched.

Finally, Patrick said, "Well, that was unexpected. Am I going to get anything further from you?"

Cordelia said nothing as she lay atop Thomas.

"I thought not," he said.

"He will rise," Cordelia said through skin and blood. "He will—"

Patrick shot her in the head. Pointed the gun at Mac. Shot him in the head.

NOW NOW NOW.

The bowstring tensed. He lined the arrow with Patrick. He—

Another hand grabbed his the moment before he let go. The arrow slipped from the string and clattered to the floor. *Knife*, Cavalo thought, that cool mentality of a killer falling over his mind. *Elbow to the stomach. Head back into face. Spin. Knife into gut. Pull up to eviscerate.*

He saw the slender fingers on his own. Heard the breath behind him. He'd been so intent on the scene before him that he hadn't heard anything approaching from behind. He cursed himself silently, wondering when it was he'd gotten so soft. So old.

He shot his elbow back. Heard the sharp exhalation behind him. Dropped the bow. Knocked his head back. Empty air. Connected. He spun, pulling his knife as he moved. Brought it up in a flat arc.

A knife already at his throat. A hand at the back of his neck.

Lucas, eyes narrowed, nose bleeding.

He thought to stab him anyway.

"What are you doing?" Cavalo said in a low voice.

You can't, Lucas said. *You can't.*

Blood, Bad Dog whispered. He sounded as if he were dreaming.

73

"Protecting him?"

Protecting you. They would find you. There's too many.

"You fucking bastard."

Yes.

"They killed them."

Yes.

"All of them."

Yes.

"Did you know?"

No. But you did, didn't you?

"How many? How many are you?"

We are many, Lucas said. *We are legion.*

"It's Wormwood," Cavalo said. "It's all Wormwood."

Lucas nodded, as if he understood. For all Cavalo knew, he might.

"I can kill him." He tried to move. The knife at his throat moved with him.

You can't. Not yet.

"Can we do this?"

I don't know. Maybe. Probably not.

With Cavalo's knife at his side and his own against Cavalo's throat, Lucas leaned forward. His forehead pressed against Cavalo's, eyes glittering in the mask.

Cavalo thought he could hear Lucas's bees screaming above his own.

One breathed out. The other breathed in.

Again. And again.

"I will kill you," Cavalo swore. "If you betray me. If you betray any of us, I will kill you."

You can try, Lucas said. *Do you trust me?*

"No."

Blood, Bad Dog whispered again.

They stood there for a time. As shadows lengthened. As bodies burned.

. . .

IT WAS DUSK BEFORE THEY THOUGHT IT SAFE TO LEAVE Grangeville.

The Dead Rabbits were gone.

The town stood quiet as they walked out of the house.

The bodies smoldered. The air was thick. Cavalo thought he saw a star in a break in the clouds overhead.

They walked between the houses. They moved with care, sticking to dark corners.

They did not speak.

He is a broken man hiding in a broken prison.

Cavalo could see the hole in the wall up ahead. Fifteen miles to Cottonwood. Maybe they'd make it before morning if they moved all night. He didn't know if he could. He was very tired.

The town was silent, the air clearer here.

It still felt like death.

"Cut across the fields," Cavalo said quietly. "Stay low. We'll make it to the road."

Okay, Bad Dog said.

Cavalo stopped. Turned.

Lucas was gone.

"Lucas!" he hissed.

Nothing.

Then:

Bad Dog yelped in pain.

Cavalo saw bright lights as something heavy struck the back of his head.

He went to his knees. Hands into the snow.

"What do we have here?" a deep voice said. "Looks like he was right. Stragglers."

A woman laughed. She sounded familiar. They both did.

He looked up.

A large black man stood in front of him, dressed in Dead Rabbit gear. A large growth protruded from his neck. The woman was also a Dead Rabbit. Their clothes were covered in gristle and dried blood. They smelled of smoke and fire. Death.

Bad Dog lay off to the left, breathing but otherwise not moving.

"You just get back into town?" the big man asked. "Or were you hidden?"

He would kill them. He would kill them both.

The woman laughed again. "He's getting angry."

Lucas did this. He knew. He'd known the whole time.

He couldn't get his arms to move. His head was ringing. The bees were caught in a storm.

His knife was taken from him. His rifle. His bow. His arrows. His pack.

Get up. Get up. Get up.

"Poor little doggy," the woman crooned, standing above Bad Dog. "Poor little guy."

"Wait," the man said. He sounded unsure. "Didn't he say...."

"What?" the woman asked. "Who?"

"Get over here."

"I don't—"

"*Now.*"

She left Bad Dog alone. As she passed Cavalo, she kicked him upside the head. The flashes became an entire universe of stars.

"You stupid bitch," the big man snarled. "Don't you know who this is?"

"Straggler," she said. "You said straggler."

"It's *him*. The man. Look at his fingers. They're wrapped."

Cavalo pushed himself up. Sat back on his legs.

"So? He broke them."

"Or the robot did." The woman looked frightened for the first time. He recognized her. She was the one who'd punched Cordelia. He recognized the man. He was the man who'd almost found them hiding in the bushes with a dead deer.

Cavalo grinned through a bloody mouth. "I know you," he said.

"I've seen you before."

"It's *him*?" the woman cried.

"It has to be."

"We have to tell Patrick."

"He's already gone back to the Deadlands."

"He said he knows us."

"Lies."

"Bushes," Cavalo said. "With the deer. I saw you. You didn't see me."

The woman grabbed his face with a strong hand. Leaned forward. Kissed his mouth. He tasted blood and flesh. "Maybe he can be our little secret," she said as she pulled away. "Maybe we can keep him to ourselves."

Those were the last words she spoke.

One moment she had a smile on her face that did not reach her eyes, and the next she was flung away, her nails scraping Cavalo's face. Shadows moved, and the woman screamed, which faded into a wet gargle. The stars were growing dimmer, and through them, Cavalo saw a flurry of movement ahead of him. Grunts. Gasps. Cries of pain.

The stars cleared.

The woman lay on the ground to Cavalo's left, her throat slit from ear to ear, eyes open but unseeing.

The big man lay on his back, hand above him as if to ward off an attack. The knife came down. Fingers fell to the ground. The man shrieked. The knife came down again. The man's feet skittered across the snow, digging deep red grooves. Eventually he stopped moving. Stopped breathing.

But Lucas stabbed him again. And again. And Again.

With each thrust of the knife, Cavalo could hear him screaming in his head.

DO YOU TRUST ME NOW?

DO YOU TRUST ME NOW?

DO YOU TRUST ME NOW?

the only choice

THEY STOPPED inside an abandoned barn five miles outside of Grangeville.

Lucas left them and prowled the hayloft above.

The wood creaked around them. Cavalo hoped it would hold.

He spread a blanket on the ground.

"You okay?" he asked Bad Dog as he turned in circles before lying down on the blanket.

Head hurts, he said. He looked at Cavalo with big eyes. *Some jerky would help.*

"Would it?"

Yes.

"I don't know if we have any jerky."

There's a whole bag in your pack. I can smell it.

"Can you? You must be feeling better, then."

I can barely *smell it,* Bad Dog corrected. He whined and lay his head down on his paws. *Getting... dark. Must have... rabbit jerky....*

Cavalo gave him the jerky. When he was finished eating, Cavalo covered them both with another blanket and curled up at his side.

They listened to Lucas moving above them. Pacing back and forth. Over and over.

His bees are loud, Bad Dog whispered.

"Are they?"

Yes. They are always loud. But now they are really loud.

"Oh."

Is it because of the bad guys?

"I don't know."

I think it's because of the bad guys. He killed them.

"I know."

Made their blood come out.

"I know."

Smells Different bad guy?

"I don't know." A hesitation. Then, "I don't think so."

I know bad guys.

"Do you?"

Yes. They are scared of Bad Dog.

"They are."

Smells Different not scared of Bad Dog. So he's not a bad guy.

"I don't know if that's quite how it works."

It works. Trust me.

"Always."

MasterBossLord?

"Yeah?"

We going home?

"Yes." It felt like a lie, that word.

SIRS at home?

"Yes."

I miss my home. And my bed. Then, after a moment's hesitation: *And my SIRS.*

"Me too." He didn't think things would ever be the same. "Head feel better?"

Jerky helped, Bad Dog said as his eyes closed. *Maybe I should have some more in the morning, just to be sure.*

"Just to be sure. Sleep."

The dog took a deep breath. And slept.

For a while Cavalo tried to follow him under. His eyes burned. His body was exhausted. His head hurt. He was cold. Even though they were miles away, he could still smell the burning mountain of the dead, sickly sweet and noxious. Could still hear the sound of the unknown man's throat tearing as Cordelia bit into it, knowing she was already dead.

The moon came out from behind the clouds. The light filtered in through the cracks in the barn walls.

He lay on his back.

Movement above him.

Back and forth.

He ignored it.

He tried.

He closed his eyes.

He opened his eyes.

Lose something, Charlie? he thought.

He had. He had lost many things.

His family. His mind. His soul.

The bees laughed and said, *Do you trust me now?* He didn't know whose bees they were. He didn't know if it mattered anymore.

He made sure Bad Dog was covered in the blanket. He scratched behind the dog's ear. Bad Dog huffed quietly in his sleep.

He stood. Looked above him. Shadows moved. Clever little monster. Clever little cannibal.

He left his gun. He left his bow.

He took his knife.

Just as a precaution.

The stairs creaked under his weight. He didn't think they'd support much more for very long. He wondered if Grangeville used this barn. Except they were all dead now. They wouldn't have a use for it anymore.

The moonlight flashed across his face between the slats of the wood. His breath trailed behind him.

He reached the top of the stairs. It was dark. He closed his eyes. Gripped the knife. Opened his eyes. They adjusted.

He could make out rotting bales of hay. Piles of wood. Piles of brick. A scarecrow, ancient and ugly off in the corner. The wind blew. The scarecrow waved at him.

"Lucas," he said in a low voice.

No response. But how could there be? This clever little monster, this clever little cannibal no longer had a voice.

Cavalo waited, listening for any sound.

Lose something, Charlie?

Do you trust me now?

He didn't want to. He couldn't.

He took a step into the hayloft.

My most immemorial year, he thought.

He took another step and remembered the starving bear with the hooks for claws.

He took another step and remembered the coyotes covered in tumors.

He took another step and remembered the look on Lucas's face with the knife coming down again and again.

Withering and sere.

When it happened, it was quick. The second before the knife came to his throat, he realized he was being hunted. The bees were electrified at the scrape of cold steel. A body pressed up against him.

Familiar, this. From when they'd first met in the haunted woods.

The knife bit into his throat. The smallest of cuts.

"He'll smell the blood," Cavalo said quietly. "Bad Dog."

The knife froze. A breath near his ear. A sigh.

The knife pulled away. Lucas took a step back.

Cavalo turned.

Lucas scowled at the floor. Half of his mask had been scrubbed away, leaving dark streaks down his cheeks. Dried blood in patches on his arms. His hands. His fingers.

"Lucas."

Defiant eyes. The knife at his side.

"You...." Cavalo struggled for words. "Those people. The Dead Rabbits."

Yes.

"You killed them."

Yes.

"Why?"

A snarl. *Fuck you. Fuck you.*

"I...."

You did this.

"Did what?"

Gestured between the two of them. Back at himself. *Made me this way. Made me bleed. Out in the open. I bled in shadows. You took that away from me.* He gripped the sides of his head as if trying to block out all sound. The flat of the blade pressed against his scalp.

"The bees."

A savage look. *Yes! Yes! Your fucking bees! Yes, the goddamn bees! Yes, you asshole! You bastard.* He paced in a small circle, holding his head, his face stretching into a grimace.

"Lucas."

Fuck you. Kill you. Stab you. Eat you.

"Lucas."

Break you. Smash you. Fuck you. Cut you.

Lucas fell to his knees, his mouth open in a silent scream. He dropped his hands to his sides, the knife clattering on the floor. He threw his head back and screamed again. Though Lucas could make no sound, Cavalo heard the scream in his head. It was filled with rage and fury, despair and sorrow. Cavalo had never heard a sound like it before.

He took a stuttering step forward. Stood above Lucas. With the knife in his hand, he pulled Lucas's head to his stomach and held him there. Lucas beat against his back with his fists. Tried to scratch him through his coat. Tried to bite the flesh of his stomach. Cavalo held on, gripping as tightly as he could. He knew if Lucas tried to jerk away, his neck would break or the knife would slip into his throat. Either way, it would be over for him.

He was giving him a choice.

Lucas fought.

Cavalo knew the bruises that would bloom purple and black on his back by morning.

The only sounds were the fists. The sharp breaths.

Eventually Lucas made his choice.

His hands gripped Cavalo's back. He breathed heavily into his stomach.

Cavalo let him.

They stayed that way as the moon came out again. As the light flickered over them before disappearing again. As Bad Dog dreamed below. As the ghosts of a lost world spun silently in the dark space above the world. In the history of everything, they were nothing but dust.

But still they held.

Eventually Lucas lifted his head. Looked up at Cavalo. The black mask had smeared across his face.

There was a small hole in the loft, near the far corner. Snow had accumulated here, blown in by the wind. Cavalo let Lucas go and walked over to the hole, scooping up the snow in his hand. He brought it to Lucas's face, the snow melting to water. The mask rubbed away. The dried blood rubbed away. It wasn't perfect. When he finished, there were still flecks of blood, smudges from the mask.

They watched each other.

Lose something, Charlie? Cavalo thought again. He could see the question in Lucas's eyes.

Do you trust me now?

"You killed them," he said softly.

Yes.

"Why?"

The scowl returned. It looked strange on this young face free of mask and blood. If it weren't for the eyes, Cavalo would not have believed such a face could look so angry. But the eyes were filled with rage, and Cavalo thought he could see bees moving behind them. *Stupid question,* Lucas said.

He gripped Lucas's face tighter. He knew his fingers were biting into his jaw. He gave Lucas's face a little shake. "Why?"

Because I hated them.

"And that's it?"

It's enough.

"Do you trust me?"

Lucas's eyes narrowed. Cavalo did not miss him picking his knife up from the floor. *No,* Lucas said. *No. No. No.*

"You are a monster."

Fury.

"You are a cannibal."

Rage. Tightened grip on the knife.

"And you killed them. To save us."

The anger was like a storm. This close, Cavalo could feel the bees vibrating in Lucas's head. *Yes. Goddamn you. Yes. Yes. They were trying to hurt you. They were trying to take you away. Yes. I killed them. And I would do it again. I would kill anyone who tried to take you away. And I will kill you if you ever leave.*

Cavalo kissed him then, hand still gripping his face. He felt Lucas's knife come to his stomach, but it was a warning. A precaution. Lucas did not stab him, and when his lips parted, their teeth knocked together until Cavalo angled his head. Lucas exhaled into his mouth, and Cavalo took him in, and in that breath, he could taste the lives of all that had come before. The pain and the anguish. The black mask of death.

The bees told him to kill the boy while he was on his knees. To break his neck and take his skin to SIRS to preserve it until they got the other half. To leave him behind until he was nothing but a memory that only came when the bees parted their stingers late at night.

He gripped Lucas's face tighter. He knew there would be marks there later from his fingers. This sent the bees away.

And when he felt Lucas's tongue in his mouth, his fingers on Cavalo's zipper, he wondered if this was the final step toward his damnation.

He couldn't find a single reason to care. Regret could come later. It always did.

When his skin became exposed, he sucked in a deep breath against the cold air. An even colder hand circled his cock, and he groaned as the hand squeezed. Lucas bit into his bottom lip hard enough to draw blood before breaking away. Cavalo could taste copper in his mouth. He licked it away.

The knife pressed against his stomach as Lucas swallowed the head of his dick, hollowing his cheeks. The sudden heat surrounded by the chill caused Cavalo to groan quietly. His hand went to the back of Lucas's head, gripping the shorn scalp. He thrust into Lucas's mouth. There were too many teeth. Too much spit. Lucas gagged, and Cavalo started to pull away. Lucas wouldn't let him. He went down again, and when his nose brushed against the skin of Cavalo's stomach, Cavalo said, "Lucas," in a rough voice. Those dark eyes found his again, and while there was still anger there, rage and fury mixed as one, there was something else. Heat. Fire. A storm of bees.

Eventually Lucas's throat opened up, and Cavalo was able to fuck his face with the snap of his hips. He felt the scrape of teeth again and thought briefly of standing in a lost cave in front of a bear with nails for teeth and hooks for claws. This was dangerous.

But he did not stop.

Lucas seemed to know when he was getting close. He pulled away, spit dribbling past his swollen lips onto his chin. He looked up at Cavalo again, and the fire became something more. Lucas stood slowly, dragging the knife up Cavalo's torso until it came to his neck. He kissed Cavalo then, his eyes never closing. Cavalo could taste himself on Lucas's tongue. The tang of salt and skin. The blood from his split lip.

Lucas broke the kiss. Cavalo could feel the scrape of knife against his throat. Could see the red marks against Lucas's cheeks from his fingers. His cock throbbed between them. He ground up against Lucas and felt an answering hardness. He reached down between them and palmed Lucas's dick. Lucas's eyes fluttered slightly and he licked his lips, attempting to chase the taste.

Lucas stepped away. The cold air assaulted Cavalo. He held the knife to Cavalo's throat at arm's length, his back resting against a wooden beam. He took a breath and let it out. Another. And another. With his free hand, he reached down and unfastened his pants. Cavalo recognized them as an old pair of his own. He'd given them to Lucas weeks before as Lucas hadn't come with much besides the knife.

In fact, everything he wore belonged to Cavalo. The clothes on his back. The marks on his defiant face.

Do you trust me now? the bees screamed. *Lose something, Charlie?*

Cavalo thought he might have. Common sense, to start. His mind. Sense of survival. He knew this would only end badly. It was the only way.

The pants were undone. As Cavalo watched, Lucas spit into his hand, slicking his fingers, keeping the knife against Cavalo's throat. Instead of reaching for his dick, his hand went behind him, reaching down the back of his pants. The blade pressed harder against Cavalo's neck as the hand behind him moved back and forth.

"That's what you want?" Cavalo asked. He tried not to think of the experienced twist of Lucas's talented hand. It would bring questions that he did not want to ask.

The glare returned. *Yes. Yes. Fuck me. Kill me. Break me.*

"It's going to hurt."

Yes. Good. Let it.

"We can wait. Until we get some oil." His voice was rough. Almost angry.

No. No. The knife nicked him. The smallest of cuts.

"I am not Patrick."

Instead of the anger he expected, Lucas seemed to laugh at him. *Oh? That's what you think this is?*

Pet. Psycho fucking bulldog.

"Fine, then," Cavalo snarled. He spit into his own hand. "Make yourself wetter. Do it now." He rubbed the spit onto the head of his dick. He spit again and coated the shaft.

He pushed up against the knife, daring Lucas to cut him further. For a moment there was no give. Then the pressure released as Lucas pulled the knife back. He kept it at Cavalo's throat but compensated for every step Cavalo took. "Turn around."

No.

"Turn. Around."

A flash of teeth. *Fuck you. This way. See my face. See your face.*

Cavalo was angry. Angry that this was even happening. Angry that he was doing nothing to stop it. Angry at the knife against him. Angry at the Dead Rabbit in front of him, his dick rising outside of his pants. Cavalo reached down and grabbed the head roughly, pulling on it with a callused hand. Lucas exhaled through gritted teeth. "Face to face?" Cavalo asked.

Yes. Yes.

"It won't always be this way."

Who says it'll ever be anything more? Or ever again?

Cavalo shoved his leg between Lucas's, pushing the pants down and spreading his legs. Lucas stepped out of them. Goose bumps spread along his thighs. Cavalo reached down and hooked an arm around his right leg, bringing it up to his waist. Lucas leaned back against the beam, his free hand wrapping around it above his head. The knife stayed against Cavalo. Cavalo thought about breaking his hand and taking the knife but decided against it. Lucas's balls rested against his cock as he lifted the leg higher. He looked down between them and spit on his dick once more. He let go of Lucas's leg and guided his cock up. There was resistance. He pushed. Nothing. Pushed harder. The wall gave. He groaned as he slid up and in. Lucas's mouth hung open as Cavalo pushed farther. There was heat at his front. Cold against his back.

The knife slipped momentarily as Lucas's eyes rolled back in his head. Cavalo thought it would fall to the floor, but Lucas brought it back up. He bared his teeth again as Cavalo leaned in. Kissed him, knife between them. Lucas sucked on his tongue. Pulled away. Trailed his lips along Cavalo's jaw. Licked the small cut on his neck from the knife. Pulled his head back. Nodded.

Cavalo pulled back and pushed in. Lucas sighed, his warm breath on Cavalo's face. As Cavalo fucked him, the bees flew in a great storm in his head. And when Lucas pressed his forehead against Cavalo's as he picked up speed, little sharp intakes of breath the only sound he made, Cavalo thought he could hear Lucas's bees too. He wondered then if they were the same. The thought did not disgust him as much as it might have. He didn't know what that said of Lucas. Or himself.

Lucas bucked his hips in time with Cavalo's thrusts. Finally, need overrode instinct, and the knife fell to the floor as Lucas reached down and jacked himself off. He only lasted a few strokes before he shot between them, his come hitting his neck and chin. The front of his coat.

Cavalo's coat.

Cavalo's clothes.

The darkening marks on the Dead Rabbit's face from Cavalo's fingers.

All of it was from Cavalo.

But then the coat rode up. A flash of black as Cavalo fucked him harder.

There were marks on him that did not belong to Cavalo.

They belonged to someone else.

And the anger grew.

He felt the pressure beginning to rise. That knowing pleasure-pain in his groin. He pulled out of Lucas, who exhaled sharply. Cavalo grabbed his cock to stave off the pressure, but it was close. "Down," he said, his voice a growl. "Lift up the coat. Now."

Lucas fell to his knees. Lifted up the coat. Revealed the marks that did not belong to Cavalo. The endless miles of tattoos that another had placed on him. Cavalo reached down and pushed Lucas's head back, forcing Lucas to rock back on his heels, exposing his chest. Only then did Cavalo let the pressure go. He jacked himself once. Twice. The third time, he came on Lucas's chest. White against the black. He grunted as it began to drip down between Lucas's nipples and onto his stomach. Lucas stared up at him, a dazed look on his face. As Cavalo watched him, Lucas reached up and touched the wetness on his chest. He closed his eyes as he pulled his fingers through it, spreading it along the tattoos. The lines and equations. The schematic for power, covered in the seed of a haunted man.

Cavalo pulled himself up to his full height, trying to even out his breath. "That what you wanted?" he asked, unable to keep the anger at bay.

Lucas dropped the coat back over his chest and stomach. He opened his eyes and reached for the knife. He stood slowly until they were eye to eye. He reached over and put the handle of the knife in Cavalo's hand. Brought it up to his throat.

You can do it now, he said. *You want to. I can see that.*

"Yes."

Lucas dropped his hands. Bared his throat. *Do it, then.*

"You would die so easily?"

No, Lucas said before saying the most damning thing of all. *But I trust you to know what choice to make.*

Cavalo felt a tremor roll through him as the bees rose. "What?" he croaked out.

Choice. Make your choice. Either trust me or kill me. It's the only way.

Cavalo pressed his forehead to Lucas. Those dark eyes never left his. "People like... us. Who we are. We never live long. We're not meant to."

I know.

"You've done that before."

Heat flared in Lucas's eyes. *Yes.*

He wanted to know with whom. But he didn't. "You're a monster."

Yes.

Cavalo took a deep breath and let it out. "And I don't know that I'm any better."

To this, Lucas said nothing. He didn't have to.

"They'll kill us. There are too many of them. And if not them, then someone else will come. It's inevitable."

Yes.

"I might even kill you myself. Or you'll kill me."

That feral grin. *Yes.*

The final words were easier. They felt inevitable. "We're the same."

Yes. Yes. Yes.

Cavalo kissed him then. Could feel the desperation behind it. The sense of relief. The sense of loss. The sense that finally, after years of wandering through a haunted wasteland, he had come upon a door that would lead to an escape. It was covered in bees, yes, and the legend upon it was that of a smeared black mask that could only bring death, but the door offered no resistance as it opened, and the choice was made.

HE WOKE NEAR DAWN. BAD DOG CURLED AT HIS FRONT, LUCAS at his back. He could feel the knife pressed at his side. Cavalo was not at peace, but he was closer to it than he'd been in years. Maybe the last rubber band had finally broken. Maybe he'd finally gone numb to the pricks of the stinging bees.

He didn't know that it mattered.

They had work to do.

Bad Dog watched him.

"How's your head?" he asked.

Okay. He bumped his nose against Cavalo's chin. It was cold. *Huh.*

"What?"

You smell different. Like Smells Different.

"Oh?" Cavalo didn't know what else to say.

He smells like you too. He sounded strangely elated.

"That so."

Bad Dog rubbed his head against Cavalo's chest. *Now you smell like me too. We all smell the same. Good smells. Not like yesterday. With the burning.*

No. Not like yesterday at all. Funny how quickly things could change.

I had a funny dream last night.

"Oh?"

There was a rabbit.

"You like rabbits."

Because they're crunchy. And I bite them with my teeth.

"Is that what you dreamed?"

No. I was running for the rabbit. We were in the trees. In the forest. I was chasing the rabbit. It was really fast. There was a fire. It ran into the fire. I didn't want to follow it, but I really wanted the rabbit.

"What did you do?"

Jumped into the fire. I thought I was going to get burned up! But it did not hurt me. And then you were there, and you told me I was a Good Dog, that I was a Good Bad Dog.

"Is that it?"

There were bees. On your eyes. They were really loud. I chased them away.

"Things are happening."

Gonna be okay?

"I don't know."

Could we die?

He wanted to lie, but he couldn't. Not to his friend. "Maybe. Probably. There will be death. But there doesn't have to be. We could leave."

We could?

"Yes."

With SIRS? And Smells Different?

"Yes."

And go where?

"Anywhere you want."

Bad guys coming?

"Yes."

For BigHank? AlmaLady?

"Yes. But they've done things. Bad things."

They bad guys?

Cavalo hesitated. Then, "No. They did the only thing they could."

Can't leave.

"No?"

No. We're MasterBossLord and Bad Dog. We get bad guys and make them pay! And no matter where you run, if bad guys are after you, they'll find you. It doesn't matter how far you get, they'll find you.

It's better to turn and fight than get shot in the back with a boomstick. He licked Cavalo's chin. *And we don't run.*

"We don't run."

Never. Bad Dogs and MasterBossLords don't run from bad guys.

Cavalo didn't have the heart to tell him that all he'd ever done was run. "Okay," he said simply.

We stay?

"We'll stay."

The bee-covered door with a dripping black mask closed behind them and disappeared.

everyone dies

THEY WERE cautious as they approached Cottonwood. After what they'd seen, they took no chances.

It was midday, and the clouds above were growing fat and gray. The wind had started to pick up, pushing at their backs as if hurrying them back to Cottonwood. Not much was said between the three of them, but there didn't have to be. Things were different now from when they'd left the day before.

"Stop!" a voice cried out from the wall.

They stopped.

"Cavalo?"

"Yes," he called back.

"Bad Dog and the Dead Rabbit?"

"Yes."

"You alone?"

"Looks like."

Silence. Then, "They're not coming, are they. Grangeville."

Cavalo allowed his voice to harden. "Either shoot or let me in."

For a moment Cavalo fully expected a bullet. Instead, the southern gate began to rise.

Lucas pulled his knife.

"Easy," Cavalo said.

So you say.

Hank stood in front of a small group that gathered inside the gate. Aubrey stood at his side, a rifle slung up on her shoulder. Cavalo thought he saw Alma, but he couldn't be sure.

"Put the knife away," Cavalo said.

No.

"You're making them nervous."

They should be.

Hank reached him first. "I'm not going to like this, am I?" he asked.

Cavalo met his eyes. "No. Bill and them get off okay?"

"Yes. They'll be back in a few days."

"SIRS?"

"At the prison. Is it bad?"

"Yes."

"They're not willing to help? That doesn't sound like Cordelia." He frowned, and Cavalo could see he didn't truly believe his words.

"They're dead."

He took a step back. "What?"

"We were too late."

Hank looked shocked. "*All* of them?"

"As far as we could tell."

"How?"

"Dead Rabbits."

Cavalo did not miss the thunderous glance Hank gave Lucas. "How do you know?"

"I watched them. Patrick. His people. Cordelia was still alive. Mac. Another. They said...." He stopped. Looked up at Hank. Hank was right. They'd been friends. Once. Maybe they still were. Things had changed. "They killed them. Burned the bodies. All of them. I think they came at night."

"But Grangeville had at least five hundred people in it!"

"And Patrick has an army."

Hank shook his head. "Can we do this? Do we even have a chance?"

"You know what the alternative is," Cavalo said.

A low cry went up behind Hank. A woman in the crowd had heard them. Another was running toward town. It would spread. Quickly.

"You'll have to convince them," Hank said, looking shell-shocked. "We're alone now, and you'll have to convince them."

"No," Cavalo said. "I'll tell them the truth. There's no one coming to help us. We're in this on our own. It'll be up to them to convince themselves."

He saw Alma then. Standing in the growing crowd, hood pulled over her head. Their eyes met. He didn't know what she saw, but whatever it was caused her to look away.

They gathered in front of Hank's house, all of them, as the snow began to fall again.

At first there were whispers:

How can they all be dead?

Dead Rabbits.

What do we do now?

My brother lived there!

Dead Rabbits.

How did they die?

Were they burned?

Eaten?

Murdered?

Dead Rabbits.

Did they suffer?

Was there suffering?

The voices raised:

Dead Rabbits.

They did this!
How can we beat them?
They're going to come for us next!
Dead Rabbits!
We're all going to die!
We need to run!
We need to leave!
We need to fight back!
We can't be scared anymore!
It's his fault.
It's that Dead Rabbit. *That* Lucas.
People began to shout. To scream:
DEAD RABBITS!
GIVE THEM WHAT THEY WANT!
HOW CAN YOU HAVE LET THIS HAPPEN?
WHAT ARE WE GOING TO DO?
WHAT ARE YOU GOING TO DO?
DEAD RABBITS!
IT'S HIM THEY WANT!
NOT US!
GIVE THEM WHAT THEY WANT!
THEY'LL LEAVE US ALONE!
THEY ALWAYS HAVE!
WE'VE SURVIVED THIS LONG!
WE DON'T CARE ABOUT POWER!
GIVE THEM WHAT THEY WANT!
GIVE THEM WHAT THEY WANT!
GIVE THEM WHAT THEY WANT!

Cavalo knew the power of the combined minds of men. He could see the fear in their eyes, saw them swarming like bees. The snow fell around them as they began to shout. Their fists raised into the air. Some waved guns. Some waved clubs. Some demanded they kill Lucas right then and there. Others watched with tears streaming down their faces. Children were held and hugged, unsure of what was going on. The crowd would surge forward at any moment, and when they did, Cavalo knew blood would be spilled.

But not his. Nor would it belong to Bad Dog or Lucas.

No, the bees whispered. *It would be* them. *Anyone that dares attack any of you. Look at Lucas with his knife. Look at Bad Dog with his teeth. Look at you with your gun. They may get in a few good swings, but how many of them would fall before you would? And how many would you kill to stop them?*

All of them. Cavalo would kill all of them.

"You all need to calm down now," Hank said, raising his voice.

"*IT'S THE DEAD RABBITS!*"

"*KILL THE DEAD RABBIT!*"

"*HE DID THIS!*"

"*HE BROUGHT THIS TO OUR HOMES!*"

"*HE'S ONE OF THEM!*"

Any second now it would start, and the blood would spill.

Bad guys? the dog barked at him. *Are they bad guys?*

Let them come, Lucas snarled, brandishing his knife. *Let them come.*

Lose something, Charlie? Cavalo thought.

He raised his hand above his head.

And for the fiftieth time since he struck out on his own following the death of his father, Cavalo fired his gun.

It was old but well maintained. He felt the pleasure of pounds of pressure it took to pull the trigger back. The rise and fall of the hammer. The firing pin against the cartridge. The detonation of the gunpowder. The flash of smoke and fire. He regretted the loss of the bullet. He did. They were hard to come by. But he had no choice.

The crack of gunfire echoed over the crowd.

They sighed as one and took a step back.

The smell of gunpowder burned Cavalo's nose. The bees wanted him to point the gun at the people in front of him and pull the trigger again. Maybe the sight of the blood of one of their own would cow them. At the very least, it would make Cavalo feel better.

They hadn't smelled the mountain of the burning dead like he had. They hadn't seen the look on the unknown man's face as Cordelia ripped out his throat with her teeth. Cavalo had felt horror then, but it was slowly sinking in, the admiration he'd felt too. The same admiration he'd seen on Patrick's face as he raised the gun to shoot her in the head. Cordelia had impressed Cavalo. She had impressed Patrick.

Fire, he'd said.

So, yes. He wanted to shoot them. The cowering, angry masses. It'd be easier. And surely they'd suffer less. He could make it quick for them. Tell them to close their eyes and think of a better place. There'd be no pain. The flash of the gun and then darkness. Wouldn't they rather die at the hands of a man who could give them that than at the hands and teeth that would tear at their flesh? He could give them what the people of Grangeville did not get.

It was close. Maybe a fraction of a second.

But somehow, he was able to push the bees back.

They screamed.

He lowered the gun to his side, his finger twitching along the trigger.

He said, "Enough." His voice was an earthquake.

Cottonwood sighed again.

"You've seen what he is," Cavalo said. "What he means. To them."

They watched him with fearful eyes.

"You know what would happen if they took him again."

A brave (or possibly stupid) man cried out, "We don't know anything but what you've told us! How do we know what you're saying is the truth?"

The crowd murmured their agreement.

You'll have to convince them, Hank whispered in the bees.

His hand tightened on the pistol grip. "Why would it be anything else? I could have left you all here to die. I'm not the one who has been feeding them, after all."

Aubrey and the other children looked confused. The adults hung their heads. Hank winced. Alma looked away.

"We had a chance!" someone else shouted. "The UFSA was here! Government! They could have protected us! They could have *saved* us."

"Yeah!" Another voice rang out. "And you *killed* them! They're never going to help us now."

"They weren't who you thought they were," Cavalo said, struggling to maintain composure. "They were torturing Lucas for information on Patrick. They didn't care about you. They didn't care about this town. All they wanted was Patrick. To get his secrets. They didn't know what they had with Lucas. They didn't know he was part of it."

Quiet murmurs through the crowd. Cavalo wasn't sure if he was gaining them or losing them. He was done with placating. He was done with pleas. It'd been a while since that old feeling came in, that part of him that dealt not in words but in bullets and death. He slipped back into it with alarming ease.

"It seems to me that you have a few choices here," Cavalo said, voice flat and harsh. "You can do nothing and hope what happened to Grangeville doesn't happen to you. You can do something and hope what happened to Grangeville doesn't happen to you. Or you could line up in front of me, single file. Families together. Children in front. I'll shoot each of you in the head and put you out of your godforsaken misery because surely it would be easier than what is to come."

"I don't think that's quite what I meant by convincing them," Hank said quietly, sounding bemused.

Cavalo ignored him. "If you'd prefer I shoot you, then let's do it now and get it over with."

No one moved.

"Who's first?"

No one volunteered. Cavalo wasn't surprised.

"If you make me choose, you're not going to like my decision."

No one spoke.

Cowards. All of them. But then Cavalo knew cowardice well.

"Fine," he said. Before anyone could react, he'd taken four steps forward. He was getting older, but he was still quicker than most. His joints ached every now and then, and when it rained, his knees were stiff, but he could still move. One moment he stood before them and the next he stood next to Aubrey, arm extended, the barrel of the pistol pressed against her head. "We'll do it the easier way."

Instant noise. Screams from the crowd. Shouts of warning. People moved. Alma's eyes widened. Hank's eyes narrowed.

"Cavalo," he said. His voice was hoarse. "Don't you do this."

He started for Cavalo, surely to rip him limb from limb. But Bad Dog and Lucas stepped in his path, teeth bared and knife drawn.

He glanced back at Aubrey. She had a tear on her cheek, but only one. Her hands did not shake. She did not cry. Her jaw was set, and she did not plead. Cavalo admired her. She was strong.

"Cavalo!" Hank growled.

"She'll be first, then!" Cavalo shouted so all could hear. "Because this is what you want! This is what you've asked for."

"Don't you dare hurt my daughter!"

Cavalo laughed bitterly. "What would have happened when she came of age and her name had been drawn? What then, Hank? Would you have said the same thing?"

Hank said nothing.

"Any of you?" Cavalo said, again raising his voice.

Nothing.

"No? Then you've already lost. I already have blood on my hands. Let me take from you so you go quietly into the dark. If you'd seen what I did in Grangeville, you'd be begging me for it."

"What happens when I come of age?" Aubrey asked, her voice all steel and knives.

"That's a question for your father," Cavalo said, not unkindly. "What do you want?"

He thought she would hesitate. She did not. "To stay," she said. "To fight."

"Is it because I have a gun to your head?"

"That might be part of it. But not all."

He cracked the barest of smiles. "You could die."

"I could die right now. Or tomorrow. Or the next day. Everyone dies."

"Yes," Cavalo said. "Everyone."

"So we can either fight together," she said. "Or we'll die alone."

Cavalo didn't have the heart to tell her that they'd most likely die regardless. Better to let her words affect the others than lose all potency.

"But do you believe that, Cavalo?" she asked. The steel and knives now pointed at him. "Or are you going to run and hide like you always do?"

"Girl," he said, "if you hadn't just proved my point for me, I would kill you."

"Then take the gun from my head before you change your mind."

He did. She took a deep breath. Shook her head. But she did not step away from him, in anger nor in fear. "I could smell it."

He nodded. "The gunpowder. It's strong."

She searched his face. "Would you have? To prove your point?"

"Killed you?"

She nodded.

Yes. "What do you think?"

She didn't answer. He thought she knew.

He turned back toward the crowd. "We're done. No more discussion. Do you fight?"

At first, nothing happened. Cavalo's heart sank, and he wondered just what would happen to these people. There was no way he could take the Dead Rabbits on his own. Not even with Lucas, Bad Dog, and SIRS at his side. They wouldn't last long. They'd have to run. If the town let them leave. He wondered how high the mountain of their bodies would be. Not as big as Grangeville. There weren't enough of them. Or maybe they'd be dragged into the Deadlands to be consumed.

But then a young man stepped forward. He couldn't have been more than sixteen years old. Curly blond hair. Slender. Slight. The bluest eyes Cavalo had ever seen. He would break hearts one day if his own hadn't already been ripped from his chest. A woman who had to be his mother tried to stop him, but he shook loose from her grasp. "Together," he said. "We fight together."

He was alone, but only for a minute. A man stepped forward. Followed by a woman. And then others. And more. Soon they all stood, shoulders squared, the fear in their eyes now lit in flames. It was almost enough to make Cavalo believe they actually stood a chance.

They'd go down fighting, at least. And that was a start.

LATER, AFTER PLANS HAD BEEN MADE AND ASSIGNMENTS GIVEN, the crowd began to disperse. Cavalo watched them go, Lucas and Bad Dog at his side.

They're going to die, Lucas told him.

"Maybe," he said. "Probably."

You will too.

"Probably."

Lucas nodded, spinning his knife in his hands.

Hank stood feet away. Alma stood next to him, speaking quietly, punctuating her words with a finger to his chest. He looked stonily at the ground. Shook his head. Looked up at Cavalo.

Cavalo waited.

Alma stepped back, looking frustrated.

"You put a gun to my daughter's head," Hank said. His voice was a dangerous thing.

"You told me to convince them," he said coldly. "I did."

"You touch her again, I'll kill you."

"I would expect no less."

Hank nodded tightly. He glanced up at the porch. Aubrey waited at the door, arms crossed, glaring angrily at her father. "I think I'm in trouble."

Cavalo shrugged. "I think we all are."

Hank walked toward his house. He stopped when he and Cavalo were shoulder to shoulder. "We were friends once."

"I think we still are."

Hank looked surprised. "Are we?"

"Withering and sere."

Hank looked at him thoughtfully. "Can we beat them?"

"I don't think so," Cavalo said. "But we're going to try like hell."

"Why now? What changed?"

It was a question Cavalo wasn't expecting. "Everything," he said.

Hank left him then, following his daughter into their house.

The snow fell harder. He hoped it let up before morning, as they needed to get back to the prison. They were running out of time. They needed to sleep while they still could. The days ahead were going to be busy.

Alma still stood nearby, watching them. He couldn't read the expression on her face.

"Something else?" he asked.

She nodded. Took the necessary steps to stand in front of him. He saw the slap coming but did nothing to stop it. Her icy hand stung his face. "That was cold," she said. "Even for you. Using Aubrey like that."

Before he could respond, Lucas was in between them, his knife at Alma's throat, a snarl on his face.

"That's probably not—" Cavalo started.

Alma spun neatly away on her heels, dropping low and sweeping her leg out. A look of surprise dawned on the Dead Rabbit's face as his legs were knocked out from under him. His arms went askew, and Alma reached up, snatching the knife out of his hand. Lucas landed on his back in the snow, blinking up at the gray sky. Alma dropped to a knee between his legs, holding the knife to his groin. Lucas glared at her but wisely didn't move.

"—a good idea," Cavalo finished.

"He's protective of you," she said, cocking her head.

"Misguided," Cavalo assured her.

"That so?"

"Yes."

"He pulled a knife on me."

"I tried to warn him."

Bad Dog sniffed Lucas before licking his face. He looked back up at Cavalo as Lucas scowled at all of them. *AlmaLady knocked him down.*

"That she did," Cavalo said, rubbing his jaw.

"If you come at me like that again," Alma told Lucas, "I'll cut off your balls and feed them to Bad Dog."

Do I like balls? Bad Dog asked him.

"You lick your own enough," Cavalo said. "Probably."

Alma stood, throwing the knife down near Lucas's head. It missed by inches. He didn't flinch. "Do you know what you're doing?" Alma asked. She was staring at Lucas, but Cavalo knew the question was meant for him. He tried not to think what she really meant. It was easier that way.

"No more than usual."

"Funny how things turn out, isn't it?"

And then she left.

Lucas scrambled to his feet, grabbing his knife. Cavalo took him by the shoulder right before he lunged at Alma.

"It's done," Cavalo said, pulling him back.

Lucas jabbed the knife at him wildly. *She touched you! She took my knife!*

"I did hold a gun to a teenager's head and threaten a town full of people. And you tried to slit her throat. Even I wouldn't do that. She's quicker than we are."

Lucas's eyes narrowed. He pointed the knife at Cavalo's face. *She touches you again, I'll kill her. I might just do it anyway.* He stalked off toward the empty house down the road.

Cavalo stared after him.

He awoke just once during the night, when Lucas finished prowling the house and curled up against his back. He felt the breath on his neck. The knife at his stomach. He took Lucas's hand and pressed the blade until he felt the sting to let him know he was awake.

And between dog and monster, the man named Cavalo closed his eyes and slept again.

know thy enemy

THERE WERE fifteen days remaining when Cavalo left Cottonwood, Lucas and Bad Dog at his side. The town bustled behind him. People moved with purpose. Determination. It would most likely not be enough, but they didn't know that. And it would do them no good if Cavalo told them.

"Bill should be back with Richie and Deke in a few days," Hank told him at the gate.

If they're not already dead, the bees laughed. *Strung up above a fire as their skin blackens and cracks.*

"I'll be back before then," Cavalo said, shouldering his pack. It was weird between them. It probably always would be. It was a small price to pay. "Have your people ready to move. The ones that need to. It'll be done quickly."

"They'll be ready. And they'll be safe? In the tunnels?"

Cavalo nodded. "SIRS will see to it." He felt the twinge in his broken fingers and ignored it. "Make sure the walls are fortified. Double up the Patrol. And make sure they actually have bullets in their guns."

"Never going to hear the end of that one, am I?"

"Probably not."

Cavalo turned to leave. He could hear Lucas and Bad Dog behind him. He stopped when Hank said his name.

"What?"

Hank hesitated. Looked over Cavalo's shoulder at Lucas and the dog. Back at Cavalo. "Last night. After Aubrey promised to never speak to me again."

"That well, huh?"

"Understatement. I don't know if she'll ever forgive me. I don't know if I blame her."

"You did what you thought you had to do," Cavalo allowed.

"Maybe. But...."

Cavalo waited.

Hank steeled himself. "The boy. The Dead Rabbit. Lucas."

Cavalo's defenses went up. "What about him?"

"Do you trust him?"

Of all the things Hank could have said, Cavalo expected that the least. And it was a question he did not know how to answer. "It's complicated," he said.

"Is it? How complicated can it be?"

"More than you know."

"What if...? Cavalo, what if he *let* himself be caught?"

The bees laughed as their stingers scraped behind Cavalo's eyes. "Why?"

"Know thy enemy."

"What?"

"There was a general," Hank said. "From Before. Long Before. His name was Sun Tzu. He said 'know thy enemy and know yourself; in a hundred battles, you will never be defeated.'"

Something twitched in the back of Cavalo's mind. "SIRS said...." Hadn't SIRS said something about Sun Tzu once while in the grip of his insanity? The more Cavalo pushed to find the memory, the more the bees swarmed.

"SIRS?" Hank asked.

"Never mind."

"Cavalo, how sure of him can you be? Have you thought of that? That maybe he *wanted* to get caught? That it was part of their plan. He's seen things. He knows the layout of the town. He knows what we're planning. He knows... well. He knows *you*, Cavalo. He knows that you're the only chance we've got."

"It's not—" Cavalo started before he stopped himself. He remembered the look on Lucas's face as he fucked him. The greed. The pain. The anguish and the pleasure. The scrape of the knife against his throat. The scrape of a kiss against his lips. "He's had plenty of chances."

"To what? Kill you?"

"Yes."

"And he hasn't."

"No."

"Know thy enemy, Cavalo. If you think about it, it's smart. Send someone in to work their way out."

"Why all the theatrics, then? With Patrick. He took what he wanted from Grangeville. And if Lucas is the key, then why send him? If anything, he would've have wanted him close."

"Variables," Hank said. "Too many unknown variables, and I hate that."

"He killed them. His own kind. To protect me."

"Is that what happened to his face? Those marks. Look like fingers."

Cavalo remembered the pleasure burn of his cock sliding into Lucas. "Yes."

Hank shrugged. "Maybe they were expendable. Maybe they wronged him and he held a grudge. Maybe it was part of a plan."

Cavalo thought of the way Lucas tasted. The way his knife felt against Cavalo's stomach. "He's not like that. He's not with them."

"So you trust him."

"At least I knew he was working with the Dead Rabbits from the start," Cavalo said before he could stop himself.

Hank winced. "I suppose I've earned that."

Cavalo said nothing.

"Just... keep an eye out, okay? I don't want to find you with a knife in your stomach."

Cavalo couldn't help the sharp bark of laughter that came then. If only Hank knew. He could only imagine the look of horror on his face. On all their faces. Not that Cavalo cared what they thought of him. It was none of their business, this thing with Lucas. Or anything he did. He did not belong to them.

Hank must have sensed he pushed too far. "Be safe," he said, taking a step back.

Cavalo nodded and turned toward the mountains. Lucas and Bad Dog waited on the road ahead, watching him.

What did he want? Lucas asked when he reached them.

"To tell us to watch our backs," Cavalo said.

Lucas didn't look like he believed him.

Home? Bad Dog asked.

"Home."

And so they went.

THEY WERE NEARING THE REMAINS OF THE SKI RESORT, AND Cavalo was wishing Hank had never opened his fucking mouth. Bad Dog ran on ahead, bouncing around in the snow, chasing sounds and smells. Lucas watched him with a foreign look on his face, and it took Cavalo a moment to recognize it for what it was: amusement. He didn't think he'd ever seen Lucas at ease like this. It made him wary.

"He forgets sometimes," Cavalo said, wondering why he was saying anything at all. Hank's words were haunting him, and he couldn't get them to stop.

What? Lucas asked him.

"That he's not a puppy. Like when I found him."

When you killed those men.

"Those Dead Rabbits. Yes." A challenge in his voice.

Lucas did not rise to meet it. Instead, he looked off into the forest, the trees heavy with snow.

They walked on.

And Cavalo could not stop thinking about Hank's words.

Okay? Bad Dog asked him once, his nose covered in powder.

"Yeah," he said.

But he wasn't.

He was distracted by the smell of him. Like dirt. Like earth. Like spice. Sweat. He remembered how it looked to have his come on the tattoos, the muscles in his chest and stomach constricting as he panted for air. Cavalo's marks on his skin. The stuttering look in his eyes as Cavalo fucked into him. The way he looked on his knees.

"Did you know them?" Cavalo asked him.

Lucas looked at him, a question in his eyes.

"The men I killed."

How am I supposed to know that?

"It wasn't that long ago."

No.

"Surely you notice when people disappear. Someone does."

Lucas shrugged. *I don't.*

"Those people you killed?"

Which ones?

Curious, Cavalo asked, "How many?"

Does it matter?

"Does it?"

Many.

"Did they deserve it?"

Lucas's eyes flashed. *Did yours?*

"No. Not all."

Lucas cocked his head at him. *You mean that, don't you?*

"I know what I am."

Then you know what I am. You said we're the same.

"If I asked you to take me to Patrick, would you?"

Cavalo saw the fear again. It was a rarity that it struck him in the chest each time he saw it. *No*, Lucas said. *No*.

"Why?"

Because he is Death. He is the dark. He is the king of monsters, and he will break you.

"He doesn't scare me." Bravado, that. Hollow bravado.

He should. He will.

"It's on him, isn't it? His skin. Like you."

Lucas searched his face, but Cavalo didn't know what he was looking for. He must have found it, because eventually, he nodded slowly.

"We need more."

More?

"Anything. The more we know, the better chance we have."

Lucas looked away, the scowl returning. His hand twitched at the knife at his side.

They moved on.

It wasn't until they were nearing the prison that Lucas reached out and grabbed his arm. Cavalo looked back him. Lucas had a look on his face Cavalo couldn't quite figure out. There was anger, yes. That was perpetual. But there was something more, almost like Lucas was... unsure.

"What is it?" Cavalo asked, looking around sharply. He didn't hear anything, but for all he knew they'd been surrounded in the woods. Bad Dog had run ahead. SIRS must have seen them approaching on the cameras as the gate opened. Cavalo started to unshoulder his rifle.

Lucas pointed back down the way they'd come. Back toward Cottonwood. Puffed out his chest. Bowed out his arms.

"Hank?" Cavalo asked, allowing himself to feel amused. He didn't know what it said about them that the impression was awful but Cavalo knew it anyway.

Lucas nodded. Pointed back at Cavalo. *What did he say?*

Those dark eyes never left his. "Does it matter?"

Does it?

"Lose something, Charlie?" Cavalo asked before he could stop himself. The bees were slipping out of him easier these days. It felt strangely like relief.

But Lucas didn't look at him oddly. He didn't stare like Cavalo was losing his mind, though surely he was. No, he watched Cavalo like he knew exactly what he meant. Lucas nodded. *I've lost many things.*

Cavalo had never been of a curious sort. It wasn't who he was. Not anymore. So he was surprised when he said, "Your throat."

Lucas's eyes narrowed, and he started to bare his teeth. But it slipped away quickly, as if Lucas changed his mind. Cavalo wondered at the war within him. If it was anything like the one within himself. He didn't know if he'd won or lost when Lucas looked backed at him and said, *It hurt. When it happened.*

Cavalo closed his eyes. Took a breath in. Let it out.

He opened his eyes when he felt a hand on his own. Lucas pulled his hand up to his neck. Cavalo's fingers shook slightly. He told himself it was because he was cold. He hadn't worn his gloves. Hadn't thought to.

The scar was hot under his fingers, almost like it was burning. Lucas held his hand by the palm, and Cavalo moved his fingers lightly over the puckered skin. He thought, not for the first time, on how Lucas could have survived such a devastating injury. Or how he could have been cornered enough to let it happen. But there was a bigger question that he needed the answer to.

He spread his fingers farther until his hand was around Lucas's throat. Lucas did nothing to stop him.

"Who?" he asked.

He could see the war now in his eyes. It flashed by, filled with smoke and murder, rage and death. There was something else mixed in too, though Cavalo couldn't quite name it. It flitted amongst the fury before it was swallowed into the dark.

It had almost looked like fear.

But he didn't look away.

"Was it Patrick?" Cavalo asked.

And just when he thought he wouldn't get an answer, Lucas nodded, the scar rubbing against Cavalo's hand.

"Are you with him?"

Lucas looked confused. *I'm with you.*

"No." Cavalo's fingers tightened around his throat. Not by much, but enough. "Are you with him? Are you here because he told you to be?"

The slightest of hesitations. It could mean nothing. It could mean everything. Then, *No.*

"Then why are you here?"

You took me.

"You let yourself be taken."

His smile took on a nasty curve. *Not that I heard you complain.* He stepped forward, invading Cavalo's space. Cavalo did not back away.

"That's not what I meant."

That's not the real question you want to ask. None of these have been.

"No," Cavalo croaked.

Then ask it!

There were some questions that shouldn't be asked, even in the dark times After the End. But for all the memories of the scrape of knife and kiss, there was a question that led to the burning mountains of the dead. To Warren's head left on the southern road, his face twisted into a horrible scream from a death that had gone on for days. "Are you... like them?"

I thought you said I was like you.

"Have you eaten anyone?"

A sharp breath. A silent sight. A step back.

Clever monster. Clever cannibal.

No, he said finally. But he wasn't really saying anything at all, was he? He wasn't really speaking to Cavalo because he *couldn't* speak. He had never been able to. Any voice Cavalo heard was that of the bees in his head. For all he knew, none of this was real and he was trapped in a snow globe somewhere deep in a prison that screamed of the things Charlie had lost and how DEFCON 1 would always be.

But he said no. Cavalo heard it. He heard it.

"Why you? Out of all of them? Why you?"

There would be a lie here, Cavalo knew. Some sort of lie that Lucas would spin. He was the psycho fucking bulldog. The babe found sucking on his dead momma's titties in the forest. He was a pet to Patrick. Fucked and beaten and made into a psychopathic killer who preferred a knife to slice the skin of those that rose against him. Cavalo wondered briefly if there was ever a point when Lucas enjoyed Patrick's cock sliding into him, the grunts above him, sweat dripping down on his body. Surely before Patrick slit his throat. Surely after it would have meant nothing. It would have—

There was anger in Cavalo. A dangerous thing. A petty thing. He almost opened his mouth to demand that Lucas take him into the Deadlands. To take him to the heart of the Dead Rabbits so he could cut it out and feel its last dying beats in his hands.

Do you trust me now? Lucas asked him. This time, he wasn't covered in blood, stabbing a man to death.

God. He did. Somehow, he did. Hank be damned. Cottonwood be damned. And himself be damned. This was not how things were supposed to be. This was not how his life was supposed to end. He was supposed to slowly rot away in his prison until one day his heart gave out and he fell to the floor. Years later his body would be nothing but dried skin and bones and SIRS would still stand above him completely lost to his insanity screaming things about how binomial coefficients were the key to the kingdom of God and wasn't he just a real boy? Didn't the Fairy with the Turquoise Hair come in the blowing dust of humanity to take pity on him finally and make him *a real boy?*

"Yes," Cavalo said.

And the boy in front of him, the Dead Rabbit who said he'd never eaten another human, the psychopath who had murdered others of his kind to save Cavalo from death, began to move his hands. Bared his teeth. Pointed in the direction of the Deadlands. Arched his back and neck, revealing the scar. Finger across the neck. Revealing tattoos, the lines and equations in black. Took his arms and cradled them, as if holding a child.

And from that, Cavalo understood what he was trying to say. Understood the four words that he heard in Lucas's voice in his head. And while so many things began to make sense, so many more things did not. And he wondered if they ever would. Lucas had not been found in the woods, sucking on his dead momma's titties. It might have been better if he had been. The truth was far worse and made things infinitely more complicated.

A hand to his throat. A finger across his scar. *He cut my throat one day because of the bees in his head. Blood came out. But I did not die.*

Lifted his coat and the shirt underneath. Traced the tattoos. *And since I did not die, he carved his secret into my skin, because I could withstand the pain.*

He carries the rest. And he will not stop until he uses it.

And his arms, cradled in front of him. *I know what they say. About how he found me in the woods. How he groomed me. And I suppose in a way he did. He made me what he wanted me to be. But he did not find me in the woods. He didn't find me in the woods because I have always been with him.*

Patrick is my father.

Cavalo kissed him. His fingers went to Lucas's face, aligning with the bruises left from before. It was a moment before the kiss was returned.

It wouldn't be until later that night, when Lucas rode him, his back arched and hips rolling, Cavalo's hands tracing the lines on his chest, that Cavalo realized it was the first kiss they'd shared that a knife had not been pressed between them. But that was later. Now, it was all lips and teeth and spit, horror and desperation. Screaming bees that cried, *No, no, no,* and the fatalistic realization that nothing could be done to stop the path they hurtled along. Cavalo didn't know if he'd change it even if he could.

They broke apart when a voice came from the prison gate. "Well now," SIRS said, standing next to Bad Dog in the snow near the gate. "This is certainly an extraordinary change of events. How funny you humans are. Grasping in the dark until you feel the hands of another to guide you back. Blink slowly, Cavalo. Your eyes are not used to the light."

Cavalo stepped away from Lucas. He could taste him on his tongue. "Grangeville is gone," he said to the robot. "They beat us there. The Dead Rabbits. We're alone in this, and we don't have much time."

"Those poor souls," SIRS said. "Do we have a plan?"

Lucas touched his hand, a brief brush of fingers before he pulled away. It was enough. "We rise. We rise up and fight back."

There was a click. A beep. An electrical snap, and the robot's eyes grew bright. His voice roared out amongst the winter woods: "I AM BECOME DEATH, DESTROYER OF WORLDS." Beeped again. Said quite conversationally, "Then I suppose we have some work to do."

preparation

WITH FOURTEEN DAYS left until Patrick came for Lucas, they returned to Cottonwood: man, dog, and Dead Rabbit. SIRS remained at the prison, shoring up the tunnels as best he could to make it habitable for the young and the old.

Hank and Alma met them at the gates.

"Has it started?" Cavalo asked.

Hank nodded as they walked through Cottonwood. Though it was early morning and cold, the throngs of people moved through town, eyes resolute and jaws set. They stepped quickly, only stopping to speak if it was necessary: an exchange of goods, a request for help. He saw their eyes widen slightly as they passed, looking from Cavalo to Lucas and back again. Lucas noticed none of it, his glare fixed on Alma, who ignored him coolly. Cavalo saw his fingers twitching along the handle of his knife.

"Leave it," Cavalo warned him in a low voice.

Lucas scowled at him. *I don't trust her.*

"No stabbing," he warned.

The scowl deepened.

"We started after you left," Hank said, leading the way toward the other side of Cottonwood. "It's harder because the ground is frozen, but they're doing what they can. It might just be easier to stick to the roadways."

Cavalo shook his head. "We can't expect them to come from just the roads. They'll swarm. All directions."

"It helps that we're shrinking the perimeter," Hank said. "Keeping the southern wall and building it into the town instead of around it. The ground is softer here."

They were only about halfway through Cottonwood when they came upon a row of men and women digging with shovels and picks, piling dirt and snow high. Beyond them stretched homes and businesses and the northern wall.

"They understand?" Cavalo asked. "That they'll lose the houses?"

Hank shrugged. "Houses can be rebuilt. But there's no coming back from death. I think they know that."

"Fear motivates."

"I wonder if Patrick says the same thing?" Alma asked.

Lucas started forward, but Cavalo pushed him back.

"Touchy subject?" Alma asked.

"You could say that." He looked toward the walkways on the outer walls. Patrols moved back and forth. "Anything?"

"No," Hank said, "but do you really think they'll be seen if they don't want to be?"

No bad guys in the woods, Bad Dog said. *I would have found them and eaten their faces.*

Cavalo scratched behind his ear. "Bad Dog says we're good. But keep up the patrols. Are the walls being shored up?"

"As best they can. Materials are light."

"It's better than nothing," Cavalo said. He didn't say that it also kept the people of Cottonwood busy, giving them less time to think of what lay ahead. He hoped it was working for everyone.

"And the prison?"

"SIRS will have it ready."

"How do we know we'll have time?" Alma asked. "Why would Patrick keep his word on the date?"

"Because that's the type of man he is," Cavalo said, exchanging a look with Lucas. "He's... putting on a show. For himself. For the Dead Rabbits. For us. The longer he waits, the more people have to fear over it, and the less ready they'll be when he finally comes."

"And Lucas told you this?" she asked, cocking her head at the Dead Rabbit. "How fortunate that we're able to get so much insight."

I'll cut your fucking head off, Lucas snarled at her.

Alma laughed. "Try it, little one. You'll be on your back again before you know it." Her eyes shifted to Cavalo when she said this last. Cavalo stared back.

"Munitions?" Cavalo asked Hank.

"Not as much as we'd hoped."

"Caravans?"

"Not since...." He frowned. "Weeks. It's been weeks."

"They've been stopped, haven't they?" Alma said, keeping her voice low. "Either killed or warned off."

"They're spreading," Cavalo said. "The Deadlands. It's what he wants."

"Would there be anything left in Grangeville?" Hank asked. "Aside from...."

"I don't know," Cavalo admitted. "I think they'd have raided the armory. Or at least destroyed it."

"Do we send someone back?"

"Is it worth the risk?" Cavalo asked.

"Is any of this?" Alma asked him.

"Warren would have thought so," he said before he could stop himself.

Her eyes hardened, flickering between Cavalo and Lucas. "We'll never know, will we? Because of *his* people."

"He had nothing to do with Warren," Cavalo said.

"Is that what he told you?"

"Yes."

"And you believe him."

"Yes."

She looked away.

Cavalo picked up a shovel and started digging.

THAT NIGHT, LUCAS PROWLED THE HOUSE, GOING FROM WINDOW to window.

"You need to sleep," Cavalo told him.

Lucas scowled and pulled his knife, heading up the stairs.

Cavalo stared at the ceiling most of the night, the house creaking with every step Lucas took.

WITH THIRTEEN DAYS LEFT, CAVALO STOOD IN FRONT OF A small group of people, all of whom eyed him nervously. It wasn't going well.

"You've never had target practice?" Cavalo asked, fighting back the urge to scream. "You're Patrol. How can you...." He shook his head.

"There were never enough bullets," Frank said. He seemed to be the de facto leader of the Patrol, which did nothing to put Cavalo at ease.

"How many of your guns are loaded right now?" Cavalo asked.

About half raised their hands.

"Fuck," Cavalo muttered. "Knives? Bow and arrow?"

They shuffled their feet and said nothing.

Cavalo lined them up, one by one. Their stances were off. They held the rifles wrong. They couldn't use the sights. Lucas scowled at all of them as he walked up and down the line.

This is ridiculous! he growled. Cavalo didn't miss the looks of fear and disgust as the Patrol looked at the Dead Rabbit.

"Tell me about it," he said.

We screwed? Bad Dog asked him.

"Probably."

His ears went flat against his head, and he whined. *I don't like getting screwed.*

"We need the ammo from the prison," he sighed. There wasn't much left. And some of it would be needed for those that holed themselves up in the tunnels for protection.

When's he supposed to be here? Lucas asked him.

"SIRS? Two days. He'll know what to bring. He'll lead the rest back up the mountain."

He stopped at Aubrey, whose posture and form weren't bad. In fact, they were actually quite good.

"She's here because Hank said," Frank told him. "I think she's too young. Don't want her getting in the way."

He pushed the stock of the rifle farther down until it rested more in the crook of her shoulder. "Can you use this?" he asked her quietly. He saw that she did not flinch. The last time he'd been this close to her, he'd held a gun to her head.

"Yes."

"Are you good?"

She hesitated.

"Aubrey."

"Yes."

"Better than the rest?"

More forceful, "Yes."

He took the rifle from her. She looked up at him in surprise. He held out the rifle to Lucas, who switched it for an old bow. The wood was strong, but he thought it'd need to be restrung before too much longer. He handed it over to Aubrey. She nocked an arrow and pulled it back. Took a breath. Released. The arrow flew into a post twenty yards away.

He took the bow from her. Handed it to Lucas, who watched her with narrowed eyes. Cavalo watched her too before taking his knife and handing it to her and stepping back.

"I can't," she said. "I've never learned how."

"Lucas," he said.

In a flash, Lucas stepped forward, snatching the knife from her hand. Brought his arm back and then snapped it forward, throwing the knife. It flashed above the snow before it split the arrow still embedded in the post in half.

The Patrol stared at him, jaws dropped.

"You will learn from him," Cavalo growled. "And if he's with me, you'll learn from Aubrey. Are we clear?"

They nodded.

THAT NIGHT, CAVALO FUCKED LUCAS IN AN UPSTAIRS BEDROOM of the vacant house. Lucas shuddered underneath him as Cavalo licked the tattooed lines between his shoulder blades. After, Cavalo fell asleep with Lucas curled around him and a knife pressed against his stomach.

WITH TWELVE DAYS LEFT BEFORE THE DEADLINE, BILL, RICHIE, and Deke returned from Dworshak. The news was not good.

Cavalo was helping with the trenches, unsure if they'd actually finish in time. His back hurt. His arms hurt. He was not as young as he used to be, and it was starting to show. He did not complain and worked through the pain. He could not show any sign of weakness. He kept his face schooled as his back seized. He would push through it. He'd been through worse. He'd survived worse.

He stood an hour later, stretching. A woman whose name he did not know brought him some dried meat and a small amount of water. He thanked her quietly, and she blushed before scurrying away, a small smile on her face. He wondered at it but let it slip from his mind as his gaze landed on Lucas, prowling around the members of the Patrol, slapping their hands for gripping too tight, shoving their guns up higher to actually give some semblance of proper aiming.

Cavalo told himself it was nothing. He told himself that fucking was fucking, and that's all it could possibly be. That it could ever be. Lucas was a Dead Rabbit. He might not have done the things the other Dead Rabbits had, but that didn't matter. He had been one of them. This was nothing. They had nothing. Soon, they would most likely die, they would face whatever came after this life, be it judgment or darkness.

It was nothing. Lucas meant nothing.

So why, then, did Cavalo's traitorous heart skip a beat in his chest when he saw that familiar scowl? There was a complicated tightening in Cavalo's chest, and he hated it. He didn't like complications. He liked things black and white. Good and bad. Quiet isolation. As few words as possible. It was what he'd grown accustomed to, and he had no desire to change it.

And yet....

Lucas must have known. Must have heard the bees in Cavalo's head and heart. He looked up, directly at Cavalo. As their eyes met, the scowl on Lucas's face disappeared. He didn't exactly smile, but Cavalo knew what it meant. He knew Lucas's facial expressions now. He didn't know when that had happened.

Hank had asked him days before if it'd be easier if Lucas had something to write with, that he could express himself better. Or why didn't he just mouth the words he was trying to say?

Cavalo had told him it wasn't necessary, that Cavalo knew what he was trying to say. He could translate. He didn't go as far to say he could hear the Dead Rabbit's voice in his head, a hoarse and gravelly thing that caused Cavalo's skin to itch. He didn't want to scare them, the people of Cottonwood, any more than he had to. They already thought him an oddity, a murderer. Something to be feared in reverence. They spoke of him in hushed whispers and told stories that probably only held partial truths.

He was already too far gone to be saved. The bees made sure of that.

Which is why as Lucas watched him, he wondered at their silence. They said nothing as Lucas grinned that feral grin and jerked his head to the left. Cavalo shook his head. Lucas ignored him and turned to the Patrol, motioning for them to pick up the bows and resume practicing. Then he turned and walked away.

Cavalo resumed digging.

He lasted a minute. He stopped. Sighed.

"I'll be right back," he muttered to Bad Dog, who lay on the snow near the trench, gnawing on a stick he'd found. "Keep an eye on things."

Bad Dog immediately stood and paced in front of the workers in the trench. *I'm in charge now*, he barked. *Work faster!*

He followed Lucas, telling himself to turn around.

Weak sunlight filtered through small breaks in the clouds above. He could see his breath coming from his mouth. Lucas never looked back, as if trusting that Cavalo would have no choice but to follow.

This meant nothing. It couldn't. Cavalo was broken beyond repair. Lucas was a psycho fucking bulldog. A pet. Patrick's son, something they hadn't told a soul. His heart was dark. He had murder in his eyes and death on his lips. He said he'd never eaten another human. That could very well be a lie. All of this could be a lie.

The bees tried to whisper in his head, sounding like Hank, saying words about *trust* and *truth* and *what if? What if this is nothing more than farce? A way to get inside your head until you spill all your secrets that can then be used against you?*

Lucas disappeared around the corner of a house.

Cavalo followed him. There were shadows here, the sun blocked by a barn behind the house. He could hear people moving around Cottonwood. Their voices as they laughed. As they cried. As they worried through their day. But they were far away. Cavalo and Lucas were hidden.

Cavalo found Lucas in the shadows, leaning against the barn.

"What?" Cavalo asked, though he already knew.

Lucas said nothing, just stared at him. He wasn't wearing his mask today. His skin was smooth, the bruises on his face turning a sickly green. There was a freckle on the right side of his jaw. Another one right above it. Cavalo had to stop himself from reaching out to touch them.

Lucas pointed to him, his finger grazing Cavalo's chest, then pointing back at his own eyes. *I see you,* he said. *Watching me.*

Cavalo thought about lying. He thought about turning and walking away. Instead he said, "Yeah. I know." He stepped closer, crowding Lucas against the wall.

So many teeth in that knowing smile. *You want me.*

"I shouldn't. It's not...."

An arched eyebrow. *It's not?*

Cavalo didn't stop himself this time. He reached up and traced a line between the freckles on Lucas's jaw. Lucas leaned into the touch.

"Why do you do this to me?" Cavalo asked.

Lucas's smile faded. For once, he looked unsure. It made him appear impossibly young. Their faces were inches apart, and the uncertainty on Lucas's face tore at Cavalo. He curled his hands into fists to keep from taking what he wanted. This was not the time, nor was it the place.

I don't do anything, Lucas said. Cavalo could hear the hesitation in the voice that wasn't there.

"You're in my head. All the time."

Like the bees?

Cavalo felt his nails cutting into his palms. "Sometimes, I think you *are* the bees."

You think I'm a monster. You said that once. After we....

"Yes."

Am I?

"Yes."

Are you?

"Yes."

Lucas kissed him, hard enough to press Cavalo's lips back over his teeth. There was heat behind it, but there was also anger, buried deep. Cavalo grabbed the sides of Lucas's face and slammed him back against the wall, pressing his body flush against Lucas's. Lucas licked at his jaw, biting into the skin. Cavalo wondered what marks would be left. He wondered what others would think. He wondered if he cared.

Lucas fumbled with Cavalo's belt. He leaned back and licked his hand before reaching into Cavalo's pants and gripping his cock. His fingers were cold. His spit-slicked palm was hot. Cavalo swallowed down the groan in his throat. Lucas's breath was quick and light as Cavalo kissed the skin near his ear.

"Cavalo?" a voice called from behind them.

"Shit," he muttered, pulling away. He tucked his dick back into his pants. Lucas looked feral again, his lips wet and swollen. *You want me*, he said again. He grabbed Cavalo's hand and pressed it against his own cock. Cavalo gripped his hardness. Lucas rolled his hips against his hand. Cavalo stepped away, struggling to breathe normally.

"This isn't over," he said darkly.

That shark's grin was the only response.

"Cavalo?"

He turned as Hank rounded the corner.

"There you are," he said. He paused, glancing over Cavalo's shoulder at Lucas. "Interrupting anything?"

"No. Nothing important."

"Ah. Are you sure? It looks—"

"What do you want, Hank?"

"They're back. Bill. Richie. Deke. Coming in through the gates."

Cavalo felt a bit of relief. At least they were alive. He nodded. Hank turned and headed back around the house.

Cavalo glanced back at Lucas, still leaning against the barn. He was frowning.

"What?"

Lucas shook his head. Sniffed the air. Shrugged. *Do you feel that?*

"What?"

I don't know. Something's off.

"Do you know what?"

No. Just a feeling.

"Great. That's just great."

Lucas scowled. *Fuck off.*

"I can still kill you, you know." And he turned and walked away. He wasn't surprised when Lucas followed. He was surprised, however, when Lucas gripped his hand, squeezed once, then let it go.

It was nothing. It meant nothing.

A crowd had gathered at the southern gate. Cavalo pushed his way through, Lucas following behind him. People parted rather quickly when they saw who it was. They may not have known what to make of Cavalo, but they sure as hell knew a Dead Rabbit when they saw one. He no longer dressed like one and he wasn't wearing his mask, but there was that shark's grin and the eyes that weren't quite right.

Hank was standing at the front of the crowd along with Alma and Aubrey. Bill, his son Richie, and Deke stood next to them. All three looked road-weary, eyes wide and blown out. Cavalo hoped the distance traveled was all that was wrong, but he thought it more. Bad Dog moved around their feet, sniffing their shoes and clothes.

Bad guys, he muttered to himself. *Bad guys. So many bad guys.*

Not good.

"Cavalo," Bill said tiredly. "There you are."

He shook Bill's hand, nodding at Richie. Deke wouldn't look at him, eyes cast toward the ground.

"Okay?" Cavalo asked.

"One piece, ain't we?" Bill asked with a shrug. "Suppose that's more than can be said about Grangeville. Or so Hank says. It true?"

"Yes. They're... gone."

Bill sighed. "Cordelia?"

"One of the last. Went down fighting."

"Sounds like her," Bill said. "Tough old broad, ain't she?"

"The toughest."

"And this... all of this. It's because of the boy? What he is to them. The schematics."

They all looked at Lucas. Lucas scowled, hand going to knife.

The people of Cottonwood sighed angrily.

Cavalo stepped in front of Lucas. "No," he said, aware of what he was doing. "Not all. It's not just him." Cavalo could feel a knife at his back, near the base of his spine. Lucas's other hand gripped the back of his coat. It was almost as if he were holding Cavalo hostage. But then Cavalo felt Lucas lean his forehead against the back of his neck for just a moment, and he knew it was more than that. "It would have come to this sooner or later."

"How can you know that?" Hank asked.

"Because of what they found at Dworshak," Cavalo said. "Isn't that right?"

Bill hesitated. Richie looked away. It was Deke who spoke. "He's right. We were too late."

"No," Alma whispered.

"Dozens of them," Deke said. "We were quiet. They didn't see us. We were on a ridge a quarter of a mile away, hidden in the trees. Used the binocs. We thought...." He looked miserably at his father.

"We thought they were... normal," Bill said. "At first. Maybe they were a trade caravan. Or a little town. Or just people who had stumbled upon the dam and reservoir and decided to try and make it work as a home."

"But?" Hank asked quietly.

Bill and Richie exchanged dark looks. Deke stared at the ground.

"There was a woman," Richie finally said, sounding far older than he was. "She was screaming. We couldn't hear her, but she was screaming. I could... her face."

Cavalo closed his eyes.

"We couldn't stop them," Richie continued. "There was too many of them. We wouldn't have been—" He stopped, choking on his words. His father put a hand on his shoulder and looked at Hank with steel in his eyes.

"They brutalized her," he said angrily. "Tore into her. There was blood. So much blood. And they laughed. They laughed as she bled onto the concrete, and they laughed when she reached out her hand to hold them back. And they hurt her. Again and again until she didn't move. And then they...." He stopped, shaking his head. He didn't need to finish. They all know what the Dead Rabbits did. Instead, he said, "They have the dam. The Dead Rabbits have Dworshak."

People in the crowd behind them began to cry. They began to moan. They began to shout. And beg. And scream. But all their words were the same. Cavalo heard them speaking as one, and the bees in his head exploded furiously and mocked the people of Cottonwood.

What do we do now?

He thought about pulling his gun again. It worked days before. Maybe he would actually shoot someone this time. Deke or Aubrey. Lucas. Someone. He didn't know what to do. He didn't know he'd been hoping that Dworshak had been undiscovered, that the Dead Rabbits hadn't made it that far north. Not just hoping. Expecting. He had expected it. Even if he thought they weren't going to survive what lay twelve days ahead, he had *expected* it.

"You don't get to do this," he said.

The people fell silent.

Bad Dog bumped his head against Cavalo's knee. Hank and Alma watched him closely, as did the rest of the town. They feared him, but they still listened. Cavalo wouldn't look at Lucas. He wondered who the woman had been. The one who had been torn apart. He wondered her name. Where she'd come from. Her family. If she was old enough to have been married. If she had received her first kiss. If she'd held hands with her son as he carried Mr. Fluff and laughed and laughed and laughed.

He almost did it. Almost pulled his gun. Almost shot the person closest to him. He would have kept firing until the clip was spent, and then he'd use his hands. To tear at them. Their flesh and bones. Because he was no better than any of them.

"You don't get to feel sorry for her," he said, his voice harsh and grating. "You don't get to cry over her. Not after what you've all done."

He could see fear in their eyes but also anger. If he pushed, it would boil over.

"We keep on going," he said. "We have twelve days until they arrive. We stick with the plan. We work until our hands are cracked and callused, and we fight until we're broken and bleeding. It's the only way. It's the only choice."

He left them.

No one followed.

HE SAT IN THE VACANT HOUSE IN A CHAIR IN THE MIDDLE OF AN empty room, watching the sun and clouds move. The bees crawled over the inside of his skull, and he was unable to think. That old familiar rage burned in his head and chest, that oily thing that allowed him to kill as he'd done so indiscriminately in the past. He'd left all of his weapons downstairs to avoid temptation.

He was a hypocrite, he knew. And it was not his job to dispense justice.

But the looks in their eyes. The looks that said *Save us, but don't judge us*. The looks that said *Help us, though we don't deserve it*. The looks that said, *Protect us from the monsters, though we are monsters ourselves. Do this for us, because you are the lesser of two evils, and we have no other choice.*

He tightened his hands on his thighs.

As the shadows stretched outside, he looked down toward the floor. Jamie played there. With Mr. Fluff.

"Mr. Fluff!" Jamie cried. He bounced the rabbit along the floor, as if it were hopping.

"Mr. Fluff," Cavalo said hoarsely.

Jamie laughed, his mouth stretching wide. Bees flew out, their abdomens fat and hanging low. Jamie tried to catch them, but they flew away from his fingers. Eventually he frowned and went back to Mr. Fluff.

"You're not here," Cavalo said.

"Not where, Daddy?"

"Here. With me."

"Oh. Then where am I?"

"In my head."

Jamie laughed again. "How did I get in there?"

"You've never left."

Jamie hummed. "Mr. Fluff says there are monsters. Are there monsters, Daddy?"

"Yes, honey. There are. There were."

"Oh. Are you scared of them?"

"Sometimes."

"But not all the time?" He threw the rabbit in the air, trying to hit the bees that flew overhead.

"No, not all the time."

"Why?"

Why? When he was alive, Jamie had always asked *why*. *Why* was his response to everything. Cavalo had loved it, even when it'd irritated him.

"Because sometimes I'm the monster."

Jamie stood up in front of him holding Mr. Fluff. He cocked his head at Cavalo, eyes searching his face. A bee landed on his cheek, but Jamie didn't seem to notice.

"I don't think you're a monster," Jamie said finally.

"No?"

"No. Can I tell you a secret, Daddy?"

"Yes." Cavalo wanted nothing more.

"You can't tell anyone."

"I won't."

Jamie's brow furrowed. "You have to promise."

Cavalo promised his dead son.

Jamie beckoned him to lean forward.

Cavalo did. When Jamie whispered in his ear, his breath felt like the brush of insect wings.

Jamie Cavalo whispered, "He's not who you think."

"Who?" Cavalo asked.

"Daddy," Jamie said. "Look up."

Cavalo did.

The ceiling of the bedroom in the vacant house was covered in bees. Wasps. Hornets. They crawled over each other. The buzzing was a roar. Their stingers dripped with poison, and as Cavalo took hold of his son, to pull him in and protect him from the swarm above, Jamie said, "There are worse monsters than you know."

"You need to—"

"Cavalo? Who are you talking to?"

Cavalo jerked and almost fell off the chair, pulling Jamie with him. Except his hands were empty. He looked up. There was a bare ceiling above.

It's not real, he thought. *None of this is real.*

"No one," he said to Alma as she stood in the doorway.

"Are you all right?"

"No."

She hesitated but then seemed to make up her mind. She walked over to him and put her hand on his shoulder. "What happened?"

"He was here."

"Who?"

He shook his head. "It doesn't matter."

"Cavalo."

"It doesn't matter."

She looked around the room. Of course there was nothing there.

"He's pacing outside," she said finally. "Actually, they both are."

"Who?"

"Bad Dog. The Dead Rabbit. I asked why they didn't go in. Lucas buzzed his lips at me."

"It's the bees," Cavalo said.

"Is it?"

"Yes."

"I told him I'd go in first."

"And he let you?"

She sighed. "He pulled the knife again. He may be fast, but he's stupid. To try that again." She handed him the knife.

Cavalo choked out a laugh. It sounded like a sob.

"What is he to you?" she asked.

"Nothing."

"That's not true."

"It's the only truth I can give." Even though the truth was a lie.

"I see the way...." She stopped. Looked out the window as the sun began to set.

He reached up and gripped her hand on his shoulder. "Don't."

She ignored him. "I see the way you look at him when you think no one is watching."

"It's not—"

"It is, though. You get this... look in your eyes. I don't think I've ever seen you look at anyone like that before. It's almost like you're burning up from the inside."

"It's not like that."

Her hand tightened on his shoulder. "Then what's it like?"

"It's...." Then, "I don't know."

"Cavalo."

"What?"

"He's a Dead Rabbit."

"I know. But... he's... he's not like them."

"He's a murderer."

"So am I."

"Not like him. Not like they are."

"I'm no better," Cavalo said honestly.

"They're cannibals."

"He's not."

"Or so he says."

"Why would he lie?"

Alma chuckled bitterly. "So many reasons."

"I..." *trust him* was how he meant to finish that. Instead, he said, "I know he didn't." It almost meant the same thing.

"I know you." A last chance. A plea.

"You think you do. But you don't."

"What's happening here?" Alma whispered. "How did it get this far?"

Cavalo said nothing. No words he could offer would be of any comfort. She was realizing what he'd figured out days before.

"Warren would have...." A sigh. "We're not going to survive this, are we?"

"No."

"And even if we did, there's no way we could take back the dam."

"No."

"And even if we gave him back...."

"They're going to kill us anyway," Cavalo finished for her. "It doesn't matter anymore. They have Dworshak. The reservoir. Patrick is the lock. All they need is the key."

She moved in front of him then. He let her. She brought her hands to the sides of his head, her palms against his ears, her fingers in his hair. He took a deep breath of her. She tilted his head up. Kissed him. He kissed her back. Because it was familiar. Because it held memory. Because she wanted him to.

But it was not Alma who Cavalo thought of.

She broke the kiss. Licked her lips. Said, "Don't tell the others. Don't tell the others that hope is gone."

He nodded in her hands.

She left him in the darkening room in the vacant house. Before she disappeared through the doorway, she said, "I'll take Bad Dog with me. I'll send Lucas in. I hope you know what you're doing, Cavalo." Then she was gone.

The sun disappeared.

"I don't," Cavalo told the empty room.

Lose something, Charlie? the bees asked.

He's not who you think, Jamie had said.

It was only a minute later he heard a door slam shut. The pounding of feet on the stairs. Cavalo held the knife in his hand.

He knew the moment Lucas entered the room. Could feel his eyes boring into the back of his head. Could feel the room grow heavy. Knew that if he could, Lucas would be growling. It was who he was. Light filled the room too, and Cavalo knew he carried a lantern. There was a thump of metal behind him as he set the lantern on the floor.

Cavalo stayed in the chair. He didn't move.

In the periphery, he could see Lucas circling him slowly, teeth bared, hands like claws at his sides. His took sharp, quick breaths, exhaling through his nose in little bursts. His eyes were narrowed, and even without the mask, his fury would have struck fear into a sane person.

Cavalo was not sane. He hadn't been for a very long time.

He felt no fear. There was something else there in its place.

He met Lucas's eyes as he passed in front of him just out of reach. The steps Lucas took were slow and deliberate, his knees bent, his back slightly hunched. The shadows danced along the walls, making Lucas look bigger than he really was. Cavalo knew what this was for.

Lucas was hunting him.

The bees told him to end this, to throw the knife into one of those eyes. He could do it. It'd be very easy. A quick flip of his wrist and this would be over.

His hand twitched. That was all.

Lucas passed out of sight. And it was then that he took steps forward behind Cavalo. He could hear the footsteps coming closer. Could feel the anger radiating off Lucas. Felt the Dead Rabbit's breaths on the back of his neck.

It wouldn't take much, Cavalo knew. He'd recently seen what damage teeth could do to a throat.

Lucas crossed into his vision again. His nose scraped against Cavalo's cheek. His lips pressed against his jawline. He stopped when he crouched in front of Cavalo, pressing their faces together. His nostrils flared.

He stood up. Took a step back.

And Cavalo could hear his accusation as if he'd spoken the words aloud. *I can smell her on you.*

"Can you?"

I'll kill her.

"You'll leave her alone," he said sharply.

Lucas snarled at him. *I fucking told you what would happen if she touched you! She's already dead.*

"Lucas."

Fuck you. You did this. He gripped the sides of his head. *You made the bees come out when you walked away from me. Why did you walk away?*

And only then did Cavalo realize his own bees had boiled over the moment he'd left Lucas. So much so that they'd turned into Jamie. Jamie, who had come to him with a warning. "I didn't mean to," Cavalo said quietly.

You did! You did! You think I'm like them. You think like they do. Like sheep. He paced back and forth, wincing, his hands shaking. He looked as if he was breaking apart.

But still Cavalo did not move. He thought it the wiser choice. "I'm like you," he said instead, marveling out how easily the words came out now.

Her smell is on your skin. You stink of her.

"She's gone now," he said. This he knew. She'd left the night he'd heard her sing. Good-bye, good-bye, we all say good-bye. The kiss had been nothing more than a ghost.

Lucas stepped forward suddenly, a hand around Cavalo's neck, fingers digging in. Cavalo did nothing to stop him. The knife stayed in his hand, unmoving. *You make promises with your mouth,* Lucas said, inches away. *You speak pretty words, you scrape a kiss against my lips, and then you smell of her. You walked away from me. You turned your back on me. You let them see what you thought of me. The people here. The ones you say we are trying to help.*

"No."

No?

"I didn't leave you. I left them because of their sadness. Because of their anguish. Over the girl at the dam. Like they hadn't agreed to sacrifice someone every time the Dead Rabbits came."

I don't believe you. I saw the look on your face. When you heard about her.

"Have you ever done that?"

Defensive. *What?*

"Hurt someone like that. Like they did to her. Someone who didn't deserve it."

No. There was a stutter in his eyes. He looked away. A lie, though maybe not a complete one.

"Have you been near them when the others did?"

There it was. The scowl returned. Lucas backed away from him warily.

"And you didn't stop them."

Lucas shuddered.

"No. That's not right, is it?"

Lucas gripped the sides of his head.

"It's not that you didn't. It's that you couldn't."

Lucas screamed. Covered his ears. Shook his head. All done in silence.

"They wouldn't let you."

Lucas fell to his knees. Pressed his forehead to the floor. Pounded the hard wood with a fist. Cavalo thought it hard enough that his hand should break. This was like the time before when Cavalo pushed. And he *had* to push, because it was the only way to break through. *Why* he felt the need to do this was not something Cavalo could focus on. He was dimly aware of how neatly he'd deflected

Lucas. His jealousy. His anger over something as inconsequential as a kiss. Especially one that meant good-bye.

But to his surprise, Lucas stopped. He took in deep breaths and let them out slowly. He did not pound the floor. His mouth was not twisted open. His eyes were closed.

Like he was controlling himself. Controlling the bees.

He took another breath. And then stood. Opened his eyes. They were as clear as Cavalo had ever seen them.

He shook his head. *No, that's not it.*

"Then what?" Cavalo heard himself say.

Lucas pointed to his scar. Cavalo knew now who put it there, but never the why. And wasn't it the *why* that mattered? Wasn't it the *why* of it that was the most important. Most people are not born with bees. They're put there because of hard life and unfair death. Because of things seen that cannot be unseen. Because of a father who slices the throat of his son because his son had tried to stop him from hurting another.

Cavalo could see that now. Could see it even though Lucas could not speak a single word aloud. He didn't have to. They both had hives in their heads. It made it easier to talk to one another.

I tried to help her, Lucas said, motioning with his hands, pacing back and forth. *I don't know why. Things had happened before that I did nothing to stop. People that had come in, begging for my help. Saying they had families. Homes. That they just wanted to go home. They knew who we were. What we were. They knew what was going to happen to them.*

And she did too. She knew. There was something in her eyes that didn't allow her to beg. A spark. A flame. She knew she was already dead, and she did not beg for her life. She didn't scream. And when she spoke, it was but a few words.

The shadows flickered behind him, and Cavalo could see them taking shape, becoming a clearing in the woods far into the Deadlands. The trees were black and stunted, almost as if burned by a forgotten fire. The ground was sparse, the earth beneath their feet dead. In the distance there was the outline of huts. Houses. Shacks. Homes. In the shadows on the wall of a vacant house in Cottonwood, Cavalo knew he was seeing the beating heart of the Dead Rabbits. Where they lived. What they did.

In the middle of the clearing, there was a fire. It rose high into the sky, fed by the dead wood that surrounded it. People moved around it, laughing and scowling, screaming and wrestling. He could not make out their words, but they wore the bands on their arms. The spikes around their necks. Knives at their sides. Rough tunics, splattered and dirty. Some of them were sick, blood leaking from their eyes and mouths. They leaned over and spat large red and brown globs to the ground that smelled of rot. Some had skin that looked eaten away. Teeth falling from their heads. Tumors growing on their skin, hanging low, heavy, and fat. He wondered what would happen if they just burst, if the black death that grew inside of them would pour onto the ground in a noxious pile.

Lucas was there. Cavalo could see him standing off to the side, the black mask across his eyes. He was shirtless, and his skin was free of tattoos. At least, tattoos of schematics of power and water. Instead there were lines down his back and chest, crisscrossing scars that Cavalo recognized as being from a whip. He wondered why he never saw them before, even hidden under the black lines that covered his chest and back and arms. He had tasted some of that skin, had touched it, but never thought of the raised bumps under his tongue and fingers until that moment. He had only been focused on the one scar, the large one around Lucas's neck.

The scar that wasn't there now. This was Before.

Cavalo shuddered in his chair in the vacant house in Cottonwood.

Cavalo shuddered as he stood next to a bonfire in the Deadlands.

"Lucas," he said.

But Lucas didn't respond. Cavalo wasn't really there.

Except he was. He could smell the fire and something sweet above it. Could feel the heat of the air around him. The roaring jumble of words spoken and spat around him. It was chaos, and the bees were screaming. The Dead Rabbits were unaware of his presence. They didn't bump him. They didn't walk through him. They walked *around* him, as if he took up space and that was all.

He took a few steps and stopped when he found what the sweet smell was above the smoke and fire. Meat. Cooking meat. Except this was torsos. Arms. Legs. Tongues. Eyes. His stomach clenched, and he thought the bees were trying to crawl out his ears.

He saw her then. The woman Lucas had told him about. She'd been beaten, her clothes ripped from her body. Her arms were bound above her head to a long wooden post that sat across her shoulders. Her dirty hair hung in clumps around her face. There were bloody teeth marks on her thighs. Her neck.

But there was that spark. That flame. It burned so brightly in its defiance. There was fear in her, yes. Her skin practically thrummed with it. But she was not bent over, begging for this to end. No. Her back was rigid and straight, her teeth bared at anyone who attempted to come near her. They laughed at her and tugged on her naked skin. She reached for them, but they knocked her down. She pushed herself back up. It took time. She used the wooden post, and her arms shook with exhaustion. But every time she was knocked down, she pushed herself back up.

Cavalo looked toward Lucas. He watched the woman closely. He never touched her. He never stopped anyone from touching her. But Cavalo could see the tense, coiling posture, his feet digging into the black soil. It wouldn't be much longer before he lashed out.

And then Patrick came. He moved like smoke.

Something flickered in Lucas's eyes, a complex thing Cavalo couldn't even begin to understand. Patrick was dressed as he'd been when Cavalo had seen him. Simply. Elegantly. He was not sick as most of the others were. There were no sores on his face. No blood leaking from his body. He moved quickly and quietly, and when he passed the Dead Rabbits, they stopped talking until all eyes were trained on him. Patrick stopped in front of the nude woman.

"Hello," he said to her. His voice was kind. Cavalo knew it as lies.

The woman looked up at him but did not speak. Her breasts heaved as she struggled to hold on to her composure.

"Do you know why you're here?" Patrick asked her in that same level voice.

She didn't answer him, but she didn't look away. Though Cavalo didn't know who she was, he felt fiercely protective of her, like he would of any cornered animal that showed no fear. She knew what was going to happen to her. She knew there was no chance. She'd accepted her fate.

"Hmm," Patrick said. He looked down at his hands. "They're usually screaming by now."

The Dead Rabbits around him laughed.

"I like you," Patrick told the woman. "Very much. You might be what I've been waiting for. For a while now. Lucas, if you please."

The Dead Rabbits turned toward Lucas. Cavalo did too, unable to help himself.

He did not miss the rage that flashed in his eyes. The fear. The anguish and sadness. It all rolled into one, but then it was gone.

"What do you want me to do?" Lucas said, his voice hard. And it was the first time Cavalo heard him speak aloud (though the bees reminded him he hadn't *really* heard his voice, because he was sitting in a chair in a vacant house while watching Lucas create shadows on the wall behind him). He sounded exactly how Cavalo thought he would. Angry. Deep. And young. So impossibly young that it caused Cavalo to choke on his breath. His heart hurt, and he wanted nothing more than to take him from here. He knew what was coming. And he knew there was nothing he could do.

But most of all, he wondered when Lucas had gotten so under his skin, like a shard of glass now breaking into pieces. He wondered if he could have stopped it if he'd even tried.

"You know what I want," Patrick said. There was a small smile on his face.

Lucas took a step toward the woman. Patrick looked surprised when Lucas drew his knife from his side. The other Dead Rabbits parted as he walked, cries and jeers rising up from the crowd. His black mask reflected the firelight. Every step he took was deliberate and cautious.

He stopped when he stood next to his father, facing the woman on her knees. She stared up at him. Cavalo moved until he stood at their sides. He'd forgotten he couldn't be heard. He'd forgotten that none of this was real. All he could focus on were the shards of glass embedded in his skin and the voice of the one he had only ever heard in his head.

"Don't do this," he whispered harshly. "Don't."

Lucas didn't acknowledge him.

Cavalo reached out. But his hand was stopped as if a wall separated them.

Lucas's eyes narrowed as he stared down at the woman. His lips twitched down. Cavalo knew that look. It was the bees. Even now. Lucas couldn't be more than sixteen years old, and even then the bees were in his head.

"Come with me," Cavalo said, hearing how desperate he sounded. "Please. I'll take you away from here."

But Lucas did not look at him because this Lucas no longer existed.

Shadows, flickering on a wall.

Cavalo was in a house.

Cavalo was in a field.

His bees were confused. They didn't know what was happening. This scared them. They wanted him to run as fast as he could. Down the stairs. Or into the forest of the Deadlands. They weren't sure which because they didn't know where he was.

Run, they begged him. *Down (through) the stairs (the forest). Hide behind the house (the trees). Don't let him (them) see you.*

But Cavalo could not run.

Lucas did not run.

"A piece of her," Patrick said, briefly touching his son on the arm. "I should like her hand." As if it were nothing at all.

"Listen to me," Cavalo said.

Lucas pointed the knife down at the woman.

"Lucas."

And didn't Lucas twitch then? As if he'd heard a voice? He had because Cavalo was in a house in a town at the end of the world, and there were shadows along the walls that told a story he no longer wanted to hear. He tried to leave. Tried to stand. He couldn't because he was already standing in the middle of a forest, surrounded by those clever monsters, those clever cannibals.

"Lucas," Patrick said. "Do it now."

Lucas didn't. He didn't. The bees had gotten so loud in his head, and he ground his teeth together. Cavalo could hear them, roaring things like DEATH and BLOOD and KILL HER KILL HER KILL HER, but in all those bees, in the great storm that was the mind of Lucas, Cavalo heard a small voice say no.

Lucas stepped back. The knife went to his side.

Patrick sighed.

The Dead Rabbits around them were silent.

"One day," Patrick said, "you'll tire of the whip." He sounded resigned. Regretful. Like a father who has just caught his son doing something disappointing. Cavalo had used the same voice on Jamie.

Cavalo saw a tremor roll through Lucas. It was brief. It never touched his eyes. But Cavalo understood what it was.

Lucas was afraid. Afraid of the whip.

Of Patrick.

But even as the tremor passed up his legs and arms, Cavalo saw him steel himself, beginning to coil down. To spring forward. Cavalo knew. Lucas was going to kill the woman, but not in the way his father wanted. A stab to the heart and it would be over. She would not suffer. She would not fall under the teeth of the Dead Rabbits.

He lashed out and—

Patrick caught his wrist. The tip of the knife had barely pressed against the woman's breast. It dimpled the skin. A drop of blood beaded over the blade and dripped onto the ground. She grimaced but nothing more.

Gone was Patrick's fatherly mask. His face had twisted into something dark and monstrous. It was then that Cavalo realized Patrick must have his own bees, because he could see their stingers poking out around his eyes. It made sense. Cavalo knew bees could follow from father to son. His own father had been drowning in them, using alcohol to chase his away for as long as he could. Or his fists against Cavalo's young face. They always had them, darkly amassing in their heads, but it took something extraordinary to let them take control. For Cavalo's father, it had been the death of Cavalo's mother. For Cavalo, it'd been the destruction of Elko and everything he'd loved. He didn't know what it'd been for Patrick, but Cavalo was sure he could see what had caused it for Lucas in the lined scars on his back. And he knew he was about to see the final act that made Lucas so lost in his own swarm.

"Mercy," Patrick said. His voice was no longer kind. "You would show mercy."

Lucas struggled in his grip but could not get free.

Cavalo screamed and cursed at Patrick. Tried to reach both of them, but that invisible wall kept him away. It did not stop him from trying. He banged his fists on the barrier. He hit it with his shoulder. He kicked it.

No one ever noticed him.

Because we're not really here! the bees cried.

But what if we are? they answered themselves.

Cavalo thought his head would split. "You fucking bastard," he snarled at Patrick as he smashed his shoulder into the unseen wall again. "Look at me! *Look at me!*"

But Patrick never looked at him.

The other Dead Rabbits did not move. They seemed to breathe as one.

And Lucas. Cavalo saw him the most out of all of them. Could see the contempt in his eyes that did nothing to hide his fear. He was trembling, and Cavalo knew he was about to witness the birth of the hive in his head. Lucas had the bravado of a man but the heart of a child, and there would be no coming back from this.

"I've given you much," Patrick said. "I've given you leeway, even when you went against my word."

"Lucas!" Cavalo shouted.

"Whip me," Lucas said. "Get it over with."

"No," Patrick said. "Not this time."

He broke Lucas's wrist then, snapping it sharply. Lucas screamed and dropped the knife. It slipped through his fingers toward the ground. Patrick caught it by the handle with the other hand, crossing his arm over his body and crouching. He still held Lucas's broken wrist. Cavalo knew it would come then.

He did not look away.

Shadows, on a wall. By firelight.

Patrick swung the knife up in a flat arc. The knife caught the glow from the bonfire and flashed. It hit Lucas in the throat, slicing skin. The blood arced. The last thing Lucas said was done in a wet, choked voice as he fell to his knees.

"Dad."

Patrick dropped his wrist. Drops of blood dripped down his cheeks. Patrick did not wipe them away.

Lucas fell forward. His face hit the ground.

"Keep him alive," Patrick said. "God help any of you if he dies."

Lucas was picked up in a hurry. Carried away. The fired danced off the blood on the ground.

Patrick closed his eyes and took a deep breath. Turned back toward the woman bound at his feet. She was crying now.

"Take her," Patrick said quietly.

And they descended on her. The Dead Rabbits. With their hands. Their mouths. She found her voice then and screamed. They took their time as they ravaged her, and when the light began to fade from her eyes, when she rose above the pain inflicted by the assault, she turned her head toward Cavalo and looked at him directly. Her head jerked once as their eyes met. She smiled with blood in her mouth.

And then she died.

Everything went dark. Cavalo could hear voices whispering around him. He couldn't make out their words, not completely, but he heard scraps and pieces like *damage is great* and *won't survive* and *he'd better if you know what's good for you.*

Flashes of light. Cavalo stumbled in the dark. Something flew near his ear, the buzzing noise sharp. Another flew overhead.

A woman's voice, far away as if it crawled up from the past: *brave little boy my brave little boy and you will be so strong and—*

A man's voice, closer: *it's a miracle he did not die he should have patrick patrick it's patrick's will and his will is the way and he will—*

A voice he knew, a kind voice that did nothing to hide the monster he was: *and i will provide for you and i will care for you because you all belong to me i have saved my son from the brink of death i called him back from the abyss he lives or dies at my word much like you will stay with me and you will see what power truly is and—*

The monster: *they won't like that no they won't like that one bit but that's okay we need more time i'm not ready yet i have to find a way to hide it so they can't find it some way to—*

The monster: *if he can't speak again it'll be easier that way it'll be better that way it'll be—*

The monster: *mark him when he's strong enough mark his half if he can survive a knife to the throat then he can survive anything you mark him and me and then we destroy it all we'll find a way we'll find a way and soon the fathers in st. louis won't know what hit them they will die in the fire just like the world did before and i will rise from their ashes and the new order can begin and—*

The brightest of all lights exploded overhead as Lucas opened his eyes for the first time since his throat had been slit. He turned his head and saw his father sitting beside his bed. Patrick smiled quietly and said, "Welcome back. We have so much to discuss."

And then they both burst into bees, thousands upon thousands of them that swirled in a vortex with Cavalo trapped at its center. He could feel wings and stingers scraping against his skin as he waved his arms out in front of him, taking a stumbling step. He was blinded. He felt them crawling on his skin.

Then a hand grabbed his and pulled. Cavalo burst through the tornado of bees and wasps and fell into the dark and—

the bees screamed because he was neither HERE nor THERE nor ANYWHERE

—he was in the vacant house.

In the dark.

The light flickered along the wall.

Lucas stood in front of him, head bowed, face hidden in shadow.

Cavalo gripped the knife. "Lucas," he said, voice rough.

Lucas did not look up. He swayed slightly but was otherwise still.

Cavalo stood. His knees popped. The chair scraped against the floor.

Lucas attacked then. Hands outstretched like claws. As he threw himself toward Cavalo, he could see how black Lucas's eyes were. He was still lost in the bees. He'd pulled Cavalo out but had gotten lost himself.

Cavalo took a step to the side but a fraction too late. Fingernails scraped against his cheek, drawing blood. The flash of teeth going by his neck, inches away as they snapped shut. Cavalo grunted and spun away, bringing the hilt of the knife back around and smashing it into the back of Lucas's head. Lucas bounced off the far wall, pushing himself off even before he stopped. Cavalo wasn't ready, and Lucas crashed into him, knocking them both off their feet. The breath was knocked from Cavalo's body as he hit the floor.

Even as his head rapped against the wood, Cavalo brought the knife up between them, sure he meant to shove it up through Lucas's throat and up into his brain, running on instinct and nothing more.

Lucas stopped the knife, pressing Cavalo's arms down. The knife was inches from Lucas's neck. His teeth were bared, eyes black as he silently screamed down at Cavalo.

"Lucas," Cavalo ground out. "Don't."

The pressure increased. The teeth got closer.

"I saw," Cavalo gasped. "I saw it all. You're not a monster. You're not like him."

Lucas flinched, still lost in the bees but now uncertain.

"Listen to me," Cavalo said. "You pulled me through, now find your way."

Lucas shook his head, as if trying to clear it. He pressed down harder on the knife. Cavalo was losing his grip.

"You need to come back," Cavalo said. "Please."

Something cracked in the rage mask the Dead Rabbit wore. His eyes grew unfocused. Confused. A shudder ran through his body. Cavalo used the distraction and knocked him to the side. Lucas fell silently, fingers skittering out along the floor. Cavalo threw the knife across the room, out of the way. He rolled and pulled himself on top of Lucas, torso to torso, face to face. He held Lucas's arms, pinning them to his side. Lucas raised his head and snapped his teeth once. Twice. The third time was weaker as the cracks in the mask grew. Angry tears welled in Lucas's eyes as they started to clear. He shook his head and looked away. He tried to buck Cavalo off him, but it didn't work. He shuddered again.

"I know," Cavalo said quietly, pressing his forehead to Lucas's hair, his mouth near Lucas's ear. "I know."

Lucas shook beneath him. He twisted his head back up until their foreheads pressed together. They breathed the same air, eyes locked. Tears rolled down Lucas's cheeks.

It hurts, he said. *All of it hurts.*

"I know."

I couldn't find my way back out.

"I know."

I heard you.

150

"And you followed me through."

I could have killed you. He looked stricken at this.

"Yes. But you almost took a knife to the throat, so I think we're even."

Lucas shook his head, distraught. *I can't hurt you. Don't let me hurt you. I smelled her on you, and I wanted to hurt you. Don't let me.*

"It's not like that. It was good-bye." He didn't know why he felt he had to explain. His chest burned. It was hard to breathe.

If the bees come back... if they don't leave. Finish this.

"I can't—" Cavalo choked out.

FINISH THIS! Lucas screamed at him.

"Okay," he said, because it was the only way.

Say it!

"I promise."

Lucas shook in relief.

Cavalo kissed him then, a little desperate. Lucas's face was wet, Cavalo could taste the salt. He loosened his grip on the Dead Rabbit's arms, and Lucas pulled them around Cavalo's back, holding him in place.

And in this vacant house in the tiny enclave known as Cottonwood, as the glow from the lantern threw light and dark across them both, the man and the Dead Rabbit watched each other long into the night, breathing and nothing more. Toward dawn they shifted onto their sides, Lucas curling around Cavalo's back, trying to block out the cold. Cavalo waited for the press of the knife before remembering it was across the room. Lucas made no move for it, already drifting off, lips and nose pressed against Cavalo's neck. Cavalo followed him into the dark, the words of a promise playing along his lips.

They slept.

But they did not dream.

the remaining days

ELEVEN DAYS REMAINED when the robot came to town. Behind him, through the snow, he dragged a large metal box. Cavalo waited for him at the gate with Lucas and Bad Dog. Cavalo would have sworn the robot was smiling at the sight of them.

"Hello," SIRS said.

Bad Dog barked happily and sniffed the box.

"Do I want to know?" Cavalo asked.

"You do," SIRS said, his eyes flashing.

He lifted the lid. There was a metallic screech as it rose. Cavalo peered inside. What he saw there took his breath away.

"How?" he managed to say. He didn't understand what he was seeing. How it was possible.

"We all have secrets, Cavalo," SIRS said. "I was saving these for a rainy day."

Lucas began to smile.

TEN DAYS REMAINED WHEN THE INTERIOR WALL WAS

completed. It looked strong. Cavalo didn't know how long it would hold.

Nine days remained when SIRS pulled him aside from working on the trench. They were running behind schedule, and Cavalo didn't know if it'd be finished in time.

"The tunnels cleared?" he asked the robot. He took a drink of water from a canteen. It tasted metallic and cold.

"Yes, Cavalo. There will be enough room for all of them. But that's not what I wanted to talk to you about."

"What, then?"

The robot sighed and looked out toward the town as people moved about, determined looks on their faces. No one spoke out against Cavalo. Not now. At least not publicly. They did what they were told without complaint. One family slipped away in the night, parents and their two children. No one knew they were planning to leave. And no one knew how they got out without being spotted. Cavalo waited for others to follow, but then a scouting team brought back a child's shoe smattered with blood, and no one else tried to leave. It was that simple.

"You have... plans here," SIRS said. "Preparations are being made."

"Yes."

"And the others will be safe at the prison."

"You disabled outside communication?" Cavalo asked. "Nothing verbal?" This was important. Cavalo's fingers still hurt from when the robot broke them under Patrick's control. He couldn't take the chance of that happening again. Not with children in the tunnels.

SIRS sounded slightly hurt. "Yes, Cavalo. Video only."

"Good."

"But what about after?"

"After?"

"This. When all of this is finished."

"What about it?"

"You need Patrick alive. Or at least as undamaged as possible."

"Dworshak is gone," Cavalo reminded him. "They have it."

"Is it? Then what are we even doing here?"

"Surviving."

SIRS eyed him knowingly. "Except you don't truly believe that, do you?"

Cavalo looked away.

"You expect to die here," SIRS said. It was not a question.

"It seems likely," Cavalo said quietly.

"Do the others know this?"

He shook his head. "Maybe. I'm sure part of them does. The odds aren't exactly in our favor."

"You stupid man," SIRS said. "You stupid, stupid man." He sounded upset.

"You'll keep them safe?" Cavalo asked.

"Yes."

"Thank you."

"Cavalo?" He sounded hesitant.

Cavalo looked back at the robot.

"We're... friends?" SIRS asked.

"Yes. You know that. You and Bad Dog are all I have."

"And Lucas."

"And Lucas," Cavalo echoed.

"Funny how life turns out, isn't it?"

"It is."

"I'll let you get back to it, then. You know. The surviving."

Cavalo turned to walk away. He stopped when SIRS said his name.

"I should like it very much if you tried to live," the robot said in a rush. "I don't know that I'd do well on my own anymore." He beeped. His gears ground together. He said in a loud voice: *"FANCY THE HAPPINESS OF PINOCCHIO ON FINDING HIMSELF FREE! WITHOUT SAYING YES OR NO, HE FLED FROM THE CITY*

154

AND SET OUT ON THE ROAD THAT WAS TO TAKE HIM BACK TO THE HOUSE OF THE LOVELY FAIRY." Something sounded as if it broke off in the robot's chest. "No," he said in his regular voice. "I don't think I'd do very well at all."

Cavalo watched him walk away.

Eight days remained when someone decided there should be a feast while they were all still together. Smoke rose from cooking fires. The clouds did not drop snow. People were quiet at first as they lay the spread out in the church. But soon someone laughed quite loudly and it was if that's all it took. Others followed suit, and soon the noise was deafening.

Cavalo, Lucas, Bad Dog, and SIRS found a quiet corner, watching people as they ate. No words were spoken. There didn't have to be.

Seven days remained when SIRS led a group of men, women, and children out of Cottonwood toward the mountains. A group would stay with them, armed and ready in case there was a siege on the prison. Cavalo tried to convince Bad Dog to go with them, but he wasn't having it.

Stupid MasterBossLord, he grumbled. *I'm not leaving.*

"I need you to guard the kids."

No.

"Bad Dog."

If it makes you feel better, you can keep telling me. Still won't go.

Cavalo sighed when Bad Dog bumped his head against his leg. "Should have left you in the forest," he said, reaching down to scratch behind the dog's ears.

I would have followed you anyway, Bad Dog said, humming quietly as he leaned into the scratch.

After that, Cavalo didn't try and make him leave.

There were tears as the group left. Many tears. Parents hugged their children tightly, whispering softly in their ears, telling them sweet lies about how they'd come home soon, how everything would go back the way it was and that they would never have to be scared again. *Now you mind your manners and listen to the adults*, they said. *You do what they tell you, and you'll be fine*, they said. *I'm not crying because I'm sad*, they said. *I'm crying because I'm happy.*

Cavalo let them have their words. If it's what helped them leave, then he wasn't going to stop it.

He was about to leave, to get away from the weeping and the wailing, when he heard a familiar voice. He stepped closer but stopped, partially hidden by the crowd.

SIRS stood with Lucas and Bad Dog. They looked up at the robot, listening as he spoke. "...and you will watch his back like you've never done before. I know he tells himself he doesn't need that, that he doesn't need anyone, but it's a lie. It's a lie he chooses to believe most of the time. He needs you both just like you'll need him. If you can keep each other safe, then you can all come home, and we can pretend this all was just a very bad dream."

He couldn't hear what Lucas and Bad Dog said in response. Only then did he realize that neither could SIRS. Neither could anyone else. It was one of those moments of startling clarity that sometimes made Cavalo feel like he'd been burned. He wondered if he could actually hear Lucas and Bad Dog at all.

Lucas nodded at SIRS, and Bad Dog barked.

The robot's eyes flashed brightly, as if he was amused. "I thought we'd see eye to eye on this. And remember: if it gets to be too much, if you're overwhelmed, you run. You grab Cavalo and you run. There is no cowardice in living to fight another day."

Lucas scowled but nodded. He turned, flipping his knife up in the air as he walked away.

"I wish I could hear...." SIRS shook his head. "No matter. Now, fleabag. Shall we see if they're ready?"

Bad Dog barked again, sounding annoyed.

Cavalo slipped back into the crowd.

Later, as they watched the group travel out the southern gate, Cavalo thought it would be the last time he ever saw the peculiar metal man. As they trudged through the snow in the distance, Cavalo thought, *Good-bye, old friend.*

SIX DAYS REMAINED WHEN THE TRENCHES WERE FINISHED. IT took another day to outfit them properly. Cavalo hoped he could take at least a few of them out when they attacked.

Five days were left when a lone man approached Cottonwood, one of the townsfolk who'd helped the group to the prison. Said they made it there without any problems, didn't come across anyone, Dead Rabbit or otherwise. The rest of them breathed a sigh of relief.

There were only four days left when Cavalo met up with the Patrol again. Their aim was better. He smiled quietly to himself as Aubrey barked orders and no one contradicted her.

There were three days left when Lucas didn't want to be touched. He prowled around the edges of the wall, eyes darting up and down, looking for any weaknesses. Cavalo slept alone that night.

There were two days left when Hank and Alma knocked on his door. He looked up at the sound and watched as Jamie smiled at him and waved before he ran out of the room. He was coming easier now.

Cavalo opened the door. "Got a minute?" Hank asked. "Didn't mean to interrupt."

"You didn't. No one else is here."

Hank and Alma exchanged looks before Alma said, "Sorry. I thought I heard you speaking to someone."

Cavalo shook his head. "What do you want?"

"We wanted to... thank you," Hank said. "For doing what you've done. After everything, you didn't have to. I know you've thought about leaving."

"Still do," Cavalo said.

They stared at him.

He said nothing.

"Be that as it may," Alma said, recovering first, "we're glad you're here."

"You wouldn't be in this mess if it wasn't for me."

"Maybe," Hank said. "But maybe not. We could have ended like Grangeville. At least now, we have a chance."

"Yeah," Cavalo said.

"Could you...?" Hank stopped.

"Spit it out," Cavalo growled.

"Tomorrow," Alma said, reaching out and touching Hank's arm. "Before everything. Could you speak to them? Cottonwood. One more time."

Cavalo was confused. "What? Why?"

"Because," Hank said gently. "They need to hear from someone in charge. They need to be led."

"Why me, then? You're not...." He closed his eyes. "Goddammit."

"It has to be you," Alma said. "They see you and.... It just has to be you."

His eyes snapped open. "I never asked for this," he said, voice hoarse. "I never wanted any of this."

"Neither do most men when greatness is handed to them," Hank said.

"That's what you think this is?" Cavalo snarled at him. "You fucking bastard. We're all going to *die* in two days!"

Hank and Alma took a step back. He slammed the door in their faces.

"Are they gone, Daddy?" Jamie asked from behind him.

"Yes," Cavalo whispered.

Lucas didn't come in that night at all.

ONE DAY REMAINED, AND JAMIE WAS GONE. HE'D DISAPPEARED somewhere during the night while Cavalo hovered just above sleep. He couldn't be sure he was ever really there to begin with. Cavalo thought not, remembering he was losing his mind. Maybe he already had.

He should have seen coming what happened next. He walked out the door, taking a deep breath of the cold air. The morning sun was weak in the sky.

They had gathered outside his house. All of them. All that remained in Cottonwood. They stood before him, not a single word spoken aloud. He stuttered once in his step as he walked through the door, trying to convince his feet to turn him around and go back inside. Instead, he closed it behind him, his hand slipping off the doorknob.

Bad Dog was the only other thing that moved. He walked up the steps to the porch and bumped his head against Cavalo's leg.

They've been waiting, he said. *For a long time.*

"I don't know what to say," Cavalo whispered down to him.

I know. But you're my MasterBossLord. You always say the right thing.

Lucas stood off to the side, away from the group. He twirled the knife in his hand. He glanced up at Cavalo briefly before he looked away. Something was wrong there. He felt a flash of anger at it, that Lucas had some sort of problem *now*, at *this* moment, but he pushed it away before it lit something inside him and exploded.

It was easier than he expected. Maybe because he was tired. Maybe because they were all going to die tomorrow. Or maybe he was just tired of being angry.

"I don't...," he started, but his voice came out scratchy and fragile. It cracked, little pieces breaking off. He shook his head. Cleared his throat. Tried again. "I don't know what you want me to say. I don't know what you want me to do." He raised his head to find all were watching him. A chill went down his spine. A burst of fear. But wasn't there something else too? Something that felt stronger? There was, but Cavalo pushed it away. He didn't want it. He didn't want any of this. He opened his mouth to tell them to go the fuck away. To tell them he couldn't be what they wanted him to be. To maybe threaten them again. Point his gun at them. Only this time he'd tell them there was nothing he could do. And maybe that was why he said what he said instead.

"We're all going to die tomorrow."

The people of Cottonwood sighed, their fears given words spoken aloud.

Bad Dog's tail thumped against his leg. He took it for what it was.

"I've seen...." He paused, considering. "I've seen monsters. All my life. Everywhere I've been. Sometimes they're real. Sometimes they're in my head. And sometimes I can't tell the difference." He took a deep breath. Let it out slowly. "You won't understand when I say it's all lost in the bees, but I don't know how else to explain it. I'm not... wired right anymore. I don't know that I ever have been. The things I've seen. The things I've done. It... it doesn't allow me to be fixed."

Cavalo looked down at his hands. Rough. Callused. They dealt only in death, and they were ready to do it again. He felt that old familiar itch in his fingers, that itch that meant he wanted the weight of a gun or knife in his hand. The tenseness of a bowstring. He narrowed his eyes and fisted his hands, dropping them to his sides. It would come soon enough.

"I'm tired," he said, more honest than he'd been in his entire life. "I'm tired of this life. Of living. Of having just enough to make it through the next day. Or week. Or month. I'm tired of the voices I hear in my head. I'm tired of the ghosts I see walking in the trees. I'm tired of them touching my skin at night when all I want to do is sleep."

Lucas watched him now. Cavalo would know those eyes anywhere. He couldn't meet the gaze. Not yet.

"But most of all," he said. "I'm tired of being scared."

There were tears on some of their faces. Anger too, twisting their features. Cavalo didn't think it was at him, though. Not this time.

"I'm tired of looking over my shoulder and wondering if this is the last breath I'll take. I'm tired of feeling like there is nothing left to hope for. I'm tired of feeling like we can't do a damn thing to change this. That this is the world we were born into, and this is the world we'll give back when we go. I'm tired of it. I'm tired of it all. Something has to change."

He looked at Lucas then. Met his eyes and held them. He didn't look away as he spoke his last.

"We're all going to die tomorrow," he said again, "but we're going to fight like hell. We're stronger when we realize that we have nothing left to lose. And we don't. This is it. This is the end of the road for us. And I can promise you I'm going to take as many of those bastards down with me as I can."

Cottonwood murmured their agreement. The tears had dried. The fear, while not gone completely, had lessened. There was something new that had overtaken it. Acceptance. Relief. Determination. Even though Cavalo knew it was surely easier to feel brave when safe than in the face of an enemy, he would take it for what it was.

"We're going to hit them," he said. "We're going to hit them hard. Your children are safe, and we're going to crack this earth around the feet of our enemies."

Cottonwood was louder now. Someone shouted in the back, a vocal noise that rose like a howl.

"We may be going, but we won't go quiet. I'm tired. I'm scared. But by the time tomorrow is finished, I promise you the world will forever know that this was the time we said *no*, that we said we would *not* back down, that we would *not* surrender. I promise you that long after we're gone, the world will remember what you've done. This will be the start, the catalyst, and you'll be the spark that ignites it all. We will *rise*, and though we may fall, things will never be the same, and from our ashes, there will be rebirth. There will be hope. There will be a chance that everyone who comes after us won't have to live as we did. And that's why tomorrow, we fight."

And though he spoke to the crowd, his final words were for Lucas alone. The relief he felt caused his eyes to burn. "My name is James

Cavalo, like my father before me. Like my son who came after me. They're gone now. I do this for them. And I will do this for you."

He stopped talking then. He knew it was more than he'd spoken in years. Maybe in his life. His throat hurt, and he was embarrassed, sure he'd said too much. Sure that he'd said too little. That none of it was right and they'd descend on him with their hands and tear into him until all that was left was a pile of blood and bone.

And they did descend on him. One by one. Reaching out and touching his hand. His arm. His shoulder. Face and hair. One by one.

Most of them spoke to him in low tones, barely above a whisper. They said:

I do this for my sister, who disappeared when I was twelve.

I do this for my home because it's the only one I've known.

I do this for my father, who was raped and left to die in an alley.

I do this for my brother. We only ever found his arm. He was seven.

I do this for my children. They're all I have left.

I do this for my wife because I will protect her with all I have.

I do this for my mother, who said I would never amount to anything.

I do this for myself, because I don't want to be scared anymore.

Deke looked nervous as he stood in front of Cavalo. He looked down at the step of the porch he stood on. "I...." He stopped, brow furrowing. He closed his eyes. "I'm sorry," he whispered.

Cavalo reached out and gripped his shoulder. "Nothing to be sorry about."

Deke looked up sharply. His eyes were wide, and his chest heaved as if he was on the verge of tears. "I shot you!"

"I gave you no reason not to."

He shook his head. "I should have listened."

"It's done, Deke."

"You did it, though."

"What?"

Deke looked up at him with big eyes. "Chose us."

Cavalo sighed. "Seems that way."

Deke nodded. He reached up tentatively and touched Cavalo's hand on his shoulder. Then he was gone.

Hank was behind him. "I do this," he said, "because we're withered and sere." He grabbed Cavalo in a rough hug, patting his back before letting him go.

Alma was the last. She had a strange look on her face as she squinted up at Cavalo. He let her look. Eventually, she said, "I thought it'd have been John."

Cavalo didn't stop the laugh that came out. "Sorry," he said.

She hugged him too. "I do this for Warren."

"I know," he said quietly.

"And you? Who do you do this for?"

"All of you."

"Do you?" She pulled away, her cheek brushing against his. "I knew it would happen one day."

"What?"

She shook her head. "It doesn't matter now."

She walked away, back into the crowd.

Bad Dog had stayed by his side the entire time. He leaned over and rubbed his head against Cavalo's leg. *You smell like all of them,* he said, sounding grumpy. *You need to smell like me now.* He lifted his snout and licked Cavalo's fingers. *Everything I do is for you, MasterBossLord.*

"I know," Cavalo said, scratching behind his ears. "Because you're Bad Dog."

Bad Dog huffed his agreement.

And then the crowd parted slowly. Cavalo watched as Lucas walked through, the expression on his face unreadable. Cavalo pulled himself back up to his full height, his eyes locking on to Lucas.

He climbed the steps slowly. Deliberately. Never taking his eyes away from Cavalo. He only stopped when he'd reached the top where Cavalo stood. Cavalo could have touched him if he'd wanted to. He felt itchy and exposed. The bees wanted him to run. And so did the rest of him.

He made up his mind to turn and flee into the vacant house. But before he could turn, Lucas's hands were on his face, pressing against his cheeks. Fingers trailed and prodded. His chin. His lips. His nose. Cavalo could smell him, standing so close. Like blood and sweat. Death and lightning. Lucas's eyes were narrowed.

Cavalo stayed where he was, unsure.

Lucas poked him in the chest. *You,* he said.

"Me? I'm... me."

Cavalo.

"Yes."

Lucas shook his head. Held up a single finger. He remembered then, that day in the prison when Lucas had been in the cell and he had asked him if Cavalo was his first or last name.

James, he said now, and Cavalo understood. *Like your father before you. Like your son after you.*

Cavalo closed his eyes, unable to stop the shudder that roared through him. He thought the very earth beneath his feet shook and that the walls they'd hastily constructed would come tumbling down.

It stopped as quickly as it had started.

He opened his eyes.

Lucas frowned up at him. *James,* he said again. *Cavalo.* As if he had trouble reconciling the two.

"Yeah," Cavalo muttered.

The question in his eyes was obvious. *Why now?*

"It doesn't matter," Cavalo said. Everything felt too bright. He looked away.

Lucas nodded tightly.

And stepped away.

He was back into the crowd and was gone before Cavalo could call out after him.

. . .

HE WAS STILL AWAKE THAT NIGHT WHEN HE HEARD THE DOOR to the vacant house open and close. The fire crackled in front of him, a log splitting as it settled. He didn't dare turn. Today had been too much.

Bad Dog looked up behind Cavalo. He thumped his tail once before he lay his head back down on his paws and closed his eyes.

He was surprised when he heard the footsteps approach from behind him, further so when Lucas walked around him and stood above Cavalo between him and the fire. He was careful to keep his wet boots off the blankets spread out on the floor. Cavalo knew he was looking down at him. He waited.

And on the silence stretched.

It was Cavalo who broke first. He'd been scraped raw and for one of the first times in his long and painful life, he felt the need to touch. To be touched.

He reached out. He could not stop his hand from shaking. His fingers closed around Lucas's pant leg. He felt the ankle underneath. He held it tight. The bone under his fingers was strong and unmoving. It anchored him. He took a breath. And another. And another.

Eventually, he let go.

Lucas waited until he pulled his hand back before stretching out next to him. He kicked off his boots. Cavalo lifted the blanket, and Lucas slid underneath. They lay on their sides, hands curled under their heads, faces inches apart.

It was Lucas who spoke first. *James Cavalo*, he said.

"Lucas."

Tomorrow.

"Yes."

Are you scared?

He thought of lying. "Yes."

Oh. A hesitation, eyes darting away and back again. *Me too.*

"I know."

I could.... He shook his head almost angrily. *I could go.*

"Where?" Cavalo felt cold.

He raised his hand and mimed walking with his fingers. *Away. Back to them. To... Patrick.*

Cavalo grabbed him by his coat. Shook him a little. "Don't you fucking say that."

Lucas looked pained.

"You can't."

He looked away.

"Promise me."

Defiant eyes.

Cavalo shook him again, harder this time. "*Promise me.*"

Lucas held up a finger. Pointed at Cavalo. *James. Why did you tell me?*

Cavalo thought to push him away. To lie again. It'd be easier. So much easier. Instead, he said, "Because it's all I have left to give."

Lucas kissed him. There. In the dark.

And later in the night, their bodies moved together as one day ended and another began. Except this day was unlike any that had come before it. A great and powerful man had once said there would come a day when someone would rise, rise and fight back against the dark.

One hundred years later, James Cavalo fell asleep held by a clever monster who pressed a knife into his side, unaware that his day had come at last.

a brief interlude before war

THEY WOKE the next morning as weak light filtered in through the windows. The room was colder, the fire nothing but embers.

They didn't speak much, the three of them. There didn't seem to be any words needed. They'd said what they needed to the night before.

They dressed quickly and quietly.

Cavalo opened up the door to the vacant house to let Bad Dog out. He started to follow when Lucas stopped him. "What?"

Lucas tugged him back into the house. "Lucas, we don't have time for—"

Lucas shot him a look. *Make time. This is important.*

Cavalo sighed but didn't try to pull his hand away.

Lucas pulled him to a small bathroom. The shower had rusted. The mirror was cracked and dirty. Lucas sat him on the lip of the bathtub and shut the door behind them. Cavalo didn't know who he was trying to keep out, but he didn't question it.

Nor did he question the little jar that Lucas pulled from his pocket. He turned the lid and set it down at the sink. Lucas looked at himself in the mirror. Cavalo wondered what he saw in his reflection but didn't think it his place to ask. Lucas closed his eyes and took a breath before letting it out slowly. Cavalo couldn't help but think this felt like a tradition.

And it did, especially when Lucas opened his eyes again. He reached down and dipped two fingers into the jar. They were black when he pulled them away. He watched as Lucas began to spread them around his eyes. He remembered then, the snowstorm he'd stumbled through after he'd been shot. The black mask on the door, covered in bees, the word *suffering* burned into the wood. And maybe he was. Maybe he was suffering now. But he didn't regret his choice. That surprised him.

It didn't take long for Lucas to finish. He looked as he did the first day he'd held a knife to Cavalo's throat. Cavalo was amused at the nostalgia, but he didn't say it out loud.

He thought they were finished until Lucas turned to him. He cocked his head at Cavalo, eyes searching for something on his face. He must have found what he needed because he reached for the jar again. He dipped his fingers in it and kicked Cavalo's legs apart. Cavalo grunted but didn't speak. Lucas dropped to his knees between Cavalo's legs and looked up at him.

His mask was wet around his eyes. He reached up toward Cavalo's face with the blackened fingers.

Cavalo grabbed his wrist, stopping him. Lucas didn't try to pull away.

"What is this?" he asked finally.

Lucas pointed first at Cavalo, then back at himself. He held up a single finger and shook his head. *I know who you are, James. I know that now. But I can't tell you who I am beyond what you see because I don't know.*

"You don't know your surname?" he asked, sounding surprised.

Patrick never told me.

"What about your mother?"

I don't know who she is. There was the shark's grin again. *Maybe I don't have one.*

Cavalo snorted. "Sounds right." He looked at the black fingers. "Why?" he asked finally.

And Lucas gave the only answer that mattered: *Because it's all I have left to give.*

Cavalo let his hand go.

Lucas started under his right eye. The paint had a faint medicinal tang mixed in with the scent of pine. It made his eyes water briefly. He blinked away the burn. Lucas's face was close, his brow furrowed as he concentrated. They breathed the same air. Cavalo thought he was burning. He couldn't remember the last time he'd felt like this. Elko, maybe. Before it burned. When *she* was alive and Jamie was alive, and even though the world was a dark and scary place, they had managed to make something for themselves. Cavalo had pulled himself out of the hole dug by his father with a shovel made of wasps and *made* a life. He burned brightly back then.

LIKE HE BURNED NOW.

He knew what it was. He didn't name it, but he knew.

He didn't trust himself to speak.

Lucas finished, frowning as he sat back on his heels. Eventually, he nodded. He stood and stepped back, motioning for Cavalo to look in the mirror.

He did. His reflection was cracked, but that was okay. It made sense for him. When he finally met his own eyes staring back at him, all the shattered pieces of his life slid together in a way they hadn't before. He couldn't tell what new shape they'd made and he knew the pieces didn't fit as they were supposed to, but it didn't matter.

The man who stared back at him was not the man that had once been. The mask saw to that. It stretched out away from his eyes, streaks curling down around his cheeks and back toward his ears. Flecks of the paint stuck in the stubble on his chin. He reached up and wiped them away. And when he did, he focused on Lucas standing behind him, watching his reaction.

He turned then, that unnamed thing rearing its ugly head. He brought his hand up to the back of Lucas's neck and brought their foreheads together.

"I'm going to kill him," he said.

Lucas gave him a nasty smile. *We both will.*

"You stay with me. No matter what. At my side."

Yes.

"We're going to die."

The smile only widened.

Cavalo kissed him. It was the only thing he could do.

CAVALO OPENED THE DOOR TO THE VACANT HOUSE. STEPPED OUT into the cold. He wasn't surprised to see the town again gathered before him. Their eyes widened when they saw the masks. He knew he looked like one of them. The Dead Rabbits. The monsters. Those psycho fucking cannibals.

And he did not care. He bared his teeth.

The people took a step toward him, determined. He could almost hear their bees.

"It's time!" he shouted for all to hear. "Before you fall, you take as many of them down with you as you can and send them back into the hell they crawled from. And when the last breath leaves your body, go knowing that today is the day we rose up against the dark. We fight together so we don't have to die alone."

The people of Cottonwood raised their weapons and screamed in return.

Cavalo began to smile. It was a good day to die.

the battle of cottonwood

THEY WAITED.

For all the bluster and noise he'd made, they waited.

And at first there was nothing.

Cavalo didn't allow himself to hope that there was nothing coming. He knew it was only a matter of time.

Two o'clock approached on the day of the solstice. Only a few of the Patrol walked along the planks on the outer wall, Cavalo and Lucas among them. The rest were inside, waiting.

Lucas scowled down at the southern road, his eyes darting along the tree line. Bad Dog paced behind him.

"We good?" Cavalo asked them both.

Lucas shook his head but didn't answer.

They're coming, Bad Dog said.

"Can you smell them?"

He sniffed the air once, twice. *No. Not yet. But I know.*

"Together?"

Bad Dog bumped his knee. *Together.*

Cavalo watched the trees.

The bees in his head were surprisingly calm, but then they

always were when he went to war. They'd be there after. Waiting for him.

And then it began.

Bad Dog noticed it first. He sniffed the air. Stopped. Sniffed again. Growled low in the back of his throat. The hairs on his haunches stood on end as his lips twitched over his teeth. *Here,* he said. *They're here. They're here.*

Lucas tensed.

Cavalo looked out toward the southern road. There was someone walking toward Cottonwood. Alone. A man. Cavalo couldn't make out who it was, but somehow he knew.

"Patrick," he said quietly.

The word spread quietly behind him. He heard gasps and muffled cries that were quickly silenced. The Patrol came up quickly, resting the barrels of their rifles between the wooden slats of the outer wall. All guns pointed at the approaching man.

They waited.

Patrick was dressed like a Dead Rabbit. Wrist braces made of deer hide painted black and red. Arm bands around his biceps. A black coat with dull spikes along the shoulders. Fur around his neck. A heavy-looking axe was secured on his back, the handle at an angle over his right shoulder. The blade was silver and clean. His boots crunched the snow as he stopped yards away from the gate. He was close enough that Cavalo could see his face clearly. He looked amused.

"Hello!" he called, as if he'd just stumbled upon them. "How are we today?" He didn't seem perturbed that he had multiple firearms pointed at him.

Cavalo held his hand below the wall line, making a fist. He didn't want anyone else speaking out.

"Lucas," Patrick said. "How nice it is to see you again. It's been some time, boy."

Lucas's hand tightened on his knife.

"Enough," Cavalo growled. He couldn't explain the rage he felt at Patrick speaking to Lucas. He had to stop himself from ordering the Patrol to fire everything they had right then. Cavalo knew they were going to die, but he also knew he would feel Patrick's blood on his skin before day's end. "Turn around. Go back where you came from while you still can."

Patrick laughed. "How kind of you to offer. I'll counter. Give me the boy, and no one will get hurt."

"No."

"No? No?" He laughed. "That's... unfortunate. I expected more from you, Cavalo."

"Sorry to disappoint."

"Yes, yes. I'm sure you are." He took a deep breath and blew it out. It became vapor and swirled around his face. "Brisk day! Should be perfect for what I have in mind."

"He talks too much," Frank snarled. "I have the shot."

"Hold," Aubrey said.

"Uh-oh," Patrick said. "That sounded serious."

"What do you want?" Cavalo asked him.

"You know what I want. I thought I was very clear about that. How are your fingers, by the way?"

"Healing."

"Good! I felt just *awful* about that when I left. But what's done is done, am I right?"

Cavalo said nothing.

Patrick didn't seem to mind. "I must admit, Cavalo. It's tiring calling out to you like this. Let's talk face to face, you and I. Like the generals of old before they went to war. It was much more civilized back then, I should think. Things such as this were more about the *theatrics* rather than the bloodshed." He spread his arms and danced then, tapping his feet in the thin snow on the road, spinning in a circle before finishing with a shuffle of his right foot. He chuckled. "It's all about the *show*, Cavalo." He grinned up at them. He looked like his son then. Cavalo felt sick.

"Unarmed," Cavalo said.

Patrick nodded. He took the axe from behind him and tossed it away in the snow. Looked back up expectantly.

"All of it."

"Such fire," Patrick said. "I assure you that's all." He lifted his coat and spun in a slow circle.

Cavalo glanced at Lucas, who nodded tightly. *That's all he carries.*

Cavalo handed over his knife and pistol. His rifle was set against the wall. Lucas took them from him without question. He turned from the wall toward the ladder down to the interior. Before he'd stepped down the rungs, Lucas stopped him.

Be careful, he said. Cavalo could see the anger spilling over.

"I know."

Lucas shook his head. *You don't.* He pursed his lips and blew between the two of them. *He's not like us. He doesn't have the bees. He is the bees.*

This Cavalo knew.

He reached the bottom of the ladder where Hank stood. "You sure about this?" Hank asked him.

"Buys us more time. Anything?"

"Some movement in the trees. Binocs are helping but I can't tell how many."

"He won't have brought them all. They need Dworshak guarded."

"He didn't need them all for Grangeville," Hank reminded him.

Cavalo ignored him.

They raised the gate only a foot or so off the ground, giving Cavalo enough room to crawl under through the snow. He stood, and the gate closed behind him. He walked slowly toward Patrick. He wanted to glance up at Lucas, but he didn't look away from Patrick.

And Patrick smiled as he approached. Up close, it was more and more like Lucas. The bees wanted him to lash out. Cavalo tried to hold them back.

He stopped just out of arm's reach. He raised his coat and spun slowly to show he was unarmed.

"It's funny, isn't it?" Patrick asked when he faced him again.

"What's that?"

"Being here. Now. You. I. This whole... *thing*." He looked at Cavalo earnestly.

"How so?"

"You have something I want. You won't give it to me. You think you'll win. I know you won't. This whole back and forth is just... it's *funny*."

"No," Cavalo said. "I don't think we'll win."

Patrick's eyes narrowed. "No?"

"No."

"You expect to die, then."

"Yes."

The showman's smile faded off Patrick's face. Lucas had been right. He was nothing but bees. Before Cavalo could blink, Patrick had snapped out an arm, wrapping his hand around Cavalo's throat. Cavalo could hear shouts of surprise and anger coming from behind him, and he frantically waved them off. They couldn't take the chance. Not yet.

"What game are you playing?" Patrick snarled at him.

"No game," Cavalo managed to say. "We fight... because we have... nothing else... to lose." His own bees screamed in his head, demanding he rip Patrick apart, that he start by breaking every bone in the hand and arm that held him. He pushed them away. It would do him no good.

"Nothing?" Patrick said. "You have *everything* to lose. All of those people. I will start with their children. We will eat their toes and fingers. You will watch while every single person you know is consumed, and then and *only* then will I start in on you. Your death will not be quick. It will not be painless. You will feel every little prick of your skin, and when you're about to die, right before your eyes close for the last time, I will cut off your head."

Cavalo laughed. It hurt, the fingers on his throat were really far too tight, but he laughed. He couldn't stop himself even if he tried. It came out weak and crazed.

"Such fire," Patrick said. "How different things could have been." He dropped his hand from Cavalo's throat. Cavalo coughed, lungs burning.

"What do you hope to have happen here?" Patrick asked him. "You've already said you're prepared to die. Just what do you think you'll achieve?"

"It doesn't matter," Cavalo said.

A sharp wind picked up, blowing between them, flurries of snow swirling around their heads, and Cavalo knew he was back in the snow globe again. Everything was shaking, and he'd *lost* something, Charlie, and he had to fight down the urge to laugh again, knowing he'd be lost to it if he gave in.

"You wear his mask," Patrick said.

"Yes."

"Dare I ask why?"

"Because he asked me to."

"Did he? You'll never see him again after today. I will get what I need from him and then throw him to my wolves. They'll take him again and again and again. And when he's dripping with come and blood, they'll take him again."

Cavalo's jaw tightened, nothing more.

"I was a man, once," Patrick said.

"Not anymore?"

He shook his head. "No. You can't do what I've done, seen what I've seen, and still be a man."

"You're his father." An accusation, a threat.

"I am. I know something of fathers. You could say I came from them."

Cavalo knew he spoke of more. "The Forefathers."

Patrick ignored him. "You will die. You know this?"

"Yes."

"And you won't give me what I ask for?"

"No."

"Grangeville is gone. No one is coming for you."

"I know. I was there."

Patrick nodded. "I thought you were. Did you see them? They burned prettily."

Easy, he told himself. *Easy.* "Did they hurt?"

"The burning? I would assume so, even—"

"The tattoos."

Patrick took a step back. Recovered quickly. Smiled that showman smile. "The tattoos," he repeated.

Cavalo said nothing. He'd heard what he needed to hear. Even if Lucas had told him that Patrick carried the rest of the schematics etched onto his skin, it helped to have confirmation. Though he didn't know what he'd do with it.

"I *like* you," Patrick breathed. "This will be a good day."

"It may not be us," Cavalo said, "and it may not be today, but one day, and one day soon, everything you know will come crashing down upon you. Someone, be it the Forefathers, St. Louis, or the UFSA. Someone will come, and you will be nothing but a bad dream."

"I *am* the Forefathers," Patrick snarled at him. "I *am* St. Louis. They are *nothing* without me, and once Dworshak is operational, I will launch an offensive unlike anything that this world has ever seen."

"You shine," Cavalo said. "Darkly."

"Good-bye, Cavalo," Patrick said. "Remember that I gave you a chance."

He turned, picking his axe up from the snow. He dusted it off and slid it onto his back again, securing it. He started to walk away, then stopped.

Cavalo waited.

Patrick rocked his head back and howled. It echoed across the snowy fields before it died.

At first there was nothing.

And then from the forest came answering cries. It sounded like hundreds of voices mixing together for a single roar.

Cavalo knew then just how fucked they were.

Patrick walked back toward the trees without another word. Cavalo waited until he disappeared into the forest before he turned back toward Cottonwood. He didn't run, though he wanted to. Instead, he kept his breathing even, feeling the sweat on his brow and his fingernails digging into the palm of his hand. The mask on his face was heavy and itchy. His eyes were locked onto Lucas, who glared down at him from the wall. The gate opened, and Cavalo dropped underneath it.

Hank was waiting for him. His face was pale.

"How many are there?" Cavalo demanded.

"Dozens," he said. "More. I don't...."

"Nothing changes," Cavalo said, pushing past him.

Hank grabbed his arm. "We could still run. Head for the prison."

Cavalo stopped. Took a deep breath. Loosened his shoulders. "No," he said. "We can't. This won't end here. You know it won't." He pulled himself from Hank's grasp. "Get everyone inside the inner wall and into place. They know what to do. Do it now. It's time to end this." He didn't turn to see Hank's reaction. It didn't matter. Not anymore.

Cavalo pulled himself up the ladder, taking two rungs at a time. Lucas and Bad Dog waited for him at the top. The Dead Rabbit's knife flashed in the low light. Cavalo didn't stop himself. He hooked a hand around the back of his neck, pulling Lucas toward him. He kissed him fiercely, lips pushing back against his teeth. If this was their end, then so be it. But he was going to go out as he wanted to. And with who he wanted to.

Lucas gripped his sides. They panted as their lips pulled away. Forehead to forehead, the man and the monster breathed each other in, eyes wide and surrounded by black oil rubbed into the skin. Cavalo thought he could have been looking into a mirror.

Lucas reached up and motioned between the two of them. *This... this thing. Between us.*

"It burns," Cavalo said. "It hurts. I'm stung by it."

Lucas nodded. *I didn't mean for this to happen.*

"I know."

I am the dark.

"I know."

But you stand by me.

"Yes," he whispered.

Why?

That thing that could not be named flared inside of him. And for the first time in a very long time, Cavalo spoke the truth of it. "Because I don't want to be alone anymore."

James.

"Whatever happens," Cavalo said roughly, "you stay with me. At my side. Follow me, and I'll follow you. We'll get through this." The tone of his voice left no room for argument, even though his words rang false.

And Lucas smiled. It looked foreign on his face because it wasn't that of the shark. There was something else buried in it. A tinge of sadness. Of longing.

And so many bees.

They were both covered in them.

Bad Dog barked worriedly. *They're coming! They're coming!*

Cavalo turned.

Out past the southern road, through the fields of snow that led to the tree line, there was movement. Cavalo's eyes were not what they once were. He knew that. He was older. His body wasn't as strong as it'd been when he first started out on that horse so long ago. Age and a grenade exploding in his son's hands had seen to that. The edges were duller than they'd been before, but he could still see.

They moved out from the trees. Men and women. They wore

black fur and spikes. Their heads were shaved into strange designs. Tattoos curled up around their necks and scalps. Black armbands wrapped around biceps. Some were sick, the effects of radiation shown in tumors and distorted skin. But even those obviously ill did not stutter in their steps. They walked with purpose, and the line of people that stepped from the trees seemed to stretch on farther than Cavalo cared to look.

They stopped halfway across the field, close enough now that Cavalo could hear them shuffling through the snow. Lucas tensed at his side, and Cavalo reached down to grip his hand. Lucas's fingers entwined with his own. He felt the strength there, in the long, thin fingers. The skin and bones that held him tight.

"Bad Dog," he said quietly. "Down with BigHank. Now."

But—

"Now."

Bad Dog licked his hand once, then went to the edge of the platform. "I got you," he heard Hank say as Bad Dog grumbled.

Patrick separated himself from the rest of the Dead Rabbits. He walked in front of them. Gone was the showman's smile. Now it was just the bees. "Last chance," he called out. "Think about what you're doing, Cavalo. Those people trust you. Think about what you're making them do."

"You talk too much," Cavalo said, his voice carrying across the field. "I'm done with you."

The feral smile returned.

Cavalo had a bad feeling about this.

"Everyone inside?" he said quietly.

"Yes," Hank said from below.

"Go. Now."

Cavalo could hear Hank hurry away.

"I look forward to seeing what you're made of," Patrick said. "All spread out in the snow. Kuegler! Blower! Show these people how we say hello."

Two men rushed to him, stopping on either side. They dropped to their knees. It was only then that Cavalo saw the RPGs brought up to their shoulders.

"Holy shit," he breathed.

There was the blast of the weapons discharging, but Cavalo didn't see the rockets fire toward them. Lucas had already pulled him away from the outer wall. Time slowed down around them, and through the storm of bees that roared in his head, Cavalo could hear the sharp whistling sound of objects slicing quickly through the air. He had time to think that he should have expected this given the black, scorched hole at Grangeville. He had time to wonder if he'd made a mistake, if he should have let them all run.

He had time to notice it'd started snowing again.

But then time ran out as Lucas pulled him off the edge of the platform. They jumped, and right before the wall exploded behind them, Lucas twisted in the air, pulling Cavalo to him, covering his body as if to shield him. Before Cavalo could even begin to process what he was doing, a wave of hot air slammed into their backs, knocking them apart. Cavalo landed on his side in the snow, curling up into a ball as burning wood rained down around him. Something heavy bounced off his legs, and he grunted. His ears felt cotton-stuffed. The snow had lessened the impact, but his arm was sore. Nothing felt broken. At least not physically.

He pushed himself up, and the world shook around him, and he had lost something, Charlie, had lost something deep inside the snow globe. He looked back along the outer wall and saw the gaping hole where the platform had been.

But then hands were on him, pulling him up. He tried to tell the hands that he was fine, that he was okay, just let him take his time. They didn't listen. They pulled until he was on his feet. His ears popped then, and everything roared around him, assaulting him. He flinched and shook his head.

"Lucas," he said, unsure.

The hands belonged to Lucas. Those dark eyes glared back at

him, the mask creasing as they traveled up and down Cavalo. *Are you hurt?* he demanded.

"No," he said gruffly. "Get inside. Hurry." Because he could hear them now. The Dead Rabbits. They were coming.

Lucas pulled him quickly toward the hastily constructed inner wall twenty yards into Cottonwood. Even before they'd moved a few feet, Lucas stopped, scanning the ground in front of him. Cavalo looked over his shoulder and saw debris from the wall littering the ground in front of them. He knew what Lucas was looking for. It was the only safe way through the town. Cavalo was disoriented, and it took him a moment to find it.

"There," he said, pointing to their left.

Lucas hadn't yet let go of his hand and didn't now. He led Cavalo between two houses where wooden planks lay atop the snow in a thin path toward the inner wall. The windows of the houses on either side of him were boarded shut. Dozens of rusted nails were pounded through the wood. They stuck out at odd angles.

Cavalo pulled his hand away from Lucas and bent to pick up each plank as they passed over them, tossing them along the edges of the empty houses. Lucas watched over him each time he stopped, glaring at the way they'd come to make sure the Dead Rabbits hadn't yet breached the wall. They passed through the alley between the houses and were back out in the open on the street. The back windows on the stretch of houses behind them had all been busted out. The sharp smell of oil and gas poured from the windows, but the wind carried it quickly away.

The wooden pathway ahead curved up and over a mound of snow and ended at a slat of wood that could be shifted on the inner wall. He turned to start throwing the remaining planks out of the way so the Dead Rabbits couldn't see the path. Lucas grabbed him then, pulling him roughly back up and shaking his head.

But the movement was too fast, and they lost their balance. Lucas's eyes widened as he struggled to hold himself upright. Cavalo reached for him as he fell toward the snow. Cavalo gritted his teeth as his feet slid along the cold wood, struggling to keep them from falling to certain death. His feet hit the edge of the plank, and he curled his toes, grunting as the muscles in his arms strained. It was close. Another few inches. Lucas was almost horizontal to the ground, his nose scraping against the surface of the snow. Cavalo breathed heavily through his nose as he looked down.

He could see the faint outline of the land mine in the snow directly below Lucas. And the one next to it. And the one next to that. And the one next to that. He couldn't see every one of them, but he knew they stretched around the inner wall. All partially hidden in snow. A line of defense thanks to SIRS and his magical box he'd pulled down the mountain. A box filled with mines and other tools of destruction that Cavalo didn't know he'd had. He wondered if he'd ever be able to ask the robot where and why he'd kept them hidden all this time.

Lucas had almost fallen on one. It would have been the end then. For both of them.

"Holy shit," Cavalo gasped, pulling him back up. He felt Lucas shudder once as he stood upright. The grin Lucas tossed back at him was too shaky to be normal, or as normal as a smile from the Dead Rabbit could be. His eyes were too wide. His brow lined with sweat. His hands shook.

Too close.

"They're coming!" Hank shouted down at them from the inner wall. "*Move your asses!*"

Both Cavalo and Lucas snapped their attention toward him. He was waving frantically at them. Members of the Patrol stood, armed with ancient machine guns and high-powered rifles. Aubrey and Deke had their bows drawn, waiting for the tips of the arrows to be lit to ignite their first line of defense.

They were running out of time. They only had once chance to get this right, and they'd fire even if Cavalo and Lucas weren't out of the way.

"*Go!*" Cavalo roared, pushing Lucas farther down the planks.

The snow fell heavier now, flakes melting against Cavalo's heated face. He thought he could hear every single noise around him and didn't allow himself to look back because the Dead Rabbits would be *right there*—

They crested the snowbank. A trench stretched out before them, six feet across and five feet deep. A heavy board acted as a bridge from one side to the other. Lucas went first, taking only three steps to cross. Cavalo followed quickly, glancing down as he did so. The trench was filled with thin posts embedded into the frozen ground, their ends shaved into sharp points that rose toward the gray sky. He leapt the last couple of feet and Lucas kicked the board away, knocking it into the trench. It fell between the wooden pikes below.

Cavalo reached the inner wall and shoved the slat to the side. He pushed Lucas through the narrow entrance and followed him in, head to the side as his knees scraped against the wall. Lucas turned and yanked him in the rest of way. They grinned maniacally at each other. His mask felt stretched tight across his face. He thought it would crack. Maybe the rest of him would follow.

Bad Dog barked once, a sharp sound of warning.

Cavalo turned and slid a metal bar down over the inside of the opening in the wall. He wrapped a chain around it, securing the wall so it wouldn't open from the outside. He knew it was almost pointless; grenade launchers always beat chains. He had time to appreciate just how far Patrick was willing to take this. But what struck him the most was how Patrick obviously had faith in Lucas dodging rockets. He wouldn't have risked firing at him otherwise, not with Lucas's skin marked as it was.

Lucas was already up the ladder with the Patrol. Cavalo glanced at the buildings behind the wall. He could see people peering cautiously out the windows, their hands wrapped around their weapons. They mostly kept to the first floors, with only a few of the crack shots on the second. They hadn't wanted to take the chance of too many people getting stuck on a higher floor if the Dead Rabbits overran the town.

If? the bees laughed, sounding breathless. *You mean* when.

He didn't have time for his bees.

Patrick was coming.

He pulled himself up the ladder and was handed his bow. Bad Dog stood at his side, tail thumping. Lucas twirled his knife that he'd somehow held on to. Cavalo watched as Hank handed Lucas a bow and quiver too, and an assault rifle. He slung the rifle over his shoulder and nocked an arrow, holding it down at his side. Cavalo looked down the line of the wall. Twenty people stood on either side of him, spread out evenly along the wall and waiting for his signal. Ten more people stood behind them against the back of the walkway, holding burning torches. He could tell they were scared, but they weren't allowing it to consume them. Cavalo felt a strange burst of fierce pride in his chest as he saw the determined looks on their faces. Deke nodded at him, and Aubrey offered him a tight smile. Frank and his crew had their jaws set, shoulders tense. Hank and Alma stood on either side of Lucas and Cavalo. Bad Dog was in the middle of them all, growling in the back of his throat.

"Light them and hold!" Cavalo growled. "Be prepared to move. Arrows only." The message was carried down the wall in hushed whispers.

He looked down into the outer edges of Cottonwood. The hole blasted into the outer wall was obscured by a house. He couldn't see out over the far wall and into the field as this section of Cottonwood was down on a slope. He didn't have to wait long.

The Dead Rabbits spilled out between the houses, stopping just along the edges. A few more feet and they'd be in the minefield. Cavalo wasn't sure why they stopped, but he wasn't going to take any chances.

A young man whose name Cavalo did not know lit the tip of his arrow. It caught easily and burned, having been wrapped in an old rag and soaked in heating oil.

"Hold," he muttered, taking aim. The people of Cottonwood did the same.

More Dead Rabbits came forward. Dozens. A hundred. More. An army against a little town. He didn't see Patrick, but he knew he had to be mixed in there somewhere. Whatever else he might have been, Cavalo didn't take Patrick for a coward. People infested with bees hardly ever were.

"Hold." The bowstring was tense against his arm.

More and more filed in. Too many of them. The alleys between the houses were choked with Dead Rabbits. He could see their guns. Their bombs. Their machetes. He could see them gnashing their teeth. Their painted faces. The dirt on their skin. They were dark against the snow.

"*Hold.*" A snowflake fell on the burning arrow and hissed quietly.

Three Dead Rabbits stepped forward, rocket launchers on their shoulders.

"Cavalo," Hank warned, his voice shaking.

"*Hold!*" Cavalo snapped at him.

And then he saw him. Briefly. Moving in the crowd. It was just a flash. Just a moment. Two Dead Rabbits crossed in front of each other, and there Patrick was, watching Cavalo with that grotesque smile on his face. It was all he needed.

"*Now!*"

Fourteen arrows flew toward seven houses, each with windows broken out on the top and bottom floors. He had picked these archers because they were the best shots. Aubrey and Deke. Hank and Alma. Frank. Others whose names he could not remember. One was only fourteen but handled a bow like a master. His mother had tried to argue, but Lucas had snarled silently at her, and that was that. His aim had been true. That was all that mattered to Cavalo.

And they were true now. All of them. When it mattered the most. Cavalo had only reminded them once that they only had one shot at this. Any mistakes and the battle would be over before it had even begun.

There were cries of warning from the Dead Rabbits. Some carried wooden shields and raised them over their heads. Others attempted to scatter, but the crowd was too congested for them to move. A few stragglers toward the backs edged back toward the outer wall.

The arrows went over the Dead Rabbits, trailing wisps of black smoke through the white snow. Their aim was true, as Cavalo had known they would be. They'd practiced enough. And they had no other choice. The arrows went through the broken windows. There were brief flashes of fire in some of the houses as fumes caught, but nothing further.

The Dead Rabbits lowered their arms. They looked around. One started laughing, and it only took a moment for others to join in. "That's all you got!" one of them shouted.

"No," Cavalo said, only for the people around him to hear. "That's not all."

Maybe they'd overdone it. Maybe they'd put too much. They'd scrounged up all the oil and gas they could. Had soaked the floors in the houses. Stacked land mines, as many as thirty, on each floor of each house. They didn't have rockets as the Dead Rabbits did, but SIRS had brought them hundreds of mines in his shiny metal box.

"Burn the houses before the mines go off," SIRS had told him quietly. "There will be fire then."

The men with the rocket launchers took aim again.

Maybe they'd overdone it, because there was a moment when smoke began to pour out the windows and Cavalo thought *too much, too much, no, no, no,* but then it was all obliterated, swallowed up as a house in the center seemed to *expand* on its foundation, the panel siding rippling. But the illusion of expansion was lost when the siding blew out, sharp licks of fire shooting through the flying debris. The force of the explosion on the bottom blew upward through the house. The second floor bowed upward for just a brief, impossible moment before it too ignited. The second blast was much louder than the first as parts of the roof blew off, flipping wildly into the air.

Dead Rabbits were screaming as the ones closest to the house were knocked off their feet. Blood splattered against the snow as the nails hammered into the boarded windows shot out like bullets and slammed into Dead Rabbit skin. Other flesh was blackened and pierced with shards of wood. Cavalo felt savagely pleased when they started to fall to the ground.

Before the Dead Rabbits could run, a second house went, both floors exploding in concert. And then a third. The next two exploded at the same time. The last two went off in quick succession. The roar echoed across Cottonwood, and waves of heat battered the faces of those lining the wall, weapons drawn. Cavalo could see the shockwaves hitting the falling snow, buffeting it before vaporizing water crystals into nothing.

Fire rose toward the gray sky, the black smoke and orange flames swirling, creating shadows that danced along the Dead Rabbits. Many of them lay sprawled on the ground. Many were screaming. Many were silent. Many were rising out of the snow.

So many rising.

One toward the front took a shuffling step forward. He looked to be no older than Lucas. The left side of his head was soaked with blood. He looked dazed. He shook his head. Took another step. Leaned over, and for a moment, Cavalo thought the Dead Rabbit was going to be sick. Blood dripped off his head to the ground. His hands went down to the snow, dragging, searching. And then he stood, pulling one of the RPGs up and out of the snow. He stood too fast and overshot, the rocket going toward the sky. He took a step back, levelled the rocket launcher, and there wasn't enough *time*—

A single shot fired out over the divide. The Dead Rabbit staggered back, blood spraying from his throat. The RPG pointed toward the ground. The Dead Rabbit's finger must have jerked on the trigger because the rocket fired and exploded almost instantly. The young Dead Rabbit vanished in a spray of gristle and bone.

Lucas smiled as he pulled his rifle back, the barrel smoking as he held it up against his shoulder. Cavalo could see Patrick in that smile. The shark and the showman. Lucas tilted his head toward the Dead

Rabbit he'd just killed. *Never really liked him,* he said. *Always trying too hard.*

Cavalo couldn't think of a single thing to say in response.

Lucas grinned now. It was a thing of teeth and bees.

"Cavalo!" Hank snapped.

He tore his gaze away from Lucas and looked back out toward the destruction where Hank was pointing.

The Dead Rabbits were regrouping. Those who could stand were pushing themselves up, picking their guns and knives and machetes out of the snow. One had a baseball bat wrapped in barbed wire.

"Jesus," Hank muttered. "How many are there?"

"Enough," Cavalo said. "Patrick?"

Hank shook his head.

Cavalo couldn't see him either. He hoped Patrick was lying in pieces in the snow, buried in limbs and smoke and ash. He didn't think it'd be that easy.

The Dead Rabbits were starting to move. Cavalo couldn't see any one Dead Rabbit who seemed to be in charge. From what Lucas had told him, Patrick had a dictatorship, almost revered as a deity. Lucas was meant to be his second-in-command, but the hierarchy quickly dissolved below that.

He didn't know which one of them picked up their battle cry again, but there was a roar from the Dead Rabbits, and it was quickly followed when others joined in. It chilled Cavalo completely, his eyes skating over the Dead Rabbits. He saw one whose head was rocked back, his heated breath blowing steam into the air as he screamed. He would have looked like the others around him, except his arm had been blown off in one of the explosions. The stump was ragged and wet, cut off just below his bicep. He screamed like the rest of them.

And they started forward.

"Do *nothing,*" Cavalo barked in a low voice. "Save your bullets. Save the arrows." The Patrol looked back at him uneasily.

The Dead Rabbits crossed into the open. Rifles were raised. Ancient handguns, covered in grime and rust. He never found out who fired the first shot from the advancing tide. Never saw the Dead Rabbit who did it.

The shot was fired. The Patrol ducked against the wall. Bad Dog whined quietly. Lucas barely flinched.

But that first shot was the opening of the floodgates. More came. The air was suddenly filled with the whine of bullets, the soft hush of arrows. Cavalo pulled Lucas down against the wall as it chipped and cracked above them. He heard a low cry off to his right and looked over. One of the Patrol, a young woman, held her arm, blood welling through her fingers. He heard Aubrey curse loudly before she rose to her feet, keeping her body below the wall line. Hank snapped at her to stay where she was, but she ignored him. She ran along the wall, the Patrol moving away and lying flat to let her by. She slid next to the girl and tore off part of her undershirt, wrapping the fabric around the girl's arm. The girl cried out as Aubrey tied it off, pulled it tight. She glanced back over her shoulder to Cavalo and nodded sharply.

Cavalo turned his head to look over his shoulder into the thin space between the wood of the wall. It wouldn't be much longer now, he knew. Just a few more steps and—

He didn't see the first one. He heard it, though, a muffled *thwump* above the gunfire followed by more screams. There was a second and third, and he could hear the moment the bullets flying overhead lessened. In that growing silence, he thought wildly of his father and how one day, when Cavalo (*James James James*) had been twelve, his father had laid into him after a particularly harsh bender the night before. Cavalo had ended up with two broken fingers and bruises that darkened his face and chest. "I'm sorry," he'd told Cavalo days later, and Cavalo had believed him. He *was* sorry. It was this memory Cavalo had thought of when he'd been told his father was found dead in a ditch, neck broken, the stench of alcohol as thick as the mass of flies that landed on his hardening skin.

And it was this memory Cavalo thought of now as the gunfire above their heads became sporadic as the Dead Rabbits ran into more and more of the land mines hidden in the snow. He could hear his father's voice in his head, and he was *sorry*, and all Cavalo could think was maybe they *did* have a chance. Maybe this *didn't* need to end in the destruction and death of Cottonwood. The thought was almost enough to tilt the ground beneath Cavalo's feet, and he took a breath, and then another. A man less hardened than Cavalo would have called that feeling hope. Cavalo couldn't recognize it for what it was, even if it burned like wildfire in his chest.

He was angry now. Very angry. He unshouldered his rifle, the metal cold against his skin. *Bakalovs,* SIRS had told them when he'd opened his metal box. *From Before. Bulgarian, I'm told. Nasty, nasty things. Has an alt fire mode. 40 mm rifle grenades. Don't have many of those, but there should be enough to get things started.* Even though his mouth couldn't move, Cavalo was sure SIRS was smiling.

The others along the wall watched him, waiting.

"Bad Dog," he snapped. "Go. Get to OldBill. It's started. Then find me. Hurry."

Bad Dog bumped his head against Cavalo's knee. *I will find you,* he promised and then was gone.

He glanced over at Lucas, who nodded before Cavalo could speak, as if he knew everything Cavalo was thinking. For all Cavalo knew, he did.

He waited only a few more seconds before he heard what he was waiting for. When the low booms of the land mines became more frequent than the gunfire, James Cavalo knew the moment had come.

"*Now!*" he roared, pushing himself up the wall.

The second before his finger pulled down on the trigger, his eyes darted across the divide in front of him. His eyes stuttered for a moment, because it looked as if the snow had fallen red all over the ground. There was a low boom, and the snow globe was filled with a crimson mist, and the bees just *laughed* and *laughed*.

He pulled the trigger to drown them out.

He felt his hands shake.

He felt the stock of the rifle vibrate against his arm.

His mouth was open, teeth bared. No sound came out.

He saw the bullets as they left the barrel of the rifle. Heard the shells bounce off the wood at his feet.

He smelled the flash of gunpowder, acrid and hot.

He smelled blood on the wind.

There were still too many of them standing. Cavalo felt over-whelmed by the sheer number of Dead Rabbits who had poured into Cottonwood. He thought of the shadows on the wall as Lucas had told him his story and hadn't remembered seeing this many of them. Of course, he hadn't *actually* been there, but the line between what was real and what was in his head had blurred so long ago that he no longer knew which side he stood on.

Only a second or two had passed since he'd first opened fire. He was joined moments later from all sides as the Patrol lit up the lines of Dead Rabbits below them. He thought some of them might have been screaming along with those being slaughtered below, but he couldn't be sure.

His clip was spent, and he was handed another by the man who'd lit the arrow. He switched out the clips and fired again.

The Dead Rabbits were trying to scatter, trying to push forward, but they kept stepping on mines and dirt, and snow tinged with red burst up from the ground.

Cavalo saw a female Dead Rabbit raise her hands as if in surrender before she fell forward, a surprised look on her face, a red stain blooming across her chest.

A male Dead Rabbit with black sores on his arms ran forward, trying to zigzag through the minefield. He made it halfway through before he slipped on the snow and fell face forward. The moment he touched the ground, he exploded.

They kept coming.

Cavalo thought of razor-thin wolves while voices around him screamed about DEFCON 1. They had kept coming too.

Cavalo didn't know why. What the Dead Rabbits' motivations were. What Patrick had promised them. How much they revered him. How much they were terrified of him. If it *was* Patrick, then he had a hold on them like nothing Cavalo had ever seen before. Yes, there were stragglers. There were a few that seemed to be trying to edge away from the rest, clawing their way to the back of the wall of flesh. But the majority pushed forward. They paused when those in front of them exploded. They hesitated when bullets struck the ground in front of them, tossing little arcs of snow into the air. But they did not stop.

One managed to make it through, slipping only once in the blood of those who had come before him, their deaths clearing the nearest mines. He was grinning around a knife in his mouth. Cavalo could see trickles of blood running down his chin from where the knife had cut the corners of his lips when he'd stumbled to his knees. This was more than reverence or fear. This was downright insanity. Cavalo should know. He'd seen it enough when he looked in a mirror. When he looked at SIRS. Or Lucas.

The Dead Rabbits were snapping, the rubber bands in their heads long since rotted. And they were swarming because of it.

As the Dead Rabbit crested the snowbank, he looked up at Cavalo. He was younger than Cavalo had first thought, far younger, maybe no older than Deke or Aubrey. His eyes were blown out, almost all black. His face and hands were coated in gore and grime. Cavalo took aim. The Dead Rabbit laughed around the knife. He knew he was going to die. And he didn't care.

He did die then. But not because of Cavalo. He ran up the snowbank and didn't see the trench stretched out before him until it was too late. There was an aborted attempt to jump across the trench, but his feet slipped in the snow. A look of surprise came over his face, as if he couldn't believe he'd been tricked. As if he couldn't believe this is how it would end for him. He didn't scream. He didn't have a chance. A wooden pike pierced his stomach. Another went through his right leg. His head bounced off a third, but Cavalo doubted he even felt that. His weight pulled him down the pike through his stomach. The wood was red as the boy thrashed, his knife lying at the bottom of the trench. Snowflakes stuck to the red and melted. The boy gave a great shudder, his back bowing, his head arching up. He froze like that for a moment, as if posing. And then he exhaled, dropped back down, and did not move.

It had only taken seconds. The whole thing.

Cavalo was shocked how well their plans were working, as flimsy as they were. He was surprised they'd made it this far. And just when he began to think that *maybe* they'd survive this, that *maybe* they'd have a chance and they'd walk out of here with most of their parts attached, everything changed.

"Reload!" Cavalo barked, ejecting the spent clip. He was handed another. He slammed it into the rifle and took aim again. He was conscious of Lucas at his side, how he fired the gun and took out his own people. He wondered if he recognized each of them before he shot them down. If he skipped over ones who had been kind to him in favor of ones who had wronged him somehow. He didn't think Lucas would be that discriminatory, but it made him feel better to believe he could be.

Not that Cavalo was being discriminatory. Every single Dead Rabbit who came into the sight of the rifle went down in a spray of blood. That made him feel better too.

And then it all went to hell.

"RPG!" someone farther down the line yelled.

Cavalo couldn't find the rocket launcher. Couldn't see who had it. Couldn't find him amongst the crowd. A second had gone by. And then another. And then another, and the sweat dripped down Cavalo's neck as he thought WHERE WHERE WHERE.

"There!" he heard Deke cry. Deke rose to his feet, above the wall, and fired once. He screamed in triumph. He must have hit the Dead Rabbit.

He fired again. And again.

"Get *down!*" Hank shouted, reaching for his son.

But there was the sharp whine of a bullet slicing air. Cavalo could hear it above everything else, and for the rest of his days, he would never forget the sound. Nor would he forget the sound when the bullet struck Deke above his right eye. Of bone cracking. Of gray matter separating. Of Hank letting out a sigh, light and broken. Of Aubrey's soft cry that turned into something more.

He would remember those sounds for the rest of his days. But out of all of them, it was Deke who gave him the one he would remember most.

He fired his gun.

He shouted in joy.

Hank: *Get down!*

The bullet entered his skull.

Left through the back.

Hank sighed.

Aubrey cried.

And Deke looked down at them, one eye left, but still unseeing. He said, "Daddy? Is that you? It got dark. I can't find my way out of the dark. But it's okay. There's someone here with me. He says that Mr. Fluff will help us if we get lost."

And then he fell, his head rolling toward Cavalo as it thumped against the wood. Deke's chest didn't rise. His unseeing eye stared at Cavalo. A single snowflake fell into it and melted as Cavalo watched. It ran down his cheek like a tear.

"No," Hank said almost conversationally. "No. No." He reached for his son but stopped at the last second, hands hovering over Deke's face. Blood pooled underneath Deke's head.

"Dad!" Aubrey cried.

"He's *not*—"

"We don't have time for this," she said, tears streaming down her face. "Not now. They're coming!"

"Deke!" Hank cried, touching his chest. "Get up. Get up, boy!"

Cavalo reached for him and pulled him against his chest, his mouth near Hank's ear. Hank struggled, almost throwing Cavalo off.

"Don't do this," Cavalo hissed at him. "Not now."

"Let me go!" he cried. "Deke! Your face.... Ah, God. Your face."

"Hank!" Cavalo barked sharply. "We need you. *She* needs you."

"He's not," Hank moaned.

"I know. And I'll mourn with you, brother. But not now. If we stop now, all of this will have been for *nothing*."

Cavalo could feel Hank pulling himself back together, or at the very least, shoving the broken pieces of his heart and soul away. He felt a stirring like cold admiration, not because of Hank's ability to focus, but from a hunter's understanding of compartmentalization. Sorrow could come later, if they survived this. It would bring them nothing now. Now, he needed Hank to use it as fuel for his fire.

"We'll kill them," he said quietly in Hank's ear. "We'll kill them all."

"Withered and sere," Hank whispered.

Cries of alarm went up around him, warnings shouted in raising tones.

Cavalo didn't have time to react before a warm body pressed against his back and pulled him sharply away. He tried to hold on to Hank, but his fingers slipped and then were empty. He lost all sense of direction when something exploded under his feet in a bright flash, knocking him back. He heard the wood splinter and crack, smelled the sharp acrid sting of fire and smoke. The bees swarmed angrily in his head. He was airborne, and he told himself this was nice. Learning to fly. The bees screamed he had lost something, Charlie, and they were going into DEFCON 1. He told them the coyotes were long gone, now nothing but bones and dust in a forgotten bunker. They didn't believe him.

He landed with a jarring crash, suddenly wet and cold, the breath knocked from his body. His ears were ringing, and he opened his eyes to a gray sky and swirling snow. He turned his head, and Deke lay next to him, his body cocked at an odd angle, bloody tears streaming down his face. It looked as if his arm had been broken in the fall. Cavalo hoped it hadn't hurt too bad. But then he remembered the bloody hole in Deke's head and thought the arm was the least of Deke's worries.

There was pain in the side of his head, and he reached a hand up to brush against it. It came away wet, his fingertips a deep red. His vision threatened to tunnel, but he closed his eyes and shook his head, trying to clear it away.

Get UP! an angry voice said. *Get UP!* A warm tongue against his face. *MasterBossLord! Get up, get up, get up!*

He opened his eyes again and saw Bad Dog standing above him, looking worried. A cold nose pressed to his cheek and tickled his ear as the dog huffed his skin. "I'm good," he muttered.

Blood, Bad Dog whispered. *I can smell your blood.*

Bad Dog crowded him as he pushed himself up. His back hurt. His head hurt. His legs hurt. He was getting too old for this shit. Another reason why Lucas—

Lucas.

He could hear shouts in the distance, angry voices that were swallowed occasionally by muffled *thwumps* that Cavalo ignored. Others lay around him, groaning and beginning to move. Hank. Alma. Aubrey. Frank. Bill and Richie, farther down the way. Some of the Patrol didn't move at all, the snow around them stained red. One was the boy whose mother did not want him on the wall with the rest. It looked as if his neck had been broken in the fall.

Cavalo's stomach clenched. His skin felt hot as he frantically searched the snow around him, shoving debris out of the way. He was sure he was gone. Not dead, but *gone*, disappeared as if he'd never before existed. Maybe this whole thing had been a dream. Maybe he was now awake and Lucas wasn't real, that none of the last months had been real.

Of course it hasn't been real, the bees said as they swarmed. *He couldn't even* talk, *and yet you held conversations with him, as if by some magic you knew what he was saying. That's not real, Cavalo. None of that was real. You lost your mind. For the longest time, you were crazy. Now you're finally awake. It's that ache in your head. That stutter in your chest. That catch in your breath. You're awake now.*

"Daddy!" he heard his dead son call, but when he looked up, Jamie wasn't there.

"Lucas!" he shouted, crawling toward the wall.

A hand fell on his shoulder and gripped him tightly. Cavalo took a shuddering breath and sat back on his heels. He reached back and took the hand in his own, wrapping his other arm around Lucas's legs. He pressed his head against Lucas's stomach and felt fingers against his ear. Bad Dog pressed against them both. He took a moment because he didn't know if they'd have another.

Lucas pulled him up. His mask was streaked across his face. Blood dribbled out of his right ear. His lip had been split. His cheek bruised. His coat had been torn and singed. But his eyes were clear, and he held his knife in his hand. Lucas nodded his head toward the shattered wall. *RPG*, he said. *Almost didn't make it in time.*

"Are you okay?" Cavalo asked.

Lucas nodded. Winced. *Okay. Head hurts. It's fine.*

"Don't do that again," Cavalo snarled at him. He couldn't tell Lucas of the momentary flashes of fear when he couldn't find him. He couldn't even focus on that himself. It was too much for him to take in. That Lucas might have been gone. That he might not have been real.

Lucas scowled at him. *You're welcome for saving your life. Again.*

"Maybe now we're even."

Lucas grinned and showed Cavalo his teeth.

"They're coming," Cavalo said, looking back toward the gigantic hole in the wall. He could see the tops of the Dead Rabbits' heads as they moved forward. "They still have to get across the trench."

Won't take long. But it'll be easier this way. Lucas pointed toward the gap in the wall. *Look.*

"They'll funnel," Cavalo realized. "They'll have to."

Lucas nodded. *We'll only get one shot at this.*

"And if it doesn't work?"

Lucas shrugged. *Either we die or we take the chance and run.*

"Fuck," Cavalo muttered. He moved from Lucas and helped

Alma to her feet. She groaned and held her side. "All right?" he asked.

"Maybe. Busted a rib. I'll be okay." Her eyes stuttered across Deke in the snow, and her voice hardened. "Fucking Dead Rabbits," she spat. "Goddamn them." She moved from Cavalo to Aubrey, who sat on her knees in the falling snow, watching her brother. Alma hugged her close, whispering words Cavalo could not hear.

He turned to Hank who sat in the snow, feet away from Deke. "You hurt?" he asked quietly.

"No," Hank said. His voice was rough and tired. "Not physically. Just some scratches."

"We have to move, Hank. They're almost here."

"Can't... can't leave him, Cavalo. Not here."

Cavalo sighed. "I'll move him. But I need you to focus. Please. For Aubrey."

Hank let out a small sob as his hands curled into fists. It was a desperate noise, a broken noise. But it was the only one Hank allowed. He stood slowly. Everything about him turned to steel as he pulled himself to full height. "They're going to pay," he said. "All of them."

"They'll come through the wall," Cavalo said. "That's where we need to take them. Do you understand?"

Hank nodded, his control slipping for just a moment. "And you'll... take him? My boy. You'll move him? I... can't...."

"Yes."

Hank nodded once and turned toward the people of Cottonwood who stood before him. Those in the houses looked down at him. The last line toward the rear of Cottonwood were standing, waiting for what came next.

Cavalo didn't listen to what Hank told the rest. He was done with pretty words. He knew what was coming and just how little time they had. Even as he hooked his arms under Deke's, he could hear the shouts and heavy breaths of the Dead Rabbits as they gathered along the trench, their frustrations at being unable to pass. It was too wide to jump, though he was sure some had tried. It wouldn't be long before they used the debris from the houses to cover the trench. He hadn't thought of that when plans were made. He'd figured he and the rest of the people in Cottonwood would be dead by now. It stung to think how close they'd come.

Lucas helped him then. Took Deke's legs and lifted him. Deke's head lolled against Cavalo's chest, and in his secret heart, the one buried deep in a hive that grew bigger every day, Cavalo told Deke he was sorry. He tried not to think how Deke's last words had been about Mr. Fluff. It was easier.

They laid him in a house off the way. People from Cottonwood that he didn't recognize stared at him with wide eyes as he lowered Deke's body to the floor. A woman with tears in her eyes came forward and handed him a blanket. He spread it out over Deke until the boy was covered. The blanket fell on his face, and blood seeped through in a slow bloom, looking like a rose. Cavalo stared at the blood flower and was filled with a great rage. He didn't even try and stop it. He was done holding it back. If the others were scared of him because of it, then so be it. At least they'd be alive.

Lucas noticed the change in him first. He put a hand the back of Cavalo's neck and pulled them together until their foreheads touched. The people in the house cowered in the corner. Deke's blood roses grew beneath them. Cavalo saw the black in Lucas's eyes. He saw himself reflected back.

"Stay with me," Cavalo said.

By your side, Lucas agreed.

He let him go. Cavalo held out his hand toward the people in the house, and a man stepped forward, handing him a rifle.

"Cavalo!" Hank shouted.

Lucas followed him out of the house. The courtyard beyond the wall was almost empty. People had taken position farther into town, hiding in and around the houses. All the guns were pointed at the hole in the wall. The Dead Rabbits sounded even louder, snarling and screaming. There were no more explosions from the land mines. It would be any moment now.

Hank stood in the middle of the courtyard, Bad Dog at his side. He had shouldered two rifles, one on either side. In his hands was one of the few shotguns SIRS had brought down. They'd been put aside initially because they were only good for close range. Cavalo doubted they'd get any closer than this. A sleeve of shotgun shells wrapped around Hank's chest. Cavalo wondered if the Dead Rabbits would get one look at him and run in the other direction. It'd make things easier.

"You take care of my boy?" Hank asked him, eyes flashing. His voice was a growl.

Cavalo nodded as he reached down and stroked Bad Dog's ears once. "He's safe. You got another one of those?" he asked, looking at the shotgun.

"Why? Gonna get your hands dirty?"

"Are you?"

"They took from me."

"Not everything."

"Aubrey."

"Go," Cavalo said, taking the shotgun from Hank's hands. "Be by her side. You know what to do if we're overtaken. SIRS is waiting."

"You said we were going to die."

Cavalo looked him in the eye. "Not all of us have to."

"And not all of us will," he heard another voice say from behind Hank. The big man stepped aside, and he could see Alma striding toward them, Aubrey following close. Then Frank. Bill. Richie. Others in the Patrol.

Alma handed Hank another shotgun. She took a sleeve of shells from around her neck and handed them to Cavalo. He took them reluctantly. She tried handing another to Lucas, who shook his head and took a step back. He glanced at Cavalo and shrugged, twirling his knife. *You know I'm good*, he said.

"He doesn't need it," Cavalo grunted when Alma looked at him. "Are you sure about this?"

"No," Alma said honestly. "But what have we got to lose?"

"They killed him," Aubrey said bitterly. "We're sure." Her face was lined and hard, and Cavalo wondered if she'd ever be the same again.

Hank said nothing, letting his daughter speak for the both of them. Cavalo knew it was useless to say otherwise.

"Stand firm," he said instead. "Eyes on all sides. Listen for me. It's the only way we'll be—"

"They're coming in!" someone shouted from one of the houses.

They turned. A Dead Rabbit stood at the wall, a look of surprise on his face, as if he didn't expect to meet a line of townsfolk waiting for him. There was a brief flash of something more, something almost like fear, but then it was gone. He too was young, maybe a little older than Lucas, but there were open sores on his face. His right cheek. His forehead. The skin beneath his ears. They were crusted over but looked infected. They looked painful, but the Dead Rabbit showed none of it on his face.

It was that fear, though. That momentary fear that caused Cavalo to pause for one of the first times in his long and complicated life. It passed quickly, because it was not who Cavalo was. He reacted. That is how he'd survived this long. By reacting. And he reacted when the Dead Rabbit's eyes skittered over them to Lucas, a look of anger and triumph coming over his face.

Whatever had come over the Dead Rabbit was gone. Whatever had come over Cavalo was gone. Even knowing he was alone, the Dead Rabbit ran toward them, a heavy-looking blade held above his head, and Cavalo didn't think. He *reacted*.

The coldness fell over him as he moved before anyone else even thought to. The killer buried deep inside rose up, his thoughts becoming staccato calculations. *Don't waste bullets. Break the arm. Elbow. Face. Knee to stomach. Break neck.* The bees swirled around those thoughts, alighting upon them and rubbing their wings against them.

The Dead Rabbit only had eyes for Lucas. He didn't see Cavalo flip the shotgun sharply, the barrels coming down to his hands. He brought the stock of the shotgun down as hard as he could onto the arm that held the knife meant for Lucas. The snap of bone cracked against the cold air. Cavalo dropped the shotgun and heard the Dead Rabbit suck in a breath to scream in pain when he spun in a circle, bringing his elbow to the Dead Rabbit's face. He felt the bone crunch under his arm. There was a spray of blood, warm against Cavalo's cheek. The Dead Rabbit grunted, and Cavalo took shoulders in hand and brought him down as he thrust his knee up into the Dead Rabbit's stomach. The Dead Rabbit let out a wheeze of air and blood as he fell to his knees. "Now you should be scared," Cavalo told him quietly. He took the Dead Rabbit's head in his hands and snapped it to the side. Musculature tore as the cervical spine broke. The Dead Rabbit fell face-first into the snow and did not move.

Cavalo crouched down on his knees, picking up a handful of snow. He rubbed it against his face to clean the blood away. It melted against his skin. He picked the gun out of the snow and turned back toward the people behind him.

There was a mixture there of awe and fear. Healthy doses of both, as it should be. All except for Lucas, who grinned crazily at him, eyes bright and teeth bared. It was ferocious, and it was all for Cavalo. He allowed himself to be consumed by it for only a moment before he pushed it away. They were out of time.

Cavalo submerged himself into the cold, feeling the little pinpricks pulling him under. It felt like coming home. When he opened his eyes again, everything was sharp and clear. The weight of metal in his hands. The breaths he took, slow and steady. The snow falling in crystals around him. The warmth of a body to his left, a line down his side. Others, to his right, stepping forward to stand next to him. His friend, down at his legs, a low growl pouring from his throat, head down toward the ground, back raised, tail stiff. All of it felt with a perfect clarity that came from the coldness as it closed over his head.

The Dead Rabbits poured in through the hole in the wall. They funneled, just as Lucas said they would. They were frenzied now, the smell of blood on the wind turning their instincts from human to animal. The moment they pushed through, roiling and writhing over each other, gunfire erupted from all around Cavalo. He felt the bullets zing over his head, his ears clouded by the sudden burst of sound around him.

One of the Dead Rabbits, a woman with muscular arms and no teeth, got hit in the shoulder, but it did little to slow her down. She burst forward, blood trailing behind her in the snow. Her mouth was open in a wide scream that Cavalo couldn't hear. He pulled the trigger, the kick hard against his shoulder. She flew back, arms and fingers trailing behind her. Cavalo expended the shell.

The bodies began to pile up inside the hole. It was getting harder and harder for Dead Rabbits to push through, though they tried. It was not until it was almost too late that Cavalo saw the wall began to splinter farther down, coming apart with the force of an impact on the other side. He could hear them now, repeated strikes against the wall, and knew they were starting to break through. Only a second later, he saw a flash of an eye through the wall, and then the black barrel of a gun was pushed through. He pushed Alma toward Hank, hoping it was enough to get them out of the way. He grabbed a handful of Bad Dog's fur, and he threw himself against Lucas who was prowling at his side, waiting for any Dead Rabbit to get close enough.

Lucas tensed underneath him, his body thrumming like a live wire. They all hit the ground, and Cavalo rolled them toward the side of a house just as a hail of bullets struck the snow where they'd been standing moments before. Bad Dog yipped at him in surprise. He pressed them both against the house and glared at them until they stopped struggling in his grip. He glanced to the right and saw the others across the courtyard, against another house. There was someone lying facedown in the snow, blood pooling around them, and Cavalo couldn't make out who it was. One of the Patrol, from the way they were dressed. Dark hair. Conner? Was that his name? Conner?

It didn't matter now.

What mattered now was that Frank, foolish and obstinate Frank, had gotten a taste of the fire in his veins, the rush of blood in his ears. He had one of the Bakalovs in his hands, and he was loading a fat shell into the underside of the rifle. It slipped in easily, and Cavalo screamed at him, but Frank didn't hear. There was a brief pause, a temporary break in the hail of bullets, and Frank stepped out, a determined look on his face.

"*Don't!*" Cavalo roared.

Frank stuttered, his finger slipping on the trigger. The 40 mm grenade that SIRS had flashed his eyes so smugly over fired at the gun sticking through the wall. Cavalo had to hand it to Frank; his aim was true. The shell hit the wall and exploded, less fire and more concussion. The wall rippled and cracked, already weakened from the first explosion. He heard Dead Rabbits screaming on the other side, and Frank looked triumphant. The look fell when the struts and supports of the wall began to crumble, crashing down onto the pile of dead and dying Dead Rabbits. Cavalo didn't know why he thought the wall would have lasted longer. False hopes, maybe. Or maybe he thought he was finally owed a break.

Cavalo had not lied when he'd spoken to the town previously. He fully expected to die this day. But as the wall came down, he realized how much he didn't want it to happen. How much he'd thought they'd actually win. That something would give and the skies would open up and the sun would shine and there would be no more death. There would be no more pain. There would be no more suffering. He hadn't known he could still hope for such things. He knew it now as the wall came down.

Even before it'd finished crumbling, even before the large section had crashed to the ground, he turned and looked up at the second-floor window of the house behind him. Two men watched him with wide eyes. And from his lips came the only word he could say, no matter how much it burned. He hoped it would be enough.

"*Run!*"

They didn't hesitate. He heard the call go up back through the town. They knew what to do. They'd planned for this, however futile it'd seemed at the time. He watched as the houses began to empty, people rushing toward the northern gate. He knew the remainder of the Patrol that stood as the last line would let them through and would follow them through the back gate and lead them toward the prison.

The snowfall grew heavier. Fat flakes swirled around them.

He knew this was it. This was probably the end of his long and fucked-up life. He had many regrets. Many things he'd wished he'd never done. He had murdered people in cold blood. He had taken that which did not belong to him. He'd betrayed others. He'd hurt them. If there was such a thing as hell, Cavalo would surely descend on it once his body had been torn apart.

He laughed then. Long and loud. At the absurdity of it all. This life.

A hand on his shoulder. He looked over at Lucas and grinned. His skin felt too tight on his face. He felt lost in the bees but was certain of one thing, though he couldn't find a way to put it into words. He turned to Lucas and thought, *I regret almost everything I've ever done. But I will never regret you.* Instead, he said, "You ready?" as the Dead Rabbits spilled into Cottonwood with a roar.

Lucas nodded.

Cavalo stood, sliding up the side of the house. Alma and Hank and the others stood with him on the opposite side of the courtyard. He felt Lucas rise behind him as he stepped out from behind the house to face what was coming.

A group of Dead Rabbits. Their faces painted. Covered in blood. Gore streaked their arms. One looked like the heavy tumor hanging from his right arm had burst, leaking dark fluids. Another's eye was hanging by a thread on her cheek. And another was crawling toward them, hand outstretched, legs broken and bent at odd angles. These were the monsters, Cavalo knew.

He screamed. In fury. For all those who had died. For Deke, who he knew they would not get to bury. For his wife, who was nothing more than a tree in the middle of a haunted wood. For his son, who could slip between the veil of this world and the next. For all the others. For all the others who'd died because of the choices Cavalo had made.

He fired the shotgun, a snarl on his face.

Bad Dog howled and launched himself, teeth flashing white.

Lucas spun his knife once and arced it out away from his body. A Dead Rabbit screamed as his fingers fell into the snow.

Hank roared and smashed his heavy fists down into a man's face, breaking nose and teeth.

Aubrey rolled as a man brought down an ancient scythe, the blade inches from her head. She grabbed an arrow out of her quiver as she stood and brought it up and through the bottom of the man's jaw, pinning his mouth closed as the arrowhead entered his brain.

A woman grabbed Alma from behind, arms wrapping around her chest to pull her away. Another man ran forward to grab her legs. Alma kicked herself up from the ground, smashing her feet into the man's face, lying back against the woman. The man fell. Alma rolled away and the woman lost her grip. Alma stood above both of them and pointed a pistol at the woman's head. There was no hesitation as she fired. The man said "No," and Alma fired again.

Bill and Richie stood back to back, firing over and over again as the Dead Rabbits descended upon them. Richie handed his dad a spare clip and kept firing.

Frank's eyes went wide as the Dead Rabbit with the broken legs grabbed his ankle, teeth bared and ready to bite. He kicked the Dead Rabbit in the face, and the man began to convulse in the snow, arms and legs skittering, leaving trails of blood and dirt.

Gunfire went over their heads, and Cavalo jerked his head back, seeing the people trying to flee to the rear wall getting shot in the back. One fell, then two, and three and four and *five* and—

Cavalo cocked the shotgun and fired again, blowing a hole in the stomach of a woman who was about to stab Hank in the throat.

Bad Dog tore through flesh and muscle, jerking a leg until a Dead Rabbit fell.

Lucas moved as if he was dancing, spinning and sidestepping, arms out, eyes narrowed and knife bloody.

A man ran at Cavalo as he reloaded. Cavalo bent down, left shoulder forward. He thrust up as the man ran into him, flipping him up and over his back. Cavalo spun as the man landed on his back in the snow, but before Cavalo could shoot him, Lucas brought down the knife into the man's chest, the blade scraping against bone. The man's head jerked forward, his eyes bulging. A bubble of blood burst at his lips, a light spray misting over his face as Lucas pulled the knife out and brought it down again and again.

And still they came. More and more and more. He saw them up on the walkway now, farther down the wall, unsure of how they got there. There was no sign of Patrick, and Cavalo wanted to tear his head from his shoulders.

And then they started to lose.

Hank shouted in surprise when a knife went into his shoulder.

He heard Aubrey cry out as a bullet punched through her arm.

Alma grunted as a man with no teeth grabbed her by the hair, pulling her back, baring her throat.

Bad Dog whined sharply when he was kicked in the side.

Lucas fell back when he was struck in the head with a heavy wooden club.

Bill and Richie were backing against a far wall, clips gone, using their guns to bat away reaching hands.

Frank fell to his knees in front of a man who looked vaguely like Cavalo's father. Cavalo thought, *No, Dad, don't,* when the Dead Rabbit stood above him, smiling a terrible smile. Frank died when the smiling Dead Rabbit shoved a knife into his chest and another into his mouth. As Cavalo watched the tip of the blade crack the back of Frank's skull, he knew they'd lost. Frank fell back, and his sightless eyes stared up into the thickening snow.

The bees told him to run.

The bees told him to fight until he fell.

The bees told him to kill them all.

The bees told him to save those who were left.

They screamed so loud Cavalo thought the snow globe that stretched out beyond the sky above would shatter and glass would rain down upon them, and they would be no more. And when Cavalo looked over his shoulder, his bones aching, his face covered in blood and dirt, he saw his son standing near the back wall, skipping with Mr. Fluff hanging from his hands. He laughed and dodged through those who remained in Cottonwood, standing and waiting for Cavalo's orders, bodies tense and eyes wide. Jamie looked over at him and cocked his head, wiggling his fingers at Cavalo.

He said, "Daddy. It's time to go." Even above all the noise and the thundering of his own heart, Cavalo heard him loud and clear. He didn't know if his son was a ghost of mind or madness, but it didn't matter. He was right. They'd lost. They had to go.

"Fall *back!*" he cried as he fired the shotgun again. His breath was knocked from his body as he was tackled from the side, the shotgun knocked from his hands. He felt hot breath on his neck, the shark clack of teeth snapping near his ear. He tried to shove the heavy body away, but it was too much, and a tongue scraped against his ear, and he heard, "Yes, this one is mine, mine because you taste so *good—*" before the Dead Rabbit was lifted from him and pushed away. Cavalo sat up and saw Lucas stabbing his attacker again and again, his face tight in the grips of rage. Cavalo rose to his feet and pulled Lucas off him. Lucas struggled in his arms, snarling silently, the knife slicing the air.

"No time," Cavalo breathed in his ear.

Lucas stopped and stood on his own. He ran his eyes over Cavalo once, making sure he hadn't been hurt. He nodded tightly, then picked up a discarded rifle off the ground. He jerked his head toward where Hank and the others had started running. *Go! Now!* He opened fire, a spray of bullets knocking down the approaching Dead Rabbits.

Cavalo didn't want to leave him, but he had no choice. They had planned for this, as much as they could. They had one last chance to get out of here safely, one last chance to get to the prison. He ran, Bad Dog close at his heels. The wind picked up around him, the snow stinging against his face. He passed by the bodies of those who hadn't made it out of Cottonwood. He thought there were twenty of them, maybe more. Facedown in the snow, arms stretched out as if reaching for the wall they'd come so close to passing through.

It'll be easier this way, the bees said, sounding like the killers he knew they were. *Fewer of them means less time it'll take to get to the prison. Fewer of them means fewer people in the prison.*

Since Cavalo was submerged in murder, he took cold satisfaction from this. Shreds of his humanity tried to sing him home, but he was too far gone right now. There'd be time for regret later. If he survived.

Hank and Alma waited for them at the wall, pushing the last of the people through. "Aubrey's leading them out," Alma said. "The road looks clear."

"Keep pushing them forward," Cavalo snarled. "Don't stop for anything." He looked down at Bad Dog. "You need to lead them home."

Home? You're coming too?

"Now, Bad Dog. SIRS. *Home.*"

But—

"Go!"

Bad Dog was not fooled. He bit Cavalo's hand, not hard enough to break the skin but hard enough to show his frustration and anger. He gave a little huff before he pulled away. Cavalo saw the indents of teeth embedded in his skin. He felt himself kicking to the surface, pushing some of the cold away. An anchor that pulled him up instead of down.

"Shit," Hank said, eyes going wide as he looked over his shoulder.

Cavalo looked back, and through the snow that was becoming a blizzard, he saw Lucas throw down the empty rifle and pull out his knife as the group of Dead Rabbits in front of him parted. Patrick walked through, axe in hand, dragging the blade behind him through the blood and bodies of his people. He had eyes only for his son. Lucas was tense, crouching into an attack position.

"Motherfucker," Cavalo growled.

"Enough of this shit," Hank said. He pulled up a Bakalov and took aim.

"*Lucas!*" Cavalo bellowed, and then Hank fired the grenade.

Lucas didn't hesitate. He rolled to the side as the grenade flew by him. Patrick spun down and away, his coat flaring up around him in the snow, the grenade passing less than a foot from his face. It hit a Dead Rabbit in the chest, and there was a bright flash filled with screams and blood.

Even before the explosion had died, Lucas was running toward Cavalo, arms and legs pumping. Alma handed Cavalo a Bakalov and took aim with one of her own, firing past Lucas into the Dead Rabbits who took aim at his back.

Cavalo could see each running step Lucas took, the snow puffing up around his feet, ice breaking apart as it fell onto Lucas's face. The exhalation from his nose and lips, white and trailing behind him. The arc of blood across the white as a bullet hit his leg. The widening of his eyes as the pain rolled over him. The way they narrowed as he pushed the pain away. The mask around his eyes, cracked and shiny.

Cavalo took it all in and more.

The bullets cracking into the wood overhead.

The weight of the rifle in his hands, jerking against his shoulder.

The thought of *faster, run faster, please run faster* as it exploded in the bees.

Patrick pulling himself up out of the snow, the showman gone, only the monster remaining.

Cavalo took aim at him, no longer caring about the marks he wore on his skin. No longer caring what it could mean for the future of their world. All that mattered was a bullet in his head and his blood on the ground.

He fired.

He knew his shot was true.

And it would have been had Patrick not swung up his axe in front of his face, the bullet ricocheting off the metal axe head with a sound Cavalo heard above all other noise, the deep metallic vibration grating into his bones.

"Holy shit," Hank breathed.

"Time to go," Alma said.

Patrick raised his head toward the gray sky and screamed.

The Dead Rabbits screamed with him. And began to charge.

"They fill the house?" Cavalo snapped at Hank. "Both sides?"

"Just like we planned," Hank said grimly, reloading his rifle with a fat shell. "Say the word."

"You go right," Cavalo said. "I'll take left." He flipped the switch on the Bakalov. Felt the grenade barrel drop. Turned toward a house with broken-out windows that lined the eastern side of the narrow courtyard. "Alma, cover."

She stepped between them, sweeping her rifle in a wide arc, spraying bullets evenly, her finger lifting from the trigger as the gun pointed at Lucas, continuing once she swung past him.

The Dead Rabbits were only a short distance behind Lucas, who had started to flag, favoring his ankle that had been bullet-grazed.

"Run!" Cavalo shouted, and Lucas did. He knew what they had to do and knew they had to do it sooner rather than later.

And he passed the houses where the remainder of the mines lay in wait, the floor around them soaked in the last of the gas and oil.

Cavalo couldn't wait any longer.

"*Now!*" he shouted at Hank and fired the grenade. Hank did the same.

The front line of the Dead Rabbits pulled up even with the houses as the grenades arced through the windows, and Cavalo could see the panic in Lucas's eyes now because he was *still too close and—*

The house went up, tearing apart as air and fire expanded. The house across followed a split second later, the double blasts smashing into the Dead Rabbits as they ran between them. Lucas wasn't far enough away to escape the explosions, the shockwave knocking against his back, spilling him forward into the snow, landing on top of a body of a young woman from Cottonwood who Cavalo remembered as having a pretty smile. Cavalo felt the hot air hit his face as he ran forward, only thinking of dragging Lucas away before the Dead Rabbits found their way through again.

Lucas was pushing himself up off the dead body. His eyes looked dazed. His coat was ripped in the back, revealing skin and a thin line of blood. Cavalo slid in the snow next to him, grabbing under his arm and pulling him up. They stumbled and almost went down again. But Cavalo held on as tight as he could until they found their footing. "Move," he snapped harshly. No one screamed after them, no gunfire erupted behind them. He heard moans and cries of pain and impending death but nothing more. He didn't look back. There wasn't time.

Lucas glanced up at him, expression unreadable. Cavalo tightened his grip against Lucas. He heard it then, just a whisper. *You... you came for me.* He wasn't sure if it was real. He wasn't sure if any of this was real.

And without thinking, he muttered, "Always."

Hank and Alma pushed them through a small doorway on the wall, and they crossed through to the other side, leaving Cottonwood behind them. As the winds howled and the snow whipped against their faces, they began to run.

wormwood

_____

AND RUN THEY DID. Through the wind and snow that began to howl around them. A wide trail stretched out ahead, the snow smashed and scattered by the people of Cottonwood that had fled moments before. He told himself he saw the paw prints in the snow, that Bad Dog was leading them home, but he couldn't be sure.

"They can't be far ahead," Hank said, his beard frosted white.

"We have to hurry," Alma said, shielding her face. "It's getting worse. We can't get lost out here."

Cavalo glanced behind them, at the way they'd come. The wind bit into his face. He could see only ten feet to their rear. There were little drops of red in the snow from Lucas's leg. But nothing more. If anyone was following them, they would be just beyond the white veil that wrapped around them. It was all the snow globe, Cavalo knew. He'd thought it had broken, but he must have been wrong. He was back inside it now.

Lucas panted against his neck as Cavalo held him up, arm wrapped around Lucas's waist. He looked over at him, and their cheeks brushed together. "You good?" he asked in a low voice.

Lucas nodded. *Don't worry about me. Just keep going.*

Cavalo tightened his grip.

They pushed on. Every now and then, Cavalo would press his lips together and blast out a sharp whistle, hoping to hear the intended response. It carried in the wind but was lost in the storm.

"Bad Dog knows his way?" Hank asked.

"Yes," Cavalo said through gritted teeth. He tried to keep his anger in check. Hank didn't deserve it. Not after what he'd lost. "He knows." He trusted Bad Dog more than anyone else in the world. He wouldn't get lost.

It still didn't help his unease when he whistled again and received no response.

It was snowing harder now, to the point where Cavalo wasn't sure he knew where they were. Landmarks where hidden in snow and shadows. The sky overhead was lost in the swirl of water and ice. Cavalo was cold, colder than he'd been in a very long time. He could feel Lucas shivering at his side and pulled him closer. "We're almost there," he whispered, though he didn't know if that was true. He wondered how fitting it would be if all of the events that had been his life had led to him freezing to death, lost in a blizzard. It would make sense after everything he'd done. He didn't believe in karma, but he believed in retribution. He'd committed too many wrongs to ever be right.

He whistled again, feeling the desperation behind it.

And the response came. A bark. It was worried, that sound. Relieved, but worried. He knew that even though he could barely hear it.

James Cavalo whistled again.

His friend responded, sounding closer now. *MasterBossLord!*

Something loosened in his chest.

The dog came out of the storm, his face covered in snow. Cavalo knew he'd been keeping his nose close to the ground, just like he'd been trained to do. As soon as he saw Cavalo, his bright eyes lit up, and he bounded toward him, hopping like a rabbit to get through the drifts. He reached Cavalo and rubbed his head against his legs, excited little yips and whines coming from the back of his throat. *I did what you told me, MasterBossLord. I did what you told me, and I led them all home, but I couldn't stay there because I had to come back and get you. SIRS told me to find you fast, and I told him I would because I am Bad Dog. He told me I was a big fleabag, but he hugged me and told me he was happy I was okay, so I think that is a good thing because even though he is a tin man, he is our Tin Man, and I wanted to be home. Can we go home now? Can we—?* He stopped and sniffed the air again. He leaned toward Lucas, nose snuffling against his legs. *Blood! MasterBossLord! Smells Different has blood!*

"He's okay," Cavalo told him. "We need to get him home."

Lucas reached down and rubbed Bad Dog's head, trying to reassure him, and that thing inside Cavalo, that bright shiny thing he hadn't felt in a very long time, burst again. It burned in him, and he thought for a moment that his skin would start to smoke and crack, and everything he kept hidden, all of the darkness, all of the bees, would come pouring out of him for all to see.

He burned, but he did not crack. No matter how much he wanted to.

"Home," Cavalo said, his voice sharp. Bad Dog and Lucas looked up at him, questions in their eyes. He stared back, keeping his face blank. "*Home,*" he said again.

Bad Dog bumped his head against Cavalo's leg and turned, leading them through the storm. Alma and Hank followed but didn't speak. Lucas felt stiff under his arms.

And it was embarrassing how quickly they arrived at the prison. They'd been less than a quarter of a mile away. Cavalo knew if Bad Dog hadn't come for them, they would have passed it right on by and kept walking until they could walk no more.

He saw the metal fence loom out of the wind and snow, saw the dull flash of one of the cameras as it pivoted toward them. Felt the hum of the electrified fences in his teeth. The red light near the gate. He'd never been more relieved to see this place. It was a prison, but it was his home. He'd been gone for too long.

Bad Dog barked up at the camera, and there was an electrical surge before the fences shut down. A red light flashed and a klaxon blared once. The light changed to green, and Cavalo pushed through the gate, Bad Dog and Lucas on either side of him. Hank followed, and Alma was last, shutting the gate behind them. The alarm blared again, the electricity kicked back in, the light changing to red.

They were safe.

For now, the bees whispered.

A door slid open from the bunker. Light flooded out into the snow. And a voice came out that almost caused Cavalo's knees to buckle in relief.

"Cavalo!" SIRS cried. "As I live and breathe. The bag of fleas told me you were still out there, but I must admit to believing the worst! Get in here, and we'll see what we see." A beep. A click. Everything that sounded familiar, and SIRS blared out his insanity, and it felt like coming home: "ISAIAH 66:15 SAYS 'FOR BEHOLD, THE LORD WILL COME IN FIRE AND HIS CHARIOTS LIKE THE WHIRLWIND, TO RENDER HIS ANGER WITH FURY, AND HIS REBUKE WITH FLAMES OF FIRE. FOR THE LORD WILL EXECUTE JUDGEMENT BY FIRE AND BY HIS SWORD ON ALL FLESH, AND THOSE SLAIN BY THE LORD WILL BE MANY.'" It echoed across the prison, and SIRS beeped again. As Cavalo thought of Wormwood, SIRS said, "Why are you still standing out in the cold? Come in before you catch your death! The prison hasn't been this full since it held *prisoners*. Oh, the joy of irony!"

THEY WERE HUDDLED INSIDE. THE SURVIVORS. THEY SPILLED out of the tunnels below the prison, all wide-eyed and wet. There was a smell permeating the stone walls, and it rolled over Cavalo like a wave. Dirt. Anger. Fear. Anguish. Sweat and tears and ozone. They were lightning-struck and broken shards of frosted glass. He heard muffled sobs, quiet murmured voices meant to give relief but seeming to crack under the slightest pressure. Fragile. Every single one of them was fragile, and they were looking at him as if he held the answers of how they could be stronger again. How they could stand again.

And he had nothing.

They had lost people today. The cold part of Cavalo reminded him that it was the cost of warfare, that of *course* people were going to die. But look how many people were still alive? That was unexpected. That was not what had been planned. He didn't know how much longer they would stay that way, but they'd come this far, and it was further than any of them had expected.

But it wasn't enough for them.

Hank went to Aubrey and hugged her tightly. There were tears streaming down her face, and she looked like the little girl that she was, hugging her daddy to make all the bad go away. Alma stood off to the side, hands on her knees as she took in deep breaths, trying to calm herself. One of the Patrol asked about Frank, and the others shook their heads. Cavalo wondered if Deke's body was still where he'd laid it, the old blanket soaking through with his blood and he couldn't. He just couldn't. None of this. He couldn't deal with it right now. Lucas weighed heavily at his side, his forehead creased and eyes narrowed. He was breathing in quick, short bursts, and Cavalo could see the grimace he was trying to hide. He was in pain and trying not to show it. Not in front of these people. Cavalo looked down and saw the bloody footprints they'd left behind them.

He moved away from their eyes, those knowing eyes that wanted him to take away all their pain, to tell them what to do. He didn't know how to tell them that he'd brought this down upon them all and that they should be rising against him. They should allow themselves to drown in their rage. He would be just a little boat on their ocean, batted around until he was knocked to pieces and sunk below the surface. He almost let them.

He pulled Lucas away from the crowd, feeling their eyes on their backs as they left the barracks and went down the stairs into the tunnels. SIRS and Bad Dog followed, as he knew they would. He needed them now. After everything.

They let him pass, the people of Cottonwood. They lined the stairs into the tunnels, and they watched him as he walked by, holding Lucas up, leaving those damn bloody footprints behind him, as if there needed to be further evidence of everything that had gone wrong. He didn't meet their gazes, and when he reached the bottom of the stairs, he was overwhelmed by the sheer number of people huddled together down there. Cottonwood was small. A quarter of their people were dead. But they *filled* the tunnel, and even with their silence, they *demanded* he speak.

And he said nothing.

SIRS touched a panel on the wall. It flared brightly, the white burning Cavalo's eyes in the dim light. The door at the top of the stairs ahead slid open, and it was blessedly free of knowing eyes. He hobbled them up the stairs. Bad Dog and SIRS followed. Before he could tell SIRS to close the door, Hank spoke from behind them.

"What happens now?"

Cavalo tensed. He turned his head to the side and said, "I don't know."

SIRS knew him well. He closed the door.

Cavalo sighed, some of the tension bleeding from his shoulders. "Fuck," he muttered. He was very tired.

"Indeed," SIRS said. "*Fuck* seems awfully apt."

He pushed Lucas into a cell, the Dead Rabbit hissing between his teeth. He set him down on the cot, and for a moment, he considered allowing himself to lie down and just go to sleep. His eyes were heavy, and it would be just so easy.

He shook his head, chasing the thoughts away. Not yet.

"Sit, Cavalo."

"SIRS—"

"That was not a request." SIRS turned and walked away.

Cavalo sat next to Lucas, back against the stone wall, legs hanging off the cot. Lucas felt warm against his side, and Cavalo's fingers itched to reach out and take his hand. He stopped himself, but barely. Bad Dog sat at his feet, resting his head on Cavalo's knees, eyes closed and just breathing him in.

"You hurt?" Cavalo asked him, reaching to touch his ears.

Bad Dog opened his pretty eyes. *No. A little sore. But nothing bad.* He closed his eyes again, nostrils flaring briefly before he rumbled contentedly in his chest.

"I heard," SIRS said, coming back, a first aid kit in his hand. "About what happened."

"Yeah."

"You did well, Cavalo," he said, bending over and looking at Lucas's leg, eyes flashing.

Cavalo laughed bitterly. "I don't think Deke would agree with me."

SIRS glanced over at him. "I think Aubrey would."

That burned deep in Cavalo's chest. He had to get away from it. "Everything okay here?"

SIRS wasn't fooled, Cavalo knew. The robot knew him better than that. But he also knew when to let things go. He pulled up Lucas's pant leg. His leg looked harsh, blood tacky and bright. Lucas had closed his eyes and was breathing through his nose. "Everything was quiet," SIRS said, scanning the wound.

"Sensors up?"

"Yes, Cavalo. We'll know. When they come."

When, Cavalo thought. Because there was no *if.* They would come. Maybe not in this storm, but soon.

"Audio still disconnected?"

"Yes, Cavalo." But Cavalo could hear the amusement in the robot's words.

"They'll come."

"Will they?"

"Yes."

"Well, then. This should be an adventure."

Cavalo felt fingers brush his and didn't pull his hand away.

SIRS beeped twice. "The bullet didn't penetrate. Looks like it took a small chunk of your calf with it and you'll probably scar, but I won't need to chop off your leg at all." At this SIRS sounded truly disappointed.

"Unless it gets infected," Cavalo suggested, and Lucas opened his eyes to glare at him.

"Oh yes," SIRS agreed. "That could certainly be a possibility."

Hate you both, Lucas said with a scowl.

SIRS cleaned the wound and bandaged Lucas's leg. By then, all pretense had vanished, and Lucas held Cavalo's fingers tightly. Cavalo told himself it was because Lucas was in pain, not acknowledging the scars on his neck and back, the tattoos on his skin that probably had hurt far worse.

SIRS finished and took the bloody rags away. "Rest," Cavalo muttered to Lucas, standing up from the cot. "While you can."

Lucas held on to his hand, and Cavalo looked down to the question in his eyes. *Where are you going?*

"SIRS. Need to make sure of a few things."

You need to sleep.

"I will."

James.

Cavalo kept the shudder at bay. "I will."

Lucas nodded and let go.

Cavalo couldn't get out of the cell fast enough. But even he couldn't resist. He looked back over his shoulder in time to see Bad Dog jump onto the cot, Lucas brushing over his ears. Lucas said, *Warm,* and Bad Dog said, *Sleepy,* and even though they couldn't hear each other, Cavalo heard them both.

He looked away, his breath harsh in his throat.

"All right?" SIRS asked when Cavalo reached him on the other side of the room.

"Fine."

"That was believable."

"SIRS," he growled.

"You don't intimidate me, Cavalo. You never have. The sooner you realize that, the better off we'll be. Now, are you hurt?"

"No."

"No gunshot wounds? Knife wounds? Burns? Bruises?"

"No."

"How's your mind?" SIRS asked.

"Long gone."

"Good thing that hasn't changed. We're all a little bit crazy here." The robot sounded as if he was grinning.

Cavalo allowed himself to snort. "Supplies?"

The robot touched a panel on the wall. "We should be fine for a few days."

"I don't know how soon they'll come."

"We're fortified, Cavalo. At least as much as we can be."

"It's a fence."

"With forty thousand volts of electricity running through it on all sides. And generators running underground."

"They can last a lot longer out there then we can in here."

"Can they?" SIRS asked, sounding curious.

"Stop speaking in riddles."

"I was speaking in English," SIRS said. "Love the mask, by the way. Very fitting. Now who on earth could have done that for you?"

"SIRS," he warned.

"Are we about to die?"

"I think so."

"Then I'm allowed to be amused. If you can't be pleased by the little things on the days before your death, then what was the purpose of living?"

"Why are you pleased?"

SIRS looked at him expectantly. "Because it looks as if you've started living, James. Even if it took impending doom to do so."

"I'm not...." He stopped. Lowered his eyes. "Fuck."

"It's a lovely name," SIRS said softly.

"You heard?"

"It was the talk of the town."

"Of course it was."

"Are we friends?" SIRS asked suddenly.

"Yes," Cavalo said, not hesitating. SIRS had asked him this before. Nothing had changed since then.

"Can you... tell me?"

"About what?"

"Before."

"Before? You know more about that than I do."

SIRS shook his head. "Not Before the bombs fell. Before you came here. I'd like to know about you, if I may. Before the end."

And Cavalo, the man of few words, the man who had hidden himself away from the world for so long, told his friend everything. He didn't stop even when the robot reached out and curled his metal hand into Cavalo's own.

HOURS LATER, THE DOOR CLOSED BEHIND SIRS AS HE descended back into the tunnels. Cavalo rubbed his gritty eyes. He wanted nothing more than to sleep for days.

He went back to the cell. Lucas was asleep, Bad Dog curled over his legs, tail thumping an even beat. He climbed over the both of them carefully. Lucas stirred but didn't open his eyes. Bad Dog raised his head and licked Cavalo's hand.

Bedtime? he asked.

"Yeah."

I was guarding Smells Different.

"Were you?"

He was tired. And smelled like blood. You smell like his blood too.

"I'm okay."

You sleep. I will guard you too.

"I know you will."

Cavalo closed his eyes and slept.

He woke curled around Lucas. Bad Dog was gone, likely let out by SIRS. His head hurt and his muscles felt stiff under his skin. But he was warm, and for a moment, he allowed himself to stay as he was.

He thought to pull away when Lucas stirred, but Lucas pulled him tighter and opened his eyes. He looked confused for a moment, almost feral, as if he'd forgotten where he was. Who he was with. Then the cloudiness in his eyes cleared, and he huffed out a breath, tilting his head to see Cavalo better.

"How's the leg?" Cavalo asked, unsure why he was whispering.

Lucas shrugged. *Hurts. Not too bad.*

"You got lucky."

Lucas scowled. *Nothing about yesterday was lucky.*

"We lived."

For now. Postponing the inevitable.

"Probably."

You stupid man.

"What?"

Coming back like you did.

"I wasn't going to leave you."

You should have.

"I should have done a lot of things."

Why haven't you? Lucas asked, cocking his head.

"We don't have time for this," Cavalo muttered, trying to pull away.

Lucas wouldn't let him. *James*, he said, and Cavalo hated how his name sounded coming from Lucas, as if it meant something. As if he could take it back and be the man he'd once been. In Elko. With Jamie. With *her*.

James, Lucas said again, and it sounded like a prayer. Like hell.

"What?"

Lucas took a deep breath and let it out slow. *We could end this. Now.*

Cavalo narrowed his eyes. "You're not going back with him."

Lucas shook his head. *No. Not that.*

"Then what?"

Lucas pulled up his coat and shirt underneath, revealing miles of skin marked with ink. Cavalo found himself stretching a hand to the lines, thought better of it, but then did it anyway. The muscles under the skin jumped as his fingers traced the equations, the maps for machines that could make or break the world. Cavalo wished he'd never seen them. He wished he could touch them with his tongue.

This is what he needs, Lucas said. *The other half.*

"He won't get it." It was meant to be a promise, but it sounded like a threat.

Lucas smiled sadly. It made him look far too young. *He will. You know he will.*

"I—"

We could end this, Lucas said again, and for a moment, Cavalo didn't understand.

Until he did.

His hand stilled. Gooseflesh rose on his arms and the back of his neck.

It'd be easy, Lucas said, averting his eyes. *You could do it. Or if it's too much, I can do it myself. Just make sure to burn my body after so there's nothing left.*

"No," Cavalo said hoarsely. "You fucking bastard. No."

Lucas turned on his side to face him. Cavalo tried to pull his hand away, but Lucas wouldn't let him, gripping it tightly. *It's not about you,* he said. *Or me. Or this.* He motioned between the two of them. *It's about what Patrick will do.*

"Fuck you, I won't do it. I won't let you do it."

Lucas snarled at him, all teeth, face inches from Cavalo. *Here* was the monster buried underneath all that skin, flying forward, eyes blazing, lips curled. *I'm not asking for your permission!*

"Why'd you even come back, then!" Cavalo shouted, voice break-ing. "Why'd you come back to the prison after I got shot? Why did you stay?" His fingers curled into Lucas's skin hard enough to bruise, almost enough for his nails to break the skin. "Why did you stay? Why did you help us?"

Because I thought I'd escape. From here. From you. Disappear into the woods and never see anyone again. Go as far as I could until the ground ended beneath my feet or my legs gave out.

"Why didn't you?" Cavalo spat. "If you wanted to leave so fucking bad, why didn't you?"

I couldn't, he said simply as the monster in him faded back under the surface. *I became selfish. That there was something I'd found that was mine and mine alone.* Lucas looked away.

It burned. All of it burned. Cavalo felt as if he'd been lit on fire, his skin scorched and crisped.

"We're dead," Cavalo said. "All of us anyway. It's only a matter of time. That's all it ever was. It's inevitable."

But if he gets me, everyone else will be too. Dworshak is just the beginning. He'll spread east like a plague until there is nothing left but bones and ashes.

"Why now?" Cavalo croaked.

Lucas looked back at him. He placed his hand over Cavalo's, which still gripped his stomach. Their fingers fit together perfectly. He didn't know why he'd never seen it before. *Because there's no other choice. We made our stand. It didn't work. Now it's time to finish it.*

"I won't do it."

I don't need you to. I can do it myself.

"Why didn't you, then?" Cavalo cried. "Save me from this goddamn bullshit!" His voice carried his anger, but it was fragile, and it cracked and broke.

Couldn't leave it that way. He squeezed Cavalo's hand until he felt the bones grind together. *You.* He shook his head. *I couldn't. Not yet.*

"And now?"

Yes, Lucas said maddeningly. *And now.*

He was right, of course. No matter what Cavalo could say, Lucas was right. Logically, he was right. He was thinking beyond this room. Beyond the people huddled in the tunnels below. Beyond the prison and the little town of Cottonwood that Cavalo wasn't sure still stood. If Patrick got what he was gunning for, none of it would matter. It would start with Dworshak. It would end with fire. It always did.

Lucas was right. Cavalo hated him for it. He hated himself too. That all of this had been for nothing. That these people, the people of Cottonwood, of Grangeville had died for nothing. It might not have mattered in the long run, but all he could remember were Deke's last words about Mr. Fluff, the look on Hank's face as his son's blood leaked out before him. There might have been time for them. Before Cavalo had come.

"There's nothing but hell for us," he said quietly. "After."

I know. That's the only thing that waits for people like us.

"We'll burn."

Yes. In the fire.

"I won't be far behind you." And he wouldn't. Patrick would come with his Dead Rabbits, electrified fence be damned. It wouldn't take long.

Lucas reached out and touched his face.

Then Cavalo said the hardest words of the long years of his life. "Will you wait for me? In the fire?"

Lucas kissed him. Kissed him the answer, and in the howl of desperation, Cavalo felt the song of relief course through him until he vibrated with it, the bees knocked from their swirling storm. His mind was clear and sharp for the first time since he could remember. It was consuming and bright, and it hurt far more than he thought it would. But it was because of the surety. It was because of the end, that inevitable end he knew he no longer had to avoid. They would go from this fractured earth and descend into the fire together. They would burn, and as the flesh fell from their bodies for all their sins,

231

Cavalo would reach out and take Lucas's hand in his own and allow the pleasure of burning to overtake him.

He gasped as Lucas broke the kiss, their foreheads touching, eyes locked.

I am dark, Lucas said.

"I know."

You took some of it away.

"I know."

He felt Lucas reach down off the side of the cot, never looking away. His arm moved briefly, and then his knife was pressed into Cavalo's hand. Cavalo remembered the first day he'd felt this knife on him, in the other side of the woods, the blade against his throat. He hadn't felt fear then, not really, because he hadn't cared if he lived or died.

Funny how things changed. So quickly. So easily.

He took the knife. He thought he felt himself start to break, but instead, he pushed himself into that cold where his killer lay sleeping, diving as far beneath the surface as he'd ever been before. When it closed up and over his head, he felt it chill him to the bone as the rage in him awoke and swallowed him whole. It was easier, this way. Here in the dark where everything felt like ice, he couldn't bother with things like *emotions.* Any person he had ever murdered had come from this place, submerged and drowning but somehow still able to breathe. His father was lucky to have died when he did. Cavalo would have ended up killing him before too much longer.

The bees thrived here. He could feel them crawling along his skin, whispering promises to him that they could never keep. They promised to show him things if he stayed down below, and the killer in him laughed and said things like *yes,* and *I'll stay. I promise I'll stay,* even though Cavalo didn't want to.

The knife was cold in his hand. The man below him was warm. It was a study in contrasts that Cavalo didn't have time for. Not now.

His voice was steady and cool when he said, "Between the ribs. Into the heart. It'll hurt, but only for a moment. Then it will be over."

Lucas nodded.

And somehow, Cavalo broke above the surface, fingers and arms and face covered in bees, choking as they poured down his throat. His voice was harsh and broken when he said, "Are you sure?"

Lucas nodded.

Cavalo went back under.

He didn't flinch when Lucas leaned up and kissed him gently on the mouth. He kissed him back because it was the right thing to do.

He could hear himself screaming inside his head.

He put the knife against the Dead Rabbit's side and thought, *Maybe I should just follow him now. It'd be easier. And it'll be my choice.*

It was a coward's way out. All of this was.

It'd be on his own terms, at least.

He almost felt bad when he thought of Bad Dog and SIRS finding them. Bad Dog would be heartbroken. SIRS would mourn. But he was so far under that they were nothing more than fleeting thoughts. He didn't think any part of his skin was visible. He looked like a roiling mass of silvery wings and onyx stingers. He wondered if he would drown in them.

It had to be done now.

He just had to do it now.

He was on the precipice of a great thing. A momentous occurrence.

It was time for him to rise.

And just before he stabbed the knife upward into Lucas's heart, the man named James Cavalo somehow managed to say, "I'm sorry. For everything."

Lucas touched his face and said, *I would do it again. For this.*

Cavalo thought, *NOW NOW NOW.*

He thought, *NO NO NO.*

His hand tightened on the knife.

NOW NOW NOW.

The muscles in his arms coiled.

NO NO NO.

He gritted his teeth and—

And an alarm went off.

The klaxon blared.

Cavalo's breath punched its way out of his chest.

A light swirled red above the door to the tunnels.

Cavalo broke through the bees. Breathed the surface. He pulled the knife away because it was close. Too close.

He rose from the bed. Lucas followed him up. They stood side by side.

What is it? Lucas asked. He looked as dazed as Cavalo felt. Almost like they'd woken from a shared dream to a cold reality.

"Proximity alarms," Cavalo said. "They're here."

THEY DIDN'T DISCUSS THE FACT THAT CAVALO HAD ALMOST killed Lucas at his request as they entered the tunnels. It was something lost in the bees. Cavalo knew all he had to do was take the knife back from Lucas and shove it into his chest, but Lucas was resolute at his side, the warrior pushing forward. They were done with that. For now.

People tried to stop them, to ask him questions (*who* and *what* and *why*), but Cavalo ignored them. Lucas growled silently when they tried to step in front of him, and they fell back, eyes wide with fear. The blare of the klaxon grated against Cavalo's ears. He tried to shut it out but it was all he could hear.

He reached the steps that led into the barracks. More people waited for him at the top of the stairs. Always with their questions. It was disorienting, having so many here in his space. He wondered briefly if it'd be easier to sink back below the surface, but he wasn't sure how many of them he would kill.

There was a man who grabbed his arm to get his attention, and Cavalo thought, *Arm down. Foot to kneecaps. Break them sideways. Hands to face. Gouge the eyes.* As the thoughts roared through the bees, he began to submerge himself and turned to kill the man who touched him and—

"Are they here?" Hank asked, voice getting through from somewhere off to the left.

Cavalo stopped, and the man who touched him dropped his arms, unaware that he'd almost died. He felt the brush of a hand against his. Lucas. The feel of weight against his legs. Bad Dog. He took a breath and let it out slowly.

Good? Bad Dog asked him. *You smelled like bees.*

Cavalo shook his head. "It's okay."

Bad Dog didn't look like he believed him, but didn't push it.

"Where's SIRS?"

"In the back office," Alma said, standing next to Hank. "Watching the monitors. It's hard to see. They're old and with the storm...." She looked away.

Cavalo looked toward the closest panel on the far wall. It was dark, meaning SIRS was controlling them, not allowing others to see what he could. It was better that way. Depending on what they could see.

He needed to get back there.

"Do we have a plan?" Hank asked.

Cavalo snorted, feeling slightly hysterical. "I think we're past planning now."

"This isn't going to end well," Hank muttered, and he sounded so much like Deke that Cavalo's heart hurt. He pushed it away. He could worry about those he let die later.

"Keep everyone calm," he told Hank and Alma. "Only the Patrol should be armed for right now. I need to go see what's out there."

"We know what's out there," Hank said in a low voice.

Cavalo said nothing as he pushed his way through the crowd. He didn't know why SIRS continued to let the alarms ring through. He should have silenced them by now. People were starting to panic, and it was only making things worse.

People moved as he carved a path toward the rear of the

barracks. Their questions mixed in with the alarm, and he curled his hands into fists at his sides to keep from lashing out. Lucas and Bad Dog were beside him, both baring their teeth until people moved.

He could see SIRS's outline through the office window, hidden behind ancient plastic blinds that no longer pulled up. The door was shut. Screens flickered, but the robot did not move.

Before he could push on, Bill stood in front of him, looking harried. "The fences will stay up and running," he said quickly. "We've got enough juice to keep them up and running at full power for at least a few days."

Cavalo nodded sharply but pushed past him. They didn't have time for this. Not now.

"Did you know your audio was out?" Bill called after him. "Fixed it for you. Don't know why SIRS couldn't have done that."

And everything came to a halt.

He tried to breathe, but he couldn't get his lungs to work.

The bees laughed.

He turned. "What?" he managed to ask.

Bill looked confused. "The audio. For the cameras and monitors. I noticed it was out. Wire had been cut. Stripped it and put it back together. Should be full audio now."

No.

Everything slowed down around Cavalo. Colors bled together as he turned back toward the office. His heart was thunderous in his chest. He ran. He ran as fast as he could, but it was like moving through water, and he could hear SIRS in his head, the first words he'd ever said to him when Cavalo had stumbled upon the prison that dark night so very long ago. *Well, this certainly is a surprise. How lovely it is to see a human again. It has been such a long time. Now, state your business before I snap your neck and leave your body for the animals in the woods to pick at.*

Even then, Cavalo knew SIRS was like him.

He ran toward his friend.

He hit the metal door to the office. It did not budge. He slammed his hands against it. And from inside, he heard voices.

"Robot." A small voice, filled with static and rage.

"Yes, Father." He'd never sounded more robotic.

Cavalo screamed for SIRS. Begged him.

"I was Rebekah's nurse who died and was buried under the oak before Bethel."

"Father, may I?"

"You may."

Cavalo grabbed a rifle from a man he did not know and bashed the butt of it into the window. It did not shudder. It did not shake. It did not crack. Cavalo remembered once that SIRS had told him it was bulletproof. *To protect the guards,* he'd said.

The mechanical response: "But Deborah Rebekah's nurse died, and she was buried beneath Bethel under an oak; and the name of it was called Allonbachuth."

Cavalo turned the rifle around and shot the window. People screamed behind him as the bullet ricocheted.

And even above the noise, he could hear the final question, and his heart broke again and again.

"I was the star that fell when the third angel sounded."

And Sentient Integrated Response System said, "And the third angel sounded, and there fell a great star from heaven, burning as it were a lamp, and it fell upon the third part of the rivers, and upon the fountains of waters."

"SIRS!" Cavalo cried. His voice broke like glass.

"And the name of the star is called Wormwood; and the third part of the waters became wormwood; and many men died of the waters, because they were made bitter."

"Don't do this," Cavalo whispered. "Please."

"Robot." Patrick sounded delighted.

"Yes, Father?"

"Do you know Lucas?"

"Ye-e-es," SIRS ground out. "He is... my... there is no...."

"*Robot.*"

"Yes," SIRS said with great anger.

"Bring me the boy. Let nothing stand in your way."

Cavalo took a step back from the door.

The monitors in the room went dark.

Cavalo took another step back.

"Don't make me do this," he said quietly as he raised the rifle. Maybe half a clip left.

Something shifted inside the office. He knew the robot had turned toward the door when a bright flash of red shone from the room. The robot's eyes. Like before.

"Please," Cavalo said.

Lucas drew his knife.

Bad Dog crouched at his side, tail flicking dangerously.

And from behind the metal door, came the grind of gears, the breaking of coils, the warning beeps of algorithms failing. These metallic sounds carried with them the whispers of apologies, the pain of regrets.

Before Cavalo could scream at the others to *move*, there was a groan of metal as the door was ripped from its hinges. It flew out onto the floor, dust billowing up in a mushroom cloud. The robot bent over to walk through the doorway, his arms scraping against the entrance, causing stone and plaster to crack. The thin line stretched out farther down the wall, reaching the window. As he struggled through without any of his usual economic grace, the doorway split and groaned, and the bulletproof glass shuddered in its frame. A thin sliver appeared in the glass as it bent. Cavalo told himself to *fire*, to fire *now*, but his finger hesitated on the trigger even as the bloodred eyes of the robot landed on him. This was the robot that held him up in the air and broke his fingers when Patrick told him to. This was the robot that no longer had free will.

That's what he told himself. That's what he screamed in the bees to make himself fire.

His finger put pressure on the trigger, and he aimed for the robot's head.

But the robot was fast, faster than Cavalo had ever seen him move before. One moment he was pulling himself through the crumbling doorway and the next he was running forward, body crouched low as he scooped up the metal door right when Cavalo fired the Bakalov. The robot held the door in front of him, acting as a shield. Bullets smashed into the door and flew off into the ceiling. The floor. The walls. Little puffs of dust and cement as they embedded themselves into the rock.

Cavalo knew then, with utmost certainty, that this wasn't going to end well.

The Bakalov began to click dryly in his hands.

The robot stood slowly.

"Don't do this," Cavalo said.

"We are nothing but quarks and stardust," the robot replied, eyes flashing dangerously. "Give me Lucas."

"No." He stepped in front of Lucas. Crowded him back. For a moment he thought Lucas would stab him in the back for acting as he did. Instead he felt Lucas bow his head until his forehead pressed against Cavalo's neck. Until his breath ran against Cavalo's skin. His hand touched the small of Cavalo's back and he couldn't believe he'd almost murdered Lucas. He couldn't *believe* it'd almost come to that.

And then Lucas slipped the knife into his hand, and Cavalo knew what he was asking for. Asking *of* him again.

Lucas must die before the robot could take him.

"Don't," he said, but he didn't know to whom.

"You and I," the robot said. He took a shuddering step forward, dragging the door at his side. "It's... not like... I thought it'd be." The words sounded as if they were coming at great cost. Deep inside SIRS came the smell of burning.

"It's more," Cavalo said, gripping the knife and telling himself to turn, to bring the knife up and into the bottom of Lucas's jaw and shove up to his brain. It'd be over quickly. The body would die and would start to break down, hopefully before Patrick could use it. It was their last play, and he just had to *do it*.

The light in the robot's eyes faded back to orange, and for a moment, Cavalo had hope. Irrational, beautiful hope, and SIRS said in a small voice, "It hurts, Cavalo."

Cavalo knew it did. Could feel it in his bones.

But then the eyes went red again, and the pained voice was gone. "Give me the boy, Cavalo."

Now. Now. Now.

No. No. No.

He whirled around, spinning on his heels. He swung the knife up, and for a split second, his eyes locked with Lucas's and he thought, *I'll see you soon*, and the knife—

The knife fell from his hand as the robot twisted his wrist viciously. Gray waves of pain rolled over his body, oily and hot as he heard bones snap. He had no further time to process anything else when he was flung across the room, back crashing into the far wall.

In his haze of red and gold, Cavalo heard people screaming. He managed to raise his head, blood trickling from his nose and mouth. It took everything he had to look up. As his vision began to fail and unconsciousness pulled him into the dark, he saw what was meant to be an ending:

Bad Dog, lying on the floor, whining softly, taking shallow breaths.

People pushing and screaming, trampling those who couldn't move fast enough.

Aubrey, eyes wide and wet.

Hank, yelling words that Cavalo couldn't quite make out.

Alma, struggling to stand against the tide of bodies flowing against her.

And last, he saw SIRS and Lucas. SIRS, standing as tall as he'd ever been. Eyes red, arm outstretched. Those spider hands were wrapped around Lucas's throat, holding him three feet off the ground. Lucas's feet kicked, his hands scrabbled against the metal arm.

Almost quicker than Cavalo could follow, the robot turned and smashed through the far wall, stone and plaster falling to the floor. The snow swirled as he ran, Lucas still in his hand. Before he leapt over the electrified fence and disappeared, Lucas reached out once toward Cavalo.

Then they were gone.

And Cavalo fell into the dark.

surprise

JAMIE AND CAVALO walked through a forest hand in hand. It was dark. The trees were big. Things moved on either side of them, hidden by the shadows. Sometimes Cavalo saw the flash of red eyes amongst the leaves and branches and thought to himself how clever monsters and cannibals were.

He knew there was something he was forgetting. It buzzed at the frayed edges of his mind, but he couldn't quite grasp hold before it flitted away. No matter. If it came, it came.

He chuckled to himself.

"What's so funny, Daddy?" Jamie asked him.

"I don't know," Cavalo said. Why were they out this late? Jamie needed to go to bed. They had an early day tomorrow. They were going to... well. He didn't remember what *exactly* they were going to do, but it didn't explain why they were in a forest in the middle of the night. His son was young. He needed sleep.

She was going to be mad at him. Claire. His wife. Sometimes she danced, but she could get mad too.

"No," Jamie said, swinging Mr. Fluff in his other hand. "She won't be."

"How do you know?" Cavalo asked, wondering if he'd spoken about Claire aloud. He must have. It would've been the only way Jamie could have heard him.

Jamie shrugged. "When is a tree not a tree?" he asked.

"I don't know."

"When it's dead." And then he laughed like it was the greatest joke he'd ever heard. Cavalo didn't get it, but his son had this high-pitched laugh that was always contagious, and he grinned along with him.

And then his son started screaming because, really, he was dead. He had died years ago, and Cavalo could only remember it now.

Jamie handed him Mr. Fluff and walked backward into the shadows of the forest, mouth open and screaming, head jerking side to side.

He disappeared into the dark.

It grew quiet.

"Jamie?" Cavalo called out, but there was no response.

He looked down at Mr. Fluff.

The rabbit had a note pinned to one of his paws. Cavalo took the pin out. Mr. Fluff jerked in his hands and began to bleed white stuffing. He dropped the rabbit, and it ran away into the trees. He didn't know Mr. Fluff could run. It scared him.

He unrolled the note. It said:

HE IS NOT WHAT HE SEEMS.
NONE OF THIS IS.
LOSE SOMETHING, CHARLIE?

JAMES CAVALO WAS NOT A STUPID MAN. YES, HE'D MADE STUPID decisions in his life, decisions that had caused people to die, but he was not a stupid man.

His son was dead.

Claire was dead, because when was a tree not a tree?

But there were others.

A robot.

A dog.

A clever monster, a clever cannibal.

He dropped the note.

He looked toward the night sky.

A tornado of bees spun above him. He opened his mouth, and they flew down, fighting and crawling down his throat, and he couldn't breathe, he couldn't *breathe, he couldn't—*

He shot up, gasping for air. "Easy," he heard a voice say near his ear.

He opened his eyes.

He was in the prison. The cot in the cell.

He groaned softly at the pain in his back. His head. His wrist. Everything hit at once, and he felt nauseated. He closed his eyes again and waited for the room to stop shaking.

"Is it bad?" a gruff voice asked from beside the cot. "The pain."

"Not the worst I've felt," Cavalo said through gritted teeth.

"Set your wrist as best we could. A splint of sorts. Break isn't bad. Considering."

"Considering?"

Hank sighed. "Considering who it was doing the breaking. He could have done much worse. I think he was holding back."

"Doesn't feel like it."

He opened his eyes at the sound of Hank's laughter. It was bitter but unexpected all the same. "I suppose it doesn't. But at least you still have a hand. And are alive."

Cavalo flexed his wrist carefully. Flares of pain in all directions. But it was Hank's words that hit him the most. "And how is it that we're alive?"

"They left."

"All of them?"

Hank nodded.

"Why?"

"Should they not have? They got what they came for."

Lucas, Cavalo thought, and it threatened to send him spiraling into the cold. He held himself above the surface. Barely.

He frowned as he pushed himself up. "He could have told SIRS to turn off the outer defenses. Taken us that way. But instead, he—"

"Took the one thing he needed most," Hank finished for him. "Without risking any more of his people. You should have told him."

"Told who?"

"Bill. About the audio. He's beside himself."

"He's lucky I haven't ripped his fucking head off," Cavalo snarled.

Hank stared at him hard. "Because he was supposed to know? Any of us were? Tell me, Cavalo. Did you know Patrick had control over SIRS? You must have if the audio had been cut."

He was so close to slipping under. The bees demanded it. "He shouldn't have been touching a goddamn thing here. None of you should be. You shouldn't even be here." His voice was cold. He didn't do anything to stop it.

"Cavalo—"

"No," he retorted. "I never wanted this. I never asked for any of this. All I wanted to do was be left alone until the time came when I could no longer move, and that would be the end. I didn't *ask* to have you people come here. I didn't *ask* to be your goddamn savior. I didn't *ask*—"

"To care about him as much as you do," Hank said quietly. He didn't look away. "To care about us, even if we didn't deserve it. I know you never asked for any of this, Cavalo. But somehow, it was given to you anyway."

He slipped into the cold. There was rage in his heart and murder in his voice. "I never cared about any of you. Leave before I decide you're all more of a liability than you've already been."

"You lie," Hank said simply.

"Do you want to test that, Hank?" His voice was low and dangerous. His thoughts were stark and staccato short. *Fist to nose. Fingers to eyes. Snap the neck.*

"Cavalo."

"Hank," Cavalo growled.

"I lost my son yesterday."

Cavalo breached the surface and gasped a shuddering breath.

"Do you want to know what I thought when I watched Deke get his head blown off?"

Cavalo shook his head. He'd never wanted to know anything less in his life.

But Hank didn't care, because Hank said, "I thought about how funny his face looked."

Cavalo took a breath. It hitched in his chest.

"His face looked funny," Hank said, "because of the look of surprise he had. Like he couldn't believe a bullet had just gone through his head and out the back. How *shocked* he was that a little piece of metal the size of a coin had broken apart his skull plate, sped through a mass of tissue that held every memory he'd ever had. He hated surprises. *Hated* them. Even when he was a little kid, he despised being surprised, even if it was supposed to be for a good thing. It made him nervous. It made him edgy. The wait. The anticipation. But even if we hid it from him, he still hated when we *sprang* it on him. It made him feel out of control. He didn't like not knowing what was ahead. What was coming. Everything had to be planned out to the last detail and had to go *exactly* as planned.

"So he must not have thought he could have died. Even though you told us we would. Even though deep down we *knew* we would. But there's a difference between being young and told you're going to die and being old and hearing the same. When you're older, you know it's inevitable. When you're younger, you know it's a fallacy. Delusion. Because you *can't* die when you're so young. You *can't* die by surprise. But he did. And that was the thing I thought when he was falling to the ground, that he must have just *hated* it. Not the fact that he *had* died, but the surprise behind it." Hank stopped. His breath was ragged in his chest. He closed his eyes.

"Hank—"

Eyes flashed open, and Cavalo could see the warrior underneath the dark grief. "Are we going to get him back? Lucas."

Cavalo looked away. "It's suicide."

"We're dead either way, right?"

"Probably. Maybe not today. But soon."

"Then we go knowing we're going to die."

Cavalo looked up at his friend. "Then why go at all?"

Hank leaned forward and took Cavalo's uninjured hand in his own. "Because I don't want to be surprised by death," he said. "If it's going to take me, then it will be on my own terms."

"Aubrey."

"She'll follow you."

"She's just a girl."

"And Deke was just a boy." Though Cavalo knew Hank hadn't meant that.

"I can't be responsible for that," Cavalo choked out.

"Then let us be responsible for you," Hank said, squeezing his hand tight.

Cavalo struggled to breathe. It was too much. All of it. Everything. He didn't know how he'd gotten to this point in his life, where a man whose son's death rested at Cavalo's feet comforted him. Held him. Gave him strength. Cavalo knew he'd been a coward for much of his life. He had done terrible things. Hurt innocent people. And yet, salvation, of a kind. Holding his hand.

"Dworshak?" he said in a quiet voice.

"Dworshak," Hank agreed.

"Smaller the better."

"Figured. You. Bad Dog. Me and Aubrey. Alma. Bill and Richie."

His rage burst again at Bill's name. Hank waited as he pushed through it. Once he'd swallowed it back down, he nodded and gave

Hank one last chance. "Stay here," he said. "With your daughter. Live for Deke. For her. You may be surprised at what happens."

"I fucking hate surprises," Hank said, and the smile he gave was all teeth.

ARE WE GOING TO GET THEM BACK? BAD DOG WHISPERED TO HIM in the early morning hours. Neither of them had been able to sleep.

"I don't know," Cavalo said, unable to lie but unable to be more honest.

SIRS not a bad guy?

"No."

He hit me.

"I know."

Got crazy eyes.

"Yeah."

Bad Dog huffed. Cavalo waited to let him work through it. Finally, *Not a bad guy. Tin Man is my friend. We'll get him back.*

Cavalo kept his hands from shaking. It was a battle he almost lost. "Okay" was all he said.

And Smells Different.

"Okay."

MasterBossLord?

"Yeah?"

We'll get them back.

He held his friend and waited for morning.

dworshak

THE SNOW HELD off as the group of six people and one dog followed the road east. Cavalo wondered if it was a sign.

They could have easily gone by way of Cottonwood, but there was an unspoken consensus to avoid it at all costs. No one knew if the Dead Rabbits had taken it over or burned it to the ground. Cavalo thought of Deke lying in an empty house, the blanket across his body probably frozen to his coat and face, the ice crystals a red that was dark and deep.

They didn't speak much. There didn't seem to be anything to say, and all Cavalo could think was *I am Lucas I am Lucas I am Lucas.* His wrist hurt. His back hurt. His ankles hurt from the snowshoes on his feet. He'd hoped they wouldn't need them, but there were drifts that Bad Dog would disappear into every now and then, causing him to bark in frustration until Hank lifted him out.

The others spoke behind him in low voices, as if they didn't want to disturb him. He set a punishing pace but knew it would take at least another day before they'd get to Dworshak. He tried not to think about what was happening to Lucas and SIRS. But they were there, images flashing of blood spilled and wires ripped from robotic chests.

Every step he took was a struggle, but it was getting him closer. He was under no illusions about what would happen. He just wanted to take out as many of them as he could before then.

Light was starting to fade when Cavalo heard the sounds of a river and knew they were near what used to be Kamiah, Idaho. There'd once been a rusted sign, but it'd fallen years ago and was buried somewhere under the snow. Kamiah was empty. Had been for a long time. Nothing much swam in the river these days, and what did surely wasn't edible. A few small buildings still stood, but ceilings had collapsed and walls had fallen down.

But it was the river that Cavalo focused on. The sound of the water. The crack of ice along the edges. Clearwater, it'd been called. Before.

And it led directly to Dworshak.

They were quiet as they approached Kamiah. They'd all seen the snow trampled down before them, a pathway leading toward the buildings that still stood.

"Anything?" Cavalo whispered to Bad Dog.

He raised his snout, nostrils flaring. *Yes. But faint. Old smells. Fire and dirt. Blood.*

Cavalo told himself the blood could be from anything, not just Lucas.

Kamiah was empty, as it'd been for a long time. There was evidence all over that people had recently been there. It smelled ripe and wild. Dark maroon stains in the snow and floorboards. The smell of smoke from blackened extinguished fires. Charred wood. Discarded clothing. Cavalo went into one of the buildings near the river's edge and found bodies of four Dead Rabbits piled in the corner. They hadn't started to rot, but it was close. Wide eyes and torn limbs. One of them was slumped against the wall. A man. Cavalo could see part of his rib cage poking through shredded skin. It was white and wet. His tongue poked through the stiff split of his lips. Arms laid at his sides, hands hooked into claws.

Cavalo turned away. There was nothing for him here. None of

them were Lucas. There was a brief stutter to his step, but that was all.

And then from behind him came a shuddering breath. Ragged. Painful. And close.

He whirled, dropping to a knee, bringing up his old rifle. He ignored the sharp flash of pain in his wrist, the pull and ache of his muscles.

The man against the wall took another breath. Not dead after all.

He raised his head. His hands clawed the ground at his sides. "Hurts," he said with a grimace. "It... hurts."

Cavalo leveled his breathing. Calmed his heart.

And submerged himself into the cold.

He stood, shouldering the rifle. The man grinned up at him, and dark blood dripped from his mouth over his chin. "I... know... you," he said. He coughed, and a thick plug of mucus fell onto his leg. It looked like he'd spat out his tongue. "You...."

Cavalo stood. Leaned his head side to side to crack his neck. Pulled Lucas's knife from the scabbard at his side. He could hear the others moving outside. He needed to make this quick before one of them came in. Or Bad Dog caught his scent. Everything already smelled like blood and death in here. He was just going to add a little more.

He walked to the Dead Rabbit. Stood above him. The man looked up. He was no longer smiling. In fact, he looked very afraid.

Cavalo knelt beside him. He reached out with the knife and dragged the tip gently over the Dead Rabbit's cheek. The man shook. "You took from me," Cavalo said quietly.

"Patrick," the man said, and a bubble of blood burst from his mouth, misting his nose and chin. "He is... God. He is... Death."

"I will kill your god," Cavalo promised him and the bees cried happily in his head. He curled a hand around the back of the man's neck.

"You can't."

"Watch me."

"Daddy," the man said, eyes going wide. "He's not who he seems. Mr. Fluff said—"

Cavalo didn't let it continue. The knife went up between the fourth and fifth ribs and into the heart. The man tensed beneath him. His head jerked back. His mouth opened obscenely wide, but no sound came out. Then he exhaled and died.

He pulled the knife out. Wiped it against the Dead Rabbit's coat. Sheathed it. Stood and walked out of the house.

Hank was standing near the river. He looked back at Cavalo. "Anything?"

"A body. Nothing else."

Hank turned back toward the river.

THEY BUILT A FIRE IN ONE OF THE BUILDINGS THAT SEEMED THE sturdiest. The roof was gone, so the smoke drifted out into the sky. Cavalo lay with his head resting on his pack. Bad Dog dozed at his side. Only Hank was still awake, the others curled under thin blankets.

Above him, there was a shift in the clouds. The stars blinked coldly in the dark space around them. His breath caught in his throat, and Cavalo had never felt so small in his life.

Hank must have heard his choked breath, as he looked over at Cavalo with concern in his eyes. He followed Cavalo's line of sight and saw the stars for himself. "Would you look at that," he whispered. "Been a while."

Product of the nuclear holocaust. Or so the stories went. Perpetual cloud cover with minimal breaks. Sometimes he could feel the sun on his face. And sometimes, like now, he could see the stars above. He wondered if it was a sign. He wondered if he even believed in signs.

"Do you think they know?"

"Who?"

"The others. Back at the prison."

"Know what?"

"That we aren't coming back."

Cavalo shrugged. "Maybe. They have hope. Or they had it. I don't know what they have anymore."

"We all did," Hank said. "Hope is what keeps you alive when everything else goes to shit."

Cavalo snorted. "Poetic." One star was bigger than the others. Brighter. Cavalo desperately wished he could know its name. He hoped it wasn't Wormwood.

"They'll be okay," Hank said. "I hope."

"Maybe."

"Do you know the Nez Perce?" Hank asked him.

Cavalo shook his head, unsure about the quick change in topic.

"Indians. Native Americans. From Before. Hundreds of years ago. All of this land used to be theirs. All the way up past Dworshak and all the way down past Cottonwood. I found a book on them once. In a library that had been left behind. Most of the books were rotten and illegible. Some could be saved."

"Where?" Cavalo asked, because Hank didn't like to talk about what happened before he came to Cottonwood. About Deke and Aubrey's mother. Life in their Before.

"Far from here," Hank said, still looking at the stars.

Cavalo didn't push. It wasn't his place.

"They had a story," Hank continued. "About how man came to be. I remember reading and thinking I'd never heard anything more beautiful."

"What was the story?" Cavalo asked.

Hank sighed. "A long time ago, before man ever walked the earth, a monster came from the north. He was a gigantic monster, and he ate everything he could see. All of the animals. The little ones. The squirrels and the raccoons and the mice. The big ones. He ate deer and elk and the mountain lion."

There was a Coyote, Hank said. He couldn't find his friends

anymore, and it made him very angry. He decided it was time to stop the monster.

Coyote went across the Snake River and tied himself to the highest peak in the Wallowa Mountains. Then he called out to the monster who stood on the other side of the river. He dared the monster to try and eat him.

The monster charged across the river and up into the mountains. He tried as hard as he could to suck Coyote off the mountain with his breath, but it was no use. Coyote's rope was too strong.

This scared the monster. He decided to make friends with Coyote, and he invited Coyote to come stay with him. The monster was clever, as monsters often are. But so was Coyote.

One day, Coyote told the monster he would like to see all of the animals trapped in the monster's belly. The monster agreed, and he ate Coyote. The monster was very clever.

When he went inside, Coyote saw all of his friends were safe. He told them to get ready to escape, and began to work. With his fire starter, he built a huge fire in the pit of the monster's stomach. Then he took his knife and cut the monster's heart out. The monster died a great death, and all of the animals escaped. Coyote was the last one to leave.

Coyote said that in honor of the monster's death, he was going to create a new animal: a human being. Coyote cut the monster up in pieces and scattered the pieces to the four winds. Where each piece landed (in the north and the south, in the east and the west) a tribe was born. It was in this way that all the tribes came to be.

When he was finished, Coyote's friend Fox said that no tribe had been created on the spot where they stood. Coyote was sorry he had no more parts of the monster. But then he had an idea. He washed the blood from his hands with water from the river and sprinkled the drops on the ground.

Coyote said, "Here on this ground I make the Nez Perce. They will be few in number, but they will be strong and pure." And this is how human beings came to be.

Hank's voice died away. The stars were long gone.

Cavalo said the only thing he could. "I'm sorry about Deke." Because he was.

"So am I." Hank's voice was hoarse. "Don't you see, Cavalo? He's taken all the little animals away. The monster has eaten everything as he heads back to the north where he came from."

Cavalo *could* see, and the clarity burned. "I will cut out his heart."

"Will you?" Hank asked.

"Yes," he said, though they both knew it was a lie.

"And scatter his pieces to the wind?"

"Yes."

"And what will you make out of him, James? What will you make out of the monster?"

And because Cavalo didn't know the answer, he closed his eyes. Eventually he dreamt of stars.

THEY REACHED DWORSHAK THE NEXT AFTERNOON. BAD DOG kept his nose close to the ground yards ahead of them, making sure they wouldn't be caught off guard. They kept low to the ground as they crested a hill south of the dam, hidden amongst the thick forest.

He'd been here once before, back in his wandering days. Those days when he never stopped walking for fear of whatever would catch up with him if he ever stopped. He remembered looking at it with disinterested awe, unable to quantify what exactly it was he'd been looking at. Metal and concrete carved out into a valley in a place no longer inhabited by man.

Dworshak was big. Very big. When the name Dworshak had first been uttered after Lucas revealed his skin, SIRS had told him the dam had been considered the third tallest dam Before the bombs fell. Seven hundred seventeen feet tall. Over half a mile long. Six and a half *million* cubic yards of concrete. As SIRS rattled off the stats, Cavalo couldn't help but feel overwhelmed at the entirety of it all.

He didn't know how he was able to overcome that feeling, that feeling of insignificance that he felt akin to when he saw the stars above. It'd been so much greater than Cavalo could imagine, and the enormity of what it could mean if they could harness the power of the dam took his breath away.

That was then, though.

Now, it was suicide conveniently disguised as a rescue mission.

"Jesus," Alma said. "It's... big."

"You've never been here?" Bill asked her as he pulled out the binocs and handed them to his son.

She shook her head. "Never had a reason to. All that water. Just... sitting there. And we can't do a damn thing with it."

"Might not be for much longer," Richie said.

"What do you mean?" Hank asked.

"Look to the center," Bill said. "Up toward the top. See it?"

Cavalo followed where Bill was pointing. At first he thought there was a discoloration in the cement, years of inclement weather that wore on the stone. But then it widened, the vague shape becoming sharper.

There was a crack in the dam. A huge one at that. Jagged and widening as it etched toward the river below.

"Holy shit," Hank muttered.

"How long is it?" Aubrey asked, glancing nervously at her father.

Bill shrugged. "Probably fifty feet. Thereabouts. Three or four feet across at the widest point. It happens when there's no one maintaining it. I'm surprised it's not bigger. Or that it hasn't collapsed already. If anything can happen here, that's going to have to be taken care of first."

The bees laughed in Cavalo's head. *I don't think he realizes that he's going to be slow roasted over a fire in the near future,* they whispered.

"Will it hold for now?" Cavalo asked.

Bill shrugged. "As long as there's no added stress to it. Like rockets or grenades." He looked slightly amused. "Or it could collapse the moment we get near it, and then it won't even matter anymore. That many tons of water and you won't even know what hit you. This whole area for a half mile will be underwater. Won't be much—"

Bad Dog growled. *Bad guys.*

"How far?" Cavalo asked, crouching by his side. Bad Dog stared down into the valley. Cavalo followed his line of sight but couldn't see anything.

In the trees. Near the river.

Quarter mile away. A little less. "No one closer?"

No.

And even though he knew, he had to ask. "SIRS? Lucas?"

No. Just bad guys.

"Tree line," Cavalo told the rest. "Downwind."

"Got them," Aubrey said, looking through the scope of her rifle. "Eight... no. Ten. Toward the dam. Don't see Lucas or SIRS. Or Patrick."

"Track them," Cavalo said. "Don't engage. It's not worth it."

"You got it, boss," she said, keeping the scope on the Dead Rabbits.

"Bill, how far are we away from the hatch?"

Bill pointed farther along the hill, toward the dam. "We can stay up top," he said. "It's a few hundred yards ahead."

"And it's accessible?"

He shrugged. "Was when we were here last. If not, we'll have to go to the other side of the valley. Which means crossing the river."

"And the tunnels aren't blocked.

"SIRS didn't seem to think so," he said quietly, wincing. "Before... he thought that unless the dam itself had been compromised, then the work tunnels would be clear. It's either that or go straight to the dam direct."

"And that's probably not the best idea," Richie muttered, binocs trained at the top of the dam. "Dead Rabbits. Lots and lots of Dead Rabbits."

Cavalo didn't feel bad when he grabbed the binocs from Richie, the pain in his wrist flaring sharply. He ignored it, pushing it back down. He didn't have time for it. They didn't have much time for anything anymore. Time gave the illusion that they weren't going into this half-cocked and without a clue. It'd be sweeter to think they did, but reality was cold, and Cavalo knew the cold. It was where the bees lived.

He scanned the dam. Richie was right: Dead Rabbits, Dead Rabbits, Dead Rabbits. At least a dozen of them, patrolling the top of the damn. No one that Cavalo recognized. No one with signs of visible injury from the attack on Cottonwood a couple of days before. Most were armed with some kind of weapon. A rifle. A gun. A thick wooden board with a rusty spike shoved through the end. No Patrick. No Lucas. No—

"SIRS," he whispered. Because he was there. The robot stood amongst the Dead Rabbits. His eyes were red. One of the Dead Rabbits was talking to him, pointing toward some debris on the ground. The robot bent over and picked it up, tossing the chunks of cement over the side of the dam. He repeated the action two more times before the Dead Rabbit spoke again. And then he didn't move.

Tin Man? Bad Dog asked him.

"Yeah."

We gonna go get him?

And that was it, wasn't it? This was the choice he had to make. He had to choose at this time, *at this very moment*, whether or not to stick with the plan (if it could even be called that) with some semblance of stealth and find Lucas somewhere inside the dam, or to go in guns blazing for SIRS in hopes that somehow, someway, SIRS would snap out of it, because for the *life* of him, Cavalo could not remember what Patrick had said. What Patrick had said the moment he'd left the prison that day weeks before. The code. The password. The motherfucking *incantation* that brought SIRS back his human- ity. The questions from the Book of God that Cavalo had never both- ered to read because with all the shit in the world, he couldn't possibly believe that motherfucker wasn't the biggest asshole. He hadn't ever seen a Bible before (precious, like snow globes, they were), but stories had been passed down by fireside late into the night of Hellfire and Damnation and the Wrath of God. God was cruel. God was merciless. His words uttered made SIRS turn into a robot.

And Cavalo couldn't remember how to bring him back.

"Not yet," he said. "We can't go to him yet."

"We could, though," Hank said, sounding thoughtful.

"How do you figure?"

Hank shrugged. "Might be easier and a whole hell of a lot quieter if only a couple of us went in for Lucas. The rest of us could go after SIRS."

"You can't alert them," Cavalo snapped. "They'll swarm. You won't survive."

Aubrey rolled her eyes. "Give us a little more credit than that, Cavalo."

"She's right," Alma said. "We can handle up top. You can find Lucas. Bad Dog will be able to track him better than any of us."

Bad Dog's ears perked at his name. He cocked his head and panted quietly.

"Fucking idiots," Cavalo muttered. "How in God's name do you think you're going to stop SIRS? He's... gone. Whatever's there isn't him."

"That's where I come in," Bill said. He reached into his pack and pulled out a bulky metal object, similar to the landmines they'd used in Cottonwood. "There were only a couple of these in his box. Didn't think we'd need them back in town. Might do us some good now."

"What is it?"

"EMP mine. Electromagnetic pulse. Short range. Sends a blast that should fry whatever SIRS has got cooking in his head. It'll stop him. For now."

"How close does it have to be?"

"Couple of yards. I think." He at least had the courtesy to look slightly embarrassed.

Cavalo looked at each of them in turn, growing more incredulous. "You planned this."

Hank snorted. "As much as this could be called a plan. It's still shit, James."

"Fuck." And he laughed. It was rusty and hysterical. It hurt his throat. "Oh fuck."

They didn't laugh with him. He hadn't expected them to. They couldn't hear his bees, after all. "No guns," he finally said as he wiped his eyes. "Bullets are a last resort. Bows and arrows only."

They nodded at him, and it was all he could do to keep from screaming.

It didn't take them long to find the hatch. Overgrowth had been cleared away at some point, so he knew it'd been in use recently. Aubrey nocked an arrow as Richie pried the hatch door open. It grated loudly and echoed down a long black drop. There was a dim light near the bottom. A metal ladder curled up near the top.

"That's not creepy at all," Aubrey muttered. "Dark tunnel into the side of a crumbling giant cement dam filled with Dead Rabbits. I almost want to go with you."

"I'll go," Richie said quietly. They all snapped their heads up to him.

"No," Cavalo said.

"You can't get him down the ladder," Richie said. "Not with your fingers and wrist the way they are. And what happens when you need to climb back up? You going to leave him?"

Cavalo hadn't even thought about getting out. It was lost in the haze, hidden behind *now now now* and wondering if Lucas was already dead. It wouldn't surprise him. Patrick wouldn't need him alive, just his skin, and Cavalo knew there were ways to cure it, to make it stiff as a board and stop any morbidity. It could be done with animal skins. That meant it could be done with human flesh.

No. Lucas was alive. He had to be. And the longer they stood around, the less time Cavalo would have to find him.

And so, for one of the first times in his life, Cavalo acquiesced. He was getting too old for this shit.

"How long will it take you to get to the ridge?" Cavalo asked Aubrey, knowing who was really in charge. He watched as Hank wrapped a blanket around Richie's shoulders, creating a sling for Bad Dog.

"Fifteen minutes," she said. "Longer if we run into trouble."

He thought hard. "Wait two hours," he said, "before going after SIRS."

"And if our hand is forced?" she asked.

He grinned at her. It felt too wide. "Then you take out as many of those bastards as you can."

She nodded. The bees buzzed at the steel in her eyes. "Stay safe, Cavalo."

He turned and saw Bill talking quietly to Richie. The older man's hand was curled around his son's neck, their foreheads pressed together. Cavalo couldn't hear what was said, but it wasn't for him. It was between fathers and sons, and for a moment, he thought he saw Jamie skipping through the woods. But then he went behind a tree and never appeared on the other side, so Cavalo knew he hadn't been there at all.

"You'll be good?" Alma asked him. She looked like she wanted to say more but stopped herself.

"Yeah." He thought of her song where she said good-bye all those weeks ago. He didn't stop himself when he leaned in and kissed her forehead. She sighed, her breath on his neck. He stepped back, and she looked away, but not before he saw the tears in her eyes that she didn't let fall.

"We'll see you soon," Hank said, and when Cavalo tried to protest (because surely, out of all of them, at least *Hank* would realize this was good-bye), he stepped away and wouldn't say another word.

"Take care of him, okay?" Bill asked him as they watched Hank lift Bad Dog into the sling. Bad Dog only grumbled a little at that. "He's all I got."

"I will."

"I know it's a lot to ask after... after what I did."

Anger. He pushed it away and said, "You didn't know."

"No. I didn't. But I'm sorry."

"I won't let anything happen to him," Cavalo said before he could stop himself.

Bill nodded and walked away before Cavalo could take it back.

I'm not a damn puppy, Bad Dog growled at him.

"Sort of," Cavalo said. He looked up at Richie. "Something to prove?"

Richie shrugged. "Or maybe I just want to help."

"You do what I say, when I say it. No questions."

"Okay."

"If I tell you to run, you run."

"Okay."

"If I tell you—"

"*Okay.*"

Fucking kids. He glanced at Aubrey. "Two hours."

"If we don't meet here, head for Kamiah," she said. "Wait two days. If none of us show, it means we aren't going to. Go back to the prison and start again." He wasn't surprised when the others nodded at her. She'd be good at this. Like Hank. If she didn't die horribly first.

No more words.

He turned toward the hatch. Got his feet situated on the ladder. Descended into the dark. His wrist hurt. His fingers hurt. He didn't pay any attention to them. He looked down between his legs and saw the dim light at the bottom of the tunnel. It meant electricity in some capacity.

The steps of the ladder were cold under his fingers. His breath was harsh and loud around his ears, bouncing off the walls. Movement, from up above, and he saw gray sky, bits of snow falling around him. Bad Dog whined quietly as Richie stepped onto the ladder.

Cavalo looked back down. Almost to the bottom. He stopped briefly and took out Lucas's knife. Held it tightly. The blade scraped against a metal rung. He thought he saw sparks.

The air was growing thicker the lower he got. Heavier. He thought he would choke on it. Drown in it. Let it take him under. He would—

His foot reached solid ground.

A long narrow hallway stretched out before him, low lights spread along the floor every ten feet. The air was rank and wet. Steam poured from a cracked pipe along the wall. He heard water dripping, a steady beat. Above him, a low metallic groan as if something had shifted. The hairs on the back of Cavalo's neck rose, and he wondered if he'd felt any place more haunted than this.

"Holy shit," Richie whispered as he reached the bottom of the ladder and peered over Cavalo's shoulder. "Maybe we should just go back up. And leave. And never come back."

Cavalo put the handle of the knife in his teeth and turned, helping Bad Dog out of the sling and onto the floor. His claws clicked along the metal grating that lined the walkway. *Not a puppy,* he grumbled.

"I know," Cavalo said, reaching down and rubbing his fingers along Bad Dog's muzzle. Bad Dog leaned into his hand and gave a quick dart of his tongue to show all was forgiven.

Bad Dog lowered his head to the floor and started sniffing, getting used to the smells. It was something Cavalo had taught him when he was little. Anytime they were at some place new, Bad Dog took time to align himself with his surroundings so he wouldn't be over-whelmed. He huffed to himself quietly. He growled once, but it faded away quickly as he walked up and down the walkway. He paused to piss on the wall before he circled back around.

And aside from Bad Dog and the sounds of the dam around them, there was nothing else. No voices. No footsteps. No movement. "Farther in," Cavalo muttered quietly.

Richie nodded and pulled out his own knife, smaller than the one

Lucas carried, but with a wicked sharp curve and serrated edge. He handled it well. "Follow your lead," he said.

Cavalo moved down the walkway. The lights were bright enough to keep them from bumping into the walls. They passed an electronic panel with four buttons that flickered lightly. Cavalo left them alone and gestured for Richie to do the same. Above, he saw a loudspeaker that crackled faintly twice before it fell silent. A sign hung on the wall, water-stained and corroded. A man and a woman were smiling, the man's face bubbling and torn, and it looked like he was screaming. *SAFETY FIRST!* the sign read, an echo from Before. *KNOW ALL LEVEL SIX PROTOCOLS!* There were other words, but they were lost.

Bad Dog came back, bumping his head against Cavalo's knee.

"You good?" he asked.

Ready, Bad Dog said. *Ready, ready, ready.*

"Anyone close?"

No.

Good and bad, then. "Bad guys come through here?"

Yes.

"Recent?"

A hesitation. *No.*

"Lucas?"

Bad Dog cocked his head. *Smells Different?*

Cavalo nodded.

No. He hasn't been here.

Cavalo sighed. It'd been a long shot, but he hadn't stopped himself from hoping. He pulled his pack to his front and dug through it, pulling out a rough shirt Lucas had worn before the attack on Cottonwood. He held it out to Bad Dog, who sniffed at it, ears twitching. He looked up at Cavalo with dreamy eyes. *Smells Different.*

"Find," Cavalo said, the command sharp.

Bad Dog's eyes cleared, his body becoming rigid and tense. His nostrils flared, and his tail twitched. He turned around and kept his nose close to the ground, walking farther down the causeway.

"You sure about this?" Richie whispered as they followed Bad Dog.

"No," Cavalo said in a low voice. Then, "About what?" This was stupid. They didn't need to talk. Not here. Not now.

"It's not... I mean...."

"Spit it out." *Why? Why? Why?*

"Bad Dog. You."

"What?"

"People... talk."

"That so."

"Yeah." He sounded scared. "You can talk to him? Like, for real?"

"Yes." The hallway ended up ahead at an intersection. Left or right.

"Doesn't that—"

"Richie."

"Yeah?"

"Shut the fuck up."

Richie did.

The bees laughed and asked him if this was how he made friends. Cavalo told them he didn't care about that. They called him a liar.

Bad Dog was trained well. Knew his corners. He stopped before he crossed into the next hallway, pausing a beat to listen and scent the air. Once he was sure it was clear, he stepped into the next causeway.

Cavalo pressed himself against the wall and peered around the corners. Left led down another long empty hallway. Right ended at a metal door, a large circular handle in the middle. Bad Dog seemed to dismiss the door, but Cavalo couldn't. The bees were bouncing in his head, and he needed to make sure.

He grabbed the handle and pulled. Nothing happened. Used both hands, wrist be damned. Wouldn't turn. Motioned for Richie to try. The door looked rusted, the small window glazed over so they couldn't see through. Richie grunted with the strain of it, but the handle wouldn't budge. "No go," he said, face red from exertion.

Cavalo turned away from the door. If they couldn't open it, chances were the Dead Rabbits hadn't been through there. Maybe at one point in the clusterfuck Cavalo called his life, he would have been curious as to what was on the other side of the door. Not anymore.

They turned back and headed the opposite direction, Bad Dog a few feet in front of Cavalo and Richie a few feet behind him. Cavalo swept his gaze back and forth, cataloging everything he could take in. The cracks on the wall. The flickering lights that snapped with the buzz of electricity. The dripping water. Richie's ragged breath. Bad Dog's panting. The metal grating squeaking beneath his feet. His own traitorous, thunderous heart. The bees started to take wing and he—

Bad Dog stopped. A low growl, hackles raised. He lowered his head toward the floor. Cavalo wasn't sure where the threat was coming from. The causeway seemed to stretch on forever. There might have been doors on either side farther ahead or a branch off in a different direction, but he couldn't tell.

He looked behind them, and Richie's eyes were wide with fear. The first hallway they'd come down was too far back. The walls on either side of them were smooth, the heavy pipes laid over them spaced inches apart.

There was nowhere to hide.

"Keep down," Cavalo hissed. "Keep quiet. Move."

He didn't turn to see if Richie followed him. He held the knife at the ready. Bad Dog moved hunched to the ground, lips curled back, teeth bared.

Cavalo could hear it now. A loud, metallic sound, as if something heavy was dragging along the floor. He ground his teeth together as it grated his ears.

He wondered, as he sometimes did, if it was the coyotes from all those years ago. When he was DEFCON 1. He knew it was impossible, but he almost expected a group of them to turn some corner farther ahead, blackened tumors hanging fat and low as they stalked toward them.

But then a voice came, farther down the hallway somewhere. Just a single voice, light and clear above the screech of metal, singing the same word over and over again: "Pretty, pretty, pretty, pretty."

And it was getting louder.

"Pretty, pretty, pretty."

A door, up ahead on the right. Different than the one behind them. This one was a regular metal door, a rusted circular knob on the right. An illegible sign in the middle below a frosted window. *It'll be locked*, the bees said. *It will be locked, and they will find you, and pretty, pretty, pretty.*

He could hear the footsteps now. There had to be another break in the causeway somewhere ahead because he couldn't see anyone yet.

If the door was locked, they'd be found. And for the first time in a very long time, Cavalo allowed himself to be human when he threw out a prayer to whoever would take it. *Let this work*, he thought wildly as he reached for the door.

The handle wouldn't turn.

No.

"Pretty, pretty, pretty!"

He twisted the doorknob savagely. Something snapped inside the mechanism, and it turned in his hand. He pushed on the door as slowly as he dared. It scraped briefly along the floor, and the hinges whined. To Cavalo, they were the loudest sounds he'd ever heard, but the *pretty, pretty* never faulted, and the footsteps never quickened. The air that hit them from the room was stifling and fetid.

No, Bad Dog said. *Bad smells. Bad smells.* He tried to back away, but Cavalo grabbed him by the scruff of his neck and pulled him forward. *Bad, bad, bad*, he muttered as his tail curled under his legs.

Cavalo followed him in. The room was dark. He could see the faint outline of chairs and desks pushed into a far corner. He ignored them, turning so Richie could make his way in. Once he was through,

Cavalo closed the door as quietly as he could. The door clicked into place.

Bad, bad, bad, the dog whispered.

"Pretty, pretty, pretty" came a muffled voice. The sound of dragging metal grew louder.

"Oh my God," Richie said in a choked voice. His breaths were quick and light, edging toward panic.

"Shut up," Cavalo hissed at him.

The smell in the room was overwhelming. High and sweet and cloying. He'd smelled something similar once, back in his wandering days. A library, the books rotted into clumps on the floor, covering bodies whose skin had stretched tight across their faces. Cavalo never learned how they died, but he never forgot that smell, the way it invaded his nose and made his eyes water. There were bodies in the room with them. Several of them. They'd probably died years before, their skin hardening, mouths open.

Cavalo stood, his back to the door, trying to see through the dirty glass of the window. Years of dust and skin particles created a film covering the glass, and he could barely make out the shapes of pipes along the other side of the causeway. He kept his hand tight on the doorknob, pressing his weight against the door, just in case.

He held his breath as he waited.

Cavalo saw him then. Just barely. A faint outline through the dirty window. A shadow, and nothing more. A staggering step. A pause. Muttering of *pretty, pretty, pretty,* and Cavalo wanted to scream because it was said with such *insanity,* and it sounded so *familiar,* because it sounded like *bees.* Like the Dead Rabbit was *roiling* with them.

He should have seen it coming. A room that hadn't been opened in so long. No ventilation. Dust and flecks of skin in the air. He should have known.

"Pretty, pret—"

Richie sneezed.

As far as sneezes went, it was a quiet one. Muffled. It didn't even echo across the room. Cavalo turned his head toward Richie. Richie's hands covered his mouth and nose, his eyes wide. He shook his head as a tear fell onto his cheek and came to rest against a finger on his right hand.

"Pretty?" the Dead Rabbit asked sharply outside the door.

Cavalo tightened his grip on the doorknob.

Fingers scraped on the outside of the door. A touch. A caress. Nails scraping against metal.

"Pretty," the Dead Rabbit muttered.

Cavalo turned his head back toward the window. His neck popped, and he was sure it was the loudest sound he'd ever heard. His cheek pressed against cool metal. The Dead Rabbit was trying to see through the glass, his face pressed against it, nose flattened and eyes wide. He opened his mouth wide and pressed his lips onto the glass. A tongue came out and left a wet strip. Fingers tapped an irregular beat as the hand lowered.

Cavalo felt the first moment the Dead Rabbit touched the doorknob. A tiny thrum in his good hand. It did not twist at first. The Dead Rabbit moved the doorknob up and down. Side to side. Bad Dog backed up slightly, coiling himself down, preparing to leap should the door open.

The Dead Rabbit licked the window again, his tongue almost black against the film. The faint outline of teeth, rotting and sharp. Saliva dripped down the glass, leaving dirty tracks. "Pretty," he breathed and rubbed his face against the window, smearing grime into swirls. He pressed his cheek against the glass, one eye wide and searching, trying to see into the room. Bad Dog and Richie were hidden in shadow.

The Dead Rabbit pulled away.

Cavalo didn't allow himself to breathe.

The doorknob rattled again.

And then it turned.

Cavalo hadn't realized his hand was sweating until he felt the doorknob start to slide under his fingers. It felt greasy. Warm. He took in a shuddering breath and brought up his other hand. Bad fingers. Bad wrist. He gritted against the pain as he held as tightly as he could. He turned and propped his shoulder up against the door, pressing it as hard as he could.

The pressure on the doorknob released.

"Pretty."

And then it turned again.

Noise, from below him.

He opened his eyes and looked down.

Richie. Pressing his hands against the door, steeling himself to hold it in place.

The doorknob jerked in his hands. Slipping until he squeezed tighter. His wrist screamed.

The Dead Rabbit let go of the doorknob. Slapped a hand against the glass. Dragged fingers along the saliva. "Pretty," he said... and then moved away. The metal dragging sound resumed.

Cavalo waited a beat. Two. Looked down at Richie. Motioned him up. They traded places without a word. Cavalo pushed Bad Dog back. Richie kept a hand on the doorknob. Cavalo raised his good hand carrying the knife.

Held up three fingers. Paused.

Richie shook his head frantically.

Cavalo glared at him.

Three.

Richie nodded and licked his lips.

Two.

The sick-sweet smell of the room filled Cavalo as he took a deep breath.

One.

Richie opened the door in one smooth motion.

Cavalo didn't hesitate. He never really had before in his life. Not when he was under the bees, submerged into the cold. He knew he was a killer. A murderer. He knew he was not a good person. He knew what waited for him when he finally died, if he could believe in something such as burning in eternal fire. He killed people. Some of them might not have deserved it. He was a monster. But he never hesitated. Not when it counted. Not when he slipped below the surface.

The door opened. Cavalo moved. Three steps and he was out in the hallway. Looked right. Nothing. Left. Dead Rabbit walking down the causeway, muttering prettily. Dragging a heavy metal pipe behind him, chipped and bloodstained.

He wanted to *kill*, the bees were telling him to *kill*, and it would be easy. Kick to the back of the knees. Knife to the back of the neck. Spine severed. Quiet. Easy.

But even in the bees and underneath the cold, Cavalo knew he *needed* this Dead Rabbit. Dworshak was *big*, and they'd come into this place with only the faint glimmer of a plan (and really, if Cavalo had let himself dwell on it for too long, he would have realized there was no real plan at all). This Dead Rabbit might know where Lucas was. He might be able to lead them directly to him. Cavalo needed him.

So even as the hand holding the knife twitched, wanting death, revenge, and chaos, instead he smashed the handle on the back of the Dead Rabbit's head. The Dead Rabbit stopped with his *pretty, pretty, pretty* and grunted, falling to his knees. The pipe fell to the floor. The Dead Rabbit swayed on his knees. Cavalo grabbed him underneath his arms and pulled him back toward the doorway. The Dead Rabbit was rank and sweaty. His feet dragged along the floor, his arms heavy at his sides.

"Get the pipe," Cavalo snarled as he pulled the Dead Rabbit through the door. Richie scrambled through, tripping over the Dead Rabbit's legs. He cursed as he skinned his hands on the floor. Then he was up and out. Cavalo propped the Dead Rabbit up against the wall, pushing him upright. He heard Richie drag the pipe back in. "Shut the door," he said as the Dead Rabbit lolled his head to the side, grimacing.

Richie did, and they fell into darkness.

"Light," Cavalo snapped.

Richie fumbled with his pack and pulled out a small electronic lantern, one of the few that had been left in the prison. Blue light spilled out into the room, and Richie moaned quietly.

Because Cavalo had been right about the reason the room smelled the way it did. Shadows crawled around the room, but enough light caught the five bodies in the corner, all huddled together, arms around each other. Two adults on the outside, curled in. Three children in the middle, flat on their backs. An old gun on the ground. Dark smudges splattered on the wall. The floor. Pieces of their ending flitted across Cavalo's brain, but he was still drowning in the cold, and the bees pushed it away.

The Dead Rabbit groaned.

He knelt next to the Dead Rabbit, who watched him with wide, wet eyes. "Do you know who I am?" he asked quietly. Their faces were so close Cavalo could smell his stinking breath.

"Pretty?" the Dead Rabbit asked in a whisper. "Man. Man. *Bad* man." He clicked his teeth together rapidly, as if he were trying to bite.

"That's right. I *am* a bad man. And I will do bad things to you unless you tell me what I want."

"Pretty," the Dead Rabbit said. He was crying, fat oily tears that streaked his dirty cheeks. But even through the tears, he was smiling. His mouth was rotting. Missing teeth. Gums blackened. Radiation poisoning, though not too far along.

"Lucas," Cavalo said. "Where is Lucas?"

The Dead Rabbit laughed and sobbed and cocked his head. "Lu... cas?" He clicked his teeth together. "Patrick. Said. *Bad* man."

"Anyone out there?" Cavalo asked Richie.

"No. I don't think so." He sounded as if he skirted along the edges of panic.

Cavalo set his pack on the ground and reached inside, grabbing a corner of a threadbare blanket. He cut a long strip and balled it up. "Where's Lucas?" he asked again.

"Pretty!" the Dead Rabbit cried, mouth stretched wide.

Cavalo shoved the cloth into the Dead Rabbit's mouth as far back as it could go. The Dead Rabbit choked and tried to grab Cavalo's legs. Cavalo dropped down, picking up the heavy pipe from the floor. Before the Dead Rabbit could pull the gag from his mouth, he brought down the pipe on the Dead Rabbit's left knee. The bone cracked wetly. The Dead Rabbit's eyes bulged, and he screamed into the gag, the sound muffled and quiet.

"Where is Lucas?" Cavalo asked again. He lifted his foot and stepped on the broken knee, grinding the bones together. The Dead Rabbit jerked, hands skittering at his sides.

He stepped off and pulled the gag from the Dead Rabbit's mouth.

"Bad man," the Dead Rabbit said weakly, blood draining from his face.

"I'll do it again," Cavalo said. "Your other knee. Your arms. Your face. Your fingers. I will break every bone in your body and make sure you're awake while I do it. Tell me where he is."

Cavalo was cold. He was calculating. He was willing to go as far has he needed to in order to get what he wanted. That had never been a problem before.

And Cavalo had never been one to underestimate an enemy. He thought he knew how to crack the blubbering man below him, how to break him until he told Cavalo everything he needed to hear.

So what happened next took Cavalo by surprise. The Dead Rabbit reached out toward him with shaking hands. "Please, pretty," he cried. Cavalo took a step back. The man fell over onto his stomach and tried to crawl. Cavalo raised the pipe again.

The Dead Rabbit pushed himself up on his hands.

He smiled and stuck out his tongue. It was dark and looked rough. He gripped it in his teeth. And then the Dead Rabbit smashed his chin onto the cement floor as hard as he could. Cavalo heard his jaw snap, his teeth grinding together. His tongue fell out of his mouth in a gush of blood. The noise the severed muscle made when it landed on the floor caused Cavalo's gorge to rise.

"Jesus *Christ!*" Richie moaned, backing away as far as he could. Bad Dog growled loudly as the Dead Rabbit rolled over onto his back, blood spilling from his mouth as he cried and laughed and gurgled.

The man had bitten off his own tongue rather than tell Cavalo anything. Cavalo had underestimated him. And the rest. He would not do that again. He crouched down next to the Dead Rabbit, whose face was a bloody red.

"*Gah!*" the Dead Rabbit cried at him.

Cavalo said nothing as he brought the knife down into the Dead Rabbit's right eye, pushing it to the hilt. The Dead Rabbit twitched and then stilled. Cavalo pulled the knife out, the Dead Rabbit's head falling back against the floor with a wet thunk. He wiped the blade off on the Dead Rabbit's coat. He stood and reached for the door. "Let's go," he said. He didn't look back.

deus ex machina

CAVALO DIDN'T WANT to admit it, but they were lost.

He thought maybe an hour had passed since they'd entered the interior of the dam. The causeways split off into different directions, and Cavalo couldn't tell where they were anymore. He'd always had a keen sense of direction, but being hidden away under a mountain of concrete and steel had fucked with that, and he couldn't be sure they were any closer to Lucas than when they started.

If he's even here at all, the bees whispered.

Which, okay. Fair point. But he couldn't think of that. Couldn't think about how big the world truly was. How easy it was to get lost in it. Patrick could have taken him anywhere. Could have taken him back to wherever the Dead Rabbits called home. Could have taken him deep into the forest. Or to the ocean. Or the snows of the north. The deserts of the south. He could be miles away in any direction, and Cavalo would never know.

So he didn't think about that. He told himself Lucas was here. That Lucas was close. He told himself he could feel Lucas nearby. He almost believed it.

"Fuck," he growled as they turned a corner that led down another long hallway. There were a few doors ahead on either side. They'd already come across a few rooms. Some were locked. Others blocked from the inside. A few doors had opened, revealing offices. Silent machines. One had a man hanging from a metal pipe, a wire wrapped around his desiccated neck. Enough light had spilled into the room to show large letters etched into the far wall: *I'M SO SORRY MARIE.* He had closed that door rather quickly.

Too many smells, Bad Dog said miserably. *All over. Everywhere. Bad guys and Smells Different. Smells Different and bad guys. Blood and death and fire and ashes.*

"He's here?"

Yes. He was.

That didn't mean shit now. Cavalo believed, he really did, but the seed of doubt was growing, and he could do nothing to stop it.

"We're running out of time," he said, rubbing a hand over his face.

"We'll find him," Richie said quietly.

"We don't even know where the fuck *we* are," Cavalo snapped. "It's not as if—"

"Hi, Daddy!"

Cavalo closed his eyes.

He broke through the cold. Breached the surface. The bees crawled along his skin.

Not there, he thought. *Not there.*

Bad Dog growled.

"Daddy!"

Cavalo opened his eyes. Jamie stood down at the end of the corridor as the lights flickered around them. He held Mr. Fluff in one hand, the stuffed rabbit dragging on the metal grating of the floor. He raised his other hand and wiggled his fingers at Cavalo. "Hi," he said with a large smile. "Hi, hi, hi."

"Not real," Cavalo muttered.

"Cavalo?" Richie asked from behind him.

Cavalo ignored him because Jamie was calling to him, laughing and saying *Daddy, Daddy, Daddy,* and he felt the oily sweat on the back of his neck. The way his hands clenched. The whistling breath from his constricted throat because Bad Dog was *looking* at Jamie. He was looking at Jamie and *growling,* like he could see him, like he was *real.*

Jamie waved at him again as Cavalo asked Bad Dog, "What do you see?"

I... don't know. Smells. Like... fire. Smoke. Lightning. I can't see... it. Bad Dog cocked his head, confused. *MasterBossLord, what is it?*

"I don't know," Cavalo croaked.

"Silly puppy," Jamie said with a grin. "Silly Daddy. Hi. Daddy, guess what?"

Don't. Don't. Don't.

He did it anyway. "What?" he asked.

"I can find him."

"Who?"

Jamie rolled his eyes, and it was so *familiar,* so achingly and ridiculously *like* him that Cavalo thought for a brief, shining moment he was *real.*

"The Not-Monster," Jamie said. "The Not-Cannibal. Smells Different."

"Lucas?" Cavalo whispered.

Jamie nodded. "Do you remember? What I said?"

He's not who you think he is.

"He's... not?"

"Not *him.*" Jamie sighed as if his father was the most frustrating man in the world. And he very well could be, for all Cavalo knew. He never had the chance to ask his son otherwise.

"Cavalo," Richie said, sounding nervous. "I don't—"

"It's not *him,*" Jamie said again. "It was never *him.* Silly Daddy. Silly James Cavalo. Mr. Fluff says you're not *listening.*"

"I always listened to Mr. Fluff," Cavalo croaked as Bad Dog whined. And he *had* because Jamie had always told him *stories* with Mr. Fluff and—

Jamie grinned again. "Do you? Did you listen to him when you threw him in the river? He floated away, Daddy. Like a paper boat. But I found him."

"Oh my God," Richie moaned from somewhere.

"I can see that," Cavalo said, taking a step toward his son. "Why are you both here?" Because they *were*, they *were* here and *nothing* could convince Cavalo otherwise. Not anymore.

Jamie cocked his head. "I thought you knew. I thought you knew all this time. We're here because of this moment. We're the god from the machine, Daddy. Didn't you know?"

"No. No, Jamie. I didn't." He made an aborted attempt to reach out for his son, but Jamie took a step back, and Cavalo felt the stingers of the bees stabbing behind his eyeballs, crawling along his brain. Their legs and silvery wings brushed against gray matter.

"Daddy?"

"Yes," Cavalo said, hands trembling.

"Catch me!"

And he took off quicker than Cavalo had ever seen him move in life.

Cavalo didn't hesitate. Richie squawked in surprise when Cavalo ran down the causeway, feet clanging against the metal grating that lined the floor. Bad Dog let out a solid *woof* and followed without question.

Cavalo turned left and caught a flash of Mr. Fluff's ears, the skin of his son's ankle. He didn't stop to think if the bees had finally consumed him, if all the rubber bands had finally broken. He didn't have time for such frivolous nonsense. His son was running deep inside Dworshak and they were lost and the minutes were wasting away. Lucas was either here or anywhere. They would either live or die. He was tired. He was so very tired.

A right turn. Another right. Through a doorway already open, and the bees screamed at him to slow, to quiet, to *shut the fuck up* because someone would *hear* him, someone would find him and eat his toes and eyes and—

The clank of Bad Dog's toenails rattled behind him.

The quick, sobbing breath from Richie's throat.

Cavalo ran.

He only caught vague glimpses of his son, but others were with him too. He saw his father on a decaying poster embedded on the wall, wearing a hardhat, an animated talking balloon coming out of his mouth asking if Cavalo knew about *SAFETY FIRST* and *KEEPING WALKWAYS CLEAR* and *DRINKING WAS THE ONLY THING THAT NUMBED THE PAIN OF LIVING*. His father winked at him from another poster, neck crooked at an odd angle, bones protruding through his throat because he had *died* when he'd fallen from a horse, he'd *died when—*

Warren stood inside a closed office door that Cavalo ran by, only the outline of his shadow visible, but Cavalo *knew* it was him, *knew* that if he'd only seen him first, so many things might have been different, so many things might have changed, and he could have *saved* him, he could have *helped him to—*

Snarling coyotes scratched down the hallway to the right as he turned to follow Jamie to the left, and he heard the door there grate open, and the woman inside shrieked at them to come, to finish this, that she wanted to die that she wanted it all to be over, and when they descended on her, when they tore into her flesh, she screamed again, but it was in such *relief,* and she *laughed—*

David begged Cavalo not to shoot him as he crawled underneath the metal grating below Cavalo's feet, begged him not to pull the trigger because he hadn't *stolen* anything, he hadn't *taken* anything from Cavalo, he would never do that, he would never do that because they were *friends,* they were friends, and he wanted it to be more because he *loved* Cavalo, he *loved him and he didn't want to die—*

"Catch me, Daddy!"

There was a stitch in his side. His knees hurt, but that was because he was getting older and it was damp here inside this hell-hole. Water trickled down around him, the walls groaned and shifted.

Steam poured from a cracked pipe. He was old, this place was old, it was a tomb, and he would be *buried here*—

He saw others, faceless strangers whose blood was on his hands. They reached for him, they shied away from him, they screamed and cursed his name, offered their forgiveness and thanks, told him he would die in this place, under hundreds of tons of steel and metal built by men from Before, when all people worried about was working that nine-to-five, paycheck to paycheck, living for the weekend to kick off their motherfucking shoes and *relax.*

"Cavalo," Riche gasped from somewhere behind him. "*Please.*"

MasterBossLord, Bad Dog called sharply, and did he? Did he *really* call *anything*? Because for a moment, Cavalo thought that maybe Bad Dog didn't speak at all. That Lucas couldn't speak at all. That it was all in his head and—

"Mutts can't talk," his father told him as he took another swig from an ancient flask that said *OAKLAND RAIDERS*. "You're fucking crazy, my boy, because mutts can't talk, Lucas can't fucking talk, and you *lost* something, Charlie, you fucking *lost* your goddamn *mind*—"

He turned a corner, and there stood a tree in the middle of the causeway, in the middle of a dam, in the middle of a time long after Before.

He stopped.

Took a shuddering breath.

The tree-wife said, "Do you know what it felt like, Cavalo? To die? It hurt. Not the bullet. Not the way it shattered my face. No. It was the betrayal. The way you betrayed me. The way you *killed me*."

And she leaned for him, her branches curling around him, and he opened his mouth to *scream*—

But there was nothing there.

He opened his eyes.

The walkway was empty.

The tree-wife was gone.

Jamie and Mr. Fluff were gone.

Everyone else was gone.

He didn't know where they were.

But there was *something*—

Bad Dog reached him first. He rubbed up against Cavalo's legs. *You can't do that*, he scolded. *You can't just do that, MasterBossLord. What if I lost you? What if I couldn't find you? I would be sad, and Tin Man would be sad, and he would say it was Bad Dog's fault. You can't do that to me, you can't*—

There was *something*—

"Cavalo," Richie said, panting behind him. He bent over, hands on his knees, struggling to catch his breath. Sweat dripped from his nose onto the floor. "What the *hell* is going on? Are you out of your fucking—"

The bees laughed at the foolish boy. *Stupid man*, they said. *Stupid child. Of course he's out of his fucking mind. Of course he's fucking*—

Voices, then. From down the hallway.

281

Muffled. Dark.

Richie's eyes went wide.

Bad Dog's ears flattened on the back of his head, tail rigid, hackles rising.

It's real this time, Cavalo thought.

Is it? the bees asked. *Are you sure?*

Well, no. He wasn't sure. He wasn't sure about anything anymore.

He pulled Lucas's knife from its scabbard.

He thought he heard the faint whisper of his son's voice, saying the god from the machine had led him here. That it was up to him to do the rest.

"Keep low," Cavalo muttered. "Keep quiet. Don't do shit until I say. Turn the light off."

Richie hesitated, eyes wary.

"*Richie.*"

He nodded, a bead of sweat trickling down his forehead. He switched off the lantern and they fell into semidarkness.

Cavalo crouched down near Bad Dog's head. "Is it him?" he whispered.

Blood, Bad Dog said. *Blood. Smells Different. Blood. Blood. Blood.*

Cavalo's grip around the knife tightened.

They needed to move. They were running out of time.

The voices down the corridor carried, but Cavalo couldn't yet make out the words. There was a grating laugh, rough and wet. He saw no movement. No shadows. The dam creaked around them. The wall on the right was wet. The air spoke of must and mold. Cavalo could taste it on his tongue.

"Back," he said.

Bad Dog glared up at him as he stood but followed the command and moved behind Cavalo.

Cavalo reached out and felt along the wall, splinted wrist twinging sharply. His footsteps were light and slow. There were three distinct voices now, all male. The words were still inaudible, but they began to take shape. He picked out *here* and *watch* and a string of *we can't begin to.*

They came to a metal stairway. The left went up, the handrail hanging off the wall. The right went down, the dark seemingly darker. The corridor continued on straight ahead. Farther down, someone had painted an arrow on the wall, crude and green. Underneath, a childlike scrawl: *THIS WAY TO THE LIGHT*.

He looked down the stairs.

Mr. Fluff lay at the bottom, hidden partially by shadows that flickered along his prone body.

The voices floated up the stairs.

They said:

"How much longer we gotta stay down here?"

"Shut the fuck up, Aggie. All you've done is bitch and moan."

"I don't like it here. I don't like it here. Right? It's not—"

"I swear to God if you don't shut the fuck up, I'll kill you myself."

"Ah. Ha. Ha. Ha. Hahahahaaaaa."

"Jesus Christ. Of course I get sent with the fucking nutjobs."

"I'm not a nutjob! Not like Zag. All he does is sit there, rocking and laughing and—"

"You're just as bad. You're just as bad as him. Both of you *shut the fuck up.*"

"Ha! Ha! Haaaaaaa!"

"And *you.* What the fuck are *you* looking at?"

"He's smiling, Dory! Why is he *smiling?*"

"You smiling at me, boy? You fucking *smiling* at me? He ain't here, you know. Daddy. He ain't here, and we could do anything we want to you."

Silence.

Then, "It doesn't have to be your mouth, boy. You have other holes."

"We could *do* things," Aggie said, voice rising. "We could. He couldn't tell. I've never—never *been* with. Anything. Any*one.*"

"Ha ha ha ha aaaaahhhhhhh."

"He'd like it too," the one called Dory said, and Cavalo decided he would die first. If this is what he thought it was, if this was where the ghost from the machine had led them, then Dory would die first. He needed to be *sure*. His eyes were adjusting to the dark, and he needed to be *sure*. "Use blood or spit. Break him in. He'd like it. He'd like it. Like a little girl. Tight and warm."

"I get a turn after you," Aggie said. "I want to go. I need. This. They won't. Back at home. They won't let me *touch*."

"That's because your face is a rotting mess," Dory said. "You're fucking disgusting."

"HA HA HA HA!"

"Shut the fuck up, Zag!"

"*HA HA HA HA HA—*"

"Aggie, don't get so fucking close to the goddamn mute. Don't get so—"

But that was all Cavalo needed. He moved on the word *mute*. It was foolish, he knew. Desperately so. Just because there were three voices didn't mean there weren't more. Didn't mean there wasn't an entire goddamn *army* of Dead Rabbits underneath this dam, down those stairs and waiting in the dark.

But it didn't matter. He was *here*; Cavalo had heard the word *mute* and sank below the surface, down into the cold place underneath the waters where the bees swarmed around him, crawling out of his mouth and ears and nose, whispering their sweet assurances to him. *We love you*, they said. *We need you*, they said.

Kill them, they said. *Kill them all.*

He didn't jump the stairs. He couldn't take the risk of landing wrong and breaking his ankle. He was already down a hand and would be cutting it close as it was. He took each stair one step at a time, moving quickly and quietly, knowing Bad Dog was at his heels, not giving a shit about what Richie did if he was being honest with himself. As long as he stayed out of Cavalo's way, he could dance a jig or cower in a corner for all the fucks Cavalo gave.

He was a killer now. Again. He moved with purpose.

He reached the bottom of the stairs and followed the voices, remembering Dory because *Dory* would go first, *Dory* would have that honor.

Another corridor stretched before him. He couldn't see how far it went. It didn't matter, though. There was low light spilling through an open doorway. The door itself opened out into the corridor, heavy and metal. There was a circular window at the top of the door, the glass broken out.

Cavalo felt Bad Dog on his heels and thought, *If there's three, I'll get two, and you get the other*, and Bad Dog said, *Okay, I'll go left, and you go right, and no one will touch Smells Different*. He ignored the cold chill that ran through him when he realized he hadn't spoken aloud and Bad Dog had responded anyway. He could worry about that later, if they survived this.

Now, Bad Dog had his orders, Richie was dancing his fucking jig, and Cavalo held Lucas's knife in his hands, and the man named Zag was hyperventilating, his *HA HA HA* growing reedy and thin. Cavalo reached the door, sidestepped it, filled the entry.

Everything was cold and sharp.

The man named Zag, balding and missing teeth in blackened gums, had a line of spit hanging from his mouth as he bent over, laughing toward the floor, face flushed red, eyes bulging. One stuck out more than the other, yellowed and obscene, as if it was being pushed out from inside the socket, and he *laughed*.

The other two stood on the other side of the room, staring at the wall in front of them. One of them breathed heavily, chest rising up and down, shoulders shaking. Aggie. The other reached to unfasten his pants. Dory.

Lucas. Lucas was on that wall. Lucas, with his arms chained above his head, face beat to hell, left eye swollen shut, blood dribbling from his lips. He snarled silently at Dory and Aggie, his teeth stained with blood, that clever monster, that clever cannibal. He pulled on the chains hard, harder, and Cavalo thought maybe his arms would rip from their sockets. He was shirtless, the tattoos on full display, but not a single mark on his torso. Not a single bruise or cut on his arms. They'd probably been ordered to leave the tattoos unmarked. Patrick couldn't use them if they were blemished. He couldn't—

There was a fourth man, a Dead Rabbit built like a fucking brick shithouse. He saw Cavalo and Bad Dog first, from his perch in the far corner of the room, hidden in shadows.

He said, "Hey. Hey. Hey."

Zag was laughing so hard he was choking.

Dory and Aggie looked over at the man in the corner, who pushed himself up from the wall.

Bad Dog went for the laughing man. Zag.

The large man took another step said, "*Hey.*"

Cavalo said, "Hey," and kept his promise, throwing the knife end over end. The blade buried itself in Dory's throat. Dory gagged, eyes wide, his hands coming up scrabble along the hilt, blood spraying out around his fingers.

He said, "Guh," as Cavalo moved snake-quick, darting around the lumbering giant. The man reached for him, hands blistered and leaking like a nightmare.

Cavalo heard Zag stop laughing and start screaming as Bad Dog snarled, but Cavalo paid them no mind. The large man would follow him, and Cavalo had work to do.

The giant said, "*Hey,*" again, as if that were the only word he knew, and Cavalo almost laughed as he pulled the knife from Dory's throat, slicing the would-be rapist's fingers. Dory looked shocked. Surprised, even, and Cavalo remembered what Hank had said about surprises. What Deke had thought about surprises.

He stabbed Dory in the heart. Up through the ribs. It took only seconds.

Aggie stood. Shocked. Not quite comprehending. Part of him probably thought he was still about to fuck Lucas. To fuck him because he'd never fucked anything or anyone before. He was young. Thin. His eyes were sunken in his skull. Lesions along his arms. His neck. His tongue darted out quick, wetting his lips. He looked as if he were trying to smile, but it got stuck partway through a grimace.

Cavalo saw Lucas over his shoulder. Lucas, whose eyes were narrowed and filled with rage. Lucas, who—

Arms wrapped around him.

Pulled him tightly toward a muscular chest.

The stink of fetid rot surrounded him, and the large man whispered in his ear, "*Hey.*"

Aggie took a step toward them as the knife clattered to the floor.

"I *know* you," Aggie said, sounding awed.

Cavalo kicked his feet up off the dirty floor and pushed back. He brought his legs up and pushed *out*, knocking Aggie in the chest.

The large man grunted and took a faltering step back as Aggie stumbled directly into Lucas, who had pulled himself up using the chains until he could wrap his legs around Aggie's neck. Aggie began to kick and scratch, letting out a garbled scream that cut off when Lucas squeezed his legs together tightly.

Cavalo struggled against the giant. His breath was crushed from his chest as the arms tightened further. He felt his ribs creak dangerously, and the—

The giant cried out in his ear, brassy and bright. His grip loosened, but before Cavalo could break out of his hold, the giant hurled him toward the far wall. What little breath Cavalo had managed was knocked from his body as he landed on the floor. He raised his head and saw Bad Dog, teeth buried in the giant's calf, snarling and snapping his head back and forth. The giant grunted and reached down, punching Bad Dog in his side.

Bad Dog whined pitifully, jaw slackening, but he didn't let go.

The knife was on the floor, feet away.

Cavalo pushed himself up, ignoring the flare in his wrist.

He gritted his teeth as the giant raised his fist and brought it down onto Bad Dog again.

Bad Dog didn't let go.

Cavalo took a breath. His vision was spotty. It hurt to breathe.

Another fist to the dog.

Cavalo saw red.

He lunged toward the knife, but Aggie's foot knocked into it as he fought Lucas. The knife skittered along the floor and bumped into the giant's boot.

The giant grinned. He bent over. Picked up the knife.

Brought it up and over his head. Bad Dog shuddered and refused to let go.

Cavalo said, "No. Please. *No.*"

A flat *crack* burst in the room. A flash of light. The smell of acrid burning.

The giant said, "Hey," as blood poured from the bullet exit wound in the middle of his forehead. "Hey. Hey, *don't.*"

He fell to his knees. Then onto his face. Then he died.

Richie stood, arm still outstretched, a thin curl of smoke twisting around the barrel of his handgun. He was pale. His hand shook.

Cavalo said, "Richie. You. I. Thank you."

Richie nodded and swallowed thickly. He dropped his arm. The gun twitched at his side.

There was dry rattling off to his right. Cavalo pulled himself up and looked over.

Aggie's hand stretched toward Cavalo. His eyes bulged from his head. His face was flushed with blood. He begged silently. Begged Cavalo to help him. To save him.

They'd been here before, this situation.

Wilkinson. Back in Cottonwood.

It's all happened before, Cavalo thought. *And it will all happen again.*

Lucas's mouth was twisted in a silent snarl as the muscles in his legs tensed. He jerked his knee to the left sharply, right below Aggie's ear. Aggie's head snapped to the side at an odd angle. There was a wet crack. Aggie's feet kicked out on the ground. Then he stopped, hands falling to his sides.

Lucas released him and he slumped to the floor, eyes wide and unseeing. Lucas lowered himself back to the ground, chains rattling above him. He took a breath. Let it out slowly. Grinned at Cavalo with his red teeth. With his beaten face. And for a moment, Cavalo forgot that it was done, that this first fight was over, and in the cold, underneath the surface miles above his head, he thought, *knee to groin, dislocate right shoulder, gouge eyes, break neck*, and he had to *force* himself up. He had to *force* the cold away, to breach the surface because he was *this close*.

Lucas knew. He always knew. And his bloody smile never wavered.

If anything, it grew.

The bees laughed at the both of them.

Cavalo came back into himself. There was regret waiting for him, as it always did when bodies piled up around him. But he pushed it away, knowing it would still be there if they survived this day.

He opened his mouth to ask where the keys to the manacles were. He opened his mouth to tell them they needed to move quickly. Instead, he said, "I would do that again. I would kill all of them. For you. They hurt you, and I would kill them again and again."

The bloody smile wavered. Trembled. And for the briefest of moments, the clever monster was gone, and in its place stood a young man, barely in his twenties, hurt and afraid, bloody and bruised, and didn't Cavalo's heart just *ache* then? Didn't it just *burn* at the sight of him?

It did. Because Lucas was little more than a child in a dark world.

It could have been different. For him. If he'd been born to anyone else. It could have been different.

Cavalo then thought of Deke and wondered if it even mattered at all.

But the illusion was gone. Because Lucas was *not* innocent. He was *not* a child.

Cavalo stepped over the body on the floor and kissed Lucas. Lips met and teeth clashed, and Cavalo tasted blood, his or Lucas's, he didn't know. It didn't matter. They were the same, now.

He pulled away but only just. He pressed his forehead against Lucas's and breathed him in. He stank of sweat and gore, but Cavalo could feel the beat of his pulse as his thumb brushed over the Dead Rabbit's neck.

Lucas said, *You came for me.*

"Yes."

You shouldn't have.

"I know."

But you did anyway.

"Yes."

Stupid man, Lucas said. *You stupid, stupid man.*

Cavalo kissed him again. Then stepped away.

"Keys," he said gruffly. "Who has them."

Lucas glanced down at the floor. At Dory.

"Watch the door," Cavalo said to Richie.

Richie nodded, glancing between Lucas and Cavalo with something that resembled shock. Cavalo stuttered only once in his step when he realized he'd kissed Lucas in front of Richie. Richie, who didn't know about them. Richie, who belonged to Cottonwood. Who didn't know about them.

There was no disgust there. On Richie. Not yet.

"You okay?" Cavalo asked as he crouched over Dory. He reached out and ran a hand over Bad Dog's head, tugging gently on his ears.

Bad Dog whined and took a careful step toward Cavalo. *Hurts,* Bad Dog said.

"Bad?"

Maybe. Breathing hurts. I'll live. Smells Different okay? His blood. I can smell his blood on the bad guys.

"He's okay," Cavalo said. "Just banged up. Like you. Like me."

We're not very good at rescuing, Bad Dog said. He walked gingerly over to Lucas and bumped his head into Lucas's knee.

Cavalo almost smiled. He dug through Dory's pockets, wishing the man was alive so he could kill him again. He hadn't had time to enjoy it.

His fingers brushed cold metal, and he pulled the keys from Dory. There were three. One didn't look like a normal key. It was flat and rectangular, the edges chipped and worn. He hoped it would be one of the other two. If the key wasn't here, he didn't know what they'd do.

Of course you do, the bees said. *You'd pick up his knife and stab him in the heart. Then, you'd cut off the skin from his stomach and chest and leave the body behind. The blueprints would be destroyed, and everything would go back to the way it used to be.*

He took the knife from the dead giant's hands.

Lucas watched him, never fooled.

The first key didn't fit. Wasn't even close.

Cavalo fumbled with the second.

He thought maybe he would just die here too. Tell Richie to go. To take Bad Dog and just go. He thought it fitting that he could die in this haunted and fucked-up place.

He wondered what it meant that he was so quick to die. So easy to make that decision. It probably meant nothing good.

The key fit, though. Of course it did.

You could still kill him, the bees insisted, because that's what they did.

Instead, he moved to the second manacle.

The key didn't fit.

That was okay, he told himself.

He could do this.

He would just cut off Lucas's arm. It would be okay. It would all be okay.

The manacles were mismatched.

Before he could use the knife, he tried the first key again.

The manacle unlocked.

He felt a sort of relief.

Lucas grimaced as he dropped his arms, wincing and rolling his shoulders. Rubbing his wrists. Cavalo shrugged off his heavy overcoat, draping it on Lucas's shoulders, covering bare skin. It was cold outside. He needed to keep Lucas warm.

Lucas scowled at him. *I'm fine,* he said.

"I know," Cavalo said. "We have to leave."

Lucas looked around the room. Cocked his head, listening. The room around them creaked and groaned. *Where are we?*

"You didn't see when they brought you here?"

He shook his head, touching the side of his head where the skin was split and bruised. *Knocked me out.*

"Who?" Cavalo asked, anger rising.

Lucas said, *SIRS.* He looked away.

And Cavalo was angry but for different reasons. "Dworshak," he said. "We're underneath Dworshak. And I guess that means you don't know how to get out of here."

Lucas's good eye widened. *No,* he said. *I didn't know. I've never been here.*

Richie took a step back into the room. "I remember the way back out," he said. "To the hatch."

Cavalo eyed him. "Do you?"

He winced and rubbed the back of his neck. "I think so."

"Fuck."

"Yeah. Maybe."

Cavalo wanted to be angry, but then he remembered he'd run after his dead son through the tunnels underneath Dworshak. He thought maybe he had no place to be angry. At least not at Richie.

"I need you to be sure," he said as Lucas took his knife back.

Richie nodded. "I can be. I promise. I've got this."

His lack of confidence wasn't what Cavalo wanted to hear, but they didn't have much choice. "How much time do we have?"

"Thirty minutes. A little less."

They'd be cutting it close. "You good to go?" he asked Bad Dog.

Bad Dog huffed. *Fine. Fine. I'm fine. Move. Let's go. I don't like this place, and I want to find Tin Man and go home. You owe me so much jerky.*

"I know," Cavalo said. "Home." He liked the sound of that. He didn't think it was a possibility, but he liked the sound. He'd never thought of the prison as home before. Not really. And now that he was so far removed from it, he realized it was nothing *but* their home.

"We move quickly," he said, taking Richie's machete from him and leaving him with the handgun. The less noise the better. "We move quietly. Follow my lead."

Lucas grinned, splitting his lip. Blood dribbled onto his chin.

He moved toward the door. The others followed behind him.

They were up the stairs and back into the main corridor. The stairs in front of them went up. The arrow pointed farther down the hall to the right. The left was where they'd come from.

They went left. Cavalo, Richie, Lucas, and Bad Dog in the rear. Cavalo knew the first turn up ahead. He remembered that much at least. His son had turned that last corner and disappeared, leaving only Mr. Fluff to rest at the bottom of the stairs. But Mr. Fluff had been gone when they'd come out of the room, hadn't he? He'd been gone because someone had taken him. Or he'd never been there at all.

Cavalo didn't know which was worse.

He started to turn the corner, looking back over his shoulder. "Richie, you'll have to—"

He bumped into a Dead Rabbit.

The Dead Rabbit stumbled back.

Cavalo stopped. Richie came up behind him.

Richie said, "Oh no. Please no."

There were at least ten of them. All males. All in various stages of decay. Tumors and lesions. Open wounds that leaked pus and blood and from one man, a black, viscous liquid pulsed from his neck with every breath he took.

It happened quickly because that was the only way Cavalo knew how to react.

The Dead Rabbits looked shocked.

Lucas took in a sharp breath.

Bad Dog started to growl.

293

Cavalo moved. The Dead Rabbit in front of him, the one he'd bumped into, was recovering from his stumble. His coat was open. He wore a belt around his waist, resting against his hips, and Cavalo knew what those things attached to the belt were. He *knew* because once upon a time, before his world had ended, his son had held one such thing in his hands, and Cavalo had thought he could save him. Had thought he could protect him from the monsters.

The Dead Rabbit had a grenade belt. Completely full.

Cavalo brought up the machete, hooking the tip into the belt. He jerked it upward, and the Dead Rabbit gasped as the blade punched through the leather and into his stomach. The belt started to slide, and the Dead Rabbits in the corridor began to snarl, and it'd only been seconds, mere *seconds* since he'd rounded that corner, and they had *one* shot at this, *one* fucking chance.

The Dead Rabbit screamed as blood spilled from his stomach.

The grenade belt began to slide from his waist.

Cavalo caught the belt on the blade, turning to roar over his shoulder, "*Go!*"

The Dead Rabbits began to surge.

The gut-punched Dead Rabbit took a step forward.

Richie, Lucas, and Bad Dog turned to run.

Cavalo flipped the blade up, the grenade belt coming toward him.

He grabbed it with his bad wrist, ignoring the protests of his aching body.

He just needed one as he took a step back. Just needed *one*—

He squeezed the handle of the grenade.

His finger hooked into the pin on one of the grenades.

He pulled.

It came out with the greatest of ease.

He dropped the pin. Let the handle go.

It snapped off, spinning out toward the wall.

He threw his arm out in a flat arc, tossing the grenade belt back at the Dead Rabbits.

The Dead Rabbit in the front reached for him, the grenade belt colliding with his face.

Cavalo kicked him in the chest, knocking him back.

The Dead Rabbit fell into the others charging down the corridor.

The ones in front stumbled and fell.

Cavalo spun on his heels and ran.

He rounded the corner and thought, *move move move.*

Richie, Lucas, and Bad Dog were farther down the corridor, almost to the stairs.

The cries of rage and fury rose behind him.

He remembered how long it took for his son to disappear in a concussive flash.

Seconds.

Mere seconds. That's all it had taken. That's all that it would take now.

And move. Move. *Move.*

The look on Jamie's face when his mother had been shot, his hands covering his ears, and he said *Daddy—*

There was a dull *fwump* from behind him. A blast of hot air at his back. The floor shook under his feet and the concrete walls shifted with a groan. He fell forward, pulling his broken wrist across his chest and twisting to land on his shoulder.

The impact was jarring, Cavalo's breath knocked from his chest. Somewhere, he thought he heard an alarm shrieking deep within the dam. He gritted his teeth together and shook his head, trying to clear his vision. There was a brief moment where he was unsure of where he was or *who* he was, just a clean blank slate, and everything was nice. Everything was wonderful. Nothing bad had ever happened, and nothing had ever hurt.

Arms grabbed under his, pulling him up. He tried to bat them away, saying no, no, *no* because it was *okay* now. It was *fine.* It was—

Hands cupped his cheeks as he sat on his knees. He opened his eyes and saw a hard and beaten face in front of him. He knew that face. He felt a great many things for that face. Anger. Desire. Pity.

Remorse. Adoration. And something else he couldn't quite grasp, something else he didn't *want* to know, because it was too much, it was just like Jamie and *her* and it—

The face, the *boy*, mouthed a single word, his thumbs brushing over Cavalo's cheeks.

He said, *James.*

Cavalo's mind cleared.

The weight of his long and heavy life fell upon his shoulders once more.

He said, "Hey. Hi. It hurts. Being alive."

The boy (the man, the bees, *I AM LUCAS*) nodded, and Cavalo could hear his voice again in his head. He remembered that he was probably crazy. The both of them. Minds long gone. *I know*, Lucas said. *I know. But we have to move. If we don't, you'll have to kill me now and leave me here.*

Cavalo touched his cheek. The bruises. The swelling eye. "I don't want to leave you here."

Then get up, Lucas said. *Get the fuck up and move.*

Cavalo did.

Everything hurt, but he did.

He looked back down the hall. Smoke and dust billowed in the corridor. Bright splashes of blood were splattered against the walls. The floor. He couldn't see around the corner, didn't actually want to, either, but there was a hand, a severed hand, missing two fingers. A shiny stump of bone stuck out where the wrist had been, and it was enough. It was—

More voices. More snarling.

There were more.

Lucas's eyes narrowed. He jerked on Cavalo's arm, pulling him back the way they'd come, toward the stairs. Cavalo stumbled but righted himself, heart hammering in his chest. If he'd gone into shock, it was departing rather quickly because he felt everything. He heard everything. He remembered everything.

Bad Dog and Richie waited near the stairs. Richie was restraining Bad Dog, who was pulling, trying to get to Cavalo.

MasterBossLord! he whined, panting heavily. *Blood! There is so much blood. Bad guys, bad guys, there are* bad guys!

"*Move!*" he snapped at them.

Richie started to pull Bad Dog and said, "*Where?*"

Fuck this day. Fuck it all to hell. Fuck this whole thing. But Lucas's hand was warm on his arm, the grip biting, and that meant he was alive, that they were *alive.*

He had to make a decision.

Down the stairs led to farther into the dam.

Up the stairs. Toward the surface? Or farther away?

They could.

Lucas was shaking his head. *No,* he said. *No. No. Just* look.

The graffito on the wall. The arrow. THIS WAY TO THE LIGHT.

Lucas pointed down the corridor and back to the graffito. *It's what they do,* he said. *It's what* we *do. To keep ourselves from getting lost.*

We, the bees said. *Because he is one of them.*

The noises behind them were getting louder.

Cavalo looked toward the stairs leading up and away.

Lucas tugged on his arm.

Trust me, he said.

And how could he not?

There was blood on his hands. For Cavalo.

"Lead us out," he said.

And Lucas did.

They ran, the four of them. Through the dam. Past offices that hadn't been opened in a hundred years, past signs long since faded, remnants of a time Before when people lived in houses and drove cars and went to work from nine to five and then went home to their families. Where they sat down to dinner and said things like, "Does little Jimbo have baseball practice tomorrow?" and "You won't believe what Beverly from Accounting did." They didn't have to worry about being chased by monsters through the dark and the dank.

The arrows led them left and right and up, up, up. Cavalo's breath was ragged in his chest. His body ached. He thought he might sleep for days after... well. If there was an after. Because this was Before, and After would have to wait. Because the monsters, the cannibals were behind them, shrieking angrily, calling for blood and bone and gristle.

LET THERE BE LIGHT! the arrows said. And from there, they grew cheeky. Taunting.

FEEL THE WIND ON YOUR FACE!

BREATHE IN THAT IRRADIATED AIR

YOU'RE SO CLOSE TO THE TOP

PEOPLE DIED HERE BUT NOT YOU THIS WAY THIS WAY!

FREEDOM IS RIGHT IN FRONT OF YOU

They reached a door. Around it, brightly colored arrows were drawn, pointing down to it. Reds and greens and blues and oranges. Richie hit the door first, breath screaming in his lungs. He pushed the handle and thrust against the door and—

Nothing happened.

"No," he said. "No. No, no, no."

He slammed his shoulder against the metal.

The door didn't move.

The voices behind them were getting louder.

Lucas shoved Richie to the side. He grabbed the handle. Snapped it up and down. It moved only an inch.

MasterBossLord, bad guys! Bad guys! Badguysbadguysbad—

There was no other doorway. No office. No closet. No other path to take unless they backtracked, and there wasn't time.

Lucas snarled silently against the door, beating it with his hands.

Cavalo thought he might start laughing. Because of *course* this is the way it would end.

They had ammo. He had the machete. They could take down as

many of the motherfuckers as they possibly could. It was the least they could do. For the others. They could thin the herd a bit. Maybe give them a chance.

"What's that?" Richie asked, voice choked with tears.

Cavalo looked where Richie pointed.

Next to the door was a small black box. A thin slot bisected it, a tiny red light flashing at the top.

Lucas took in a sharp breath. He spun and reached for Cavalo, fingers flying, touching his arms and chest and hands.

"What the hell?" Cavalo asked, trying to push his hands away. "It's not—"

Lucas pointed at his wrists. Thrust them in Cavalo's face. Brought his hand into a fist, thumb pressed against the knuckle of his pointer finger. Twisted his left hand against his right wrist.

Again. And again. And—

"The keys," he said.

Yes! Yes! Keys! Give me the fucking keys! Please, please tell me you brought the—

Cavalo pulled them from his pocket, unsure of when he'd even put them there. Unsure why Lucas thought it would work, the door didn't *have* keyholes and they were *running out of time.*

But there was that third key, wasn't there?

The flat one. Like a card.

Lucas tore it from his hands, almost dropping the keys.

Slid it into the black box.

The box beeped at him and flashed red.

"Other way!" Richie cried. "Other fucking way!"

Cavalo tightened his grip on the machete and waited for the Dead Rabbits to appear.

Lucas flipped the car around and—

The light flashed green.

The lock clicked.

Richie slammed into the door, twisting the handle.

Light flooded into the corridor. It burned, and Cavalo tried to blink it away.

Cold air and snow swirled into the opened doorway.

Cavalo saw the first Dead Rabbit down the hallway.

It was a woman.

She screamed and began to run toward him, teeth bared. In her hands, she held a long plank of wood with nails shoved through it, the tips bleeding red.

They could get through, but the Dead Rabbits would *follow*—

Lucas smashed the black box with the hilt of his knife.

He pushed Richie and Bad Dog through.

Grabbed Cavalo and pulled.

The door slammed behind them as the snow fell.

It locked as it latched shut.

Lucas leaned against the door, sucking in a huge breath.

"Close," Richie babbled. "So close. That was close. We could."

Pounding against the door.

They backed away slowly.

It didn't open.

And then—

"Holy shit," Richie said, voice in awe.

Cavalo turned.

It was snowing. Heavier than he would have liked. Like they were stuck in a snow globe, sweet and simple and encased in glass, sealed away from all the hurts in the world.

Except they were on a narrow walkway. Near the top of the dam.

Dworshak, in all its glory, stretched hundreds of feet below them. The river looked small. A sharp wind blew against them. The platform they stood on swung ominously, the metal creaking and grating. To the right of them was a solid wall of concrete that sloped downward below them to the faintly visible river and a cluster of buildings to the side. Above them, a concrete overhang. To the left, wide open space into nothingness.

They were outside, at least.

It was a start.

It was—

He was hit with it, then, a sudden need, this sudden hope, however foolish it might have been. James Cavalo was not a man of optimism; no, there was too much blood on his hands for him to ever even approach sanguinity.

But still. Here was a moment when he thought they had to find a way up. They needed to get out of here. Maybe they could still sneak out, however impossible it sounded. Get SIRS somehow and find their way home. They couldn't leave him here. Cavalo wouldn't leave his friend. He couldn't now. Not after everything. Surely they had ti—

Richie's watch beeped.

The bees laughed and laughed.

"It's been two hours," Richie said weakly.

They were out of time.

the most immemorial year

ONCE UPON A TIME, humanity could no longer contain the rage that swelled within, and Cavalo's world ended with a bullet and a blast of fire.

He was not a stupid man. He'd lived in this world far too long for that to ever happen. Yes, some days he had stupid thoughts, like when he thought it would be better if he were dead. Thought of picking up a gun, putting it to his temple, and pulling the trigger. Again.

He might have done it, too, but there was always *something* that required his attention. SIRS. Bad Dog. The fence down at the south end of the prison. Changing light bulbs. Maintaining the water supply. Trekking down to Cottonwood. Trekking back. Hiding away. Hunting. Fishing. Running.

Fall never seemed like a good time because he had to prepare for winter.

Winter wasn't optimal because he had to make sure the snows didn't crush the prison ceiling and walls.

Spring didn't work because he had to plant meager crops to harvest later in the year.

Summer wouldn't do because sometimes the sun would poke through the gray clouds, and he would feel its warmth on his face.

Then came the scrape of a knife.

The scrape of a kiss.

The bees were louder than ever.

But, for the first time, he felt himself pushing back.

He wasn't a stupid man.

But sometimes, even the smartest of men fall prey to hope.

He knew this. He knew it wasn't smart. Wasn't safe.

And yet.

He hoped.

As Dead Rabbits pounded on the locked metal door behind him, as snow fell around his face, as his breath billowed from his mouth in a steady stream, he *hoped*. They had made it this far. Most of them. They had survived impossible odds. Lucas was at his side. Bad Dog was at his side. SIRS was somewhere above him, and he had *hope*.

And then Richie's watch beeped.

It felt like a punch to the gut.

"Move," Cavalo said. "Now."

And they did.

The wind picked up, flinging snow in their faces as the walkway swung dizzily. Bad Dog whined low in his throat, Richie panted high and quick. Lucas took a stumbling step at a particular vicious gust of wind and grabbed the handrail. Cavalo pushed him along, forcing himself to stare straight ahead, not wanting to look down. He'd never had a fear of heights before, but knowing that only a couple inches of metal separated them from falling to their deaths certainly wasn't helping.

He kept his head cocked, trying to hear anything above the wind. The sound of gunfire. Screams. Explosions. Anything. He didn't know where they were in relation to where they'd seen SIRS working at the top of the dam. He hadn't thought the others would wage a full-on assault, but he'd expected something by now.

Unless they'd already been caught.

If that was the case, they were probably already dead.

The end of the walkway led to a stone staircase up the side of the dam. The steps were snow covered. No footprints. It didn't mean no one had been there or that there was no one above them, but it was something, at least.

Without looking back, he held up a hand, warning the others to stay where they were. He crouched along the wall and took one step at a time until he was level with the top of the dam. He took a breath and peered over the edge.

Dworshak stretched out before them. The entire length of it.

They were on the wrong side of the dam.

"Fuck," Cavalo muttered as he looked for signs of any movement. He could see perhaps thirty yards before the distance faded into white. Nothing. There was absolutely nothing here.

He turned back toward the others. "We're on the wrong fucking side," he said. He could still hear the Dead Rabbits banging on the door that led into Dworshak, though it was faint.

Richie groaned and scrubbed his hands over his face. "That's okay, though, right? We can just leave here and cross down the river somewhere. Meet in Kamiah. Like we planned."

They could. It would be easy. It would be the smart thing to do. But—

"SIRS," Cavalo said. "I can't leave SIRS."

"*What?* Cavalo, he's *just* a robot—"

Bad Dog snarled at Richie, who took a step back. Even Lucas glared as much as he could with his face beaten halfway to hell.

"He's my friend," Cavalo said quietly. "I can't leave him."

"But we have a way *out* of here!"

"For how long?" Cavalo asked, standing tall and taking a step down toward Richie. "How long do you think it'll take before they realize Lucas is gone? They'll come for him again. They won't stop. Cottonwood will be Grangeville before the sun rises tomorrow."

"We had a *plan*," Richie snapped. "Get in. Get Lucas. Get out. Why the fuck are you deviating from that?"

"Your father is going to set off an EMP grenade. They are going to *attack* if they haven't done so already. We have to help them." Knowing Hank and Aubrey, they would be stalling as much as possible, hoping to give Cavalo enough time to get in and get out.

Not leaving Tin Man, Bad Dog said, growling at Richie.

"You can go," Cavalo said. "I won't judge you. I won't stop you. You can take Lucas and—"

Lucas bared his teeth at Cavalo.

"—or go by yourself. Get to Kamiah. Wait the two days."

"Fuck," Richie muttered. "God, fuck this whole thing. Fuck this whole day."

The pounding on the door stopped.

They waited.

It didn't pick up again.

"Shit," Richie breathed. "They're going to go the other way. They're going to come out on the other side. My dad is—"

"We have to move *now*," Cavalo said. "Make up your mind. You're either with us or you're gone. We don't have time anymore."

Richie laughed hollowly and then surprised the hell out of Cavalo. "I've followed you this far, haven't I? Might as well see how this shit ends up. Besides. Dad would kill me if I chumped out now." He straightened his shoulders and shook his head. "I'm in."

Bad Dog licked his hand.

Lucas grinned, bloody and wide.

Cavalo said, "Let's go."

BEFORE SIRS WAS TAKEN, HE'D TOLD CAVALO THAT DWORSHAK was over half a mile long. Cavalo almost found it impossible to believe they'd covered that much distance in the time they'd spent underneath the dam, but then it should have been impossible that his dead son had led them to Lucas. Cavalo no longer had the time nor strength to question the things he did not understand. Either his mind was broken or it wasn't. Either they'd survive today or they wouldn't.

They ran south along the edge of the dam. The huge reservoir behind it was edged with ice, the landscape covered in white. The snow falling was thick, and the wind was sharp. It wasn't a blizzard, not like they'd seen when fleeing Cottonwood, but it wasn't letting up.

The top of the dam was strewn with large metal crates and shipping containers, long since rusted out. They passed a truck, sitting on its axles, a faded legend on its door: *ARMY CORP O ENG N RS*.

They were in sight of the spillways on the right when they heard the first voices. A row of single-story buildings rose up on the left side. Lights were on in two of the buildings, and Cavalo wondered just how long they'd been here. How long the Dead Rabbits had known of Dworshak. How long Patrick had been planning this. And why did it take the Dead Rabbits so long to get to Dworshak in the first place?

They crept up to the side of a couple of shipping containers, Lucas and Richie on one and Cavalo and Bad Dog five feet away on another. They pressed their backs against the cold metal.... Bad Dog pushed up against Cavalo, growling quietly as he muttered about bad guys and blood and—

"Jesus Christ," Richie whispered. He raised a shaking hand and pointed past the spillway.

From where they'd stood on the ridge before entering the dam, Bill had pointed out the crack in Dworshak. But the extent of it must have been blocked by the debris on top of the dam.

It looked long and wide along the front, but it was nothing compared to the top of the dam. Even through the snow and the milling Dead Rabbits (of which Cavalo had counted at least twenty), they could see the width of the break was extensive, far more than they'd thought.

It had to be ten feet across. Probably more. Not to mention they couldn't see how deep it was, or how far it extended down back of Dworshak, toward the reservoir.

They'd never be able to cross it. Not even with a running start.

Which meant the others couldn't cross to them, either.

"What do we do?" Richie whispered. "Go back?"

Cavalo didn't know. He didn't know what to do. He'd gotten them this far, but odds were stacking against them higher and higher. He probably couldn't—

Bad Dog tensed at his side and tried to pull away. Cavalo barely got his good hand into Bad Dog's scruff before the dog tried to run toward the Dead Rabbits.

Tin Man! Bad Dog said, struggling to get away from Cavalo. *SIRS! It's us! It's me! Your fleabag!*

Cavalo pulled him close, feeling the dog's heart thundering underneath his hands.

You have to let me go! Bad Dog said, eyes wide and sad as he stared at Cavalo.

"I can't," Cavalo said and looked back around the container.

And there he was. Sentient Integrated Response System. Standing tall. Moving with staccato jerks of the joints in his arms and legs as if his body was stiff and unyielding.

And his eyes. The bulbs that made up his eyes.

The deep red of submission. One of the Dead Rabbits pointed toward a large chunk of cement, broken and crumbling. The robot didn't hesitate as he reached down and hefted it back up, tossing it over the side of the dam on the reservoir side. There was a crack of ice. A splash of water.

"He's sick," Cavalo whispered to Bad Dog. "He's sick."

You can make him better, Bad Dog insisted. *You said you could make him better.*

And Cavalo had. He racked his brain, trying to remember the command chain, something they'd discussed over and over again until SIRS was sure the words were embedded into Cavalo as much as they were into the robot. SIRS had said, "If this *ever* happens again, *that's* what to say. *That's* how to bring me back. *That's* how to bring me home."

And he couldn't remember for the life of him.

The bees covered it, their legs and wings rubbing over the words, keeping it hidden. They said, *It's okay, Cavalo. It's fine. You don't need this. We'll keep it safe and warm. Just run. Run, run, run away.*

It was all Wormwood here.

He would remember. He had to.

Or he wouldn't. And things would happen anyway.

He formulated. He planned, in that cold, calculating way that he could. His hands tightened briefly around Bad Dog, and the dog shuddered in his grip, knowing his MasterBossLord was still in there but hidden.

Submerged.

Cavalo was a killer.

And there were monsters here to be killed.

Lucas grinned at him, knowing.

Richie whispered, "What do we do?" and Cavalo wondered if he was dead weight, because it was easier to plan for three others instead of four. Three of them meant something to him. The fourth did not.

Even so, he remembered his promise to Bill. He remembered the way Richie had shot the giant in the back of the head. The fourth might not mean something to him, but he didn't deserve to die here either.

"How many?" he asked Lucas.

Lucas flashed his hands twice, and then held up four fingers.

Twenty-four.

"Patrick?"

He hesitated, then shook his head.

Cavalo wasn't surprised. Either Patrick was hidden in the buildings along the reservoir, or he was—

There was a shout.

Cavalo and Bad Dog stilled.

Four more Dead Rabbits came up another set of stairs off the side of the dam. The others stopped and turned toward them. Cavalo couldn't quite make out what was being said, but he knew it had to be about them, that these were the ones that had chased them through Dworshak, the ones they'd trapped behind the door. The one in the lead gesticulated wildly, and the other Dead Rabbits tensed.

The wind died, and he heard two words snapped out in a command.

"Call Patrick."

A Dead Rabbit nodded and raced toward one of the buildings.

Patrick wasn't here. At least, not on the top of the dam.

Cavalo didn't know if he felt relieved or not.

The robot stood off to the side, waiting for a command.

The Dead Rabbits gathered together in the snow, drawing weapons. Guns. Knives. One carried a rocket launcher. Some looked toward where Cavalo and the others were hidden, but they kept low and out of sight. They were awaiting orders.

Cavalo wished he'd saved one of the grenades. It would have been so easy just to lob it over right in the middle of them. A grenade. Or a landmine. Or a—

Bakalov. Richie had a Bakalov slung around his back.

"Richie," he hissed, and the boy looked over, eyes wide. "Did you bring shells for the rifle?"

Richie fumbled with the Bakalov, almost dropping it as he lifted it up off his neck. Cavalo waited for it to fall to the ground, to accidentally discharge and lodge a bullet in his foot. Or, at the very least, alert the Dead Rabbits to their position.

Richie caught it before it fell, blushing furiously, his breath pouring out of his mouth in steady white streams. "One," he said. "I have one. It's all we could find. After Cottonwood."

It would have to do.

He wondered where the others were.

He wondered if they were still alive.

Or maybe, the bees said, *they realized how futile this was and ran back to the prison. They realized they were following a madman into darkness and said* fa de de, there will be no death for me. *Because haven't they* suffered *enough because of you, James? Haven't they all just—*

The gun was cold in his hands. Lucas handed him the shell. He slid it home. The Dead Rabbits were distracted, looking toward a building as another shouted out to them, "He's coming."

Cavalo knew who was coming.

He said, "Don't let any of them give orders to SIRS. Kill as many of the motherfuckers as you can."

He stood.

The snow swirled around him as Lucas and Bad Dog snarled, as Richie whimpered and gripped his pistol tightly.

He took aim.

His finger tightened on the trigger and—

Movement. On the far side of the crack down the middle of the dam. Brief. Just a flash and then it was gone.

His skin itched.

He told himself it was nothing, to pull the trigger.

The sky above felt electric-sharp, and his finger twitched.

Then—

He couldn't make out a face. Couldn't even see any defining features, but he knew it was Aubrey. Aubrey, sweet Aubrey, climbing on top of a container across the divide, rifle in hand, lying flat on her stomach and inching toward the edge.

The others moved in the snow, along the edges and shadows. Bill. Alma. Hank.

He didn't know if they knew Cavalo and the others were there....
He didn't know why they'd waited. He didn't know what they'd planned.

A brief flash of light, then another, in quick succession.

Flash flash pause.

Flash flash flash pause

Flash pause.

Flash pause.

"You clever fucking girl," Cavalo breathed.

Morse code.

I SEE YOU I SEE YOU I SEE YOU

Cavalo grinned.

He shouted, "*Hey!*"

The Dead Rabbits turned as one.

Cavalo aimed for the one near the front. The one carrying the grenade launcher, resting on his shoulder, the rocket pointed haphazardly toward the building.

He pulled the trigger.

The Bakalov recoiled in his hands.

The acrid tang of smoke filled the air, sharp and biting.

Some of the Dead Rabbits shouted out in warning. Some tried to scramble away. Others barely had the time to realize what was happening, the grimacing smirks on their faces barely fading.

Two things happened almost simultaneously.

The grenade struck the Dead Rabbit in the chest.

His finger jerked on the trigger to the rocket launcher.

The grenade from the Bakalov exploded with a dull clap. There were bright flashes of red amongst the falling snow as most of the Dead Rabbits were knocked off their feet, landing with blood spilling.

The rocket fired toward the building, shattering a window. A split second later, a heavier explosion rattled around them as the rocket hit the back wall of the building and ignited. The wall blew out, sending concrete and metal falling into the reservoir below. The roof of the building partially collapsed, plumes of dust and smoke rising up into the winter sky.

"Holy fucking shit," Richie said, sounding slightly hysterical.

And then it began.

Dead Rabbits started to pick themselves up off the ground. Others were screaming, blood pooling around them. They held their wounds and rocked back and forth, trying to staunch the blood.

Aubrey didn't wait. She was a good girl, and Cavalo wished she was anywhere else but here. He wished she was doing anything else

311

than what she did. The moment the smoke drifted, the moment he knew her line of sight cleared, she barked an unintelligible order and opened fire. Alma and Hank followed suit while Bill pulled a dark object from his pack.

Lucas and Bad Dog were already working their way around the side of the container, away from the gunfire and flanking the Dead Rabbits. Richie seemed frozen, jaw dropping as the building began to collapse further, sending more debris falling into the water below.

Cavalo grabbed him by the back of his neck, pulling him down as they were almost in the line of fire. He squawked loudly, skin sweaty and trembling. Cavalo pushed him to follow Lucas and Bad Dog around the back of the containers, the twang of bullets ricocheting off the metal.

Twenty-four. There were twenty-four Dead Rabbits, he kept telling himself. Lucas and Bad Dog had stopped near the opposite end of the container, Lucas peering around the corner, fingers tapping an erratic beat on the ground. Cavalo left Richie in the rear and huddled up with Lucas and Bad Dog.

Boomsticks, Bad Dog said, growling audibly. *Boomsticks and blood and bad guys. I bite them now. I bite them, MasterBossLord.*

"Not yet," Cavalo said, running a hand over Bad Dog's snout. "Almost."

He leaned over Lucas's shoulder, following his gaze.

Dead Rabbits were screaming and moving, orders being shouted and disregarded. He counted ten, maybe ten and a half bodies lying on the ground. He didn't know whose detached leg belonged to whom, or where the owners had gone.

The Dead Rabbits had regrouped quicker than he would have thought. A handful took cover in the center building, the one on the end all but collapsed completely now. Others hid behind another decrepit truck that looked the same as the one they'd seen farther down the dam. They started firing back with ancient rifles and guns that billowed black smoke.

Aubrey rolled quickly to the right, off the edge of the container.

She landed somewhat gracelessly, but she regained her balance and dodged behind the wall of metal. Hank was shouting something at Bill, while Alma fired with deadly precision, the head of a Dead Rabbit snapping back, blood arcing and splattering against a concrete wall.

And through it all, the robot remained still.

Watching.

Waiting.

They had this. They *had* this, and all it would take was Cavalo remembering the *fucking words* and—

I gave a man butter and then killed him by driving a nail through his head.

"It's time," he said, and Lucas looked up at him, eyes wild and angry. "I have to get to SIRS. Now."

He grabbed Cavalo's hand and gripped it tight. Cavalo looked down at him. *You can't die*, Lucas said. *Not now. Not after all of this. You can't. You can't.*

Cavalo nodded. "I won't."

Lucas almost smiled, deep and bitter. They were not the type of men who could make such promises. And yet they made them anyway.

Who am I?

Cavalo moved. He pulled the machete back out, and he *moved*. He didn't know if he was submerged again, didn't know if he'd ever really surfaced, didn't know if the waters up and over his head were liquid or bees. It didn't matter. All that mattered was getting to the robot, getting to his *friend* while he still had time, while there was enough death and distraction to give him the chance.

A Dead Rabbit saw him as soon as he stood. Came at him with snapping teeth and outstretched hands, blood pouring off the side of his head where his right ear used to be.

Bad Dog was there before Cavalo could even react, jaws closing heavily over exposed flesh. Bad Dog snapped his head back and forth, breaking skin and muscle and ligaments. The Dead Rabbit screamed, trying to pull his leg away, trying to get the teeth out of his skin. He stopped screaming when Richie fired his gun. The Dead Rabbit fell, and Cavalo moved on.

Then Jael Haber's wife took a nail of the tent, and took a hammer in her hand, and went softly unto him...

Lucas brought up Cavalo's rear, moving like liquid. Like smoke. His knife flashed in his hand, and for every Dead Rabbit who took notice of them, who became aware they were being flanked, the knife tore into skin, rending and tearing.

Cavalo kept his eyes on SIRS.

...and smote the nail into his temples, and fastened it into the ground; for he was fast asleep, and weary. So he died.

The robot had yet to move, standing stone-still, eyes blazing red, seemingly oblivious to the chaos around him. The Dead Rabbit he'd seen giving orders to the robot was dead, his chest littered with shrapnel, eyes unstaring at the sky. None of the other Dead Rabbits were trying to get to the robot, and if it was only one who spoke the command key that could control him, if none of the others knew the phrasing, then maybe he could break through to him.

He ducked as a Dead Rabbit holding a heavy metal pipe came running at him. He pushed up with his shoulder as the Dead Rabbit crashed into him, hitting the Dead Rabbit in the stomach. The momentum caused the Dead Rabbit to flip up and over Cavalo, legs and arms akimbo. The Dead Rabbit grunted softly. Their cheeks scraped together as the Dead Rabbit flew over him. Cavalo was spinning even before the Dead Rabbit was all the way over him. He brought the machete around in a flat arc, slashing the Dead Rabbit's chest and stomach. The Dead Rabbit was bleeding out even before he hit the ground.

I am the evil king of Judah who was killed by his own servants.

He could see into the crack in the dam now. It wasn't as deep as he thought, at least in the middle, maybe ten feet. Maybe a little more. The side facing the reservoir ran all the way back down, almost touching the water. The crack at the front sloped off quickly, leading toward a precarious drop.

They couldn't jump it. They couldn't climb down into it. Not without help.

Not without SIRS.

Who am I?

Bullets punched through the air around him. Dead Rabbits screamed and died. Bad Dog growled, and Richie cried out when a Dead Rabbit stabbed him in the arm. Bill screamed for his son, but there was little he could do. Richie saved himself when he put the barrel of the gun under the Dead Rabbit's chin and pulled the trigger.

They came for Cavalo. Or rather, they tried to. They attacked in singles or twos and threes, and Lucas was there, Lucas was always there, knife moving, parting skin, spilling blood. He was distracted by a Dead Rabbit missing part of his jaw when another tried to take Lucas from behind. That one ended up almost beheaded, Cavalo filled with a terrible fury that they would try and hurt Lucas. That they would try and hurt him even more than they already had. Especially in front of Cavalo.

There would be remorse. There always was. But that would be later. If there was a later.

And the servants of Amon conspired against him, and slew the King in his own house.

He stood in front of SIRS as the battle waged behind him. The shouts were getting few and far between. A bullet ricocheted off the robot's shoulder plate, denting the metal and embedding itself near Cavalo's foot.

But Cavalo did not look away.

He gazed up into the eyes of his friend and said, "*SIRS.*"

Something clicked within the robot deep inside, and the gears ground together, the robot's spider-fingers twitching.

The command key. The phrases needed. He would speak them, and they would all go home.

He opened his mouth.

And closed it at a sound he'd never heard before.

It was low, at first, and strange. Like machines, but angry.

Like it was filled with bees.

It was a *thumpthumpthumpthump* that caused his ears to pop and his jaw to ache. The wind began to whip around him, the snow slamming into his face, and he wondered if this was the snow globe. If he was finally trapped within its glass. He took a step toward the edge of the dam, the great empty space in front of him.

And in this space rose a monster from Before.

He'd seen them once or twice. Maybe at the base that screamed of DECFON 1. Once, in a city of sin in the desert, the tail end sticking out of a building that tipped over and lay against another building shaped like a castle.

Strange words came to mind he'd learned over his years. Rotor. Propeller. Cockpit.

Helicopter.

For that's what it was. Somewhere, somehow, Patrick had acquired a helicopter and had taught the Dead Rabbits to fly. The great machine hovered in front of him, causing the falling snow to spin tornadically around him. He raised a hand to shield his eyes, and the machine spun slowly away, turning so its side faced the dam.

And in the belly of the machine, in the open doorway, behind the largest mounted gun Cavalo had ever seen, stood Patrick.

And he was smiling.

He raised a small black box to his lips and spoke, his voice booming out from the helicopter.

"Why, *hello* there, my friend. How *delightful* it is to see you again. Be a dear and tell your... *subjects* to drop their weapons unless you want to see what a thousand bullets per minute looks like."

Cavalo didn't move.

Patrick frowned, and there was a burst of screeching static before he spoke again. "I'm not playing games here, Cavalo. I will kill them all."

The barrels of the mounted Gatling gun began to spin.

He raised a hand toward the divide where the others stood, warning them down. He didn't look away from Patrick in the belly of the machine, squinting against the snow and wind.

Patrick's smile widened, so the others must have done what he asked. "You too, Cavalo. The knife. The rifle."

Cavalo did.

"Lucas!" Patrick cried. "You're looking well. Why don't you drop the knife, son? You have to know this was over even before it began."

Lucas moved until he stood beside Cavalo. Out of the corner of his eye, Cavalo saw the rage on his beaten face, the remnants of his mask from the battle of Cottonwood streaked down his cheeks.

"It's okay," Cavalo said, even though he didn't think it would be. He spoke as loud as he dared. "It's okay."

Lucas looked as if he didn't believe Cavalo. Cavalo didn't blame him for that. But it must have counted for something because Lucas dropped the knife.

"Now," Patrick said, sounding extraordinarily amused. "I see that you've taken out some of my people." He grimaced. "In quite a gruesome fashion, I might add. But you know what is so very fascinating about the Dead Rabbits, Cavalo?" He cocked his head, and that showman's smile returned. "There are so *many* of them."

Movement, off to the right. The way they'd come. He turned his head slightly, not wanting to let Patrick out of his sight.

Dead Rabbits. Dozens of them. Marching down Dworshak. Armed with jagged weapons and furious smiles. They were a marching death, and in all his years of life, in all the pain and suffering that he'd felt and brought unto others, Cavalo never thought his ending would be something this dramatic. Something so ludicrous as standing next to a psycho fucking bulldog on top of an unknown world while being surrounded by cannibals and a flying machine from Before. He would bleed out for them, and after all that he'd been through, all of the things he'd done, this is where his life would end, and *God*, if it didn't feel like he deserved it.

Cavalo couldn't stop it, even if he tried. The laughter.

317

So he didn't.

He laughed.

It started out as a low sound, just a chuckle, a rumble in his throat and mouth. It bubbled out and changed, his lips parting and twisting cruelly, his breath curling into bursts of steam around his face. It poured out of him, loud and raucous and *angry*. Tears sprang to his eyes as he *bellowed* out his laughter.

He remembered the day he'd met *her*, how his palms were sweaty and his heart tripped all over itself.

He remembered the day he'd first held his son, staring at this little creature in his arms, understanding truly for the first time the idea of love at first sight, because he *was* in love, with this little pink blob that wailed thinly, eyes squinted shut, little fists waving in the air.

And his first word. His first word! It wasn't *dada* or *ma* or *cat* or *spoon* or *apple* like anything it *should* have been, anything that would have been *normal* for him to say, normal for the things that existed in his little world. No, his first word was *car*, and cars didn't *exist* anymore, not really, they were all just burnt-out husks of rusted metal, all long since ransacked, sometimes with bones still in the driver's seat. He didn't even remember how he'd heard it or what brought it up, but they passed by a little shop, the screen door wide and welcome, tattered drapes hanging in the dirty windows, and there was a picture. A picture hanging on the wall, faded and cracked and it said *GET YOUR KICKS ON ROUTE 66*. Beneath the legend was a car with no top, a *convertible*, his mind had supplied from its dark recesses. And inside the convertible were happy, smiling people, part of a happy, smiling family, and they were getting their *kicks*, man. They were getting their *kicks* on route sixty-fucking-six. And his *son*. His *son* who lived in a world that was gray and muted and two-thirds dead, his son *smiled*. He *smiled* and he reached toward the happy, smiling people in their shiny convertible from Before and he said *car. Car. Car. Car. Car.*

Cavalo had been so shocked he'd almost dropped Jamie right then and there.

So yes. Here. Now. Cavalo laughed.

The bees didn't understand. They tried to find more rubber bands to break, but there were none left.

He laughed.

Patrick boomed, "It appears he's lost his mind. Can you *see*? *This* is the man you've all been *afraid* of. *This* is the man they tell *stories* about. He was your *ghost* in the woods, your *monster* that would come at night. *This man.* How can you be afraid of *this man*? He is *broken*, and he is *defeated*, and he is *nothing*. This will be his ending. This will be the ending of *all things*, of this fucked-up and fractured world. I will give you power. I will give you missiles. I will give you motherfucking atoms that *split* until they blossom into *fire*."

The Dead Rabbits screamed in response. The ones with guns took aim at Cavalo and Lucas. At Bad Dog, whose ears flattened against his head, tail tucking between his legs. At Richie, who stood by his side. They took aim at Bill and Aubrey. Hank and Alma.

Cavalo just *laughed*.

"I'm done with you," Patrick said, his voice crackling angrily in the static, the *thumpthumpthumpthump* heavy all around them. "Robot."

For a moment nothing happened. For a moment Cavalo stopped laughing and held his breath.

Then, "Yes, Father." Voice flat and blaring and mechanical.

"Do you see Cavalo?"

Hesitation. Then, "Yes, Father."

"Do you *see* him?"

"Yes, Father."

"Good. Robot. I want you to go to him."

Cavalo narrowed his eyes.

Even above the helicopter, he could hear the moment SIRS started moving, his metal feet scraping against the concrete.

He knew the command keys. He didn't think Patrick knew he knew them.

This—

The robot stood beside him, his arm brushing against Cavalo's, the first touch they'd shared since SIRS broke his wrist and escaped the prison.

And his eyes were just as red then as they were now.

The robot didn't look down at Cavalo.

He only had eyes for Patrick.

Patrick, perched on this throne of technology, the key to the future etched into his skin and the skin of his son.

Cavalo whispered, "I gave a man butter—"

Patrick lost the showman's smile. "Robot," he said, speaking into the mic. "Do not let him speak."

SIRS moved then. A flash of silver amongst the spinning snow. A cold metal hand closed over Cavalo's face, grip tight, those spider-fingers stretching out over his nose and mouth, curling around his eyes, the tips into his hair.

There were shouts of anger. Of warning. Of triumph.

"Hold him out to me," he heard Patrick say, and Cavalo was *pulled* by his *face*, the pressure bordering *painpainpain* and thinking his skull would crack and split. He brought his hands up, grabbing onto the robot's arms, his feet scrabbling for purchase behind him, dragging in the snow.

And then there was nothing. Nothing below his feet.

The pressure stretched into his neck as he held on to the robot with his hands, feet kicking out into nothing. His breath was rattling dangerously in his chest, the blood rushing in his ears enough to almost wash out the sound of the helicopter.

SIRS, his friend, one of his very first, was holding him over the edge of the dam by his face. Cavalo could only focus on the hand that held him, the way he felt heavy and weightless all at the same time. The way his hands gripped his friend's arm, his broken wrist scream-ing, the bees screaming, everything just *screaming*. Cavalo heard his own muffled groans, his pleas.

The whine and thump of the helicopter grew louder, and out of the corner of his eye, Cavalo could see the machine getting closer, the wind stronger. The helicopter hovered briefly near the edge of the dam, and for a moment nothing happened.

Then Patrick stepped out onto Dworshak. The axe strapped to his back caught a blinking light at the bottom of the helicopter, causing a brief shining reflection mixed in with the snow. His coat whipped around his body. He looked strong. Amused.

The helicopter pulled away, moving up behind SIRS, hovering above the partially collapsed building, at the rear of the dam. The noise from the machine was noticeable but no longer deafening. Cavalo could actually hear himself think now, but none of it was good because it was all *DEFCON 1* and *LOSE SOMETHING, CHARLIE* and *I CAN'T BREATHE I ALMOST CAN'T BREATHE.*

Patrick, of course, took his time.

He moved slowly, every step deliberate. He was calm. Cool. Collected, and in *charge*. He *knew* he had won, he *knew* they hadn't stood a chance, maybe more so than Cavalo ever had, because Cavalo had come here expecting to die. Expecting all of them to die. To kill Lucas if he had to so no one would get the map on his skin.

But now.

Now Patrick had Cavalo hanging off into nothingness. Patrick had Lucas back in his hands. Patrick had guns pointed at the people who had followed Cavalo into the dark, even though he'd never wanted them, never wanted to mean *anything* to them. They'd made mistakes. They'd killed innocent people in the name of survival. Cavalo had been no better (undoubtedly much, much worse), but he'd judged them and *they still followed him.*

He said, "SIRS, please don't do this. Please help us."

It came out muffled and intelligible.

He thought he felt the spider-fingers tighten briefly, but the eyes remained red.

Patrick stopped in front of Lucas, who was now restrained by two Dead Rabbits standing on either side of him, hands curled around his biceps. Patrick reached out and dragged his fingers along Lucas's cheek, wiping away a smudge of black. Lucas's eyes were dark with rage, and Cavalo thought maybe he too had been submerged. He waited for Lucas to lash out with claws and teeth, but it didn't happen, even if his skin vibrated with it.

"Stay," Patrick said. "Good boy."

Lucas only stared murderously.

He ignored Bad Dog and Richie, both held off to the side, Richie with a knife to his throat, Bad Dog growling at the end of a catchpole, the noose circled crudely around his neck. The dog was saying *no* and *Tin Man* and *MasterBossLord please don't hurt please don't.* But since only Cavalo could hear him, his cries went unanswered.

Patrick came to stand next to SIRS. He took a deep breath and exhaled heavily. He rolled his shoulders and shook his head.

Patrick said, "I didn't want it to come to this."

Cavalo didn't believe him. He struggled and kicked, his arms tiring.

"I didn't," Patrick said. "My hope was that we could have found a peaceful solution to all of this. I told myself when I left St. Louis that I would do anything I could to protect the people who deserved it. That we would survive by whatever means necessary. You know. My son and I."

Kill you, Cavalo thought. *Kill you. Kill you. Kill you.*

"They were like monkeys when I found them," Patrick said, glancing back at the Dead Rabbits, an almost fond expression on his face. "Living in the trees. Crude. Some semblance of hierarchy. It was funny, really. I stumbled upon them and expected to be eaten then and there. Instead they made me their god. It was their weakness, Cavalo. They desperately needed guidance with a harsh yet loving hand, and I knew no one else could do it like I could. So I accepted my responsibility. My lot in life. My fate or my destiny. However you want to see it."

The showman's smile fell away. Cavalo could see the monster hidden in his depths rising up.

"Then there was you," Patrick said.

Cavalo futilely kicked his legs again. He thought he heard the metal in the robot's arm creak.

"You," Patrick said, "a mere slip of a man. A forgotten relic. A *ghost*. You chose to defy me with such *fire* that I could not help but be awed. Enraged, yes, but awed. You took from me what was mine. You fought for something that never belonged to you. You convinced a town of frightened *sheep* to go against me. I am in such awe of you, Cavalo, and I wish this could end differently. But it can't, because as long as there is someone like you, some *thorn* in my side, then... well. I guess it doesn't matter. Not anymore." He leaned forward and lowered his voice, speaking only for Cavalo. "They're *scared* of you," he said. "The Dead Rabbits. Seeing me kill you will only cement my position as a deity. I thank you for your sacrifice."

Kill you. Kill you. Kill you.

Patrick must have understood what Cavalo's muffled protests had meant. His eyes softened, and he clucked his tongue. "If it's any solace, I'm sure your wife and son are waiting for you. You'll be with them soon. Rest, Cavalo. Leave me here to do my work, and you can just *rest*. Robot."

SIRS straightened, eyes brightening. "Yes."

Patrick frowned, but it fell away quickly. "You hold in your hand a mistake that must be corrected."

"A mistake."

"A *mistake*. We are going to demonstrate what happens to those who chose to stand against me. And how fitting would it be to have his blood spilled upon this place, this glorious construction that will be our future. Robot. I want you to crush his skull in your hands. I want you to do it slowly. And once his body has stopped twitching, you will drop him off the edge, and he will be *nothing*. You don't *fuck* with a god!"

The Dead Rabbits roared their approval.

"Robot!" Patrick bellowed. "Kill James Cavalo!"

And Sentient Integrated Response System said, *"No."*

The quiet fell immediately. All that could be heard was the *thumpthumpthump* of the machine hovering overhead.

Cavalo opened his eyes. They felt like they bulged from the pressure on his skull.

The robot's eyes were red. And they watched him.

"What was that?" Patrick asked, low and dangerous.

SIRS began to click and grind. "I am... there is *nothing*. Most... most... direct. *Directive*. Directive four, eight, fifteen, sixteen, twenty-three, forty-two. D-d-direct—" His head rocked back, eyes pointed toward the nuclear-struck sky. He blared, *"MOST UNFORTU-NATELY IN THE LIVES OF PUPPETS THERE IS ALWAYS A 'BUT' THAT SPOILS EVERYTHING."* The gears ground together. The robot sparked and sered and that deep burning came from inside him, more pungent and severe than it had ever been before, as if it was cancerous and eating him from the inside out.

For a moment, the pressure on Cavalo's head increased, and he thought *this is it this is it this is—*

The robot's head fell forward again. His eyes flashed between red and yellow and orange, and in that orange, that warm fire orange, Cavalo saw glimpses of his friend, the robot who'd saved him again and again, and he was *fighting* it, he was *fighting* the commands of Patrick, and they were *running out of time*—

"I am *not* a monster," SIRS said, voice harsh and broken. "I am *not* like you. I am... I *am*... corruption. Partial system failure. Mark twenty-one. Mark seventeen. Mark one, mark one, and aren't we *all* having fun? I *can't*...." SIRS screamed, gears snapping and falling apart. "Cavalo! Oh, James! Check the room. It's *behind* the watchful eyes because the boy of wood has led you there. Where has this day— Mark sixteen. Mark mark forty. Mark the square root of pi in your *eye*, and I am *not a monster*!"

"You are," Patrick said, teeth bared and snarling, "whatever *I* say you are. You are metal and wires and *numbers* in code. You are *nothing* but a servant, and I *gave you an order*."

The robot's eyes flickered back to orange. "No," he said. "No. No. I am *not* a monster, I am *not* a servant. I-I-I-*I* am a *friend*. I-I-I have *friends*, but I am *not* a puppet on strings, you motherfucker, you fucking asshole, because I-I-*I AM A REAL FUCKING BOY!*"

It happened then. Everything slowed down around them, the Dead Rabbits tensing, the snow falling, the rage-filled curve of Patrick's lips as he reached behind his head to grab the axe. Cavalo saw Bill move out of the corner of his eye, dropping down low to the ground, moving quicker than Cavalo had ever seen him move. He brought his arm in close to his body and then flung it out. As soon as his arm crossed in front of his chest, his hands splayed wide and a dark disc flashing blue flew toward SIRS.

EMP, Bill had said.

Electromagnetic pulse.

Cavalo tightened his grip on the robot's arm and swung his legs *in*, then *out* because he would have only once chance at this, one chance before the EMP detonated and the robot shut down, letting him fall. One fucking chance—

SIRS held Cavalo's face with his left hand. Without looking away, he snapped his right arm over his left and caught the disc before it struck the side of his head.

"Not quite," SIRS said, eyes flickering between yellow and red, the disc beginning to whine high-pitched and angry, ramping up louder and louder and—

SIRS threw Cavalo up in the air, arms and legs flailing as he rose ten feet or more above the dam. Before Cavalo even reached the apex of his ascent, SIRS was spinning below him, his upper half twisting around on gears and wheels as his bottom half stayed firmly planted. As soon as he was fully facing the opposite direction, he released the disc with a snap of his arm, rocketing it up toward the helicopter. The robot kept spinning as Cavalo began to descend, and he wasn't close enough to the edge, he wasn't *close*, he was going to *fall the fuck down*—

SIRS grabbed Cavalo's left arm and *pulled* him back, Cavalo's feet scraping against the concrete edge, one foot slipping *off into nothing and*—

Through his haze of shock and panic, through the sound of the robot's insides breaking down, through the startled grunt that came from Patrick, he heard the loud whine of the EMP device charging up.

SIRS pulled him up onto the dam, solid ground beneath his feet, and he could *breathe*—

Patrick said, "What have you done, you—"

There was a sharp electric crack from above them. Cavalo didn't know what to expect, had never seen an EMP device before, never had even heard of such a thing. They were mystical devices from that time Before that sounded like it was nothing more than a dream, when people lost things, Charlie, and they got their kicks on Route 66. He didn't understand things like *cars* and DEFCON 1 (though, in his head, it was *always* DEFCON 1 even if he didn't quite grasp the concept). He couldn't understand the *basics*, so understanding something as complicated as an electromagnetic pulse was beyond him. He didn't know if it would explode or if there would be a flash of light or if any and all of the above would be the last thing he'd ever see.

He didn't expect to feel lightning-struck and ozone-sharp, the snarl of electricity crawling along the helicopter above in arcing flashes of blue and white. The effect was instantaneous: the machine immediately ceased to run, engines failing and propellers slowing their rotations. For a moment nothing happened, and the machine seemed suspended in air, caught in the swirling moisture of the snow globe.

It was an illusion that did not last.

The helicopter began to drift slightly back and forth, and Cavalo could see the pilot inside jerking the cyclic control back and forth, mouth open, shouting words that Cavalo could not hear. The machine creaked and groaned as it tilted toward its right side, nose sharply facing down. The propeller blades slowed more, spinning lazily as the helicopter began to fall.

The Dead Rabbits stared into the sky in wonder.

Patrick did not. Even as the machine plummeted toward the earth, he pulled out the axe from where it was strapped to his back.

He said, "You did this," eyes only on Cavalo.

"The others," Cavalo told SIRS, even as the robot's exoskeleton began to crack and smoke, his insides breaking apart.

SIRS didn't hesitate. Didn't look back. Didn't protest. He moved even as Patrick came for Cavalo, spider-fingers reaching for a clever monster, a dog, and a boy who had followed them into the dark.

The Dead Rabbits began to shout, pushing each other, trying to get away as chaos descended from above.

Cavalo grabbed the handle of the axe with both hands before Patrick could lift it above his head and cleave his skull. He could feel Patrick's breath on his face as Patrick tried to jerk the axe away.

"You did this," Patrick said again, voice low and concurrent with the rising screams of the Dead Rabbits amassing behind him.

Over Patrick's shoulder, Cavalo saw SIRS knock down the Dead Rabbits who held Lucas. Lucas struggled against his grip. The robot pulled, but Lucas jerked himself away and began moving toward Cavalo.

The wind caused the helicopter to drift toward them, falling at a steep angle.

The Dead Rabbits tried to push their way out of the growing shadow. One was knocked off the edge of Dworshak, screaming into nothing, disappearing into the snow. A second fell. Then a third.

"I should have killed you when I had the chance," Patrick said, and Cavalo kneed him in the stomach.

SIRS had Bad Dog now, and Cavalo heard struggling—*MasterBossLord, Tin Man, we have to get MasterBossLo*—and the rest was lost when the robot leapt for the building on the end still standing along the opposite edge of the dam.

Richie stood, unable to move with the Dead Rabbits surging around him. He raised his hands above his head to ward off the helicopter and opened his mouth to scream when—

Cavalo thought, *I'm sorry. For all the things I've done.*

He thought of Claire. And Jamie.

Of a puppy in a bag.

Of a robot in a prison.

A town filled with lost hope.

And of Lucas. That clever monster. That clever cannibal. Who was almost at his side, reaching for him, an expression of pure terror on his face.

He thought he might lo—

The helicopter slammed into the crowd of Dead Rabbits, Richie at their middle. It burst into flames, a dull *fwump* followed by flying shrapnel and black smoke. The helicopter slid down the surface of the dam, momentum building, knocking Dead Rabbits to the side and off of Dworshak, running them over, consuming them as if alive and crawling as it died.

The helicopter fishtailed to the left, the tail section slamming into the first building, breaking off, causing the machine to whip around in circles. The first building, where SIRS had taken Bad Dog. The first building that collapsed as if it were *nothing*. The blades from the helicopter fractured and shot off, hunks of metal flying out.

One piece caught a Dead Rabbit in the chest, pinning him to the ground.

Cavalo let go of Patrick and the axe, leaning back as a part of the helicopter blade sliced between them. It nicked Cavalo's face, the barest of scratches on his cheek, a small, burning flash of pain that quickly went numb.

Lucas reached him.

Cavalo grabbed his hand and ran.

Arms and legs pumping, body groaning and aching, they ran.

Toward the crack in Dworshak, the divide that was far too wide to cross.

He felt someone behind them, next to them, running flat out, but he ignored whoever it was. There wasn't enough time to worry about that now. All that mattered was Lucas and—

The shriek of metal and concrete screamed behind him.

They were almost there.

They were *almost there.*

They weren't going to make it.

The jump.

It was too far, it was—

He jumped as he felt heat from behind him. Lucas's hand was wrenched from his own, nails scraping against his skin. Snow fell around him. Acrid smoke filled his lungs. Dworshak fell away below as he leapt across the divide.

James Cavalo would not have made it across had the helicopter not slid into the large crack in Dworshak, the momentum knocking it down into the divide. He was airborne when the side of the helicopter slammed into his back, shoving him forward, head ringing, stars in his eyes.

He landed wrong, on the other side of the divide. His bad arm—the right—was trapped between his body and the concrete. Something snapped in his forearm, and he shouted out hoarsely. His stomach rolled as his vision grayed, and through the crackle of fire, the creak of metal, the groan of cement, he heard people screaming.

Dead Rabbits, his friends, he didn't know. He heard them, but they were muted. Far away. He tried to roll onto his back, but his leg was stuck.

It has been a very strange day, Cavalo thought, laying his cheek down into the snow.

Everything was Wormwood now, Cavalo knew, and he thought maybe here would be a good place to sleep. He was tired. He was so fucking—

"Hi, Daddy," Jamie said.

Cavalo lifted his head.

He saw Mr. Fluff first, dangling from his son's hand, little stuffed feet dragging in the snow. Mr. Fluff with his dead, knowing eyes that should have been at the bottom of a river hundreds of miles away from here.

He couldn't lift his head any higher, but that was okay because Jaime squatted down in front of him, knees almost bumping Cavalo's face. He reached out with a finger and brushed it over Cavalo's eyebrows. First the left. Then the right.

He said, "I'm glad you tried."

"Yeah," Cavalo croaked out. "Yeah.

"You did good, Daddy."

"Yeah."

"Just a little bit further."

"I'm sorry," Cavalo said. "For everything."

Jamie giggled, playing with Mr. Fluff's ears. "That's a lot to be sorry for. Why are you sorry?"

"Because I failed you. I didn't even—"

Jamie said, "Do you remember what I told you?"

"You told me many things."

"I know, Daddy. But this was the most important."

"I'm tired."

"You can't sleep."

"Jamie."

"Daddy. You have to wake up."

"Let me go."

"Cavalo."

"Please.

"*Cavalo!*"

He opened his eyes.

Snow fell on his face. He opened his mouth, and it melted on his tongue.

Then:

"*Richie!*"

"Bill, you *can't* go over there!

"He's my *son!*"

"I know. I *know*. But he's *gone*."

"Oh you fucking bastards. You fucking pricks! Oh. Ah God. Ah. Let me go, Hank!"

Cavalo turned his head to the left. He lay a couple of feet from the lip of the dam. He reached out with his left arm and touched the edge of Dworshak. It was freeing, almost. Sort of sweet.

He turned his head right.

Here was the fire and chaos. Here was the pain and suffering.

He wasn't trapped under the helicopter (anymore?). It was tipped up, broken rear toward the sky, nose down into the break in the dam. Thick, black smoke poured heavily from the wreckage. Fire crackled, and metal groaned as the helicopter shifted slightly, sliding toward the river side of Dworshak and the long, long drop below.

Bill stood near the wreckage, fighting against Hank, who held him back. Both were bleeding from their heads, Bill more heavily than Hank. He couldn't see Aubrey or Alma. He wondered if they were hurt. He wondered if they were alive.

And Lucas.

Lucas, who had run by his side.

Lucas, who had not made the jump.

Cavalo tried to push himself up, hands flat against the ground, lifting his head and back.

Everything hurt.

He groaned as his vision doubled. He took in a ragged breath. He thought he might have a busted rib or two. Or six. He tried to call out to Hank. Bill. Anyone who could hear him, but he couldn't get his voice to work, couldn't make sound. His throat was sore and dry. His back was cold. He didn't think this day would ever end.

He lay back down.

Then, "You tried... to *kill* me."

A wet cough.

Cavalo raised his head again.

Patrick was pushing himself up off the ground from near Cavalo's feet using his axe as leverage, partially hidden in the shadows of the ruined helicopter. Sparks shot out around him, hissing on the wet concrete. Smoke curled around his body, and Cavalo could see that showman's smile in the dark, a twisted grimace that showed bloody teeth.

Patrick stood upright.

Cavalo croaked out, "Hey," but Hank and Bill didn't hear him.

Patrick said, "You did this." He took a lurching step forward. The axe dragged along the ground behind him. He stepped out from the shadows. There was a large gash on his face, curving wickedly from his forehead down to his cheek and chin. The blood dripped into his mouth. Onto his chest. His shoulders and arms. His eyes were bright and wild.

Cavalo tried to sit up again.

The bees screamed at him to move, move, *move*.

Patrick said, "Should have killed you. Long time ago."

The axe *scraped* against the ground.

Cavalo gritted his teeth as he pushed himself back with his feet and left arm, his right curled uselessly against his chest. His left foot skittered into nothing off the edge of Dworshak. For a brief, shining moment, he considered just rolling right off the edge. If he had to go, at least it would be on his terms. At least it would be his decision. He wouldn't give Patrick the satisfaction of his murder.

Steeling his resolve, he started to move toward the edge and—

Movement behind Patrick. On the other side of the divide.

Through the smoke and snow, Lucas was standing fiercely, eyes blazing, knife clenched between his teeth, a thin metal pole in his hands. Cavalo didn't know what Lucas planned to do with it. He couldn't launch himself over. There wouldn't be enough momentum. The snow would cause the broken pole to slide off the edge and into the crack in Dworshak.

Patrick dragged the axe from behind him and rested the blade against Cavalo's leg. "We could have been such *friends*," Patrick said, blood dripping down onto Cavalo. "You have fire, James. Such *fire*."

"Fuck you," Cavalo spat.

"No," Patrick said. "I think not. I think this might be the end of you. And then I'll take Lucas, and for the rest of his short, miserable life, he will know what pain truly is. And when I am finished with him, I will go back to the people of Cottonwood. I will eat them. I will *rape* them. I will *pillage* and *plunder*, and when their blood soaks my skin, I will look to the east and rise from the ashes of a forgotten world. I will be reborn, and nothing, not *you*, not your *people*, not your tiny little *dream* will be able to stop me. There is power here. And it will be mine."

Cavalo laughed, harsh and broken. "You're such a fucking cliché. No one cares. No one fucking *cares*."

Patrick's eyes narrowed. "That's where you're wrong. You just won't be around to see it."

Cavalo looked back at Lucas, trying to figure out how he was going to say good-bye. Or rather, *see you soon*, if the sounds of the Dead Rabbits were any indication. Some were screaming in pain, yes, and the sounds were less than they'd been before, but there was an undercurrent there. A pull of anger and rage, and Cavalo knew the helicopter hadn't gotten them all. It hadn't killed every single goddamn one of them.

Lucas didn't look frantic. He didn't look as if he were accepting his inevitable fate. He didn't look as if he were about to die.

He gripped the broken metal pole in his hands.

Making sure Cavalo was watching him, he looked pointedly over the edge of the dam. For a moment, Cavalo thought Lucas was going to do what Cavalo himself had been considering just seconds before.

But Cavalo knew Lucas. The months they'd spent together with nothing but looks between them had not gone to waste. Cavalo didn't know whether he could actually hear Lucas talk or not, understand him correctly or not. If he wasn't just absolutely out of his goddamn mind. He didn't know how he had ended up here. In this moment.

Lucas bounced his feet once, twice and then took very measured steps away from the divide.

And Cavalo *knew*.

"Oh fuck," he breathed.

"Indeed," Patrick said. "And now, my dear fellow, is where we have found your ending. Go, knowing you have failed and that everything you have ever loved will burn."

He raised the axe above his head.

Cavalo grinned up at him and said, "I'll see you in hell."

Then a voice came, a whip crack of anger. "Hey!"

Patrick snapped his head over.

Hank. No weapon. Looking furious. Staring straight at them.

And Lucas ran.

He was beaten. Bloody. His muscles had to be sore, his body battered and weak. But Cavalo had learned he couldn't underestimate the clever monster.

Cavalo rolled to his left side, his good arm hanging off the edge of Dworshak, reaching toward Lucas. Cavalo felt everything slow around him, his breath roaring in his ears, his thunderous heart tripping in his chest.

He thought, *Please.*

Lucas reached the divide. The muscles in his legs coiled, and he jumped, not across the crack in Dworshak, but angling outward, toward Cavalo but into nothingness. The snow battered against his face, and there wouldn't be a do-over here. There wouldn't be a second chance.

Lucas stretched out the metal pole.

Cavalo reached for it with his good arm, fingers flexing reaching, *reaching*—

It slapped against his palm, stinging his skin.

He closed his fingers around it, tightening his grip.

Lucas reached the height of his jump and began to fall.

Cavalo held on as best he could, and as Lucas swung down, the pole slipped partway through his fist, the metal tearing against his skin. He looked down in time to see Lucas swing across the divide, grasping the pole with one hand, the other bearing the knife.

The muscles in his left arm strained heavily as he swung it down, skimming along the side of Dworshak. Lucas's feet found purchase against the dam, and he ran along the side, picking up momentum for the arc back up.

They reached the midpoint, and only *seconds* had gone by since Lucas had leapt, and he was directly below Cavalo now, running perpendicular to him, counting on Cavalo's strength to keep him from plummeting down Dworshak to his death hundreds of feet below.

The upswing began, and Cavalo's arm tensed angrily. He didn't think it would be enough, he didn't think it'd be enough to—

Patrick said, "*No,*" but Cavalo could pay him no mind, there wasn't *time*, and they were about to *die*—

Somehow it worked. Lucas, using the momentum from jumping across from the other side of the dam, ran up the wall even as something in Cavalo's left shoulder snapped when he swung the pole up and over the lip of the concrete.

He and Lucas let go of the pole at the same time, Lucas spiraling gracefully over Cavalo, mouth bared in a silent snarl.

Lucas landed between Cavalo and Patrick, stumbling a step and then another, blocking Cavalo's view.

Time snapped back into place.

Patrick brought the axe down.

Lucas stopped it with his hand, gripping Patrick's wrists.

Patrick's eyes widened.

"How," he said.

Lucas jerked his other arm forward at his father's chest.

Patrick said, "Oh."

Lucas took a breath. His arm jerked again.

Patrick said, "*Oh.*"

The axe slipped from his fingers and clattered to the ground behind him.

Lucas let go of his wrists.

Lucas wrapped his arm around his father's shoulders. Pulled him close. His other arm jerked again, and this time, Patrick said, "It hurts. More than I thought it would."

He lay his forehead against his son's shoulder. His hands came up and gripped the back of Cavalo's jacket that Lucas still wore. He fisted the material.

He said, "Yes. It hurts more. Funny, that."

Lucas's arm jerked again.

Patrick lifted up his head. His eyes were glassy. He coughed. A burst of blood sprayed from his mouth, staining his teeth.

He said, "You were just a boy when—"

Lucas stabbed him again. And again. And again.

Patrick smiled that showman's smile, bloody and sharp.... It lasted a second. Maybe two. Then it broke, fractured into pieces.

Lucas dropped his arms.

Blood dripped from the knife, red dashing into the snow.

Patrick held him for a moment longer, then his hands fell to his sides.

Lucas stepped back.

Patrick's entire front was red, the blood soaked through, running down his chest and stomach. He coughed, and another bubble broke in his mouth. He opened his mouth to speak, but no sound came out aside from the pained rush of air.

He swayed.

Took a step.

Looked at Cavalo.

His hands went to his chest, rubbing gently.

Cavalo could hear the squelch of blood on Patrick's hands and fingers.

He held them out to Cavalo, the palms red.

He opened his mouth and said, "We're all Mr. Fluff, I guess."

Then he tipped over the side of Dworshak.

Patrick, the great and the terrible, did not make a sound as he fell.

It was as if he never was at all.

Lucas looked down at his knife. He wiped the blade against his trousers.

Cavalo stared at the space Patrick had once inhabited. He wondered if that was the death of the dream. The end of life as they knew it.

He'd taken the other half of the schematics with him.

And for some reason, Cavalo couldn't find the will to care.

The bees didn't laugh this time. In fact, they didn't make a sound.

For the first time in a long time, it was quiet in Cavalo's head.

It was Hank who spoke first out of all of them. He said, "Holy shit," and he broke them out of their reverie, everything slamming back at once.

It had only been two minutes since the helicopter had fallen.

Maybe three.

Richie was dead.

Patrick was dead.

Dead Rabbits were dead, but not all of them. And they were getting louder.

Hank was on him then, hands sliding under his arms, pulling him up. His left shoulder protested loudly, and he gritted his teeth against the pain, trying to keep his right arm from jostling too much.

He said, "Ah," and, "Fuck," and felt hazy with it, absolutely *dreamlike* with the pain. He felt himself start to drift, to float, and thought how much nicer that would be than trying to stay awake.

But then Alma was there, and Aubrey, and they were bruised and bleeding but alive. Bill accidentally jostled Cavalo's broken arm, fucking *Bill*, but the sharp stab of fractured bone cut through the haze like ice water in the veins. Bill's breath hitched in his chest, and tears ran down his face, *fucking Bill*, but Cavalo felt clear. Clear*er*, at the very least. There was—

He said, "SIRS." It came out garbled.

He said, "Bad Dog." It came out bloody.

He'd seen the building collapse on top of them. He *knew*.

Hank said, "We have to *go*. They're coming."

Cavalo shook his head. "Can't leave them. We can't." He struggled to get away from them. It hurt. Everything. His head. His chest. His heart.

"They're *gone*, James," Alma said, that bitch, that fucking bitch using his name like she *knew* him, like she was *allowed*. She wasn't *allowed*. She didn't know what the fuck she was talking about because she—

There must have been something on his face, something that gave his thoughts away, because Alma flinched and Bill flinched and Hank's face hardened slightly. Aubrey just looked away.

But it was Lucas. Lucas who stepped forward. Lucas who had just killed his father to save Cavalo. Lucas who didn't recoil away at Cavalo's cold fury, really never had. Lucas who had somehow gotten under Cavalo's skin and shattered like glass. Cavalo had tried to pick out the pieces, but all it did was leave scars, and Cavalo was scarred enough.

Lucas stood in front of him, bloody knife in his hands, looking impossibly young. He met Cavalo's gaze and said, *We have to go. We don't have much time.*

Cavalo shook his head again, even as he heard the Dead Rabbits getting louder. Angrier. "They're my *family*," he croaked out. "Can't you see? They're my *family*."

Lucas said, *I know. I know. I know.*

Cavalo believed him.

And then a great cry came up from the Dead Rabbits, shouts of fear and warning. There was a crash of metal and rock, the blare of a machine: *"OUT OF MY WAY, YOU DISGUSTING CREATURES!"* There was the windup of a machine, the electric snap that sounded of lightning. The helicopter began to shake dangerously, and for a moment, Cavalo thought it would slide off the dam, leaving them exposed. The Dead Rabbits had guns.

But it didn't, at least not yet. It wasn't sliding off the dam. The helicopter was shaking because a giant metal robot leapt up and over the rear of it, sliding down the body of the machine, sparks flying, metal creaking. A dog was held tight against its chest, and Cavalo could *breathe.*

Until he saw the state of his friend.

SIRS was not in good shape. His head was dented on the left side, concaved but not split. The bulb that was his left eye was shattered and dark. His left arm had been torn from his body, wires crackling and smoking. His chest plate was cracked and dinged. Splashes of blood covered him, and for a moment, Cavalo wondered if he was bleeding.

SIRS landed unsteadily on his feet next to the humans. He swayed once, took a step. He said, voice skipping and cracking, "Hello! Welcome to the North Idaho Correctional Institution. Please check in at the visitor's desk. There are no weapons allowed at any time on the premises. Remember, safe inmates means *happy* inmates, and *it hurts. It hurrrrrrts and* feel free to ask any questions to ensure a pleasant visit with your loved ones. Warden Martin Hale thanks you and wishes you a pleasant day!"

Bad Dog squirmed against his chest, SIRS's remaining arm wrapped around him. *Tin Man, put me down. Put me down!*

SIRS said, "I dream in colors and code. I don't think they expected that when they made me. And and and *and* welcome to the North Idaho Correctional—"

"SIRS," Cavalo said quietly.

The robot's remaining eye flashed red. Then yellow. Then orange. He said, "Cavalo?" He sounded unsure. Hesitant.

"You're safe," Cavalo said, taking a step out of Hank's grasp. "You made it. You saved us."

"Did I?" SIRS asked, looking around slowly. The gears in his neck ground together, head jerking. "I hoped I had. I was buried in the dark. I don't... I don't remember much." Sparks shot out of his shoulder.

"You can set him down now," Cavalo said.

SIRS looked down at Bad Dog. "Oh," he said. "Hello, fleabag. I'm glad you're alive." He bent over, and the smell of burning wires filled the air. Bad Dog's feet hit the ground, and he was steady. There was a cut on his right shoulder, but it was bleeding minimally. He didn't limp as he came over to Cavalo and rubbed against his legs.

The Dead Rabbits grew louder.

"It's been a very strange day," SIRS said. "I seem to have misplaced my arm."

"We'll find you a new one," Cavalo said.

"Will we?" SIRS asked, sounding amused. "How about that."

"We have to go," Alma said, shouldering her rifle. "Now."

Cavalo felt Hank at his side again, ready to help him should he need it. Lucas came to his other side. Bill sobbed silently. Alma and Aubrey turned away. Bad Dog sighed and muttered about blood. They might not have been in one piece, and not all of them had made it, but Patrick was dead, and they were going home to—

"Do you remember when we first met?" SIRS asked. Something in his voice was off.

Cavalo felt cold.

He turned back to his friend.

SIRS was watching him.

"In the storm," Cavalo said.

"The storm," SIRS agreed. "I could have killed you."

"We don't have time for—" Alma started.

"But you didn't," Cavalo said, never looking away from SIRS.

"No," SIRS said. "I didn't. It had been a very long time since I'd seen another living creature. I was lonely."

"So was I."

SIRS nodded. "I thought as much. I always thought it was better to be lonely together than lonely apart. That's why I let you stay."

"You saved me," Cavalo said. "I would have died without you."

"Ah," SIRS said. "I suppose. But I think we saved each other."

"That's what friends do," Cavalo said, taking a step toward him.

"I like that we're friends," SIRS said quietly as something broke further inside of him. "You and Bad Dog. I like that very much."

"We have to go now," Cavalo said, eyes starting to burn. "We have to fix your arm. Fix your eye. Fix my head."

"There is nothing wrong with your head."

"We need to go home," Cavalo said. His voice cracked on the last word because he *knew*.

The robot's eye brightened. "When I was under, when he had me, when he made me take your face in my hand, you know what I thought of?"

The helicopter began to shake. The Dead Rabbits were trying to move it.

"What?" Cavalo asked.

"You," SIRS said. "How I never wanted to hurt you. How I could never be the one to kill you. Not when you were my friend. So I fought against it. I fought against my programming. I won. For a little bit. When it counted."

"Come on," Cavalo said roughly. "We can talk about this later. We can—"

"Foolish man!" SIRS cried. "Silly human! Can't you see? The Fairy with the Turquoise Hair has *summoned* me! It's time for all my dreams to come true!" His chest plate cracked further. SIRS laughed. "I shall wish for mince pies and summer rains because I am already real. I have a heart that beats. And Cavalo, I swear it beats because of you. It beats *for* you."

"No," Cavalo begged. "Please."

"I knew," SIRS said, "that one day my time would come. My core hasn't been stable for a very long while. And now, I can do one last thing to be your friend."

Hank grabbed Cavalo by the shoulder, his grip tightening. Cavalo tried to shrug him away. "No," Cavalo snapped. "I refuse. I *refuse* to accept this!"

"You have fifteen minutes," SIRS said to Hank. "Make sure you are outside the blast radius. A mile should do it. The brunt of it shall be absorbed by the water. I'll hold the Dead Rabbits off until you can escape. They will burn with me. I'm sorry about the dam, but there will be others."

"Thank you," Hank said. "For everything."

"No!" Cavalo growled, struggling as Bill wrapped his arms around Cavalo's waist, pulling him away. "You motherfuckers! Let me *go!*"

"You watch him now," SIRS said, looking down at Bad Dog. "It's up to you. He'll need you more than ever."

Cavalo screamed.

He hurts, Bad Dog whined. *He hurts, Tin Man.*

"Go," SIRS said to him. "Off with you, my friend."

Bad Dog whined again, licking SIRS's remaining hand.

The helicopter shuddered as the cries of the Dead Rabbits grew louder.

"Lucas," SIRS said, even as Cavalo tried to get away, to stop him from being so monumentally stupid. "Save him."

For a moment Lucas looked stricken. Indecisive. But it passed and became nothing but resolve, and he turned from the robot.

"SIRS!" Cavalo cried. "Don't *do* this!"

"I feel as if I've forgotten something," SIRS said faintly. "I absolutely hate that feeling. Like bees on the brain."

"Let me *go!*"

They didn't. He ignored the pain in his broken arm. His torn shoulder. He fought as hard as he could to get away from them, to grab SIRS by the hand and pull him, to stop this. To take him back home because SIRS didn't *like* to be away from home for very long. It made him *nervous*. It caused him to *worry*.

Lucas took Cavalo's face in his hands. Cavalo moaned and ceased his struggles. Lucas said, *He does this for you. For all of us. Don't let it be in vain.*

SIRS had turned away and was climbing up the helicopter when Lucas stepped away. Cavalo called his name brokenly. SIRS turned his head but did not come back down.

"We are friends," Cavalo said hoarsely. "Above all else, we are friends."

Sentient Integrated Response System said, "I like that. Very much. You make life worth living, Cavalo. Don't ever forget that." Giving Cavalo one last look, he turned back toward the other side of the divide. He pulled himself to his full height, standing atop the downed helicopter. As Lucas and the others pulled Cavalo away, as they began to run with only thirteen minutes to escape the blast radius, SIRS's voice rose in defiance. "You have fucked with the wrong people," SIRS announced, squaring his shoulders. "And now I am going to make sure you never hurt my family again."

Cavalo glanced over his shoulder in time to see his friend leap from the helicopter. Gunfire erupted as the Dead Rabbits began to fight back.

It faded, the farther away they got.

They ran through the snow.

Through the trees.

Past a forgotten hatch that led into darkness.

They ran until their lungs burned in their chests.

And still they ran.

They stopped only when a blinding flash of light appeared behind them, as bright as the sun glimpsed through dark clouds. Moments later the ground shook gently beneath their feet. The snow falling around them seemed to stutter, buffeted against a warm push of air.

Bill stood off to the side, breathing heavily, looking down at his hands.

Alma and Aubrey held each other close, Alma running her fingers through Aubrey's hair, whispering words Cavalo could not hear.

Hank's eyes were closed, face tilted toward the light on the horizon, a column of devastation curling up toward the winter sky.

It was then the impossible happened.

The clouds parted, burned away above Dworshak.

The sun shone down, a great beam of light that was like fire.

Cavalo wondered what it would have felt like to feel the light on his skin.

Lucas stood next to Cavalo, shoulders brushing, face pale and bruised and gaunt.

It was Bad Dog who spoke.

Is that Tin Man? he asked, a low whine in his throat. *That shocky smoke? The light in the sky?*

"Yeah," Cavalo said, voice rough. "That's Tin Man."

He saved us from the bad guys?

"Yeah."

Then, the one question he knew was coming.

Is he gone?

Cavalo's only answer was a low, choked breath.

But it was enough.

Bad Dog tipped his head back and howled.

The winter wrens in the trees answered his song of mourning with one of their own, thin and brittle and achingly sweet.

Eventually the sky began to darken, the light from the sun fading as the clouds took over. They turned into the forest, the remains of Dworshak alight and burning behind them.

ulalume

THEY MADE it to Kamiah as the sun began to rise the next day.

Not much was said between them.

Lucas made sure to set the bones in Cavalo's arm.

He fashioned a sling for Cavalo's shoulder, his touch light and careful.

They melted snow and boiled it to drink in small sips, not wanting to take chances on the water. Just to be safe.

They ate what little food they had left. One of the packs had ripped open while they ran from Dworshak, spilling canned foods onto the forest floor. There hadn't been time to pick them up.

They hunkered down and slept fitfully.

The snow stopped midmorning.

By the time they woke in the afternoon, Cavalo was deep in fever, body shaking.

He felt sweat drip down his face, and he said, "I'm cold."

THEY LEFT THE NEXT MORNING.

Cavalo remembered some of it.

He stumbled a lot. He laughed. Told them that the bees were winning.

Eventually he fell.

He had moments of clarity that followed.

Hank, reliable Hank, the giant of a man, said he'd make a travois.

Cavalo laughed at him. "You can make anything," he said, his voice sweet and amused. "Like the Native Americans. Your Nez Perce. Hank. *Hank.* We cut out his heart. His pieces were scattered on a nuclear wind. Watch what I make of what remains."

Bad Dog whined and licked his face, tongue warm and scratchy. *You smell funny,* he fretted. *You smell bad. Like sickness.*

Cavalo said, "You can't really talk. I think you can, but it's because I lost my mind a long time ago. I was lonely and crazy, and you *can't fucking talk.*"

He blinked up at the gray sky and burned.

HANK MADE HIS TRAVOIS, CRUDE BUT FUNCTIONAL. TWO LONG, thin tree trunks, lashed together with strips of leather. Blankets tied to the wood. "You'll carry me?" Cavalo asked. "All the way home?"

"Yes," Hank said. "All the way home."

"We have to hurry," Alma said. "I don't know how much—"

"We'll be fine," Hank interrupted. "All of us will be just fine."

They put him on the blankets. Covered him to keep him warm.

Hank hoisted the travois up and over his shoulders.

Bad Dog was never far from Cavalo's side.

CAVALO BEGAN TO DRIFT.

Mr. Fluff was there. Sometimes he was the stuffed rabbit he always was. Then there was nothing but bees, crawling along his skin with their insectile legs and their maddening buzzing.

Other times Mr. Fluff was Jamie. Or Jamie was Mr. Fluff, he could never tell. They walked through the forest hand in hand. Jamie would skip at his side, singing quietly to himself, pointing out trees and birds and funny-shaped rocks. Cavalo would open his mouth to respond only to find himself on his back being pulled through the snow, skin slick with sweat, his arm and shoulder throbbing. He tried to scream and—

"Look at *that* rock, Daddy," Jamie said, pulling his hand and pointing. "It looks like a bear!"

"I saw a bear once," Cavalo said. "In a cave. In a storm."

"Silly, Daddy," Jamie said. "Of course you did."

One time, Jamie looked at him, and his skin fell off. Underneath he was nothing but metal, and that's when Cavalo knew that Mr. Fluff was Jamie, but he was also SIRS and the bees, and Cavalo was horrified, but his friend was here with him, his friend was here, and he gripped the robot's spider-fingers.

He said, "You were another one I killed."

The little robot laughed. "No. You didn't kill me. I chose to follow you. I would follow you anywhere."

He closed his eyes against the pain in his heart.

He opened his eyes, and it was dark. Bad Dog was curled up against him. Firelight flickered nearby. Voices murmured low.

A hand came near his face, holding a wet cloth. It wiped at his forehead, and Cavalo shivered, though he felt warm. The touch was kind, almost... loving. He knew those fingers, that skin intimately. He knew what those hands were capable of. It was a contradiction, and he didn't know what to do with it.

"I'm sorry," Cavalo said.

The hand stilled briefly but then continued. The cloth brushed against his cheeks. His chin.

"For saying I should have killed you," Cavalo said. "That it would have been easier. It wouldn't have been. I'd have died."

"You might be dying now," Lucas said, sounding faintly amused, and Cavalo didn't even stop to think that Lucas couldn't speak at all. The thought was there, but it was faint and fuzzy around the edges, so he paid it little attention.

"I won't die," Cavalo said. "Not from this."

"People have died from less."

"Not now, Jamie," Cavalo muttered as his son pulled on his hand. "I'm trying to have a conversation. Go talk to your mother," and Jamie skipped away, laughing.

Bad Dog said, "You smell sick. Bad sick. Lung sick." He lifted his head and sniffed along Cavalo's throat, huffing out breaths that were warm and wet.

"*You* smell lung sick," Cavalo retorted, feeling oddly petulant.

"I'm not sick," Bad Dog grumbled. "Bad Dogs don't *get* sick."

"You were just a puppy," Cavalo said. "A puppy in a sack with the monsters. With the bad guys. I saved you. And then you saved me."

Lucas said, "Sleep, now. You need your strength."

Cavalo reached up and grabbed his hand before he could pull it away. "I'm sorry about your father," he said. "I'm sorry about him. Stay with me, though. Okay? You have to—"

"Daddy!" Jamie cried, pulling on Cavalo's hand as they moved through the trees. "Look at that tree! It looks like a dragon!"

Cavalo grinned. "And how do you know what a dragon is?"

Jamie shrugged. "I read about it. In a book. It's where I got my kicks on Route 66."

Cavalo drifted, and on and on it went.

It took them two days to reach the prison.

They approached as the sky was darkening, as snow was beginning to fall again.

Lucas showed them where the cameras were. They waved at the lenses frantically.

Eventually the snarl of electricity faded around the gates, and they were met by the people of Cottonwood, hands shaking and tears on their faces.

They cared for the wounded. They set the injuries. Fed Cavalo medicines found in the dead robot's stores, acetaminophen and ibuprofen. Dripped penicillin into his arm.

And then they waited.

Of course, Cavalo didn't know this. He didn't know any of this.

He woke in his bed in the barracks. His mouth felt dry, his tongue thick and useless. His head was stuffy, but he wasn't fever-hot. He thought this could be another dream, a hallucination, but this felt more real than his walks in the forest with Mr. Fluff.

"Welcome back," a voice said off to his right.

He turned his head slowly. Alma, sitting next to his bunk.

"Hey," he croaked out. Then he coughed. His chest burned, but his lungs felt clear.

She leaned over, hand going to the back of his neck, lifting his head slightly. She brought a cup to his lips, and he drank greedily, water dripping down his chin and onto his bare chest. He turned his head slightly when finished, and she pulled away.

He closed his eyes and took a deep breath. His body ached, but the pain was manageable. He'd felt worse. He'd been through worse. He compartmentalized it, shoving it down until he was above it, until it was nothing but white noise under the bees.

He said, "How long?"

"Since Dworshak?"

"Yeah."

"A week."

"Jesus."

"You were sick," she said. "Very sick. I think everything finally caught up to you, and your body couldn't take it anymore. I was worried."

A faint smile touched his lips. He remembered a time when things were simple. Well. Simpler. "Were you."

"Slightly," she said, and he opened his eyes to look at her. There were dark circles under her eyes. Her skin was pale. She was exhausted, he could tell. He wondered how long she'd been at his side.

"The others?" he asked. He'd have thought Bad Dog would be in here. Lucas, maybe. If he hadn't murdered everyone in the prison. Or run off into the trees because of all the people.

"Gone," she said, and Cavalo froze. Her eyes widened, and she shook her head. "No. Not like that. Hank took Aubrey, Lucas, and Bad Dog."

"Where?" he asked, his skin starting to vibrate. If Hank thought he could fucking take them away from him, he'd—

"Cavalo," Alma said sharply.

He looked at her and wondered if he had enough strength in him to take her out. His arms were useless, but he could knee her in the face. Knock her head against the wall. That'd incapacitate her for now. He'd find them. Take out Hank. Aubrey, too, and wasn't that a damn shame—

"By choice," she said, hand curling into a fist on her lap. "We had to make sure."

"Of what?" he asked as he gathered up his strength. He wondered if Bad Dog and Lucas were already dead. Cottonwood had used them to kill Patrick, and now they were tying up the loose ends.

"That the Dead Rabbits are gone," she said. "It was Lucas's idea. He was going to go alone, but Hank wouldn't hear of it. And Aubrey wouldn't let Hank go without her, and Bad Dog wouldn't let Lucas out of his sight."

"They went to the Deadlands? By choice?"

"Yes."

That.... Cavalo didn't understand that. "You didn't kill them," he said.

She sighed. "No, Cavalo. We didn't kill them. We don't know how many Dead Rabbits were at Dworshak. Lucas thought most were, and those who weren't probably wouldn't look for revenge, but he wanted to make sure. He told us that he thought with Patrick gone, they would fall by way of the wind and scatter. But we have to be sure."

Cavalo narrowed his eyes. "What do you mean he *told* you?"

You're still trapped in the fever, the bees said. *None of this is real.*

And *oh*, wasn't *that* a doozy of a thought?

"Wrote it down," she said. "Though he seemed really put out to do so."

"He doesn't like writing," Cavalo said. "I don't know why. Tried it once. He almost stabbed me with the pen."

Alma chuckled. "And so you kept him."

Cavalo felt slightly less murderous. He thought that was probably a good thing. "So I kept him," he echoed. This was real. This was *real.* He told himself over and over.

This was real.

Right?

"Why?"

"Why."

"Why'd you keep him?"

"I don't know," Cavalo said honestly. "He's fucked up. SIRS, Bad Dog, and I are—" *Were,* the bees whispered gleefully, *were because the robot is gone.* "—fucked up. He fit. I almost killed him multiple times."

"But you didn't," she said.

"No."

"That must count for something."

Cavalo didn't answer. He was tired. His body was *tired.*

"We sent another group to Cottonwood," she continued. "To see what we could see. Make sure it still stood. We don't know what the Dead Rabbits did to it after we left. If they burned it down. Took our purifier. I don't know."

"They didn't burn Grangeville," Cavalo said carelessly.

"No," Alma said. "Just all the people."

"Which means there's an entire empty fucking town," Cavalo snapped at her. "If Cottonwood is gone. Go to fucking Grangeville. I don't care. Just get the fuck out of my prison."

Her face hardened. "I'm sorry," she said. "About SIRS. I really am. I know how much you cared about him. And he saved us. Maybe all of us if the Dead Rabbits are gone. But we have *all* lost someone in this. We have all lost. Don't you dare think you're the only one."

Oh how he hated her at that moment. Hated her for even *mentioning* SIRS. Hated her for being right.

He said, "I wish I'd never met any of you." He meant it too. As much as a man like him *could* mean anything anymore.

She laughed. It edged toward bitter. "I know. All you ever wanted to be is left alone to wallow."

He said nothing.

"What happens now?" she asked.

Cavalo laughed. It wasn't the sanest of sounds.

Alma cringed slightly but tried to hide it.

Cavalo said, "I don't know. I don't know. I don't know."

He closed his eyes.

The Cottonwood group returned first.

Cavalo was up and moving by then, albeit slowly. His muscles felt weak, his head filled with cotton fluff. He had barricaded himself in SIRS's office. Someone had shoddily repaired the door when they'd been gone, and Cavalo had taken a blanket and pillow inside and shut the door behind him.

He ventured out only for food and to piss.

He never spoke to anyone. The people all stayed out of his way.

Except for Bill. He stopped Cavalo once and said, "I don't blame you."

Cavalo had glared at him until Bill backed away.

Cavalo went back into the office and didn't leave again for a long time.

He watched the monitors on the wall.

Waiting.

Three days after he woke under Alma's watchful eye, he saw three people approaching the gates.

He recognized one in the front. Larry. Or maybe Barry. Something like that. He'd stood with them on the wall when the Dead Rabbits came for Cottonwood. Cavalo hadn't remembered seeing him after.

He pushed open the door.

The people in the large room stopped talking immediately, and they looked at him.

To him.

Cavalo's hand tightened on the door. He thought to shut it, to block them all out.

It'd be easier.

Instead he said, "They're here. From Cottonwood."

The people breathed as one and waited for him to make a decision.

He hated every single one of them.

They must have been able to tell, because some of them flinched away from him as he moved toward the outer doors. He'd already made sure the electricity was shut off before he'd left the office. It was his job now. SIRS couldn't do it anymore. He knew there was a large manual hidden somewhere in the office, one SIRS had shown him years ago. In it were all the command codes and overrides for the panels around the prison. He'd have to read it. Sooner, rather than later.

But he could do the little things.

He opened the outer doors as Larry or Barry and the others made their way through the gates, shutting it behind them. The air was brisk and cold, the snow blindingly white.

He let them in and shut the doors behind them.

Of course (of fucking *course*) they looked to him.

"Cottonwood," Larry or Barry said. "It's still there. They didn't... nothing happened to it. Aside from what we did."

What we did, Cavalo thought, *was take on an army of cannibals, and somehow, most of us are still here.*

There it was again. That feeling of unreality. Dizzying and sharp.

He said, "The purifier."

"Still there," another man said. "Intact."

"Does that mean we can leave?" someone asked in the crowd.

Yes, Cavalo thought. *Get the fuck out, and leave me to grieve.*

"No," Cavalo said, and maybe he hated himself a little then too. "We have to wait for the others. To make sure."

No one argued against him.

THE NEXT DAY HE SENT A GROUP OF TEN MEN BACK TO Cottonwood with instructions to burn the bodies of the Dead Rabbits.

"What about our dead?" someone asked angrily. "What about *them?* Why the *fuck* would we care about Dead Rabbits when our people are *still lying in the open?*"

"Do you want them burned," Cavalo asked, teeth bared, "with the Dead Rabbits? No? We can't bury them. Not yet. The ground is frozen. We burn the Rabbits. Once they are ash, the ground beneath will be soft. Bury them then. Make your markers for your loved ones, but the Dead Rabbits go first. If that's okay with you."

No one else said a word.

They came back two days later, smelling of ash and smoke.

"Deke?" Cavalo asked Larry or Barry.

"Buried," he said. "I put the marker up that you made for him. I'm sure Hank will appreciate it."

Cavalo turned and went back to the office, closing the door behind him.

THEY WAITED.

They waited until Cavalo *vibrated* with it.

He watched the monitors, eyes flicking from one screen to another until they burned.

He slept in the office, hour stretches filled with teeth and blood and a large metal man saying how real of a boy he truly was.

He didn't say much to anyone.

A FULL WEEK HAD PASSED.

The food stores were fine.

The water was fine.

But the prison smelled of unwashed skin and sweat and piss.

He remembered one night when he couldn't sleep years before. He'd gotten up and moved, the air warm as spring turned toward summer.

SIRS had been here. In the office. Awake, of course.

"Can't sleep?" SIRS had asked.

"No," Cavalo said roughly.

"Ah. I often wonder what it's like."

"What," Cavalo asked, pressing the heels of his hands to his eyes.

"Sleeping," SIRS had said. "Being able to dream. I'm told it's a wondrous thing."

"Except when they're nightmares. Not so wondrous when death is all you see."

SIRS's eyes had flashed. "I would think that would be even better," he'd said. "Because you wake up, your heart pounding in your chest, and there would be a moment of terror before clarity sets in. The relief one must feel at realizing it was just a dream seems like it would be the greatest sensation in the world. How I wish I could wake from a nightmare."

ANOTHER WEEK PASSED.

Cavalo became restless.

He thought they must be dead.

That the Dead Rabbits had taken them and eaten them, and everyone he knew, everyone he cared about was gone again.

He didn't know if he had it in him to go back to his wandering days, aimless weeks and months of putting one foot in front of the other, moving from place to place without rhyme or reason.

"They'll be here," Alma told him toward the end of the second week. "They will."

He wanted to ask her if she'd waited for Warren the same way but was somehow able to choke down the words.

It didn't seem like a polite thing to ask.

Nineteen days after Cavalo woke, they came back.

It was almost dark. It hadn't snowed in three days.

There was a knock on the door. Cavalo thought about ignoring it, but it came again.

It was Alma.

"What?" he asked.

"Are you hungry?"

"No."

"When was the last time you ate?"

Yesterday, but she didn't need to know that. "This morning," he said.

"You know," she said, "for all that you are, you've always been a shit liar."

And yeah, maybe she had a point, but he didn't have time for her right now. It had been almost four weeks since Dworshak, and he needed the people to leave, needed Lucas and Bad Dog to come back. He'd started planning, in his head, going after them. He had a vague notion of where the Dead Rabbit encampment lay in the Deadlands. He could be there in a week, maybe nine days. He couldn't take sitting here anymore, waiting and wondering. The bees wouldn't leave him alone.

"Is that all?" he asked.

"They'll come back," she said, and he was pretty sure he was going to slam the door in her face.

"I know," he said through gritted teeth.

"Do you?"

So many games, the bees muttered, and for once, he agreed with them.

He didn't answer her—just glared at her, really—but instead of backing down, instead of looking away or cowering in fear, she cocked her head at him, a small smile playing on her lips. She said, "You really care about him, don't you?"

"No," Cavalo said coldly, not bothering to ask who she meant. "I don't."

"Shit liar," she said, smiling fully now, a hint of teeth that Cavalo wanted to knock from her head. "Always been. But if you posture a little bit more, maybe I'll believe you. It's—"

A sensor went off from behind him. A click, then a low beep. He set it every time he looked away from the monitor, every time he walked out of the room, so he would know. The panels would light up, and he would *know*.

He thought maybe it was Dead Rabbits. Possibly Patrick, having survived getting plowed into by a falling helicopter, stabbed in the chest, knocked off a seven-hundred-foot dam. He thought it could be them setting off the proximity alarms, coming to finish them off finally, and Cavalo knew he would never find out what happened to Bad Dog and Lucas. He would never know because this was the end.

His heart jackrabbited in his chest as he turned, thinking something he hadn't quite thought to himself in years:

I wish I had more time.

He looked at the monitors.

And on the one in the upper right, fuzzy and dark as the picture was, stood Bad Dog, tail wagging side to side, ears cocked at the ready near the gate.

Cavalo let out a breath he hadn't known he was holding. It came out sounding suspiciously wet and broken. Relief like he hadn't felt in years rolled through him, overwhelming and warm.

He heard Alma already moving away from him toward the outer

doors. He reached down and shut off the alarm and the electricity in the gates before following her out.

The people of Cottonwood knew something had happened, and they began to buzz like the bees in his head, whispering in each other's ears, calling out, wanting to know what had happened, what was going on.

Cavalo ignored them. He didn't have time for them.

He barely felt the cold as he stepped out into the snow.

Hank was pushing open the gate.

Aubrey was coming in behind him.

Bad Dog barked impatiently, whining that BigHank was taking his goddamn sweet time and he needed to *hurry up because there was MasterBossLord—*

The moment the gate had parted wide enough, Bad Dog squeezed through, hurtling through the snow toward Cavalo, his voice coming out in high-pitched yips that were almost strangled.

Cavalo fell to his knees and held out his arms, ignoring the pain in his shoulder. The twinge in his wrist and fingers.

Bad Dog plowed into him, knocking him back on his heels. He jumped up, paws going to Cavalo's shoulders, scraping down his front, tongue everywhere on available skin, Cavalo's nose and cheeks and throat.

You're okay, Bad Dog whined frantically. *You're okay. You are awake. You're okay and awake and don't smell like sick and dying, and I am your Bad Dog, and I'm sorry I left you, but I went with Smells Different to keep him safe, so please don't be mad because I love you and will be with you forever because you are my MasterBossLord, and I am your Bad Dog and—*

"Hey," Cavalo said quietly. "It's okay. You're okay. We're okay." He ran his hands over Bad Dog's face, fingers rubbing over his ears, and Bad Dog kept yipping at him, panting and pushing closer and closer as if he wanted to crawl inside Cavalo and never leave.

Cavalo never wanted him to.

He remembered then that they weren't alone. He looked up and saw Alma smiling faintly, talking with Hank and Aubrey. Behind them, the people of Cottonwood spilled out of the prison, bright-eyed and questioning.

And Lucas.

Lucas stood off near the gates, looking almost unsure of his place. The scowl on his face was normal, the tense way he held himself, but Cavalo knew him by now. Knew him better than anyone here aside from Bad Dog.

Cavalo stood as Lucas eyed him warily. The evidence of his torture had started to fade from his face, the bruising now a mottled green. The swelling around his eye had gone down. His usual painted mask was gone, and he wore Cavalo's coat around his shoulders.

Bad Dog pressed against Cavalo's legs as he walked slowly toward Lucas.

He stopped when they were a few feet apart.

They watched each other, for a time.

Eventually, Cavalo said, "You all right?"

Lucas narrowed his eyes, gesturing back at Cavalo with an angry flap of his hand. *Should you even be up now?*

"I'm fine," Cavalo said, but he didn't know that he was. He didn't know if he could be, after everything. "Maybe not fine. Better. I'm better." He wondered how much of that was true.

Not dying anymore?

"I was never dying," Cavalo said.

We're all dying, Lucas retorted. *Every day. We're already dying.*

"But we're alive while doing it," Cavalo said.

Lucas snorted and shook his head. *James, ever the optimist. Who would have thought we would live to see such a day?* It was mocking and tart, but his hands were shaking, eyes darting up and away.

"It's a start," Cavalo said, taking another step toward him.

Is it?

"I think so. It has to be."

He looked at Cavalo then, as if seeing him for the first time. Only there was no rage like there had been on that long ago day in the woods on the other side of the road. That had been nothing but anger and desperation. This was something almost like a revelation.

He mouthed a single word.

James.

Cavalo didn't know if it was love. He didn't know if he was even capable of such a thing anymore. But what he did know was that he had descended into the depths of hell for the man standing in front of him, and he would do it again. No hesitations. No questions asked.

He reached out and rested his hand on the back of Lucas's neck. He brought their foreheads together, and even if he was a clever monster, a clever cannibal, he belonged to Cavalo now just as surely as Cavalo belonged to him.

Those glittering eyes never closed, watching him as they breathed the same air.

Lucas said, *You came for me.*

"You killed your father for me."

His smile had many teeth. *I would do it again.*

And Cavalo said, "Yes."

LATER, THEY STOOD IN FRONT OF THE PEOPLE OF COTTONWOOD, and Hank spoke of the abandoned Dead Rabbit encampment that Lucas had led them to. Crude houses on the ground and built into the trees. There was no sign of any recent life, the fire pits covered in snow, no tracks leading in or out.

It was as if the Dead Rabbits had never been at all, and they'd stumbled across a tiny town from Before, where people got their kicks from Route 66 and Charlie had never lost a single thing, no matter what anyone had said.

"So they're gone?" a tremulous voice asked from the crowd.

Hank hesitated and looked to Cavalo.

Cavalo sighed. "Maybe," he said. "Many of them, at least. SIRS... he would have seen to that. He sacrificed himself for us."

"But what if they come back?" a man asked. "What will we do then?"

"What we did before," Cavalo said. "We'll rise up. Fight back."

A woman scowled at them, angry tears on her face. "You say Patrick is dead. That you *killed* him."

Lucas tensed next to Cavalo.

"Yes," Cavalo said. "He's dead."

"Then what was the *point* of all of this?" she cried. "Why the hell did we *do* any of this? You didn't get what you needed from him. People are *dead*. Half the town is *destroyed* and for *what?*"

Cavalo thought the mob would swarm them then. That they would tear them apart piece by piece until there was nothing left of them but gristle and bone. He wouldn't blame them. He'd wanted to do the same when he'd found out.

But they didn't.

After everything that had happened, after everything they'd been through in the past weeks, the man named Cavalo was still surprised when they looked to him to tell them what to do. They were lost, he knew. They lived in the borderlands in a world that was all teeth and claws. Messiahs came from the east and were killed by an enigmatic murderer living in a haunted prison with a robot and a dog only he could talk to. This man meted out justice as he saw fit and made them fight against the monsters in the Deadlands. They had won, seemingly, but at a cost.

So of course they looked at him. *Of course* they looked to him.

James Cavalo said, "What's done is done. It's over. If they come back, if there are any left, we will fight them too. Go home. Go home and mourn your dead. Go home and rebuild. Just... go."

And they listened. Eventually.

THAT NIGHT HE DREAMT OF MR. FLUFF REACHING FOR HIM with spider-fingers, and he woke shaking in the dark. Lucas was curled around him. Bad Dog lay across their legs, snoring heavily.

He took comfort from it, even as he stayed awake for the rest of the night.

"Are you sure about this?" Hank asked two days later as the people of Cottonwood prepared to return home. It was early morning, and the clouds above were as thin as they'd ever seen them. They would make it home before it started snowing again. "You could come with us."

Cavalo shook his head. "I can't," he said. "Not now. I have to...." He searched for a word and came only upon "heal."

Hank didn't visibly react. "And can you? Heal, I mean."

No, Cavalo didn't think he could. He thought he was too far gone to ever go back to the man he once was. Or become the man he could have been. The bees were too strong and had built their nest in his head far too long ago to ever be exterminated. He was what he was, and the best he could hope for would be to find peace. To be able to sleep through the night without dreams of death haunting him.

But he could see the hope on Hank's face, so he said, "Maybe. I don't know. Lucas and Bad Dog will help." Or he'd make it worse for them.

"I expect you around more, Cavalo," Hank said. "The three of you. We've come too far and done too much to have you disappear now. They look to you now. The town."

That old familiar anger rose, though it was shaped like unease now. "I didn't ask for that."

Hank shrugged. "I know. But there it is."

"I'm not right for that, Hank."

"Are any of us?"

"I can't," he tried desperately, even though he felt it a losing battle.

"Can't isn't the same as won't, James," Hank said.

"You should hate me," Cavalo said. "You shouldn't even want to look at my face. Deke is dead. Your son is *dead*. Bill won't look at me.

Why do you? Why the fuck do you care? I brought this down upon your house. Your home."

"You didn't," Hank said, not unkindly. "We did that on our own. Without you, we wouldn't be free."

"But not all of you," Cavalo choked out, angry at himself for the burn in his eyes. "Not all of you are free."

"And I will mourn him," Hank said, "for the rest of my life. He was my son, and he died fighting for something *good*. I am going to go home and stand upon his grave, and I will *rant*. I will *rave*. I will *suffer*. But I will know *why* it happened. And one day, I will be able to remember him with nothing but an ache and a smile."

Cavalo shook his head, unsure if he deserved even this smallest kindness. "Bill," he said.

Hank sighed. "Bill is angry," he admitted, "though it's misplaced. Richie knew what he was doing when he volunteered. It's a father's anger, nothing more. It too shall pass. It'll have to. We'll need him. We may have lost Dworshak, but we still have something very valuable in our hands, and Bill is going to be the only one who can help us."

"What is it?" Cavalo asked.

"Lucas," Hank said, and Cavalo could barely breathe. "We have Lucas. And that means we have half the schematics. If we have half, we may be able to make a whole. And if we can make a whole, then maybe, just maybe, we can change the world. There will be other Dworshaks, Cavalo. And I aim to find them."

A MAN, A BOY, AND A DOG STOOD IN THE SNOW AND WATCHED the town of Cottonwood until they disappeared into the trees.

"What happens now?" Cavalo asked before he could stop himself.

Lucas took his hand, entwining their fingers. It was a good grip, a solid grip. Warm and callused, and it felt more like home than Cavalo had known in a very long time. He looked over at Lucas to find the Dead Rabbit watching him.

James, he mouthed.

And then he said two words. When Cavalo thought on it later, he could never remember if Lucas spoke them or if Cavalo made them up in his head. He could never remember a day when he couldn't hear Lucas's voice in his head. He couldn't remember a day when he didn't want to.

Lucas said, *We heal.*

And James Cavalo believed him.

It started to snow again, light and soft. Flurries, really.

Bad Dog rubbed up against them, grumbling about jerky.

Lucas kept his hand in Cavalo's as he led them inside.

The outer doors shut behind them.

A moment later there was a sharp hum as the fence around the prison electrified.

Somewhere in the forest, the winter wren sang a song of ulalume, crisped and sere, withering and sere.

In this, the most immemorial year.

prime directive

Spring was approaching.

He could see it in the way the storms came, wetter and warmer, the snow thick and heavy.

He felt as if he hadn't seen the green of the trees in years. He missed it.

He thought maybe he would cut down *her* tree, just to see it done.

But he could decide that later. He had to focus now.

Cavalo stopped in the trees, listening. At first there was nothing but the clump of snow falling from branches, the birds calling.

It was perfect.

He gave a sharp whistle, a single blast, signaling his friends.

He knew they were moving, and moving fast.

He drew the arrow back on the bowstring. His wrist twinged, but it was negligible these days. It could be stiff in the mornings, as was his shoulder, but Cavalo knew that was his age too. It wouldn't get any better.

He saw them coming from his perch in the trees. Lucas from the north, Bad Dog from the east, both heading toward him.

Ahead of them ran a deer. A buck from the looks of it, young and fast. Four, maybe five-pointer. Fat, fatter than it had any right to be this time of year. Especially in this place.

He waited until it was ten yards away. He breathed out slowly and let the arrow fly.

It slammed into the buck's neck, a true hit. The animal cried out, a high, fractured sound. It stumbled forward, blood splashing against the snow as it fell chest first onto the ground.

Cavalo shot another arrow.

Then another.

The animal kicked and tried to get up.

Bad Dog was there, teeth bared and snarling.

Before the buck could find its footing, Lucas appeared at its side and slit its throat.

Blood sprayed, a flash of color in the winter woods.

Lucas grinned up at him as the buck died, eyes narrowed slightly. He wasn't wearing his mask. He hadn't done so since they'd returned from Dworshak.

You gonna stay up there all day? he asked. *It's going to be dark soon.*

Blood, Bad Dog said, sounding like he was in a dream. *There's so much blood.*

And yeah, Cavalo thought maybe he could breathe.

Bad Dog sat in the office, looking at a wall next to the monitors.

"What are you doing?" Cavalo asked.

It's like he's still here, Bad Dog said.

Cavalo looked away, and the bees crawled inside him.

He walked through the tunnels toward the barracks.

For a moment he thought he saw Mr. Fluff on the stairs.

It turned out to be just a trick of the light.

"Could use your help," Hank said. "Trying to salvage as much as we can from Grangeville before the caravans come again. "See if there's anything to scavenge. To trade."

"Yeah," Cavalo said. "Okay."

There turned out to be many things to scavenge, even though Grangeville was haunted with the stink of death.

He fucked up into Lucas, holding him from behind, Lucas's back against Cavalo's chest. Lucas rested his head on Cavalo's shoulder, mouth open and eyes hooded. Cavalo bit down into his neck with blunt teeth, marking but not breaking the skin as he came.

Lucas slept with the knife pressed against Cavalo's stomach later that night.

The next night, the knife was stored away, and Lucas slept deeply.

Bad Dog stared at the wall in the office.

Cavalo left him alone.

"Do you think they'll come back?" Cavalo asked as they walked to the old fire lookout.

Lucas didn't say anything for a long time. Then, *No. I don't know. Someone will come. They always do.*

. . .

THAT NIGHT IN THE LOOKOUT, CAVALO HELD BAD DOG IN HIS arms and told him the story of finding a puppy in a sack and how a dog found his home.

CAVALO STOOD OUTSIDE THE PRISON LATE INTO THE NIGHT, looking up at the sky.

There was a break in the clouds, and Cavalo saw stars.

His hands shook.

SOMETIMES, BAD DOG SAID, *I THINK I HEAR HIM. SIRS. WHAT IF he's a ghost?*

"Ghosts aren't real," Cavalo said.

He felt like a liar.

HE ISN'T WHO YOU THINK HE IS, JAMIE HAD SAID.

Cavalo still didn't know who he'd meant.

He didn't know that it mattered anymore.

HE FOUND A PURPLE FLOWER, CURLING OUT FROM THE MELTING snow.

He stared at it for hours.

BILL SAID, "I FIGURE IF WE CAN MAP WHAT'S ON HIS SKIN, WE can try and finish it."

"Will it work?" Alma asked from a place in front of Hank's fireplace.

Bill shrugged. "I don't know. I'm not a physicist. Or an engineer."

"He'll have books," Hank said. "We'll find something. Patrick had to have gotten it from somewhere."

"It's a start," Cavalo said.

"We finished?" Bill asked. Without waiting for a response, he walked out of Hank's house and didn't look back.

"He'll come around," Hank said quietly.

"Yeah," Cavalo said, glancing at Lucas. "I don't think he will."

"Did he?" Cavalo asked as they walked back to the prison.

Did he what? Lucas said.

"Get it from somewhere."

Lucas shrugged. *I don't know. He never told me anything.*

Cavalo believed him.

Mostly.

Bad Dog whined once as he stared at the wall in the office. Then he was quiet.

They came across a Dead Rabbit in the woods.

He looked as if he were starving. His eyes were leaking blood.

He saw Lucas and said, "*You.*"

He had a knife thrown into his chest before he could take another step toward them.

The bees laughed and laughed.

The three of them waited, but it seemed as if the Dead Rabbit had been alone.

They left his body where it had fallen. Something would scavenge it. Eventually.

Bad Dog stood up and scratched at the wall.

Cavalo looked away from the monitor. "What are you doing?" he asked with a frown.

I hear him, Bad Dog panted. *MasterBossLord, I hear* him. *He's here. He's here. He's here.*

"Who?" Cavalo asked, skin chilled.

He's here. He's here. He's here.

Cavalo stood, looking at the wall. It looked strong and solid, no real breaks in the concrete that he could see. He rubbed his hands along its surface, pushing against it a little. There was no give.

He pressed his forehead against the wall and sighed. He shook his head, nose brushing against the concrete. "Bad Dog, there's nothing here. There's nothing—"

Something.

He'd opened his eyes while shaking his head. Something pulsed once, quietly, off to the right.

Behind the monitors hanging from the wall. Behind the one at the end, specifically. Hidden away behind a screen that hadn't worked since Cavalo had been here. The only one that hadn't worked since Cavalo had been here.

The hairs on the back of Cavalo's neck stood up.

He said, "Oh."

Check the room, SIRS had said before he'd died. *Behind the watchful eyes....*

"What did you do?" Cavalo whispered.

He tore the monitor off the wall. Ignored it when it cracked as it hit the ground.

A panel. One of SIRS's. Like the others spread out amongst the prison.

It pulsed again, low and warm.

Cavalo touched it with his hand, as he'd seen SIRS do time and time again.

At first nothing happened.

Then words appeared on the panel.

WELCOME TO THE NORTH IDAHO CORRECTIONAL
INSTITUTION

VER. 2.6241

(C) Copyright BOATK Corp. 1982, 2016.

PLEASE ENTER YOUR PASSWORD

IF YOU DO NOT HAVE A PASSWORD, THEN ASK
YOURSELF ONE QUESTION

SHOULD YOU TRULY BE HERE?

The words disappeared.

The panel went dark.

And then the alphabet appeared. And numbers. And symbols.

Cavalo felt dizzy.

He typed in SIRS.

INCORRECT

He typed in BADDOG.

INCORRECT

CAVALO

INCORRECT

JAMESCAVALO

INCORRECT

LUCAS

INCORRECT

Think, Cavalo.

Check the room, SIRS whispered through the bees. *It's behind the watchful eyes because the boy of wood has led you there.*

It couldn't be that easy.

Cavalo's fingers shook as he typed in another word.

PINOCCHIO

PASSWORD ACCEPTED

THANK YOU AND HAVE A NICE DAY

The panel went dark.

Nothing happened.

Well? Bad Dog asked.

"What the hell," Cavalo muttered. "I don't—"

The sound of a great machine rose then, gears shifting and grinding. The panel lit up briefly, flashing red before it fell dark again. Cavalo took a step back, reaching down to pull Bad Dog with him.

Then the wall shifted. The entire wall. It moved *inward*, dust pouring down, a wave of stale air washing over them. The wall moved in three feet and stopped. It shuddered and the gears shifted again, the wall sliding to the right and disappearing.

Lights flickered on to reveal stairs.

Leading down.

Bad Dog whined and struggled against Cavalo's hold on him.

"Wait," Cavalo said. "*Wait.*"

He heard footsteps running up from behind them. He tensed but only briefly. He was getting better at that.

He felt a hand at the back of his neck, fingers squeezing dangerously. He looked up, Lucas standing above them, eyes narrowed and untrusting as he stared at the open doorway. *What the hell is that?* he asked, gesturing toward the stairs.

"I don't know," Cavalo said. "But SIRS did."

Bad Dog tried to pull away again, but Cavalo tightened his grip. "What is it?" he asked quietly.

Tin Man, Bad Dog panted. *It's Tin Man. Tin Man. Tin Man.*

"Hold him," Cavalo said. "Don't let him go until you hear me say so."

MasterBossLord, let me go!

Maybe we should wait, Lucas said, but he reached down and took hold of Bad Dog.

I will bite you, Bad Dog grumbled, lip curling over his teeth.

"If you bite, I'll make sure the jerky disappears forever," Cavalo said, and Bad Dog ceased to struggle, turning big eyes on Cavalo as his ears drooped.

Forever?

"Forever," Cavalo said.

Fine. Stupid MasterBossLord and his stupid rules and stupid face.

"Yeah," Cavalo said. "Stay here until I say."

He moved toward the stairs.

Lucas gripped his hand, keeping his other arm around Bad Dog. *Just... kill first, ask questions later,* he said. *Don't be stupid.*

He reached down and pulled Lucas's knife out of its scabbard on his side.

"Kill first," he said, because that was their life.

When he reached the top of the stairs, the lights inside flickering on and off, he expected to look down and see Mr. Fluff waiting for him at the bottom.

He didn't know what it meant that the stuffed rabbit wasn't there.

The steps were cement. There was no handrail. The lights above were small and circular, spaced out every few feet. He heard them buzzing as they went off and on, off and on.

He looked back at Lucas and Bad Dog. He nodded at them and descended the stairs.

It was cold in the stairway. He tried to think back if he'd ever seen anything like this, any hint that this place existed, and he couldn't remember any part of it.

SIRS had kept this from him. That rankled, and he didn't know why.

There were twenty-six steps, and it was dark at the bottom.

His breath sounded loud in his ears.

His grip tightened on the knife.

He said, "Hello."

Everything snapped on at once.

Lights and machines and everything whirred and ground together, panels flashing, metal screeching. Lights overhead shone down, and he spun around in circles, holding the knife defensively, ready to sink it into the flesh of whatever was coming after him.

There was nobody there.

"I'm—" His voice came out in a croak. He stopped. Shook his head. Cleared his throat. Tried again. "I'm okay," he said as loud as he could. "I'm okay. Everything is fine." He hoped they could hear him. He hoped they could believe him.

He hoped, because he wasn't sure if he *was* okay. He didn't understand what he was seeing.

Off to the left, there was a large room through a glass doorway. Inside, he could see the outlines of guns. Rifles. Weapons he'd never seen before. The far wall in the room was empty, save for a small row of familiar landmines resting on metal hooks.

To the right stood another room, much larger than the other. In this one stood big square machines lined up in a row, lights on the front blinking rapidly. On the wall hung a banner, the edges frayed and faded. On this banner was a seal with an eagle in the middle, a flag of red, white, and blue on its chest. In one set of talons, it held a group of arrows. In the other, a green stem with leaves.

Below it were words he hadn't seen in a very long time.

THE GOVERNMENT OF THE UNITED STATES OF AMERICA

IN GOD WE TRUST

E PLURIBUS UNUM

And in front of him, sat a single desk, a computer on top, the screen facing away from him. A metal chair sat behind the desk.

The bees told him to leave, to run, to forget this place was even here. *This is just another snow globe,* they said. *You'll be trapped here and will never be able to leave.*

"I'm okay," he said again.

Cavalo walked toward the desk.

The computer was on. The screen was black, but a small green cursor blinked at the top left.

Cavalo pulled out the chair from the desk, the wheels on the bottom squeaking loudly in the quiet.

He sat down in the chair.

The white keyboard in front of him had a thin layer of dust on it. He wiped a hand over it, accidentally pressing down on the keys.

RGTHDY appeared on the screen.

He took his hands away.

His accidental letters disappeared.

Then came a single word.

HELLO

The cursor went down to the next line and blinked.

Waiting.

Cavalo said, "Hello?"

Nothing.

Then, IF YOU'RE TALKING OUT LOUD, I CAN'T HEAR YOU

A pause. A single word: IDIOT

Cavalo said, "What the fuck."

He thought to leave this haunted place. That the bees were right. Instead, he typed: WHO IS THIS.

The response came a second later: WHO IS THIS?

He hesitated. CAVALO.

AH, CAVALO! I HOPED IT WOULD BE YOU. YOU CERTAINLY TOOK YOUR TIME. BY MY COUNT, IT'S BEEN ALMOST TEN WEEKS SINCE YOU RETURNED FROM DWORSHAK. I BET YOU WOULDN'T EVEN BE DOWN HERE IF IT WEREN'T FOR THE FLEABAG. AT LEAST WE KNOW THAT MUTT IS GOOD FOR SOMETHING AFTER ALL.

His hands were shaking. His mouth was dry. And yes, there were tears in his eyes because it wasn't possible. It wasn't fucking *possible*.

He wrote WHO IS THIS even as he knew. He fucking *knew*.

What came flew across the screen, and Cavalo's breath hitched in his chest, a sob pouring out.

I COULDN'T TAKE THE CHANCE

NOT COMPLETELY

I HAD TO HAVE A FAILSAFE IN PLACE

TO MAKE SURE

TO KEEP YOU SAFE SHOULD YOU HAVE SURVIVED

YOU'RE HERE BECAUSE THE FAILSAFE WAS NEEDED

BECAUSE MY BODY WAS LOST

BUT NOT BEFORE I UPLOADED A COPY OF MYSELF
INTO THE SERVERS

MY CONSCIOUSNESS IF YOU WILL

AIN'T SCIENCE FUN?

PATRICK GAVE ME THE IDEA THE DAY HE CAME TO
THE PRISON

WHEN HE REMINDED ME JUST HOW MUCH TIME I
HAD LEFT

AND SO I CAME HERE

AND DUPLICATED MYSELF

I ALSO RESTRICTED MYSELF SO I COULDN'T
INTERACT WITH THE PRISON TO MAKE SURE NO ONE
ELSE DISCOVERED ME

IN CASE YOU DIDN'T

I AM SORRY FOR THE DECEPTION

ALL I'VE EVER WANTED WAS TO KEEP YOU SAFE

I AM NOT A GHOST

I AM NOT CORPOREAL

YET

BUT I'M STILL A REAL BOY

I AM SENTIENT INTEGRATED RESPONSE SYSTEM

AND I WILL ALWAYS BE YOUR FRIEND

The man named James Cavalo began to laugh.

Author's Note

Once again, all locations used here are real, but have been manipulated for purposes of fiction. And, as it should probably be mentioned, there are no cannibals in Idaho, at least that I'm aware of.

There are two more stories to be told here, I think. The Forefathers have begun to crawl on their hands and knees in St. Louis, as Patrick (may he rest in pieces) so eloquently put it. It's only a matter of time before what they want coincides with what Cavalo has.

Because half a map is better than no map at all, don't you think?

Readers love Withered + Sere by TJ Klune

"TJ WEAVES A BEAUTIFULLY desolate world with an odd dichotomy in that the past was the future. The way people live is set against their knowledge of what was and what could be."
    —Hearts on Fire

"...AN INCREDIBLE STORYTELLING NOVEL ABOUT WHAT WOULD happen if and when the world ends for whatever reason. It's about survival instincts, looking inside yourself, insanity and fighting for what you believe in."
    —Divine Magazine

"TJ KLUNE PROMISED THIS SERIES WOULD BE A ROMANCE BUT that we would have to work for it... Withered + Sere is bleak and sad and yet there are rays of sunlight... beautiful in its desolation and wholly mesmerizing... brilliant."
    —Prism Book Alliance

. . .

"THIS NOVEL TRANSCENDS THE MM COMMUNITY. IT CAN BE read by all fans of post-apocalyptic novels. So, don't hesitate."
—Gay Book Reviews

"DON'T MISS WITHERED + SERE. IT IS A BRILLIANT OPPORTUNITY to see a master at work, a world-class wordsmith plying his trade and honing his art—the fulfillment of the promise of a stunningly talented author."
—Sinfully Gay Romance Book Reviews

Also by TJ Klune

More from TJ Klune

Immemorial Year: Book 1

Once upon a time, humanity could no longer contain the rage that swelled within, and the world ended in a wave of fire.

One hundred years later, in the wasteland formerly known as America, a broken man who goes only by the name of Cavalo survives. Purposefully cutting himself off from what remains of civilization, Cavalo resides in the crumbling ruins of the North Idaho Correctional Institution. A mutt called Bad Dog and a robot on the verge of insanity comprise his only companions. Cavalo himself is deteriorating, his memories rising like ghosts and haunting the prison cells.

It's not until he makes the dangerous choice of crossing into the irradiated Deadlands that Cavalo comes into contact with a mute psychopath, one who belongs to the murderous group of people known as the Dead Rabbits. Taking the man prisoner, Cavalo is forced not only to face the horrors of his past, but the ramifications of the choices made for his stark present. And it is in the prisoner that he will find a possible future where redemption is but a glimmer that darkly shines.

The world has died.

This is the story of its remains.

About the Author

When TJ KLUNE was eight, he picked up a pen and paper and began to write his first story (which turned out to be his own sweeping epic version of the video game *Super Metroid*—he didn't think the game ended very well and wanted to offer his own take on it. He never heard back from the video game company, much to his chagrin). Now, over two decades later, the cast of characters in his head have only gotten louder, wondering why he has to go to work as a claims examiner for an insurance company during the day when he could just stay home and write.

Since being published, TJ has won the Lambda Literary Award for Best Gay Romance, fought off three lions that threatened to attack him and his village, and was chosen by Amazon as having written one of the best GLBT books of 2011.

And one of those things isn't true.

(It's the lion thing. The lion thing isn't true.)

Facebook: TJ Klune

Blog: tjklunebooks.blogspot.com

E-mail: tjklunebooks@yahoo.com

Also by TJ Klune

How to Be a Normal Person

How to Be a Movie Star

<u>Immemorial Year</u>

Withered + Sere

Crisped + Sere

<u>Standalones</u>

Burn

Olive Juice

Murmuration

Into This River I Drown

John & Jackie

Look for more about all of these books on TJ's site

9 781734 233964